# IMPERIAL ENTANGLEMENTS

# IMPERIAL ENTANGLEMENTS

## TERMINATE THE OTHER WORLD!

## BOOK 3

Icalos

Podium

Cover design by Husa

ISBN: 978-1-0394-5491-0

Published in 2024 by Podium Publishing
www.podiumentertainment.com

Podium

# IMPERIAL ENTANGLEMENTS

## PROLOGUE

# Bad Dreams

A woman raced through dark and damp catacombs, her snakelike lower half twisting and propelling her as fast as she could go. She hadn't had time to equip her armor, so she was clad only in the traveling clothes she normally wore. As a result, she was bleeding from wounds all over, but she ignored the cuts as she sped through the halls.

A group of robed, hooded figures barred her way, carrying short swords and daggers well suited to their cramped surroundings, a giant snake monster slithering in front of them. The monster opened its jaws with a hiss and spat out a cloud of green mist. The woman vanished under the assault . . . only for a metal lance to thrust out of the fog and pierce the snake straight through the head. The figures ran forward with their weapons raised, but the woman's snakelike tail whipped around and knocked them off their feet, her lance sweeping across the floor and across the figure's stomachs. They cried out as she cut them all in one go then leaped out of the mist and over their heads, continuing on her path. She seemed no worse for wear from the struggle, the latest of many.

Finally, she reached her destination. She came to a large chamber where another group of hooded figures stood around a large ritual enchantment carved into the floor. One of them dragged a young woman toward the center.

The woman who had just arrived reached out and called the young woman's name, rushing toward the group. A hooded figure chanted, and a massive magic circle formed on the ground. A multiheaded hydra appeared in the room and began to snap at the woman. She snarled and swung her lance, piercing one of its heads.

"Out of my way!"

But the other heads snapped at her and forced her back. Her way was blocked.

The young woman made eye contact with her and gave a sad smile. She whispered, "I'm sorry."

And then . . .

* * *

"NO!"

The snake woman sat up with a shout. She blinked and panted for breath as her hand gripped the lance at the side of her bed. She frowned and took a deep breath, then she gritted her teeth and glanced over at the bottle at the side of her bed.

It had been a long time since she'd dreamed of that day. Years, even. But now, she had dreamed it again for the third time this week. And she knew why.

She glanced at the letter on the desk.

She heaved a sigh and let go of her lance, dropping it on the floor of her room. Then she groaned, grabbed the bottle, and tanked the rest of its contents in one go.

# 1

# Tiberius's Friends

*"And here I thought Dwarves and Mélusine could hold their drink."*

—Legate Limitanei per Velusitum Quintus Coruncanius Censorius, after the twelfth incident involving a certain diving company.

NSLICE-00P, her contracted Exploratores Ateia Niraemia and Taog Sutharlan, and her Dobhar guard, Estrith Edilddaughter, crested a hill and came into view of their next destination, an urban sprawl of stone that NSLICE-00P predicted could house around one hundred thousand people or so, given the population densities she had observed thus far.

The city was built between a mountain range and a large river, with a vast swamp in its rear, and thus had only one easy entrance. Layers of walls guarded this entrance, new and smaller layers extending out where the city had expanded. Ships moved up and down the river as wagons and pedestrians streamed through large gates in the walls. A massive Legion keep was built into the closest mountain, jutting out of a cliff face and towering over the city, while large stone gates nearby led to the Dwarven colony in the mountain itself.

This was Velusitum, the capital of a proper Imperial province.

As they approached, Ateia took a deep breath. "Seero, can we talk?"

NSLICE-00P halted her march and turned to face the girl.

"Affirmative."

Ateia nodded and took another deep breath. "Seero . . . would you mind if we avoided the Exploratores for now?"

NSLICE-00P's robotic eye flickered. "Requesting Elaboration." NSLICE-00P predicted that request as inefficient. One of her primary goals for traveling to Velusitum was to access the greater resources and records the Exploratores of the province's capital were said to possess. She could not do so if she did not make contact with said Exploratores.

On the other hand, Ateia's strategic goals aligned with her own, since they both had missing people they wanted to find. So, NSLICE-00P didn't reject the proposal out of hand and instead waited to see if Ateia had a reasonable explanation.

The girl frowned.

"Magister Tiberius told us to be wary of the Magister Exploratore per Utrad, and that he had some friends in Velusitum who might help us. I was thinking we should meet with them first."

NSLICE-00P's robotic eye flickered for a moment.

"Analysis complete. Friendly Ateia's request determined as reasonable. This unit is willing to defer querying local Exploratores assets in favor of making contact with potential friendlies."

While NSLICE-00P did wish to continue on with her search, she was aware that there were unknown factions which might be hostile to Ateia. Hostile actions toward Ateia would now draw NSLICE-00P into conflict with otherwise unaligned third parties in light of her new major directive. Therefore, since the group had some confirmed friendlies they could contact instead, taking some time to gather intel on the local authorities was predicted to reduce the risk of unnecessary conflict. Besides, it would also give her a chance to deploy her own intelligence assets and establish a local network.

Ateia nodded back at her. "Thanks, Seero. I'm sorry for delaying you."

The group made their way into Velusitum and quickly found an inn. Between the people of Velusitum and the Otter Burrow, NSLICE-00P gained two Dungeon levels over the course of the night, reaching Dungeon level one hundred and eight.

The next morning, Ateia tried talking to the innkeeper.

"Agedia of the Mélusine or Vafum Broadbane of Khalbuldor, huh? Only the Aesdes know where Agedia is at any given time, but Vafum's heading up a diver company in Khalbuldor, I hear. He should be there. Though, whether that miser will deign to meet with you is another story. As for Agedia . . . go around and start fights in taverns, and she'll appear somehow."

The innkeeper shook his head while Taog gave Ateia a look, but she just shrugged.

"It's that or we bet on the Exploratores. Magister Tiberius seems to trust them."

Taog nodded, and the group moved out. NSLICE-00P deployed her covert subordinates along the way, with their new and improved stealth mini drone golems.

Normally, 01R would take off running immediately, rushing to fulfill the wise-mighty-gracious boss-queen's order at maximum haste, but today, he waited. He stood in place, looking at the drone golem in front of him. He frowned.

The new cyber-rats and drone golems were useful, for sure. They had many more eyes now, and each of them had their own subordinate golem to command. There was nothing wrong with that in and of itself. 01R was only grateful that the boss-queen's army was growing.

But . . . his disloyal heart could not help but dread the implications.

The boss-queen had summoned them more help . . . which implied that she thought they needed the help. Which meant . . . 01R was not fulfilling his duty effectively enough. Oh, the gracious and kind boss-queen had never said anything to that effect, but 01R did not wish to wait for her rebuke. He wanted to help her, not wait for her to help him. His previous way of searching . . . was not enough. Not anymore.

So, he took a moment and pondered. What could he do to do more? How could he better fulfill the boss-queen's will? How could he reduce her burdens?

He sighed and ordered the drone to activate. It vanished from view as it rose into the air, and then both rat and drone started to scan the area. He didn't know, so he would continue on as before. But he swore in his heart he would find a way. He would become better.

The wise-mighty-gracious boss-queen deserved no less.

The group made their way toward the mountain range on the side of Velusitum. There, they found massive stone gates built directly into the cliff face, giving way to tunnels leading deeper into the mountain. The gates were open, and wagons full of trade goods drove in both directions. NSLICE-00P detected numerous Earth-attribute signatures moving underneath the ground, and to either side of every gate, short, stocky guards took positions with metal armor covered in runes.

This was the Dwarven colony of Khalbuldor.

The Dwarves were an independent ally of the Empire rather than a client race, so the colony was not officially considered part of Velusitum. This was a partnership that went back to the earliest days of the Empire, such that almost every province had at least one Dwarven colony within its borders.

The Dwarf guard raised an eyebrow as he looked over the group. "What business do the Exploratores have in Khalbuldor? I thought you all were off at the front."

Ateia shrugged. "A mission of our own. We're looking for Vafum Broadbane."

The guard frowned. "Got the short end of the straw, eh?"

Ateia raised an eyebrow. "Do you know him?"

The guard shook his head. "Ain't a Dwarf in Khalbuldor who doesn't at this point. Some sort of trouble with the dungeon shut down his operations, so the miser's been complaining in the tavern ever since. Refuses to let anyone else drink in peace, he does."

Ateia and Taog exchanged glances, and Taog heaved a sigh. "Wonderful."

The group made their way into Khalbuldor. A huge, spacious cavern had been dug into the mountain, reinforced by massive stone pillars decorated in runes and carvings. Short stone structures covered the floors and the walls. NSLICE-00P still observed humans and other species, but the majority of people in this place were the short, stocky, bearded Dwarves. The air was filled with the sounds of forging as countless blacksmiths and craftsmen plied their trade. There were even large structures reminiscent of factories. NSLICE-00P observed loading docks where the Earth-attribute train cars were loaded with crates.

The group continued on, searching for the tavern. They did not have to search for long, as they heard the shouting long before they found the building. Taog raised an eyebrow as he watched all the pedestrians give the building a wide berth, then heaved a sigh as Ateia approached it.

"You calling me a weakling?! I'll have you know I took down the Green Wyvern! I can handle a little worm!"

"I'm calling you an idiot! That 'little worm' already tanned your hide!"

"That's because *YOU* cheaped out on the weapons! Get me a real weapon already, and I'll have it down pat!"

"That's because *YOU* can't be bothered to take care of anything I buy you! You've broken five, *FIVE* enchanted mana iron lances in the past year alone, you stupid snake!"

"Because *YOU* keep buying from the lowest bidder! It's not *MY* fault if your cheap crap can't handle my skills!"

"It is ABSOLUTELY your fault! *MOST* people can use one mana iron weapon for years, at a minimum!"

"Cheapskate!"

"Musclebrain!"

Ateia took a deep breath before opening the door. A collection of different races sat at the bar, drinking among themselves. Behind them, a man and a woman were shouting at one another. The man was a Dwarf with black hair wearing a fancy robe. The woman had long golden hair and well-used plate armor. She also had the lower body of a snake covered in green scales.

Both were flushed and holding half-empty mugs. Not their first, judging by the mugs on the floor and tables around them.

The barkeeper glanced over at the newcomers and shrugged.

"Bar is, in fact, open, if you don't mind a bit of noise. They're annoying, but they won't start a real fight. Broadbane's too cheap to pay for damages."

Ateia's eyes widened.

"Ah . . . is that . . . Vafum Broadbane?"

The pair stopped shouting and glanced over. The dwarf scoffed while the snake woman froze.

"Aye, that's my name. Now shove off. I don't owe anyone money, and we aren't taking any orders while the bloody dungeon's closed."

Ateia shook her head. "My name is Ateia Niraemia. Magister Exploratore per Turannia Tiberius sent me."

The room went silent. The snake woman coughed, took a deep breath, crouched down . . . and then leapt across the room all at once. She landed right in front of Ateia and grabbed her hands.

"Wow! Tibbers sent you?! How is he?! Not drinking too much, I hope?! Does he talk about me?!" Suddenly, her eyes narrowed. "Wait . . . you're not his girlfriend, are you?! He . . . He can't! You're too young!"

Ateia shook her head with all her might, and the snake woman smiled.

"Ah, I knew it! Good old Tibbers would never do something like that! Barman, a round for my new friends! Come in. Drink, drink, and tell me more!"

Suddenly, the stone floor rose up, forming a giant hand. The hand picked up the snake woman and dropped her on the other side of the room.

Vafum Broadbane stepped forward, shaking his head.

"Shove off, Agedia! Gush on your crush to someone who cares! Better yet, just move to Turannia already and stop bugging me!"

Agedia glared at him.

"You know I don't do well in cold rain!"

Vafum shook his head and cursed, then looked over the group. His eyes widened. "Wait, Ateia Niraemia, you said? With a half-Wulver boy and a wandering knight–looking lass?"

Ateia nodded.

"Yes, that's us."

"Ah, crap."

Agedia suddenly shot up, no longer flushed. Vafum motioned, and the pair sat in one of the booths. NSLICE-00P's group moved to join them as Vafum heaved a sigh.

"Look, Tiberius warned us you bunch would be coming. But . . . your timing's a bit awkward."

Taog frowned. "What do you mean?"

Agedia's eyes narrowed. "Something's going on in Utrad; we aren't sure what. Magister Caelinus has been off at the border for a while now. He normally doesn't have this much trouble with the Centaurs. The Legion's been ignoring new dungeons, letting them pop up around the cities like they're apt to do. But the Magister Exploratore and the guard have been working overtime cleaning up bandits, criminals, and officials they say are corrupt. I think they've made record arrests this year."

Ateia tilted her head. "I mean, isn't that their job?"

Vafum shook his. "Officially, yes, but everyone knows how it works. Small bandit groups aren't normally a high priority, and crime is only illegal if you can't afford the bribe. It feels like Utrad's trying extra hard to clear the field, to keep everything spotless as far as people are concerned, at the cost of letting the dungeons go unchecked."

Agedia nodded. "Normally, something like that happens when one of the province's higher-ups is planning a big play and doesn't want anyone left who can cause trouble."

Taog narrowed his eyes. "What kind of play?"

Vafum frowned. "That's the thing, kid, we don't know. A new invasion to expand the province? A purge of political rivals? A big, expensive infrastructure project to revolutionize the economy? A march on Corvanus to usurp the throne? It could be any number of things. Normally, I'd be hearing some gossip from the merchants and officials I do business with, but Khalbuldor's dungeon is shut down. And everyone knows I hate gossip, so I ain't hearing crap while my diving company's out of work."

Agedia nodded. "Normally, I could make my way around the taverns and find some guard with too much to drink and too much to say, but they're sealed up tight. The Legate Legio per Velusitum is cracking down on his men, and the comitatenses and Exploratores are all out of town. And the bookworm officials all run when I come to drink, the cowards."

Vafum crossed his arms. "Maybe if you could visit a bar without starting a brawl, you might have a better reputation."

Agedia glared at him. "Says the one stuck here drinking all day. At least *I'm* trying to do some work!"

Vafum shook his head, biting back his reply. "So yeah, we don't know what's going on, only that it's something big, and both of us are basically grounded at the time." He heaved a sigh. "Look . . . I owe Tiberius for a lot. He said you're looking for some folks. I'd love to help, but I'm not sure it's smart. If I start asking for favors while I'm out of work, it'll raise questions. And right now, that might draw the wrong kind of attention to you."

Agedia smirked. "Only because you're such a miser."

Vafum scowled. "And obviously, the drunkard is of no help unless the people you're searching for live in a bar."

"What was that?!"

Ateia rubbed her chin. "You said there's a problem in the dungeon? What's going on?"

Vafum sighed. "An adamant bull worm showed up and decided to make our local dungeon its home. Huge, covered in armor tougher than steel, impervious to Fire or Earth Magic. Likes to feast on metal. A Dwarf's worst nightmare. Now, normally, a monster like this showing up in one of the province's few sanctioned metal dungeons would whip the Imperials into a frenzy, and the Legion would spare no time or effort to kill the bloody thing. But all the comitatenses and Exploratores are away, wouldn't you know it, and Khalbuldor ain't got a champion who can kill something like this. So, we're stuck waiting until either Magister Caelinus gets back or one of the Dwarf cities can send reinforcements."

Ateia and Taog exchanged glances. ". . . Could you help us if someone dealt with the worm?"

Vafum narrowed his eyes. "Stop right there, girlie. Even this idiot with muscles where her brain should be couldn't leave a scratch on that thing. So don't get stupid ideas into your head."

Agedia crossed her arms. "I totally could have taken it if *YOU* would just get me a good weapon!"

Vafum scoffed. "Your idea of a 'good weapon' is one made of dragon scales and mithril! *I* could kill the bloody thing if I could afford something like that, no magic required!"

And so, the two started arguing once again while Ateia turned to NSLICE-00P.

"So, Seero. How do you feel about hunting an adamant bull worm?"

"Response: This unit has no particular feelings regarding entity 'Adamant Bull Worm.' This unit has no data on said entity and cannot predict probability of a successful termination. Recommendation: This unit proposes covert reconnaissance."

Ateia grinned. "Works for me! Taog?"

Taog stared into the distance. "Normally, I'd advise against us running off against some clearly super dangerous monster. But . . . it's Seero. So . . . whatever Seero says."

"It's decided, then!"

And so, the group got up and left the bar as the shouting grew louder once again.

But the shouting died down a short time after the group had left. Vafum waved to the barman, who wordlessly brought another pair of drinks. Vafum took them and handed one to Agedia.

"Agedia . . . are you okay? That . . . That was the lass, wasn't she?"

A frown formed on Agedia's face. She didn't say anything, but Vafum caught a slight quiver in her eyes.

Then she slammed her tail against the ground and threw her head back, drinking the entire cup in her hand in one go. Once she finished, she stood up and began slithering out of the tavern, not swaying or staggering in the slightest.

"I'm . . . going to go after them. They'll need a guide."

Vafum watched her go as his face fell.

"Agedia . . ."

He sighed and tanked his own drink.

# 2

# What Do You Mean, "Don't Terminate?"

*"NSLICE units are notably more flexible than pure robots and have some ability to interpret a commander's intentions beyond the letter of their orders. They are not, however, mind readers, and their sheer loyalty means they will execute a command even if they do not understand it. So, if they are given a confusing or unclear order, they will attempt to decipher it as best they know how, which may NOT be in line with what the issuer intended. It is, therefore, the responsibility of the handlers to be as precise and specific with their orders as the situation allows. Broad and open-ended orders—for example, to 'terminate all potential hostiles'—are to be strictly avoided."*

—A memo from Dr. Ottosen after an incident involving NSLICE units and a refugee camp.

As the group made their way toward the dungeon, something shot through the air above them, landing with a crash in the middle of the street. All the Dwarves walking around them jumped . . . then walked off cursing as they saw what it was.

Agedia had arrived, now with a helmet on her head and a mana iron lance on her back.

"There, found you all! Heading to the dungeon, are we?"

Ateia shrugged. Agedia grinned . . . and promptly turned around, heading forward.

"Well, let's get going, then!"

Ateia and Taog stood there, blinking, but NSLICE-00P kept walking, so they moved to follow suit. Ateia walked up next to Agedia.

"Um, Miss Agedia."

Agedia winced. "Ugh, that makes me sound old. Just call me Agedia!"

Ateia slowly nodded. "Okay, Agedia, you're coming with us?"

The woman shrugged. "Oh, Vafum said something about 'stopping idiot kids from committing suicide,' but that's boring, and I owe that stupid worm a rematch. And Tibbers also told us not to mess with the shiny girl, so I'm curious to see what she can do."

Agedia's eyes suddenly narrowed.

"You bunch *have* been in a dungeon before, right? You aren't *actually* suicidal idiots, right?"

Ateia shrugged while Taog looked off into the distance. "Yep. Seero's something of an expert, so we'll stay close to her."

The woman nodded. "Works for me. Let me show you around, then."

And so, the group made their way deeper into Khalbuldor. Eventually, they reached an open plaza surrounded by a small wall. A number of large structures were built with entrances directly in the wall, while guards rested on top. At the center of the plaza, a stone cave jutted from the ground, with large metal doors facing their direction.

As they approached the walls, two guards eyed them, but once they saw Agedia, they shrugged and went back to their board game. Agedia turned to face them.

"Welcome to the dungeon of Khalbuldor, the Mines of Might. You bunch ready?"

Ateia and Taog nodded. Estrith gripped her spear. 00B, 00F, and the canus monsters all growled. And NSLICE-00P activated her helmet.

"Engaging dungeon termination protocols."

Taog suddenly jumped, rushing in front of NSLICE-00P.

"Wait, Seero! You can't destroy this dungeon!"

"Requesting Elaboration: Why can't this unit terminate the dungeon?"

"This is an approved dungeon, vetted and sanctioned by the Empire! It's supposed to be here. The Empire uses it to train and gather resources! And it's a *HUGE* crime to destroy one!"

NSLICE-00P's robotic eye flickered.

"Acknowledgement: This dungeon has been designated a strategic asset of entity Empire and is subject to nonintervention protocols. Requesting assistance with protocol updates. Previous records indicate a 99.99 percent probability of encountering hostility from the dungeon's subordinate monsters, and this unit's protocols indicate the appropriate response is to terminate the threat. This response appears to be incompatible with the nonintervention protocols, and so would prevent this unit from entering the dungeon."

Taog held his head as he tried to parse her words. "So . . . you're wondering what to do if we get attacked by dungeon monsters?"

"Affirmative."

Taog heaved a sigh. "You can kill the dungeon monsters, Seero. Just don't kill the dungeon master or destroy the core."

"Objection: Dungeon cores consistently produce hostile monsters. Hostility and potential danger remain as long as the dungeon core is left operational."

"That's the point, Seero!"

"Requesting Clarification: This unit does not understand."

Taog held his head and groaned. "Look, Seero, you can grow stronger and receive loot if you kill the monsters. You've noticed that, right?"

"Affirmative."

Taog nodded. "Right, so, that's very useful to the Empire. A handful of dungeons that have no history of sending their monsters to attack the outside world are allowed to remain so that the Empire can hunt the monsters on a regular basis. We *want* a source of monsters to fight, as long as it's not overly dangerous to the nearby settlement."

NSLICE-00P's robotic eye flickered as she analyzed the statement. She compared it to prior records . . . and found it reasonable. When working for her original organization, she, too, had conducted raids with the intention of acquiring new NSLICE bases where she wasn't expected to terminate the entire target settlement. She just hadn't considered that as she tried to adapt her protocols to her new circumstances, since she had been focused on self-preservation.

"Acknowledgement: Updating protocols. Parameters set: Single target termination, self-defense from immediate hostiles only, excepting target monster."

Taog closed his eyes and exhaled his breath.

Agedia raised an eyebrow and spoke to Ateia. "Your friend . . . likes to destroy dungeons, does she?"

Ateia nodded. "Yes. Yes, she does."

Agedia grinned. "I'm excited to see what she can do, then. Let's get going!"

01R crawled through a side alley, sticking to the shadows. His drone flew overhead with its Invisibility active, scanning the faces of the passing crowd. He heaved a sigh.

01R didn't particularly enjoy sneaking, but he knew that was what the wise-mighty-gracious boss-queen had summoned him for. Previously, he'd had the challenge of pushing that stealth to the limit. Of trying to get as close to the man-things as possible, to get the best position while still remaining undetected so he could scan as many of their faces as he could.

But these new golems . . . had taken even that challenge away.

Their stealth enchantments, being engraved directly into their hulls, could remain active practically indefinitely. The golems didn't have to spend mana or attention forming their own magic circles from scratch, they just had to channel some power through the engraving, and it would activate on its own. So, they could maintain Invisibility at a fraction of the cost it took the normal monsters. And since they could also fly . . . the golems could very easily acquire an ideal position to scan the crowd.

So 01R was finding himself spending more time commanding the golem than he was sneaking. It was just more efficient that way. His eyes couldn't see anything the golem wouldn't.

Which meant . . . he was unnecessary. Anyone could command the golem and achieve the same results he was. The . . . *traitorous monster-thing* that disrespected the boss-queen with his every word could do the job, though 01R had no doubt he would find a way to fail at even that simple task.

The point being, 01R was dissatisfied with his current efforts. So, he thought to himself, what more could he do? What could he use his own body for to better accomplish his mission?

It was at that time that he heard a crash and a squeak behind him.

He turned to look. Something had leapt from a nearby window and crashed into the alley behind 01R. The sacred records informed him of what it was.

**Monster Rat (Level 2)**

A small, little rat, hardly different from their mundane ancestors, save for the slight mana signature 01R's sensors detected. It shook its head, gathering itself from the crash, when its eyes caught sight of 01R.

It froze.

"W-What are you . . . ?"

Just then, a dark shadow leapt into the alley. The rat monster squeaked and ran for its life, quickly rushing toward 01R and hiding behind his back. 01R frowned but turned to face the newcomer instead.

He saw black fur like the dead of night. He saw wicked scimitars designed to rip flesh from bone. He saw glowing yellow orbs whose gaze spelled death for all they laid upon.

He saw a cat.

The cat narrowed its eyes on him. It crouched down, adjusting its stance, and then pounced at 01R. The rat monster behind him prepared to run once 01R started to move, but instead, the rat's eyes widened.

01R didn't move.

The cat swiped its paw at him. 01R lifted his own, catching the cat's and stopping it dead. The cat blinked at him. The rat monster froze.

01R then pushed, the blessed armor of the boss-queen assisting him. The cat's paw swung up, causing it to fall backward as it lost its balance, and 01R stepped on the cat's torso, crossing his arms and looking it in the eyes. The eye of the boss-queen in his head flashed red.

"I am not your prey-meal. I am a servant of the wise-mighty-gracious boss-queen, yes-yes. Do not make-repeat that mistake again. If you wish-desire to do battle, then I will oblige, yes-yes. But know that I will not display-offer mercy again, yes-yes."

The cat meowed at him. 01R stepped off of it and waited. The cat flipped back over and backed away. Looking over him, it tensed its muscles, then turned its head and ran away. 01R shrugged and turned around. He looked down at the rat trembling on the ground.

"Now, who are you?"

The rat continued trembling in place.

"Y-You defeated-overcame the vicious cat-thing, just like that? W-What monster-terror are you?" It glanced over his armor. "Maybe some kind of rat-thing knight, yes-yes?"

Ateia frowned. They had traveled three floors already . . . and hadn't found a single monster or chest. Even the traps were limited to simple pitfalls, with none of the normal arrows or spikes. Just empty stone caverns and tunnels, with gouges in the walls where once metal ores grew.

"This is weird. Hasn't this dungeon been around for a while? Why is it so empty?"

Agedia narrowed her eyes.

"Because it's in danger. This dungeon may have been around for a while, but it largely limited itself to Metal- and Earth-attribute monsters. I think it realized we like it to be predictable; that's probably why the Empire approved of it in the first place. But that also means it wasn't prepared for a threat like this, so it's withdrawing from the earlier floors and saving its strength to defend itself."

She looked around. "At the very least, that means we shouldn't encounter any resistance from the dungeon itself. But it does mean the first thing we'll encounter will probably be that stupidly tough, metal-crunching worm. Are you bunch ready for that?"

Ateia and Taog nodded. Estrith just scoffed and hefted her spear. NSLICE-00P . . . stepped around the corner with her monsters and then came back alone. Agedia blinked at that but shrugged. She didn't know much about monster tamers, after all.

"Okay, then let's move. Quickly and quietly."

And so, the group began to run through the empty dungeon . . .

# 3

# Terminate the Adamant Bull Worm!

*"We should take the mines and push them somewhere else. That'd be bloody easier than getting eaten by one of those monsters."*

—Dwarven Captain Barildrid Silversword on viable responses to an adamant bull worm attack.

Agedia led the group down along the fastest path, turning toward Estrith along the way.

"Hey, you're a Dobhar, right? You're the first one I've met! I thought the Dobhar never left the North Seas. How did you end up here?"

Estrith scowled at her, but her instincts warned her about this woman, so she replied. "Unspeakable humiliations the likes of which you've never known."

Agedia nodded. "Ah, you lost and got subjugated, huh? Sorry to hear that. You get used to it eventually, though. Took my people about two hundred years or so? But it's not all bad. Enchanted heaters are nice, and I hear the food's a lot better than what we used to make."

Estrith glared at her then looked away, refusing to interact with the Mélusine any further. Agedia shrugged and turned to NSLICE-00P.

"What about you, shiny girl? Where are you from? I've never seen armor like that."

"Answer: This unit currently lacks a home base. Previous home bases were destroyed or had the designation removed. Specific details on this unit's armor are classified."

"Ah, don't want to talk about it, huh? That's fine. How'd you end up here?"

"Answer: A forced relocation upon conclusion of a mission."

Agedia nodded. "Ah, yeah, I've hit teleport traps before. Rough stuff. Like drinking too much, except without the fun parts."

They had just arrived on the twentieth floor when Agedia stopped. Narrowing her eyes, she drew her lance.

"We're close. Can you see it?"

NSLICE-00P zoomed in. They were in a straight and narrow hall that led to a large circular chamber. She could see a large mass of tough, black chitin curled together, corresponding to a massive energy signature on her mana sensors.

"Affirmative."

NSLICE-00P turned to face her group.

"Observation: Mana readings exceed recordings of NSLICE Uscfrea. Request: This unit requests all friendlies wait in a secure location. This unit cannot guarantee safety at tactical ranges. Command: Friendly Estrith, please ensure friendlies Ateia and Taog's safety."

Estrith frowned, gritting her teeth. Her first instinct was to lash out and refuse the usurper's comparison to her king, but she held her tongue. If there was one thing she could admit, it was that the queen of the Dobhar was strong. The usurper was in her right to make such claims.

Also, if this monster was stronger than her king . . . then there was a chance the usurper might lose. And Estrith could not intervene in a battle between such powerful opponents. It would be . . . such a pity if that were to happen. Yes, she would just have to wait here, as the queen of the Dobhar commanded, and leave her to whatever fate awaited. It couldn't be helped.

Agedia turned to her. "What are you planning, shiny girl? You going to take that stupid worm alone?"

"Response: This unit will conduct covert reconnaissance and commence with termination if the probability of success is reasonably high."

Agedia frowned but nodded. "Well, if you're sure. I'll hang back for now and intervene if you start attacking."

"Affirmative."

With that, NSLICE-00P activated her Invisibility spell and made her way toward the chamber.

*The spell shape Armor is now Level 2!*

NSLICE-00P activated her sensors, trying to scan the creature's hide for composition, likely defensive ability, and potential weak points, but the moment she stepped into the chamber, the creature began to stir, untangling itself and revealing its form. It was a massive worm, nine feet in diameter and about forty-five feet in length, with a black stonelike exoskeleton. It opened its circular mouth, revealing diamondlike teeth.

| Species | Description |
|---|---|
| Adamant Bull Worm (Level 107) | **A huge worm monster that feeds on metals and minerals. Not a picky eater, though, will settle for flesh just fine. Big, wiggly, and eats everything. Its chitin is said to be as hard as adamant, though few have been able or willing to put that claim to the test.** |

It turned its maw toward NSLICE-00P and the entrance. She quietly moved out of the way.

The worm turned its maw, still facing directly toward NSLICE-00P. Her danger predictions began to rise.

What NSLICE-00P wasn't aware of was that the adamant bull worm didn't rely on sight to begin with, so an Invisibility spell had little effect on it. And since it fed on metals, it had a knack for detecting such things. Especially rare and valuable metals it hadn't consumed before.

Like the Iesnuorium in NSLICE-00P's Equalizer.

Vafum hypothetically could have told NSLICE-00P this, but he wasn't here. And, unfortunately, Agedia generally relied on her teammates for such things. They handled the planning and the research; she handled hitting things really, *really* hard, so it slipped her mind that Invisibility wouldn't be effective against the worm. Plus, given the prevalence of non-visual senses and magical detection methods, she assumed an experienced dungeon destroyer like NSLICE-00P wouldn't rely solely on Invisibility in the first place.

The worm let out a roar and began rushing toward her. Fortunately, NSLICE-00P had activated her repulsors once it became clear the worm could track her, and she flew into the air, readying her guns and missiles, along with several magic circles.

Reconnaissance-in-force it was.

But the worm curled up and rushed up the wall of the room, launching itself backward into the air toward the cyborg.

"DIE, YOU STUPID WORM!"

Agedia rushed into the room, curling her tail down like a spring while holding her lance and tensing every muscle in her body. She began to glow slightly as she activated a skill, and then shot forward like a bolt from a ballista. Her lance crashed right into the side of the worm's head.

"UGH, NOT AGAIN!"

There was a loud clang, and the head of the lance bent and cracked. But the worm was knocked off course, allowing NSLICE-00P to boost out of the way and take her distance. And then she began to bombard the worm with machine guns, missiles, and Bolt spells of every different attribute she had, analyzing the impact on the worm's HP barrier.

The machine guns did very little, and even the missiles didn't get very far. Fire, Earth, and Metal Magic had no effect either. However, Holy and Water seemed to perform beyond even optimistic predictions.

Magic circles formed and fused together, and then jets of water glowing with golden-and-silver light blasted the creature, who shrieked and spun about. It curled around, trying to avoid the jets, before launching itself in the air once again. NSLICE-00P dodged and fired the Equalizer while the worm was still midair, focusing the jets on the target.

The monster shrieked again, but its hide was extremely thick, and its sheer bulk was an obstacle in and of itself. It would take NSLICE-00P a while to cut through it.

And of course, the moment the monster landed on the ground, it twisted and curled, preventing the cyborg from striking the same spot.

"Adapting strategy. Determining efficient means of Water-based termination. Recommendation: Friendly units should retreat from the area."

Agedia launched herself again, striking the worm once more, but it ignored her this time, and the tip of her damaged lance snapped off.

"Ugh, stupid shoddy lance, stupid miserly Dwarf. But I'm still not going to leave you here alone!"

NSLICE-00P dodged out of the way, then began forming dozens of magic circles in the air. They began to glow bright as she Supercharged each of them to the limit.

"Warning: This unit is about to activate attacks with a wide area of effect. Please vacate target area to avoid friendly fire."

Agedia blinked at the sight.

"Oh. Um . . . bye then!"

She started slithering back toward the entrance hall, then NSLICE-00P formed a barrier over the entrance and around herself before activating the magic circles.

*The spell shape Blast is now Level 8!*
*The skill Water Magic is now Level 7!*
*The skill Holy Magic is now Level 12!*

NSLICE-00P used the simplest spell that produced a large quantity of the element, and the entire room filled with glowing Holy Water. The worm started writhing about, bubbles escaping its maw as it shrieked. It tried to smash through the walls and floors, but the barriers of the dungeon were not made of simple stone or metal. And since worms breathed through their skin, some of said water began to seep into the creature. NSLICE-00P lost control over the water as it passed through the creature's HP barrier, but it still alerted her to the locations of the pores on the creature's body.

She formed new magic circles for Holy Water Beams directly over the creature's HP barrier, blasting the water around it into jets. She randomly adjusted the portion of the spell related to the Beam shape, causing most of the circles to sputter out. But eventually, one succeeded, and the jet grew larger. She then iterated on that circle until the Beam shrank instead.

*You have learned the spell shape Spike!*
*The spell shape Spike is now Level 5!*
*You have learned how to adjust spell shape sizes!*
*The skill Spell Shaping has leveled twice and is now Level 18! New spell shape choice available!*
*Mana Control increased by 10 and is now 185!*

She formed dozens of Holy Water Spike magic circles, adjusting the shape to form tiny needles, as small as she could make them. And then, she launched them toward the pores on the monster with as much speed and power as she could force into the projectiles.

*The skill Spell Penetration has leveled three times and is now Level 6!*
*The skill Geomancy has leveled three times and is now Level 5!*
*The skill Heroic Challenger is now Level 2!*
*The skill Water Magic is now Level 8!*
*The skill Spell Fusion is now Level 9!*

And since she was continuously bombarding the worm with enough Holy Water spells to flood the room, Geomancy was working overtime. She pushed more mana into the Geomancy and Spell Penetration skills to boost the effects, with Heroic Challenger further stripping the monster's defenses.

The Holy Water needles began to pierce through the monster's HP and strike through flesh. The worm's shrieks grew, and bright red blood started to taint the water, but it could not stop the barrage coming from all directions, nor the Holy Water drowning and purifying it all at once. And since it lacked mobility in the water, it couldn't catch NSLICE-00P.

This fight could only end in one way.

*You have slain Adamant Bull Worm (Level 107)!*
*Gained 79 Personal XP, 23 Dungeon XP!*
*Level up! You are now at Personal Level 64!*

**Powerful monster record obtained. Monster lineage unlocked.**
**Earth-Eater Worm-type subordinates may now be summoned!**

"Mission Report: Target terminated."

01R crossed his arms as he looked down at the rat. He personally didn't know what a knight was, though he knew the man-things often called the wise-mighty-gracious boss-queen as such.

"I am not worthy-deserving of such a title, though it is the ideal I strive-work toward, yes-yes."

"I-I see. What warren-burrow are you from? This is Boss Cravenfang's territory-domain; I didn't know he got a new enforcer-warrior, yes-yes."

01R narrowed his eyes.

"I serve-acknowledge none but the wise-mighty-gracious boss-queen. Do not insult-affront me again."

The rat monster shrieked and covered its head.

"Apologies, forgive-ignore this lowly one! W-Who is this boss-queen? T-The only woman-lady boss I know is Boss Heartfinger, yes-yes."

01R opened his mouth before pausing. The boss-queen had instructed them to remain incognito and not to reveal any dungeon-related information. As much as he wanted, he could not declare her glorious name to outsiders.

"The wise-mighty boss-queen's name is too glorious to be stated-spoken casually. Simply know-understand that I serve a higher boss-queen than any of these . . . pretender-imposters."

The rat on the ground trembled.

"Y-You . . . I heard-learned there were newcomers, but a new boss . . . Oh, Boss Cravenfang will not be happy-pleased, no-no."

01R scoffed. He cared little for such a pretender, save to put him in his place for daring to call himself a boss.

But then . . . 01R froze. The . . . *traitorous thing's* poisonous words sounded through his head. The pathetic mutterings about loyal subordinate-minions and building kingdoms. And here was a pathetic thing that did not know the boss-queen's wisdom or power or grace . . . a whole burrow of them that apparently controlled this area as their domain.

01R grinned as an idea began to form in his head. A way he could better fulfill the boss-queen's will.

"You there, what is your name-title?"

The rat's trembling grew, and its ears fell flat against its head.

"S-Snuan Covenwalker."

01R leaned in closer.

"Snuan Covenwalker, tell me about this pretender-imposter Cravenfang."

# 4

# Terminate . . . err . . . Save the Mines of Might!

*"AHAHAHAHAHAHAHAHAHAHAHA! Hahaha, ha. I'm sorry. It's just, that was a funny joke. Because surely you were joking, right?"*

—Traveling author and former Exploratore Placus Paesentius Statius, on the plausibility of taming an adamant bull worm.

Agedia came back into the room as NSLICE-00P let the water fade, the dungeon draining the remainder via magic. The Mélusine nodded at NSLICE-00P.

"Nice fight, that was some spell. You some kind of battlemage, then?"

"Requesting Clarification: Please define term: 'Battlemage'."

Agedia tilted her head but shrugged.

"They don't have those where you're from? Uses magic as their main thing but can take a hit if needed. Understands the importance of armor."

NSLICE-00P's robotic eye flickered. According to combat data, she had, in fact, mainly used magic in the majority of engagements since arriving in this place. Her defenses were reasonable, and her protocols contained a great deal of data regarding armor.

"Response: By the stated definition, *battlemage* is a reasonably accurate descriptor for this unit."

The rest of the group then made their way into the room, staring for a moment at the bloody mess of the adamant bull worm. NSLICE-00P was about to start leaving, since the target had been terminated and she was not supposed to terminate the dungeon at large, when a hidden door opened at the side of the room. NSLICE-00P whirled toward it, weapons and magic circles at the ready.

A mana signature had suddenly appeared in the room just as the door opened; one that NSLICE-00P hadn't detected previously.

"Peace! I mean-intend you no harm!"

Out walked a short, squat, and hunched-over being. It had pink skin, a rodentlike face, and two large front teeth. It was unarmed and had both of its paws held up.

**Naked Mole-Ratkin (Level 12)**

Agedia's eyes narrowed on it.

"Is that so? Talk quickly, then."

"I come from the Great Master, the Lord of the Mines of Might. He has watched-observed your victory over that foul creature over there and wishes to know if you are hunting-slaying them."

Taog frowned at that. "*Them*?"

The Naked Mole-Ratkin nodded.

"There are three, in fact. This one was left behind to guard the rear, but there are two more, pushing deeper into the Great Master's realm. He would request your assistance in defeating them and will reward you greatly if you do."

"Acknowledged. Mission Update: Additional targets identified. Reengaging termination protocols. Please guide this unit to target locations."

Ateia and Taog turned to Agedia as NSLICE-00P started following the monster to the door on the other side of the room.

"What do you think, Agedia?"

Agedia rubbed her chin and shrugged.

"Could be a trap, but unlikely if the dungeon's been threatened like this. And if there *are* more worms, that's what we're here for."

With that, the rest of the group followed suit as well . . .

Further inside the dungeon, two adamant bull worms rampaged inside a large room. Golems formed of magic metals rose to oppose them with glimmering spears, mighty war hammers, and shining bows, but the worms' tough hides deflected the blows, and their diamond teeth crushed the golems to scrap metal.

And behind the worms, a hooded figure cackled.

It was all coming together. Utrad had been strangely on guard recently, and its Magister Exploratore had always been a crafty one. It had taken a great deal of thought, work, and patience to pull this off.

But he wasn't the Herald of Tremors for nothing!

Adamant bull worms. The scourge of the Dwarf clans, miners, and blacksmiths everywhere. Known for being completely untamable, and therefore, considered a natural disaster that no one would realize he was controlling. It had, in fact, been an absolute pain to take control of this bunch. If not for the powers he gained directly from the Domides he served, it would have been impossible for him as well. Even then, he was barely controlling the creatures. All he could do was point them in a direction and *possibly* avoid being eaten.

But, well, that was the point of his mission, after all. The Realms of Mana were a place of wonder, where anything was possible. Where godlike powers could be obtained, if only one could pierce the veil between the Material Plane and the Source.

He patted the bag at his side, where an enchanted dagger lay. Soon, he would pierce that veil just a bit more and gain access to power like he could never imagine. And Magister Caelinus would return to find his capital's main source of magic metals no longer available to him.

The Herald of Tremors grinned. Yes, it had all come together. Magister Caelinus and the Magister Exploratore were both away with the bulk of their forces. Neither the Mines of Might nor the Dwarves of Khalbuldor could defeat adamant bull worms without assistance from the Empire. No one could stop him now!

"Observation: Human detected. Appears to be unconcerned with target monsters."

"Yes, he's the one leading-commanding them."

"Significant shift in mission parameters detected. Pausing termination protocols. Reanalyzing mission consequences for primary directive in light of targets being tamed monsters."

The Herald of Tremors turned around and blinked. There was some sort of armored knight walking into the room, right next to one of those horrid rodentkin he'd encountered at the start of the dungeon.

Was it an ambush? The knight was completely covered in metal, so could have been a kind of living armor, but he hadn't seen one of that design before, and it appeared to be conversing with the monster. He frowned. In any case, they could not be allowed to interfere.

"Kill them!"

One of the adamant bull worms turned away from the golems ahead and spun around, rushing toward the newcomers.

"Hostile intent detected. Reengaging termination protocols."

Suddenly, dozens of glowing magic circles filled the air. The Herald of Tremors's eyes widened. He barely had time to throw up a barrier before a massive flood filled the room. His worms began shrieking and writhing.

He frowned and started to cast a spell of his own. A mage of this caliber was unexpected, but he was a Herald of the Realms of Mana! He had made a bargain with a Domides and could directly draw upon the power of its realm! No mundane mage relying on the ambient mana in this world could match his might—

His eyes widened. His barrier was hissing and dissolving, and he noticed the water had a silver and golden glow to it.

This spell was filled with Holy mana. The mana granted to heroes and saints. The mana that would directly oppose the powers of the Realms of Mana should it make its way past the veil.

The one weakness of his vaunted powers.

As the water began leaking into his barrier, his mind raced, trying to determine which of his powers and spells could overturn this situation. But he wouldn't get the chance.

"Hostile spell detected. Equalizer engaged."

A rainbow beam shot through the water and struck his barrier. The barrier shattered, as well as the magic circle he had been forming. The last thing he saw was a magic circle forming in the water right in front of his face . . .

*You have slain Human (Level 75)!*
*Gained 7 Personal XP, 3 Dungeon XP!*
*You have slain two Adamant Bull Worms!*
*Gained 163 Personal XP, 53 Dungeon XP!*
*You have leveled up 2 Personal levels!*
*You are now at Personal Level 66!*
*The skill Water Magic is now Level 9!*
*The spell shape Blast is now Level 9!*
*The spell shape Spike has leveled twice and is now Level 7!*
*The skill Spell Penetration has leveled twice and is now Level 8!*
*The skill Geomancy has leveled twice and is now Level 7!*
*The skill Heroic Challenger is now Level 3!*

NSLICE-00P let the water drain away before dropping the barriers she had used to protect the Naked Mole-Ratkin, as well as the dungeon's golems.

"Mission Update: All targets in this location terminated. Please guide this unit to the next target location."

The Naked Mole-Ratkin, who was trembling and backing away now, jumped.

"A-Ah, t-that was the last of them."

"Mission Update: All known targets terminated. Mission accomplished."

Agedia and the rest joined her just as two golems appeared from a door on the far side of the room, carrying two chests. They placed the massive golden one in front of NSLICE-00P and the large silver chest in front of Agedia. The Naked Mole-Ratkin then spoke.

"T-The Great Master thanks you for your assistance-help. Your rewards, as promised-offered."

NSLICE-00P scanned the chest for traps and then opened it. Inside, she found a rod made of silvery metal, about three feet long, with a white gemstone at the top.

| Name | Description |
|---|---|
| **Rod of Command** | **A rod used to command golems. This one may control up to ten at once. May take control of unbound golems via physical contact. Also functions as a potent spell focus, particularly for Earth and Metal Magic.** |

NSLICE-00P scheduled the rod for investigation at the next available time. If this rod was involved in the command, communication, and control of golems, then it could have implications for mana-driven communication infrastructure.

Agedia, on the other hand, was hugging some new lance while Estrith tried to look away, but she couldn't help glancing at the weapon.

The Naked Mole-Ratkin began to back away from them. "Now, p-please leave, if you don't mind. T-The Great Master says the presence of a hero this deep makes . . . his monsters uncomfortable-worried."

Snuan led 01R into the sewers, trembling with every step. She, as 01R had learned, was clearly looking for any opportunity to escape, but 01R was keeping a close eye on her, so she had no chance to run.

Approaching a crack in one of the walls, they stepped inside, and 01R found himself inside a tunnel with multiple paths branching off in different directions. An easy place to get lost . . . or ambushed.

That is, if the wise-mighty-gracious boss-queen had not shared her wisdom with him. The cybernetic components he was blessed with could draw a map with perfect accuracy and run sensor scans to detect any life-forms. He would see any treachery long before it arrived.

"Well, lead-guide on, yes-yes."

Snuan trembled but had no choice but to obey. 01R noted with approval that she led him on a straight path, not attempting to twist him around or lose him in the tunnels. Whether that was out of honesty, fear, or knowledge that there were defenses further inside, he could not say, but he would have hated to waste time on such things. Soon, his sensors began to detect a large concentration of thermal and mana signatures, as well as a couple very familiar ones.

He raised an eyebrow.

"Wait. There is something I must see-check, yes-yes."

Snuan stopped as 01R turned down another tunnel, just before making contact with the signatures. Snuan tried to creep away, but 01R turned to face her.

"Come-follow along now, yes-yes."

Snuan's ears fell, but she obeyed.

Walking halfway down the tunnel, 01R stopped, crossing his arms.

"Show-reveal yourself. I know you are there, yes-yes."

A dark figure crawled along the roof, lowering itself on a thread. Snuan yelped as the figure came into view and turned to run, but 01R reached back without looking and placed a paw on her shoulder, holding the trembling rat in place.

"What are you doing here, 02S?"

"I'd like to ask you the same, 01R. I wouldn't have thought *you* would be playing with the locals."

01R narrowed his eyes at the cyber-spider.

"The wise-mighty-gracious boss-queen saw fit to speak-interact with the other man-things, to show them grace rather than to prey-consume them as is her right. I simply follow-emulate her example. So, what are you doing-plotting here, 02S?"

02S chittered with her mandibles. "Protecting the boss's possessions, of course."

"Possessions? Yes, everything-everywhere *should* belong to the wise-mighty-gracious boss-queen, but I doubt there is anything down here she has already claimed—" 01R froze and started to tremble. ". . . He didn't."

02S giggled, and 01R slapped a paw on his face.

"He did. The snack was captured by the locals mere moments after we split up."

01R groaned. "Why didn't he tell-warn anyone?!"

02S giggled again.

"Why do you think? He broke his communication protocols earlier, and no one pays attention to his reports in the first place. Besides, you know he's probably thinking something stupid again."

01R heaved a massive sigh.

". . . So we have to save-rescue him now too."

"Eh, I wanted to watch him squirm a bit more, but I guess."

01R just slapped his face again and heaved another sigh as 02S giggled.

INTERLUDE

# The Might of the Legion

Agedia walked over to the adamant bull worms, taking out a large knife, and began cutting away. It took a while, but eventually, she got a piece of its exoskeleton. Sighing, she shook her head. Normally, she would want to butcher the entire thing—monster parts could be very expensive and made for some excellent gear—but the dungeon wanted them to leave, so she thought she better not overstay their welcome. Besides . . . it would all belong to NSLICE-00P anyways, who didn't seem particularly interested in the corpses.

Agedia shook her head before walking over to the man who had been in the room. She glanced at the dungeon monsters. "Sorry, but I'm going to need to take this. We'll need the body and belongings to report on what happened here. But I can't carry three adamant bull worms back, so I think you're getting the better end of this."

The Naked Mole-Ratkin nodded. "The Great Master says-declares that is acceptable."

Agedia nodded in thanks and hoisted the corpse over her shoulder, then the group made their way out of the dungeon. Agedia's eyes narrowed as she carried the weight.

The situation had become a lot more complicated. She had only accompanied the group to keep them safe and see NSLICE-00P's capabilities for herself, but it turned out this was not a natural disaster but an intentional attack. Taming an adamant bull worm, much less three, was no normal feat. In fact, Agedia could only think of two possible types of people who could pull it off. The first would be heroes with access to some special taming skill she had never heard of.

The other?

The other would mean that the fight that Agedia had put to a close years ago had come to her very backyard.

Her heart pounded and her body trembled at the thought. But whatever she felt about the matter, she could not ignore it when it happened right in front of her eyes. Much less when the girl happened to have visited at the same time.

She took a deep breath as she tried to calm her beating heart. The road ahead was deeply troubling . . . but at least there was one silver lining.

NSLICE-00P, Ateia's companion, was *far* more powerful than she had expected.

The council of Khalbuldor gathered around a large stone table. A pouch of belongings, including an enchanted dagger, rested on top, next to a piece of exoskeleton.

One of the Dwarves crossed his arms.

"And we believe the alcoholic snake on this? How did she even take down an adamant bull worm? How are we sure she didn't just dream it up in a drunken haze?"

Another Dwarf narrowed his eyes.

"Mind your words, Yudric. Personality defects aside, there is no question as to Agedia of the Mélusine's might or accomplishments. She and Broadbane have contributed greatly to Khalbuldor. And I heard she recruited the help of an Amicitia Populi Elteni."

Yudric scoffed. "From Turannia."

The second Dwarf shook his head. "You betray your ignorance of all things beyond metal, Master Smith. Word is this person defeated Uscfrea Spellbreaker in single combat. Turannia may be weak, but the king of the Dobhar was not."

A third Dwarf chuckled. "Besides, Yudric, we all know Agedia can hold her drink. You should know that best of all, after you challenged her and lost."

Yudric scowled, but the head of the council raised his hand.

"We can discuss the Mélusine later. We saw that accursed worm enter the dungeon, and we know Agedia returned with a piece of its body. We all know you don't shave a piece off an adamant bull worm while it's still alive. I think we can believe that the monster—or monsters, as Agedia claimed—have been dealt with, and have someone scout the dungeon to confirm it's back in operation. All in agreement?"

All the Dwarves at the table nodded and agreed. Yudric scowled and muttered but begrudgingly nodded his head. The head of the council's eyes turned grave.

"Then . . . what do we make of this?"

He pointed to the items on the table, and the council went silent. Eventually, he turned to Yudric.

"Master Smith, what do you make of the weapon?"

Yudric glared at the enchanted dagger on the table. He took a deep breath. "I don't know."

The second Dwarf raised an eyebrow. "You don't know? That's surprising, Master Smith. Are you sure your dislike of the Mélusine warrior isn't impacting your motivation?"

Yudric barked at the Dwarf, "Watch your tone and your accusations, Thabumlir Noblejaw, lest I sully my hammer with your blood! I *always* respect the metal, regardless of where or from whom it came from. I have forged countless masterpieces from materials you cannot dream of! I have studied the metal my entire life and earned my title from the sweat of my brow, the accomplishments of my hand, and the knowledge that I gathered, unlike *some* people who rely on the honor of their forefathers. So, believe me, I do NOT state my ignorance lightly. It is not that I do not know anything about this dagger. It is that I could not determine the first thing about it."

The council went silent once more. A third Dwarf's eyes widened. "Master Smith . . . you mean to say . . . ?"

Yudric nodded slowly. "The Aesdes themselves could not identify the name or characteristics of this weapon. It is not of this world. I suspect it came directly from the Realms of Mana, and not the nice ones."

The council did not respond, save to call for drinks. Eventually, Thabumlir whispered, "So Magister Caelinus was right . . ."

The head of the council rested his elbows on the table and crossed his hands in front of his face. "It . . . would appear so. And we have but one response."

He looked around at each member of the council. One by one, each of them slowly nodded. He took a deep breath.

"Send word to the magister. The Dwarves of Khalbuldor have made their decision . . ."

On the borders of the Utrad Province, a thousand hooves thundered and shook the ground. Muscular human torsos wrapped in leathers and furs blended into the horse bodies. They galloped across the field, turning this way and that, flowing like streams of water. They pulled back the strings of mighty bows crafted from the bones of mighty monsters and the wood of magical trees.

The Centaurs and the tribes they had subjugated charged forth, crossing the Somno Secta River that marked the edge of the Empire and the Wild Lands, unleashing a hail of arrows that blotted out the sun.

Before them stood a wall of metal. Giants and Minotaurs and particularly large humans hoisted towering metal shields. The shields glowed, and mana drifted off of them, merging together into a continuous barrier. The arrows seemed to turn toward the shields and bounce harmlessly off them.

Underneath the arms of the towering Legion bulwarks, Legion sharpshooters took aim with enchanted crossbows, unleashing a counter volley from the gaps in the shields. Centaurs cried and fell. Bolts and boulders from siege weapons far behind the lines crashed down from above, breaking apart the Centaurs' movements.

The Centaurs split to the side, and a wall of wood charged the legion lines. The Pastor Silvarum marched onward, crossbow bolts having no impact on the living trees.

A centurion shouted a command, and the sharpshooters fell back, replaced with battlemages who pointed their staves between the shields and chanted, volleys of Fireballs shooting through the air. The front lines of the Pastor Silvarum caught ablaze and began to flail about, crashing into the Centaurs around them.

As the battle raged, a heavy fog rose from the Somno Secta and covered the Centaur force. Singing voices rang through the mist while the Centaurs ran amok, crashing into one another.

The Auxiliary Aqua rose from the river. Selkies chanted and blinded the enemy with fog as Sirens raised their mana-laden voices. Fishkin and Crocodilekin stepped onto the banks, lifting spears and harpoons.

And then a horn blew through the air. The Legion's archers and mages and siege weapons halted their fire.

The knights of the Empire charged into the fray from the flank, covered from head to toe in solid metal armor. They rode on all manner of beasts—hippogriffs and unicorns and giant wolves and massive lizards. Some rode on horses that had a shine in their eyes and that cut across the ground almost as if in flight. The riders lifted swords and lances of metal and bone: some, golden and silvery metals engraved with magic circles; others, the remains of mighty monsters repurposed by their slayers. They rushed into the fog and crashed into the confused Centaurs, slaughtering all they encountered.

The Legion sharpshooters and mages took to the rear as the Legion slayers moved forward, lowering halberds to form a wall of spears. They let out a cry and charged the front, just as the Auxiliary Aqua attacked the rear.

The Centaur war chief tried to rally his fleeing warriors and gather his elites for a counterattack, but suddenly, he fell over, the blade of a Dimindium Pendem assassin lodged in his heart.

Magister Caelinus watched from a nearby hill as the Centaur force broke and routed. Just then, someone walked up to him. A man with goat horns and hooved legs, wearing the light armor of the Exploratores.

"Magister Vibius, is there something to report?"

Magister Exploratore Vibius's mouth curled into a smile. "Indeed there is. The Dwarves of Khalbuldor have sent word. They've pledged their support."

Magister Caelinus let out a hum and rubbed his chin. "I see. Is there anything else we should take care of first?"

Magister Vibius shrugged. "There *is* the issue of the Amicitia Populi Elteni."

Magister Caelinus raised an eyebrow. "The one from Turannia? The wandering mercenary?"

Vibius nodded. "The report claims she's quite formidable and can take down a full-grown ursanus in a single blow. Rector Aemilia may not have exaggerated all that much, after all. What's more, she's currently in Velusitum, in the company of two Exploratores from Turannia. They are on a mission on her behalf, and so have refused my call to arms."

Magister Caelinus narrowed his eyes. "Will it be a problem?"

Vibius shrugged. "To be determined. But . . . it appears she was the one who handled that adamant bull worm in the Mines of Might, after which the Dwarves of Khalbuldor saw reason. So perhaps there is an opportunity instead?"

Magister Caelinus rubbed his chin again as he looked over the field and the fleeing Centaurs. He took a deep breath. "No helping it now. The Dwarves are on board, and we just broke the Centaurs; we'll need to move soon. Head over there and see what you can do about the mercenary. Someone like that could be a serious asset . . . or a major risk. Whatever you do, just make sure it's settled by the time I return."

Vibius gave his signature sly smile. "It shall be done . . . Magister."

Magister Caelinus shook his head as Vibius snuck away. He gazed out at the banner of the Legion and his triumphant troops celebrating their victory.

"If only . . ."

# 5

# Establishing Priorities

*Priority Number One: Protect the lives of designated VIPs.*
*Priority Number Two: Prevent proprietary technology from falling into nonaffiliated hands.*
*Priority Number Three: Execute orders by affiliated command personnel in accordance with the chain of command.*
*[. . .]*
*Priority Number Seventy-Six: Survive and return to mission commander.*

—NSLICE Standard Mission Priorities.

After Vafum begrudgingly bought everyone a meal, NSLICE-00P made her way back to the inn. It was late at night, and the others had gone to sleep. NSLICE-00P was still operating at full efficiency, though, and had work to do.

Which was figuring out what work she *should* do.

Up to this point, NSLICE-00P had been mainly reacting to events and local circumstances. She upgraded when circumstances demanded it, she took opportunities as they presented themselves, and she moved as situations dictated. This, perhaps, was to be expected. She was an enforcer, enacting her masters' will and responding to situations on the ground.

But the scenario had changed. NSLICE-00P had acquired great gains and great revelations on the way to Velusitum, and so had a great many opportunities and upgrades before her. Exploring Metal Magic, Mana Crafting, Enchanting, and the Item Foundry to reverse engineer her own technology without corresponding industrial infrastructure, analyzing new nonstandard materials and what implications they might have for her physical weapon arsenal, continuing to expand her magical arsenal, investigating Illusion Magic and how it might reinforce her emotional controls, or utilizing the foreign system to upgrade her implants were just a few.

Likewise, she was now the lead unit of an entire NSLICE network. She had work to do there as well: upgrading existing cyborg units, processing new units, and exploring the new options for fully automated units, as well as researching options for expanding the range of communications so the range individual units could operate apart from her. And then there was the software aspect of adapting NSLICE network-scale protocols to local conditions and the current mission set.

Not to mention the defense, development, and command of the NSLICE home base that had been established in Turannia, centered on the Otter Burrow dungeon. Or managing diplomatic relations with the local factions. Or upgrading the capabilities of the friendlies so that they could fulfill the new major directive without personal assistance from her.

In other words, NSLICE-00P now had too many opportunities and tasks on her plate to simply react to each one in turn. She needed to organize and prioritize which would be the most efficient for her needs. And she needed to do so in light of her primary, critical, and major directives.

Her robotic eye began flickering rapidly as she got to work.

First of all, she redefined her primary task in light of the directives. Her primary objective was to search for and report to the first located persons of interest while maintaining the safety of friendlies Ateia and Taog and preserving the Dobhar race if at all possible. Her secondary objective was to improve her own capabilities to ensure her own survival under local conditions. Her tertiary objective was to expand the capabilities of the NSLICE network and rebuild or replace industrial and communication infrastructure necessary to maintain it.

Next, she reclassified herself. She was not just an enforcer anymore, and it was no longer efficient for her to act like one. She designated herself as the acting command unit for the NSLICE network, a key maintenance and production facility, and the primary combat asset. She didn't particularly have protocols for the first two designations, but it would allow her to shift her calculations away from her previous behavior.

She then analyzed the state of the primary directive and the various means she now had to pursue it. The most important intel she had gained were the various pieces of evidence that she was not on Earth, and the failure of the Banishment spell. She needed to understand this place: what it was, where it was, and what relationship it had with Earth, if any. She needed to know if she was on some isolated place on Earth, a different planet, a different part of the universe, or a different universe entirely. If she had moved through space or time or both or none. Only then could she know, for sure, what her specific short-term goals should be. Whether to continue searching this place . . . or to search for a way to leave it.

Her heart rate sped up slightly at that thought, but she cast a Calm spell on herself and carried on, setting her new objective as researching the reality around her. To explore the Banishment spell and other magics that might be related. To explore magic and mana itself, as well as the foreign system, as they all seemed integrated and critical to the fundamental nature of her current surroundings. And to investigate the space around her, how it differed from Earth, and so how it might be related to it.

Exploring magic could also aid with recalibrating her emotional controls, and would expand her combat abilities as well, so it was an efficient task to focus her attention on.

As for searching this location and the local society for the persons of interest directly, she would defer that task to the Empire. The Empire clearly had long-range communications and large-scale organizations available, and so would be more efficient at a search than she would, even accounting for the new NSLICE network. So, it was more efficient to rely on them than to walk around herself. The most important thing she needed to do regarding the local search was maintain cordial relations with the Empire.

In other words, she would remain by Ateia and Taog and avoid hostility against the Empire if at all possible. This would also allow her to ensure her friendlies' safety.

The NSLICE network could continue searching her immediate surroundings, and she would continue expanding it, though at a lower priority. The NSLICE network was more trustworthy compared to an unaffiliated faction, but it would not match the observed scale of the Empire anytime soon. Expanding the network would be a long-term objective she would work on as opportunity arose, but not an immediate priority unless circumstances required its specific capabilities.

The same went for replicating industrial infrastructure and the investigation of nonstandard materials. At the end of the day, she could both produce new NSLICE units and upgrade her own components via the foreign system. The ability to do so manually was just another option, not truly a new capability. Perhaps friendly Melion could be tasked with this if integrated into the NSLICE network, as they had already expressed interest in working as a maintenance personnel.

It was at that moment that there was a quiet knock on her door.

"Seero, are you awake?"

NSLICE-00P opened the door to find Ateia outside.

"Affirmative. Query: Does friendly Ateia have a query or status update for this unit?"

Ateia shook her head.

"I just wanted to talk. It's been a while since we've had a chance to chat."

NSLICE-00P's robotic eye flickered. She originally planned to explore the Banishment spell next. Maintaining relations with friendly Ateia was important, though a lower priority than understanding reality around her if Ateia had no important updates or queries.

However, NSLICE-00P's organic components indicated that a conversation was desirable, and that she should regularly check-in on friendly units in any case. Her cybernetic components . . . ultimately acquiesced. With the Calm protocol active, they detected no physiological anomalies or excessive emotions in the organic components that would interfere with that analysis. And besides, NSLICE-00P didn't require all of her processing power to conduct conversation, so she could devote a thread to spell analysis anyways.

"Affirmative."

Ateia smiled at her. "Thanks, Seero. It's kind of been crazy, you know? Finding out my dad's been using a fake name, that he never told me who he really was. And . . . the idea that I have enemies out there. I'm sorry we haven't talked much since. I just . . . was distracted."

"Observation: Compartmentalization of classified intelligence is standard procedure."

Ateia nodded. "Taog said as much, but it still hurts, you know?"

NSLICE-00P scanned Ateia's body but found it in optimal condition, minus standard end-of-day fatigue. "Requesting Clarification: This unit cannot detect any physical damage within friendly Ateia. Please specify the nature and location of the injuries."

Ateia shook her head. "I mean . . . emotionally, Seero."

NSLICE-00P's robotic eye flickered, and her cybernetic components dropped the separate thread. "Request: Please describe the state of friendly Ateia's emotions, the underlying causes, and any known treatment methods."

NSLICE-00P realized something. If she gathered data on a full organic's emotional experience, she could better analyze her own organic components and so better recalibrate her emotional controls. It was a way to gather data on organics that did not involve setting her own organic components loose. She did have some basic psychology knowledge, but if there was anything she had learned since arriving here, it was that her previously programmed protocols were much less efficient than data gathered from real-world incidents.

Her programmed knowledge mainly dealt with combat morale, in any case. And recalibrating her emotional controls could prevent the rise of unexpected directives, or even unexpected critical mission failure. When also considering the need to maintain relations with Imperial contacts and prevent damage to her friendlies, NSLICE-00P calculated this conversation as higher priority than an immediate analysis of the Banishment spell, and so gave it her full attention.

Ateia tilted her head but started to speak, describing what was in her heart. And NSLICE-00P listened all the while.

* * *

01R made his way into the space filled with heat signatures, dragging along a trembling Snuan. He found a large cavern, large enough to fit a small man-thing, filled with rat monsters scurrying every which way, bringing in food and random trinkets from countless tunnels. To the side of the cavern was a metal cage holding a trembling Rattingtale, rat monsters poking at his armor. At the center of the cavern was a small chair teetering on top of a pile of junk.

Sitting on top of the chair was a Ratkin, a hunched humanoid rat that towered over the others. He was a hulk of a Ratkin, with a massive gullet that made 01R wonder if he could even move, wearing a metal bracelet like a crown on top of his head.

"Minions! Bring-Fetch me my food! It is time for supper, yes-yes! And hurry it up with that intruder-outsider! I want-desire that shiny armor, yes-yes!"

01R cleared his throat, and all the rats and the Ratkin stopped what they were doing, turning toward him. Rattingtale's eyes widened while Snuan hissed at him, "W-What are you doing-thinking?! We need to sneak-creep, yes-yes! We'll be killed-slayed, yes-yes!"

The Ratkin chuckled. "Well, well, well, what do we have-possess here? Another intruder-outsider, yes-yes? And this one came to give-offer himself, yes-yes."

01R crossed his arms. "I believe you stole-took something that belongs to the wise-mighty-gracious boss-queen. I, 01R, her warrior-servant, have come to retrieve it, as well as to claim-obtain your loyalty for the boss-queen, as is right and proper."

The Ratkin narrowed his eyes.

"Do you, now?" He slowly rose to his feet. "You dare to come here and insult-offend me, the powerful-deadly Boss Cravenfang, in my own home-palace? You will all die-perish for this! And then I will break-destroy your 'boss-queen' and show everyone this land belongs to Boss Cravenfang, yes-yes!"

01R's robotic eye turned red. "So you have chosen . . . death."

Boss Cravenfang pointed at 01R and Snuan. "Kill-slay them!"

The rat monsters rushed forward as Snuan screamed. 01R extended his metal claws and charged into the fray, meeting the first rat's slash with his own, his metal claws cutting through it with ease.

*You have slain Monster Rat (Level 3)!*
*Gained 7 XP!*

And so, the fight began.

INTERLUDE

# The Alert Is Sent! The Boss-Queen's Servants Call for Aid!

*"Fortunate? No, Legate, we could not be any less fortunate. Our foes may be weak, but you're about to learn that quantity has a quality all its own."*

—Dux Comitatense Manilia Statia, on discovering the target corrupted dungeon's Verminflood affinity.

01R stood in the center of a pile of bodies, blood coating his fangs. He frowned. These monsters were weaklings who had barely gained their mana cores. Some were not even monsters at all yet. They provided him no challenge, and little experience. Killing them was just a waste.

Fortunately, their self-preservation instincts had finally kicked in, and though they surrounded him, they did not approach any longer.

"What-What are you all doing? Kill-slay the outsider!"

The rat monsters trembled and glanced around, pointing at each other, only to duck and hide behind their peers. 01R turned away from them and began walking toward Boss Cravenfang.

"You coward-weaklings! Must I do-finish everything myself?!"

01R narrowed his eyes.

"I see you are afraid-worried, yes-yes. Come, I will make your death swift-quick."

Boss Cravenfang snarled at 01R and reached into the pile under his throne, pulling out a small knife, which in his hands seemed more like a longsword, and a buckler.

"Die-perish, you weakling!"

Boss Cravenfang leapt at 01R with speed unexpected from his bulk. 01R's eyes widened as he leapt back, the tip of the blade barely passing in front of his snout. 01R had just landed and was going to leap forward, but Boss Cravenfang kept moving forth and thrust the buckler into 01R, knocking the cyber-rat back. 01R had just reset his stance when Boss Cravenfang swung his blade once again, forcing 01R to dodge yet again.

01R smiled. "Now *this* is a fight-battle, yes-yes!"

Boss Cravenfang moved to bash the rat with his shield when 01R flickered and vanished. Activating his Dash skill, he moved behind the Ratkin, swiping with his claws. But Boss Cravenfang whipped around, swinging both his weapons wildly, and the side of the buckler caught 01R's paws, knocking him off course. Boss Cravenfang then managed to catch 01R with his blade. He didn't penetrate the cyber-rat's armor, but he still left a deep scratch in the metal.

Boss Cravenfang scowled as 01R leapt back. His sword began to glow.

His next attack came much more quickly, with his sword leaving a trail of light as he activated a skill. 01R's sensors reported dangerous levels of mana, and he barely managed to dodge with his own Dash skill. 01R channeled mana to his own claws to counter, but Boss Cravenfang was swinging his blade around as quickly as he could. 01R couldn't find an opportunity, and he couldn't risk taking a blow from the glowing knife.

01R frowned.

The cybernetic components granted to him by the boss-queen were powerful, but they were only amplifying his base strength. And the sacred records told him Boss Cravenfang was level twenty-three, a nine-level difference from the current 01R, as well as a Ratkin with innately higher strength than a monster rat. 01R could not defeat him in a direct contest of power. 01R had an edge in speed, but due to the level difference, not a high enough one to slip past the Ratkin's guard. If he could not find an opening, he would lose.

He also lacked the weaponry the boss-queen's own components granted her. He *could* use some of her magic spells, but he had no personal skill with them, and his mana was a drop in the bucket compared to the boss-queen's. He would burn up all his mana on a spell that would merely distract the Ratkin.

And worst of all, Boss Cravenfang was not like the foes 01R had faced in the corrupted dungeon. He had not been born as a high-level monster, relying purely on some innate instinct and the dungeon's commands. He had clawed his way up by his own strength, wit, and determination. He had the real experience to go along with his levels.

01R gnashed his teeth as he ducked under a blade, only for Boss Cravenfang to kick him away. 01R was much weaker than he thought. He talked much about displaying the might of the boss-queen's servants . . . only to find himself dependent on her power.

And then a message passed in front of 01R's eyes.

*"I, like, already got the snack, you know? You can leave whenever now."*

01R frowned as he replied.

*"Not yet! I must prove myself worthy-deserving of the wise-mighty-gracious boss-queen, yes-yes!"*

*"Okay, but you should probably look behind you. Boss won't be happy if you die, you know?"*

01R glanced behind him as he dodged another blow. The rat monsters were making a solid formation behind 01R, cutting off his path of retreat.

He gritted his teeth. His stomach boiled at the very thought of retreat.

But 02S was right. The boss-queen, above all, valued their lives. And his, more than most, belonged to her. He could not waste it on his own pride. He would endure anything for the sake of his boss-queen, even the humiliation of cowardice.

Channeling mana to his claws, 01R prepared to leap at Boss Cravenfang once more, who grinned and prepared to swing his blade.

And then 01R jumped backward, rushing through the crowd of monster rats. Boss Cravenfang blinked before snarling, "Don't you dare run-flee! After him!"

The monster rats closed in on 01R . . . only to trip on invisible threads laid by 02S. 01R barely escaped the grasp of the crowds, fleeing into the nearest tunnel.

He gnashed his teeth, but he did that which the *traitorous thing* did not. He sent a priority alert to all the other covert units, alerting them there were organized and hostile monsters in the area . . .

As NSLICE-00P talked with Ateia, she caught a priority alert from 01R. It appeared he had encountered a hostile faction of monsters.

She analyzed the situation.

While the fact that the monsters were organized was concerning and brought into question if nonintervention protocols might be relevant, hostilities had already broken out, and terminating the threat was now the appropriate response.

She weighed intervening herself, but ultimately deemed that the NSLICE network's combat assets could handle the situation if appropriately deployed. She ordered reinforcements to head toward 01R's direction, deployed the units specialized for that purpose, and then set a thread to monitor 01R's status while she continued her own business.

Rattingtale stared ahead as he lay wrapped upon the wretched spider-thing's back. She had quietly removed him from the cage as the traitorous 01R engaged the evil rat-things. She now carried him out of the tunnels and back into the sewers, where she placed him down and untied him.

He raised an eyebrow. "You are . . . not going to eat-consume me?"

She giggled. "Do you want me to?"

Rattingtale had a flash of panic, but simply shook his head and sighed. If he thought about it, this spider-thing could have eaten him at any time. But she would not. Not as long as the boss-queen commanded otherwise.

He took a deep breath.

It had all gone wrong. When he'd met the other rat-things, he had cried in joy. He had found more of his kin, free from the strange man-thing's influence. He thought that surely it would be a simple matter to convince them to aid him. Surely, they would acknowledge his superiority and help him reclaim his rightful place.

They had not. Instead, he'd met a Ratkin far larger and stronger than himself who saw him as nothing more than a slave . . . or a meal. And since he had not gone with the boss-queen's peons, none of them knew where he was. None of them cared. He was helpless and alone.

Or so he thought.

01R stepped out of the tunnel, nodding at 02S. Rattingtale looked the traitor in the eye.

". . . What-What are you doing here? Why did you intervene-interfere?"

01R frowned and crossed his arms. "I *was* planning-hoping to use these lessers in service of the wise-mighty-gracious boss-queen. But *someone* got themselves captured-apprehended and required rescue."

Rattingtale glared at him. "Quiet, you traitor-betrayer! You would not help-save me! You just want-need an excuse for your own failure!"

01R scoffed and turned away. "I would kill-slay you myself if you did not belong to the wise-mighty-gracious boss-queen, yes-yes. Thank her for her grace-mercy. It is only because she has claimed you that we watch-guard you at all."

02S giggled. "And because it's fun to watch you suffer."

Rattingtale frowned. He was about to respond when he heard countless footsteps. His ears moved back against his head. "S-Shouldn't we run-flee?"

01R's eyes narrowed. "This is where we hold-defend our ground, yes-yes."

Rattingtale gulped as 02S spread threads over the entrance. The monster rats soon came into view, charging toward the crack in the wall. Some tripped and fell over 02S's threads while others were caught in her webs, but still, they rushed forward.

01R stepped into the gap and extended his claws.

"02S, guard-defend the . . . *thing*."

She giggled and stepped over him, and then the fight was on. 01R slashed and slashed, but he was only one rat. Even if the monster rats couldn't hurt him, they could move around him. 02S tossed webs at them and bit any who approached, but they were many, and now driven by the presence of their boss at the rear.

They swarmed over 01R, holding him down with the weight of numbers. They had surrounded 02S and were picking at her legs. Rattingtale closed his eyes.

Then he heard the howls.

The canus minors, now converted to cyber-dogs, rushed into the sewers. 00C bowled over the monster rats to 02S's rear and barked at the other two. 01C and 02C unleashed breaths of fire and water, pushing the monster rats back from 02S's side. 00F pounced from the shadows, unleashing mana-filled claw strikes that cut through the rats holding 01R down.

And then they heard a mighty roar. 00B crashed into the entrance to the tunnels, knocking aside monster rats as he raced toward Boss Cravenfang. The Ratkin frowned at the bear monster charging toward him, and being an exemplar of his kin, he made his ancestors proud.

He turned and fled down the nearest tunnel.

And ran straight into a spider's web.

Someone gave a dramatic sigh. "Can you, like, not start a war please? This is, like, so much work or something."

Boss Cravenfang was thus immobilized and could not move his shield to block. He could do nothing but scream in terror as the bear's mighty paws crashed upon his head.

01R sighed and shook his head, turning to the other monsters.

"Thank you for your aid-assistance. I am ashamed at my weakness-pitifulness."

00B grunted and happily patted 01R's shoulder. But the bear did not know his own strength from his latest levels and smashed 01R into the ground.

The cyber-rat groaned. ". . . It seems I have much training-growing to do before our next spar, yes-yes."

Rattingtale was watching all this in silence when another monster rat stepped out from the shadows, hands raised. The canus monsters growled at her while 00F prepared to pounce, but 01R raised a hand. He picked himself off the ground and crossed his arms.

"Snuan? What are you doing-intending here? I thought you ran-flee, yes-yes."

The monster rat glared at him.

"I want-desire to, yes-yes! But you went and dragged-pulled me out in front of the boss and then attacked-murdered him, yes-yes! Now I have nowhere else left to go-return! So, let me into your boss-queen's colony, yes-yes!"

She looked around at all the other monsters and trembled.

"It seems much . . . safer-secure, yes-yes."

Rattingtale frowned as 01R grilled the other rat, demanding her eternal loyalty for the boss-queen. She wanted to join this slavery willingly, it seemed. All because it was safer-secure, huh?

He glanced around at all the monsters who had come to fight. Who had defeated the foe who had imprisoned him immediately. The traitorous 01R who had intervened instead of leaving him to die. The wretched spider-thing who had protected him instead of eating him alive.

He had . . . a lot to think about.

# 6

# Shifting Focus

*"Cooperation with unaffiliated parties is to be avoided if at all possible, but is permitted if necessary for mission completion or fulfillment of a major or higher-priority directive. Units should still avoid leaking classified intel, and should be prepared to terminate cooperating units once the situation permits."*

—NSLICE protocols on temporary alliances.

As 01R instructed Snuan on the loyalty necessary to become one of the wise-mighty-gracious boss-queen's servants, he suddenly felt the boss-queen's attention on him. His robotic eye started to glow . . . and then projected an image of the boss-queen herself. Snuan jumped and fell on her back, clearly awed by the sheer magnificence of the boss-queen.

"Surrender request acknowledged. Offer: All parties intending to surrender should review and sign the following contract."

With that, the hologram cut off, and a magic contract appeared before the rat.

Snuan trembled. "You there! Rat-Knight-thing! You didn't say-mention you worked for a man-thing!"

01R just stared off into the distance. "The wise-mighty-gracious boss-queen . . . spoke-commanded through me . . . Oh, what did you say-ask? Ah, that is because the wise-mighty-gracious boss-queen is obviously above all the lesser man-things, and should not be associated with them, yes-yes."

One of the cyber-dogs, 01C, tilted their head and barked. 01R crossed his arms.

"Those two man-things she associates-interacts with? I . . . am not sure-certain. They seem lesser to me as well, but the boss-queen gave-offered them a contract sometime earlier, yes-yes? She must have-possess plans for them I cannot see, yes-yes."

Meanwhile, Snuan trembled, imagining all the horrors man-things were said to inflict upon captured monster rats. Being fed to larger pets. Being experimented on by mad wizards. Being dressed up and paraded around as an exercise in humiliation.

But Snuan also glanced around her, at the spider-things and cat-thing and dog-things and bear-thing that were all watching her. Her ears went flat against her head. She glared at 01R.

"I better not be eaten-consumed!"

She signed the contract.

That night, after separating from NSLICE-00P and the rest, Agedia slithered into the tavern. Vafum was still sitting there, alone at this point, and he already had a pair of mugs ready as he waved Agedia over. She sat down with a sigh and then started drinking. Vafum let her finish before he began.

"So . . ."

Agedia sighed again and stared at the bottom of her cup. "It's . . . definitely her. I can . . . Well, it's all too familiar."

He took a deep breath. "You going to be okay? I can take the lead on this if you need me to."

Agedia frowned but shook her head. ". . . I don't know. But you taking the lead on anything of the sort will draw all the wrong sorts of attention. I guess the Aesdes have a sense of humor, because circumstances being what they are, it *has* to be me."

He watched her for a moment before continuing. "Well then, what do you think of the lot?"

She gave a small smirk. "Tibbers undersold shiny girl."

Vafum raised an eyebrow. "Really? She's *that* strong? Tiberius told us she took down Spellbreaker alone."

Agedia nodded. "Three adamant bull worms and their handler, and she didn't even break a sweat."

His eyes widened. "Wait, *handler*?"

Agedia's eyes narrowed as she nodded. Vafum swore and waved the barman for another round of drinks. Only after both of them had emptied their new mugs did Agedia continue.

". . . It's them. It has to be. Nothing else makes sense."

Vafum slowly nodded. "And the girl?"

Agedia shook her head.

"They wouldn't have been so surprised by us if they were after her, which means they definitely don't know who she is, thank the Aesdes. But she is *definitely* not strong enough yet. Shiny girl can take care of her to some extent, but . . ." She took a deep breath, and her face turned dark. "We all know a tough bodyguard isn't enough."

Vafum didn't respond, instead ordering another round of drinks.

* * *

The next morning, the group was making their way back to Khalbuldor when they were halted by the guards, who led them to the Council Hall, where the council of Khalbuldor was waiting for them. They were brought to an audience hall, where the council sat on thrones arranged in a semicircle. The leader nodded at them.

"Thank you, NSLICE-00P and company. You've done us a great service."

"Acknowledged."

The leader nodded to the side, and a Dwarf attendant brought a tray. On top of it was a bag and a pendant.

"Please, accept our gratitude, and a token of our friendship."

"Affirmative."

NSLICE-00P took the bag, which was filled with coins, and the pendant.

"Know that you are always welcome in Khalbuldor from now on, as well as any other hold that acknowledges us. We hope this is the start of a beneficial friendship."

"Acknowledged."

And so, the group made their way back to the tavern to meet up with Vafum and Agedia. NSLICE-00P displayed the persons of interest, and the two of them took down notes while Vafum heaved a sigh.

"I'll do what I can, lass. It may take a bit to get around; I'll need to get the company back up and running first."

"Acknowledged."

Vafum then glanced around and motioned for the three to move closer. Leaning in, he whispered to them, "We do know something about the Exploratores' chap, though."

Ateia's eyes widened, and she started to smile until she saw the look in Vafum's eye.

"There's a problem, though. The shiny lass will probably be fine, but the two of you are a bit weak to be pulling on that thread. I'd recommend you train for a bit before leaping into the world of intrigue. Won't stop you from getting stabbed in a dark alley, but at least you might survive the dagger."

Agedia nodded. "How about I show you all around the dungeon? The good spots, now that we're not on the clock."

Ateia frowned, then looked at NSLICE-00P. "Well, we were going to check in with the Exploratores, but what do you think, Seero?"

"Analysis: Increasing the capabilities and resilience of friendlies Ateia and Taog is desirable and will not interfere with this unit's current objectives. Conclusion: This unit finds this course of action acceptable."

Ateia glanced over at Taog. He frowned and rubbed his chin.

"Personally, I wouldn't mind getting a bit stronger."

Ateia took a deep breath. More and more, she was wondering who exactly her father was. But she had waited for years for him now. These questions could wait a while longer.

"In that case, we would be grateful if you could show us around."

NSLICE-00P requested a return to Velusitum before braving the dungeon, and Ateia and Taog agreed, using the time to double-check their supplies. Meanwhile, NSLICE-00P moved toward where her monsters had fought the night before and gathered her combat-focused units into the Monster Hangar, along with new friendly Snuan.

Snuan cursed and flailed about at the sudden Transfer.

"W-What is happening-occurring?! Where am I?!"

"Answer: This unit has gathered friendly Snuan Covenwalker to the Monster Hangar for transit. This unit is preparing for a subordinate upgrade routine. Friendly Snuan is a high-priority unit, since she has not integrated with the NSLICE network."

"I-Integrated? W-What do you mean-intend by *integrated*?!"

"Answer: Monster unit evolutions appear to include options for installing cybernetic components."

Snuan paused, her eyes widening when she heard the word *evolutions*. "Oh. Why didn't you say-speak so? Um, t-thank you?"

It was at that moment that 01R contacted her. "Wise-mighty-gracious boss-queen, forgive my insolence, but I have a request-plea."

"Acknowledgement: Please state the request."

01R bowed his head. "Please allow this unworthy one to fight-train with the others."

"Observation: NSLICE-01R's combat capabilities are calculated as sufficient for a covert unit. Please state the rationale for additional upgrade routines."

01R looked down, gritting his teeth. "I am . . . unworthy-undeserving of your consideration, wise-mighty-gracious boss-queen, yes-yes. I am no better than any other when it comes to sneak-creeping; not at all worthy of the attention you have lavished-wasted upon me. I thought to do more by recruiting-conquering these rat-things in your name . . . but instead, I learned-discovered how weak I truly am."

00B cried softly and nuzzled 01R with his nose. 01R rubbed a paw on the bear's head but shook his head. "I have done-tried my best, but the truth is, you are already stronger-mightier than me, yes-yes."

And then, a truly unexpected voice joined the conversation.

"I, the Great-High . . . Ahem. I would also like to request-ask for this."

Everyone in the sewer turned to stare at Rattingtale.

"The traitor . . . the other rat-thing, 01R, is right-correct, yes-yes. I . . . *We* . . . cannot do-achieve much as we are now."

01R's eyes narrowed. "What are you planning-plotting, *traitorous thing*?"

Rattingtale just stared at the ground. "I . . . am not sure-certain anymore."

NSLICE-00P's robotic eye flickered. By her analysis, the combat specialized units of the NSLICE network had proven their worth, and the covert units had demonstrated they could defend themselves until reinforcements arrived. Additional combat potential for the covert units was not necessary.

However, the NSLICE network itself had shifted in capabilities, unit specialization, and overall role regarding her primary objectives. The stealth mini drone golems had proven as or more capable than rat and spider monsters in the observation role, were noticeably more cost-efficient in terms of hangar space and mana upkeep, were significantly more expendable as fully automated units, and did not provoke inherent hostility from the local society.

As for the network's overall role, NSLICE-00P had lowered the priority on searching the immediate area for the persons of interest, so the need for covert units had dropped accordingly. And with the additional directive of protecting the friendlies, combat assets had risen in comparative value.

"Analysis concluded. Statement: This unit finds NSLICE-01R's request to be reasonable, and covert units will be included in the upgrade routine. Command: Please prepare for transit."

NSLICE-00P worked out a schedule once more and transferred about half the covert team to the Monster Hangar, including 01R and Rattingtale. 01R bowed his head low.

"Thank you, wise-mighty-gracious boss-queen. I swear-vow I will become worthy of your boons."

Agedia took the group and showed them around. The Mines of Might had recovered from the attack, and the lower floors were now filled with monsters and ore veins once again. She showed them the paths to take when they wanted to bypass earlier floors, and where they could hunt for the best balance of safety and profit. Ateia and Taog then spent the rest of the day hunting under Agedia and NSLICE-00P's watchful eyes.

That night, NSLICE-00P spent some time analyzing the Banishment spell, but she made little progress. Not only was the spell noticeably more complicated than the others, it had entirely different structures. She could not simply slot in a shape like she did with other circles. She did identify a part related to the Holy attribute, but it was connected to the rest of the spell with a different method, and attempting to slot another attribute in just caused the spell to fail. She tried casting the spell again, but nothing occurred when the magic circle activated, so she couldn't observe its mechanisms either. She concluded she needed more appropriate targets, or more similar magic circles, before she could glean any useful data from the analysis.

And so, she engaged standby sentry mode for the night, deciding to determine her next steps in the morning.

# 7

# Divining the Answer

*"To see the present, one only needs to pass their sight through space. To see the past, one needs to pass through both space and time, but at the very least, the history of a place, person, or object is recorded upon them and offers a guide. To see the future? The future is unsettled and still in motion. There are countless possible futures even for the next minute in this room. To see the future requires one to address every single one of these and then try to guess which is most likely. There's a reason even the Aesdes barely dabble in such things."*

—Magister Arcanum Novia Pantensa during a lecture at the Imperial Academy Arcanum.

The next morning, the group returned to the dungeon. They were just at the entrance when NSLICE-00P spoke up.

"Request: Can entity Agedia guard the friendlies today?"

Agedia tilted her head. "Sure, but what will you be doing?"

NSLICE-00P pointed to 00B and the others. "Explanation: Due to the level difference, friendlies Ateia and Taog have a different optimal upgrade location from other subordinate units."

Ateia frowned for a second but then nodded, smiling at 00B. "Ah, that makes sense. Yeah, go ahead and train your monsters, Seero. We'll be fine."

Taog looked incredibly worried but shook his head. "Seero . . . don't destroy the dungeon or anything, okay?"

"Affirmative."

He slowly nodded. "And . . . stay safe, okay?"

"Acknowledged."

NSLICE-00P then deployed one of her drone golems, which flew in between Ateia and Taog before vanishing from view.

"Statement: This unit has deployed an autonomous unit to monitor the friendlies' progress and will move to reinforce should the friendlies be at risk of termination. This unit requests the friendlies avoid excessive risk, as it will take this unit some time to arrive in that case."

Taog nodded back at that. "Sounds good. We'll be careful. Thanks, Seero."

And so, the two groups split up and made their way to their respective destinations in the dungeon. Once they had split, NSLICE-00P deployed the covert monsters, along with Melion, and got to work.

01R ducked as a spearhead stabbed past his head, barely missing his ears. In front of him was a Naked Mole-Ratkin with a scrap iron chest plate and an iron spear. Dashing forward, he extended his claws for a counter; however, just as he was about to strike, a warning blared in his head from the NSLICE network. Another Naked Mole-Ratkin to his opponent's side turned and thrust its own spear toward him, and 01R was forced to retreat, his opponent pressing the advantage and moving to spear him before he could land.

Just then, a thread latched onto his back. 01R launched into the air, up and above the spear, as one of the spiders, 03S, pulled him up. 03S then swung him forward, and 01R landed on his opponent's face. He was in no position for a decent attack, but still clawed at his enemy as he was able. The monster dropped its spear and tried to grab the cyber-rat, and in doing so, left itself open. 01C rushed into the gap in the spears and grabbed the Naked Mole-Ratkin's leg, pulling it to the ground and away from its comrades. The rat and spider monsters then set upon the foe, including the trembling Rattingtale and Snuan. The other mole-rats moved to attack, but the canus monsters warded them off.

Such process repeated until their foes were defeated. The wise-mighty-gracious boss-queen had adjusted her strategy and no longer saw fit to gift them with free kills. They were now to earn their own victories, the boss-queen only intervening should one of them fall into mortal peril.

01R approved of this change. The boss-queen had been granting him and his fellow monsters gifts they did not deserve from the day he was born. It was high time they started contributing *something*, if not to the boss-queen then at least to their own growth.

What 01R did not approve of was his own performance. He looked down at his claws and clenched his paws. More and more, he felt the limits of his species. Even with the assistance of the cybernetic components, he still could not match a basic humanoid monster in strength. Even Naked Mole-Ratkin of a lower level than him could overpower him if he contested them directly, and his advantages in speed and agility were hindered by his small size. He could move as fast as he liked, but the sheer difference in reach meant the larger opponents still had time to react regardless.

He could not continue on as he was. A basic increase in stats may have been enough to defeat a mundane predator, but it was not sufficient against other monsters and magical creatures. He needed an edge. Something to overcome the limitations of his species.

It was then that Snuan came up to him, hiding behind his form. She was eyeing 00F as she did, while the cyber-cat watched her in return. 01R sighed. There seemed to be a trend of cowardice among his fellow rat monsters that originated from the outside world. Yet more proof of the boss-queen's superiority.

"Hey-Hey, when do I get some of that shiny-pretty armor?"

01R crossed his arms and scoffed. "When you are worthy-deserving of it, yes-yes."

Snuan glared at him.

"Don't be callous-cruel! I'm in great danger-peril, yes-yes! The only one! Everyone else has that shiny-pretty armor, yes-yes!"

01R shook his head.

"I am not. This armor is not equipment-gear. It came-appeared from an evolution, so you must raise-grow your levels before you may acquire it, yes-yes."

Snuan continued glaring at him but said no more. 01R sighed and shook his head once more. He still was . . . *conflicted* about outsiders like this growing more like the boss-queen. But if the *traitorous thing* had been granted the boss-queen's armor, then he could accept this rat-thing receiving it as well. She at least did not speak treason and blasphemy with her every word. Besides, it was only natural that all would seek to become more like the boss-queen . . .

01R froze. He started to tremble. He had realized his mistake.

All this time, he had been focusing on *himself*. His strength as a mere monster rat, his attributes, and his claws. But the boss-queen did not simply fight like any old man-thing. No, she was something more, and that was thanks to her cybernetic components. Her armor was more than just defense. It contained weapons and powers and even her physical attributes. It boosted her thinking, her magic, and her senses. It turned the boss-queen *into* the weapon.

The boss-queen had declared ALL her monsters receive these components at first opportunity. It was clear she intended for them all to become more like her. So why was 01R insisting on acting like a mere monster rat? Why was he not trying to become even more like his boss-queen?

01R felt chastised as he, for the first time, opened the Implants menu in the sacred records.

| Available Implants | | | |
|---|---|---|---|
| **Name** | **Cost** | **Mana Upkeep** | **Description** |
| **New Implant Slot** | **3** | **--** | **Adds additional slots for implants.<br>+2 HP<br>+2 Mana** |
| **Internal Weapons Bays** | **5** | **None for implant. Upkeep will be added for each weapon/trap installed.** | **May integrate weapons into cybernetic components. Dungeon master may also install available dungeon traps. Will reduce maximum mana to maintain or reload the weapon in question. Cost will depend on the weapon or trap.<br>Please note that some traps and weapons may be unavailable based on your size.** |
| **Repulsors** | **5** | **1 (May use more to boost power.)** | **Enables flight and tactical boosts.** |
| **Energy Channels** | **5** | **None. Costs mana to use.** | **Enables user to channel internal energy into external attacks.** |

He shook as he read through the options. There, waiting for him all along, was a solution to his dilemma. The moment he decided to become more like the boss-queen, he found a way to overcome the limitations of his species.

**You have unlocked an Additional Implant Slot! Max HP and Mana increased!**
**You have unlocked the Repulsors implant!**

While part of him wanted new weapons, the warning on his size gave him pause, so the internal weapons bays would likely not help him overcome his limitations. On the other hand, he had seen the boss-queen utilize energy channels to great effect, but he knew his place. His mana reserves and Density could not be compared to the infinite might of the boss-queen.

But repulsors, on the other hand, would revolutionize his mobility. Not only would he move much faster than before, but he would be able to fly in the air. He could increase his angles of attack and increase the powers of his claws by striking at higher speeds. Even just 03S swinging him around had enabled him to bypass the enemy's defenses, so what if he was flying on his own power, aiming his attacks for maximum effect?

01R watched as circles formed on his paws and metal protrusions formed on his back. He could feel his power coursing through these new parts, ready to activate on his command.

Crouching down, he sent the order. His new parts began to hum and glow as he prepared to leap . . . and then suddenly, 01R vanished and slammed straight into the roof before unceremoniously falling to the ground.

Snuan looked at him and frowned.

"You know what? I think-believe I'll wait a bit before getting that dangerous-scary armor, yes-yes."

After a good amount of subordinate upgrades, NSLICE-00P left the dungeon and regrouped with her friendlies. They ingested organic fuel together, and then returned to the inn to rest. Ateia and Taog were exhausted and went straight to bed, leaving NSLICE-00P to her own devices. This time, she decided to investigate a new spell.

| Holy Spells | | |
|---|---|---|
| Name | Level | Description |
| Divination | 1 | Attempt to read the state of the world. May reveal things that were, things that are, or things that yet may be. What, exactly, none can predict, only that what is revealed should not be dismissed. |

The description was somewhat vague, but it seemed to imply the spell would grant the user more data. Since it was also a spell in the Holy school of magic that was not part of the modular spellcasting, NSLICE-00P predicted it could potentially provide related data to the Banishment spell. So, she went ahead and tried to cast it.

As the spell activated, NSLICE-00P felt her mana reach out and make contact with the mana in her surroundings. Not the mana in the air or the mana in the ground or in the people around her, but with something deeper lying below the surface.

"Establishing connection. Opening port for data transfer. Activating data-gathering protocols."

NSLICE-00P attempted to boost the connection and acquire data as the spell implied . . .

Suddenly, her head was on fire.

A massive stream of mana and data poured in through the connection established by the spell, rushing into her mind. Within seconds, her memory overflowed, and her cybernetic components cut her consciousness in response. NSLICE-00P's robotic eye shut off, and she fell to the ground.

# 8

# Premonitions

*"Great care must be taken during Divinations. When you are separating your mind and senses from your physical present, it is all too easy to become separated from reality, and to mistake hopes—or fears—as truth."*

—Celestial Elf Sage Ningainë, on the fate of Aodetar "Kinslayer."

NSLICE-00P found herself surrounded by darkness and heat. She tried to activate her protocols . . . but they did not respond. She tried to bring up her logs . . . but they did not appear. In fact, now that she paid attention, her *entire UI* was missing.

Looking around, she suddenly started coughing. The air was thick with smoke. All around her, fires raged. A city was burning, despite being constructed of stone. And for some reason, her filters weren't working. She tried to engage her helmet, but with her UI missing, nothing occurred. She tried to reach for her helmet and move it manually . . . but she couldn't feel the helmet. She couldn't feel anything, in fact.

Looking down, her organic eye widened. Her arm was missing. *All* of her cybernetic components were missing.

Her heart started pounding, and there were no emotional controls to counteract it.

And then, she heard a voice.

*Help me, Seero.*

She didn't recognize it, but the voice still demanded her attention, increasing her heart rate and blood pressure. She looked around, searching for the source. She tried to activate her sensors before remembering her situation. But then, she saw something.

The shape of a person, shining with bright golden-and-silver light such that their features couldn't be seen. They reached out their hand toward NSLICE-00P.

*Help me, Seero!*

NSLICE-00P tried to reach out her hand, but she had no limbs to reach with. She tried to activate her repulsors, but those were missing as well. She tried to cast a spell, but her mind couldn't remember the shape of the magic circles. With nothing else she could do, she opened her mouth to shout, but she couldn't remember the words.

And then, the figure was wrapped in flame and shadow, and NSLICE-00P saw them no more. Then the fire grew, engulfing the city around it.

Finally, she found her voice and cried out as the flames reached her too . . .

NSLICE-00P's organic eye shot open. Her heart was still pounding, but she didn't see any more smoke or fire. Instead, she saw the floor of her room in the inn, and a furry paw patting her head. Her robotic eye flickered on a moment later, and the tension in her chest eased slightly as her UI snapped on in her sight.

*"System reboot successful. All systems online. Running diagnostics . . ."*

NSLICE-00P's organic eye blinked as her cybernetic components checked over her systems. She glanced around. 00B was standing over her, crying and pawing at her face. Her other monsters were also standing around her.

"Boss-queen! Are you fine-okay?!"

NSLICE-00P opened her mouth, pausing for a second until a gap in her diagnostics allowed her to calculate a response.

"Status . . . Report: All systems . . . appear operational. Full diagnostics . . . in progress."

00B cried again while the cyber-dogs started licking her. 01R frowned but heaved a sigh of relief. NSLICE-00P finished her diagnostics, confirming there was no lasting damage, and then opened the logs to determine what happened.

It appeared she had *severely* underestimated what the Divination spell meant by "read the state of the world." What had happened was that the spell had hit her with a mana package containing the world's *entire* present state, with no discernable limit on scale or scope. And NSLICE-00P, having activated data-gathering protocols, opened up the connection formed by the spell and requested more. And since she also possessed a dungeon core that could read data from mana, the connection dumped a truly staggering amount of raw data on her, rather than letting the spell parse it on its own. She did not have a specific query, either, so the connection had merely thrown as much of that raw data at her as it could. Her memory had overloaded while receiving atomic- and subatomic-level data on the state of the atmosphere.

NSLICE-00P began to dump the data. It would not be useful to her as it was, and learning to parse it was beyond the scope of her current hardware.

Finally, she checked on the state of her organic hardware.

She found her heart was beating at an abnormally high rate, her organic eye was open wider than it should be, and her emotional state was in severe flux. Her organic components had seen something while her cybernetic half was rebooting, which she now reviewed. On the surface, those images could not have been real, as the loss of her cybernetic components would have resulted in termination of the remaining organic parts.

Yet, her organic half did not want to let those images go, considering them as important intel. NSLICE-00P could not rule it out as a side effect of the spell, or even as part of the data package. And the fact that the situation she saw appeared impossible was not actually conclusive. She had already observed several phenomena that were impossible by regular physics.

So, she reactivated her emotional controls, reinforcing them with a Calm spell, but also filed away the images for later review. Once she did, the emotional controls successfully activated, and her organic components returned to their baseline state.

And then, she filed away the Divination spell as potentially dangerous and not to be used without further investigation.

"Status Report: Diagnostics complete. All systems online and fully operational. Abnormalities detected in organic components. Emotional controls operating at 78.56 percent effectiveness."

All her monsters sighed in relief as 01R looked her in the eyes. "Is there any way we might serve-assist, wise-mighty-gracious boss-queen?"

"Response: Negative. No outstanding damage or danger remains. This unit will enact standby sentry mode and conduct maintenance to restore optimal operation. Recommending all units without outstanding orders do likewise."

01R frowned but nodded. "As you order-command, wise-mighty-gracious boss-queen. Please alert-inform us if there is anything we can do."

"Affirmative."

And with that, the monsters returned to the hangar, save for 00B, who curled up at NSLICE-00P's feet. NSLICE-00P closed her human eye and attempted to enter standby sentry mode. It took her an abnormally long time to enter the state due to fluctuations in her organic components.

And so, several days passed. NSLICE-00P spent the daytime training her subordinates as Ateia and Taog trained with Agedia. She spent her free time analyzing the Banishment and Divination spell circles but did not attempt to cast either. Unfortunately, she made little progress in deciphering the magic circles, much less determining how to manage the data delivery. She determined she would require more data from external sources, preferably a local expert. The foreign system occasionally seemed to miss important details in its descriptions, after all.

With that in mind, NSLICE-00P reviewed her subordinates, analyzing if it would be efficient to move on from the current upgrade routine:

| **Subordinates** | | | | |
|---|---|---|---|---|
| **Total Subordinates: 34/34** | | | | |
| **Name** | **Species** | **Level** | **Mana Upkeep** | |
| **Rattingtale** | **Cyber-Rat** | **16** | **1** | **Check Status** |
| **Lilussees** | **Cyber-Spider** | **17** | **1** | **Check Status** |
| **(TEMPORARY) Ateia Niraemia** | **Human** | **30** | **--** | **(Status locked)** |
| **(TEMPORARY) Taog Sutharlan** | **Human/ Wulver** | **29** | **--** | **(Status locked)** |
| **01R** | **Cyber-Rat** | **17** | **1** | **Check Status** |
| **02R** | **Cyber-Rat** | **14** | **1** | **Check Status** |
| **03R** | **Cyber-Rat** | **15** | **1** | **Check Status** |
| **04R** | **Cyber-Rat** | **15** | **1** | **Check Status** |
| **05R** | **Cyber-Rat** | **14** | **1** | **Check Status** |
| **06R** | **Cyber-Rat** | **11** | **1** | **Check Status** |
| **07R** | **Cyber-Rat** | **10** | **1** | **Check Status** |
| **08R** | **Cyber-Rat** | **12** | **1** | **Check Status** |
| **09R** | **Cyber-Rat** | **9** | **1** | **Check Status** |
| **10R** | **Cyber-Rat** | **8** | **1** | **Check Status** |
| **01S** | **Cyber-Spider** | **16** | **1** | **Check Status** |
| **02S** | **Cyber-Spider** | **15** | **1** | **Check Status** |
| **03S** | **Cyber-Spider** | **14** | **1** | **Check Status** |
| **04S** | **Cyber-Spider** | **9** | **1** | **Check Status** |
| **05S** | **Cyber-Spider** | **10** | **1** | **Check Status** |

| 06S | Cyber-Spider | 8 | 1 | Check Status |
|---|---|---|---|---|
| 07S | Cyber-Spider | 11 | 1 | Check Status |
| 08S | Cyber-Spider | 9 | 1 | Check Status |
| 09S | Cyber-Spider | 10 | 1 | Check Status |
| 10S | Cyber-Spider | 11 | 1 | Check Status |
| 00B | Cyber-Bear Cub | 19 | 5 | Check Status |
| Uscfrea Ymmason | Dobhar | 95 | -- | Check Status |
| Estrith Edilddaughter | Dobhar | 62 | -- | Check Status |
| Aldreda Aetheludaughter | Sacred Otterkin | 1 | -- | Check Status |
| 00C | Cyber-Dog | 12 | 4 | Check Status |
| 01C | Cyber-Dog Ignis | 10 | 5 | Check Status |
| 02C | Cyber-Dog Aqua | 11 | 5 | Check Status |
| 00F | Cyber-Cat | 11 | 4 | Check Status |
| Melion | Metal Slime | 65 | 15 | Check Status |
| Ceitidh Greumach | Wulver | 32 | -- | Check Status |
| Snuan Covenwalker | Monster Rat | 8 | 1 | Check Status |

They had all grown in levels, but it wasn't enough. Ultimately, her subordinates were still relatively weak compared to the average opponents she had faced. Ateia and Taog were not predicted to defeat most of the adversaries she had on record, either. Subordinate upgrade routines were still the most efficient course of action at present. Finding and consulting a local expert on Banishment or

Divination would be helpful, but her friendlies weren't aware of any such experts in the immediate vicinity. Likewise, NSLICE-00P wasn't certain Banishment was directly relevant to her primary directive.

As for Divination, she wasn't sure it would ever be possible to effectively parse such a massive quantity of data. Unless she could gain better insights into the spell itself, it might be faster to simply search every inch of this place by foot. As such, guaranteed progress on a major directive was valued higher for now.

Still, for some reason, NSLICE-00P continued to analyze their current routine against possible alternatives. And her organic components continued to request further analysis. And the images from before continued to flash through her mind, despite her attempts to archive them . . .

Ateia and Taog's group was currently battling against a squad of elite Naked Mole-Ratkin. Agedia stood in the front, warding foes off so the pair could take them down a few at a time. Ateia's arrows struck true, with an occasional Light Arrow piercing the ones with tougher armor.

Taog stood to the side. He had traded out his shield for the Dark Blade NSLICE-00P had given him, now holding two swords. It did mean it was dangerous for him to challenge foes head-on, but in the majority of their battles so far, Taog had not been tough enough to perform the vanguard role, in any case. If he insisted on that role, he would end up falling behind, so he searched for other ways to contribute to the battle.

Taog infused his mana into the Dark Blade, creating a dark aura around it, and slashed at a Mole-Ratkin, taking it down. He then slashed a second monster with his other blade, but it got caught in his opponent's armor. He was forced to let it go as the Naked Mole-Ratkin swung a pickaxe at his head. He ducked underneath and jabbed the Dark Blade into a gap in the monster's armor, then reclaimed his sword.

He frowned at it. He glanced at the Dark Blade, then back at his other sword. He tried to feel his mana in the infusion around the Dark Blade, then infused the other blade, trying to replicate the same aura. The blade glowed with a normal mana infusion, but the aura around it started to dim . . .

"Taog!"

Taog looked up, and his eyes widened. A spear was headed right toward his face.

He leapt back, but not far enough, and the spear scratched his cheek. The Naked Mole-Ratkin moved to press its advantage when Agedia's lance pierced right through its chest. Agedia then spun the lance around with the monster still on it and took out the rest of the Mole-Ratkin in one swing. She crossed her arms and frowned.

"Let's call it a day. You two have been going at this nonstop for a while now, you know? You probably need to rest a bit."

Ateia came over to Taog. Taking out a bandage and a weak healing potion, she began dressing his wound.

"Are you okay? You know, it's best to experiment outside of live combat."

Taog shook his head and sighed. "Fine, just . . ." He looked down at his swords. "I feel like I was on the verge of something."

But Agedia was right. It was simply foolish to get distracted like that, and he should have waited until they left the dungeon to experiment. They *had* been fighting every day for a while, so perhaps the fatigue was getting to him.

Once Ateia finished with his wound, he nodded and stood up, and then the group went home for the day.

The pair had split with Agedia and were just arriving at the inn. NSLICE-00P hadn't arrived just yet, but they were a bit early today, so they were sure she would show up in a bit. NSLICE-00P always arrived precisely on time, after all.

But as the two walked toward the door, they were approached by a man. A man with the cloak and emblem of the Exploratores.

"Exploratores Ateia Niraemia and Taog Sutharlan?"

Ateia turned and raised an eyebrow. "Yes, that's us. Can we help you?"

The man nodded.

"Exploratore Quintis Umbrius Fullofaudes. Magister Vibius requires your presence at the Exploratores HQ."

Ateia crossed her arms. "Hm, can it wait? We were about to meet our companion in a bit."

Exploratore Fullofaudes shook his head.

"Exploratores business, so he needs to speak with you two alone. He said he will not interfere with your mission regarding the Amicitia Populi Elteni. He also said he is not asking."

Ateia and Taog exchanged glances. He frowned but shrugged. He didn't like this Exploratore's tone, but . . . they had no good reason to refuse an order from the local Magister Exploratore, so there wasn't really a choice. Ateia turned and nodded.

"Very well. Lead the way, then."

Exploratore Fullofaudes nodded.

"Thank you. Let's get going."

# 9

# A Dark Secret

*"The Empire . . . is far more fragile than you know. You've no idea the lengths we must go to hold it together. The things I've seen, the things I've done . . . I no longer wonder if the Aesdes will forgive me, for I know they will not. All I wish for, now, is that you'll be able to enjoy the fragile, ephemeral peace that was bought at prices I hope you'll never know."*

—Exploratore Quirinia Hilaris, attempting to convince her granddaughter not to join the Exploratores.

Exploratore Fullofaudes led them to the Exploratores HQ and stopped. He looked up into the air, focusing on a seemingly empty location high up in the sky.

"Here we are. We'll have to request you leave your hidden companion behind. And a word of advice? Invisibility isn't that useful if you aren't hiding your mana."

Ateia and Taog's eyes widened slightly. The drone golem NSLICE-00P had ordered to watch the pair did not respond, but it also stopped moving, maintaining its place up in the sky as NSLICE-00P ordered it to comply. Exploratore Fullofaudes nodded then led the pair inside.

The two were led up to a large office with beautiful carvings along the door. Opening it, they stepped inside. The office was richly adorned with silk curtains, cushions made from the finest monster wool, one shelf full of artifacts, treasures, and trophies, and another filled with bottles each worth more than several Exploratores' yearly incomes. And sitting behind a magnificent desk was Magister Exploratore per Utrad Vibius Vatinius Balbillus himself. He wore fine silk clothes underneath the Exploratores cloak and insignia and had goat horns coming from his forehead. He gave them both a smile with slanted eyes.

"Exploratore Ateia Niraemia, at your service, sir."

"Exploratore Taog Sutharlan, here as you ordered, sir."

"Welcome, welcome. Have a seat, you two."

Ateia and Taog sat as requested. Magister Vibius nodded and reached under his desk, pulling out two pouches. The coins inside clinked together as he placed them on the desk.

"First things first, I owe you two my thanks. I've heard you've been hard at work cleaning up my province while I was occupied with the front."

Ateia nodded. "Just doing our duty, sir."

Magister Vibius's grin grew. "Perhaps so. Still, good work is to be rewarded. Consider this the Imperial bounty for that situation in Khalbuldor's dungeon."

Ateia and Taog glanced at one another, then slowly took the pouches. Vibius resumed speaking once they did.

"Now then, I hear you're on a mission for an Amicitia Populi Elteni? Why don't you tell me more about your quest, and I'll see if I can help."

Ateia and Taog glanced at one another and frowned, but then slowly started to speak. They were on guard, but Magister Vibius didn't ask them any pointed questions or probe into NSLICE-00P. He simply stated what he already knew about their mission and asked what they had done so far and what other information they'd like to share. Eventually, Ateia and Taog started to relax.

It was at that point that Magister Vibius's smile dropped.

"Now then, let me explain why you two are here. Exploratores Ateia Niraemia and Taog Sutharlan, we need your help."

Taog raised an eyebrow at that. "Forgive me, sir, but what do you need *our* help with? Surely, we aren't the most experienced Exploratores you have?"

Magister Vibius shook his head. "No, but due to recent events, I know you are trustworthy, and that makes all the difference. Do you know what this is?"

Magister Vibius reached into his desk and pulled out a box covered in glowing magic symbols. He channeled his mana through them and unlocked the box, opening the lid to reveal a dagger covered in red engravings. Even from across the desk, Ateia and Taog could feel heat emanating from it. Ateia frowned.

"I mean, it's obviously an enchanted dagger of some kind, but I can't tell more than that."

Magister Vibius nodded and rested his elbows on his desk, crossing his hands in front of his face. "What do you two know about the Cults of Mana?"

Taog frowned. "Not much, just that they're some strange folk who worship the Domides instead of the Aesdes. Crazy wizards trying to access the Source more directly or something like that?"

Magister Vibius nodded. "Well, you're not wrong, but that is merely what the public has been allowed to know."

Taog raised an eyebrow. "*Allowed* to know?"

Magister Vibius smiled at him for a moment. "Indeed. The public, the Legion, even the Exploratores. They've all heard the silly little tales of the silly little cultists. But they would not find it so silly if they learned the *truth*."

Ateia's eyes widened slightly. "Magister?"

Magister Vibius rose from his chair and turned toward the window behind him, his back facing the pair. He paused for a moment before speaking in a soft voice.

"What if I told you the Empire is now under the control of one of these cults?"

Ateia frowned. "That's impossible. The Emperor would never allow it."

Magister Vibius nodded. "A true Emperor, yes. I cannot speak for the Southern and Eastern Courts, but the Northern Court has lacked a true Emperor for some time now, ever since General Priscillianus killed Emperor Herius, and Herius's son got himself killed in Turannia, of all places. The man sitting upon the throne now is but a puppet appointed by the south and the east, and helpless before the whims of his own court. He no longer has any real power."

Taog furrowed his brow. "What about the Exploratores or the inquisitors? Surely they wouldn't let some cult infiltrate the court?"

Magister Vibius shook his head. "Ah, you still believe the Exploratores have power, do you? I hate to burst the young folks' bubble, but the Exploratores don't have any *real* power. We occupy a transient place in the Imperial hierarchy where we don't report to anyone but the Emperor but we also don't command anyone. Our mandate and jurisdiction are vague and constantly shifting. As such, our power is *entirely* dependent on our ability to convince the powers that be to let us act, so, for the most part, we only end up acting as is convenient for said powers. And if the powers themselves are corrupted? Then best of luck taking them down as an Exploratore. Even the Hero of Elteno just got lucky; he was in the right place at the right time. I have no confidence *he* could replicate his own feats on demand."

"And the inquisitors?"

Magister Vibius shrugged. "An inquisitor *could* help. But 'inquisitor' is a special role appointed by the Emperor with a clearly defined mandate. Without a strong Emperor, you will not get many inquisitors, and it is all too easy for those in power to adjust that mandate to exclude themselves."

Ateia and Taog fell silent. Magister Vibius sighed.

"I'm sorry to say this, but the Empire is *much* weaker and *much* more corrupt than anyone believes at first. All some cult needed to gain influence was a few key connections and an excess of Idrint. And the Legion? The Exploratores? We're struggling just to keep up with the new dungeons, monster waves, and barbarian incursions, so what can we do if our own leaders have turned against us?"

Magister Vibius turned to face them once more, looking them in the eye.

"But it doesn't have to be that way."

Taking a seat, he pointed to the dagger. "Magister Caelinus became aware of these people some time ago and recruited me to investigate. We've been moving slowly and carefully ever since, finding allies, building support, and weeding out their agents wherever we could find them. We'll never be completely free of them, but we've cleaned out Utrad's leadership at the very least. This province is run entirely by people who still believe in the Empire, or at the very least are not actively working to subvert it."

Magister Vibius's face turned dark. "But that will not be enough. The Northern Court moves against the magister, and he cannot defy appointments from above. They will send their agents into positions of power and will work to undo all that we've done. In fact, they are already here."

Ateia and Taog's eyes widened as they looked at the dagger. Ateia spoke softly. "You mean, that guy in the dungeon?"

Magister Vibius nodded. "There are . . . *rumors* circulating in certain circles. An uptick in mana storms and Rifts, more corrupted dungeons on the outskirts of the Empire than have been seen in centuries. And rumor has it that someone is behind it. That there are dark rituals being researched which can break down the very walls of the world, or that could even corrupt a dungeon by force."

He pointed to the dagger. "Now I am sure. This dagger is something we picked up from a purge of the cult a year ago. It is not of this world and resists the very power of the Aesdes themselves. We, thus, couldn't identify it, other than that it likely comes from the Realms of Mana—one opposed to the Aesdes. And then, mere days ago, a second dagger was found, identical to this one. Found, in fact, in the pockets of a man secretly assaulting the Mines of Might with supposedly untamable adamant bull worms."

Ateia and Taog's eyes went as wide as they could go. Magister Vibius nodded.

"That's right. I believe that man you encountered was attempting to corrupt the Mines of Might, which would have devastated Velusitum and destroyed Utrad's primary source of mana iron. You and your friend put a stop to the plot, and for that, you have our sincerest gratitude."

Ateia trembled. "How . . . How is this possible? If this . . . *cult* is opposed to the Aesdes and taking over the Empire, why haven't the Aesdes done something? Couldn't they have sent a message to the shrines, or something?"

Magister Vibius shook his head. "The Aesdes are fair, but they are distant. They do not interfere directly in the affairs of the living; they focus on maintaining the world itself. They would not oppose such a cult directly. At most, they would empower a hero or two to oppose them."

At that, Ateia and Taog glanced at one another, and Magister Vibius smiled slightly.

"I see you two understand now, right? You've seen and heard of this cult's doings, and now, you find yourselves directly opposed to them. They will not take your interference lightly, unintentional as it may have been, and likewise, you cannot leave them at large if you wish to protect the Empire and its people."

Ateia gulped but slowly nodded. "No, I suppose we can't."

Magister Vibius nodded back. "And neither can we. Now that the cult has moved against Utrad, Magister Caelinus must move against them openly. And it is clear the Northern Court is in their grasp and can no longer be trusted."

Taog looked him in the eye. "What are you going to do?"

Magister Vibius met his gaze. "Protect Utrad—and the Empire—from all its enemies. Foreign . . . and domestic."

Taog's mind raced. He thought of the cult. He thought of what Vafum and Agedia had said. He thought of Turannia's comitatenses being called to Utrad, ignoring the incursions into Turannia. His eyes narrowed. "You . . . You're planning a rebellion."

Magister Vibius smiled at him. "Clever, Exploratore Taog. But not exactly. If the Northern Court is under the control of treasonous cultists, then it is the duty of the loyal to oppose them, is it not? Magister Caelinus has no ambition other than to protect the people he has been charged with. Join us, you and your friend, and let us defeat our mutual enemies. Together, we can destroy the cult and restore peace and prosperity to the Empire."

Taog rose to his feet, pulling Ateia up.

"I've heard enough. Stories about cults or no, we're not getting caught up in a rebellion. Our friend isn't going to care either. We'll go on our way, then, and pretend this conversation never happened."

Magister Vibius shook his head. "Ah, I'm a bit disappointed. You don't seem to understand the situation, do you?"

Taog pulled Ateia to the door. "I understand just fine."

Magister Vibius grinned and snapped his fingers. "Do you, now?"

Suddenly, concealed Exploratores appeared in the room and knocked the two teens to the ground. Magister Vibius sneered at the two.

"After all, whoever said you could leave?"

# 10

# The Status of the Friendlies

*"I suppose we should clarify that the no negotiations protocol does not override protocols on collateral damage."*

—Dr. Gaute Ottosen, after NSLICE units "resolved" a hostage situation.

When NSLICE-00P returned to the inn, she did not find her friendlies. However, she knew from the drone assigned to them that they had some business with the Exploratores. Logs from the drones and the mana connection from her contract with them indicated they were still at the Exploratores HQ, so NSLICE-00P did not react even as the night went on. She was busy investigating the Exploratore's comments on her drones' inadequate stealth measures.

So, it was not until the next morning that NSLICE-00P realized the situation was abnormal.

Taking Estrith, she moved to the Exploratores HQ to check in on the friendlies and determine their status. The staff greeted her politely and led her to the office of the Magister Exploratore. Magister Vibius stood up with a smile, walking forward to shake her hand.

"Ah, you must be NSLICE-00P! Welcome, welcome. I've heard much about you, and am glad we finally have the chance to meet."

"Greeting: Hello, this unit is designated NSLICE-00P. It is nice to meet you."

Estrith simply glared at the man. Magister Vibius ushered them in and took his seat.

"Now, how may I help you today, NSLICE-00P?"

"Request: This unit requests a status report on friendlies Ateia Niraemia and Taog Sutharlan. To this unit's knowledge, they remained at this location overnight after being requested for Exploratores business."

Magister Vibius nodded. "Yes, I have need of them. They will be working on a classified mission here at the headquarters for the foreseeable future. I apologize for the inconvenience; I am aware they were assisting with your mission. If it pleases you, I can assign some other Exploratores to cover for them in the meantime? We have some veterans here who could undoubtedly aid your quest."

NSLICE-00P's robotic eye flickered. Since a local search of the immediate area was no longer a priority, a personal guide from the Exploratores wasn't especially necessary. At this point, Ateia and Taog's presence was mostly for the sake of the major directive. As for assistance from the Exploratores, NSLICE-00P calculated it would be more efficient to have them search through their records and the rest of the Empire than it would be to have them follow her around.

"Negative Response: Immediate replacement of the friendlies is not necessary at this time. Statement: It is a major directive of this unit to ensure the safety of friendlies Ateia Niraemia and Taog Sutharlan. Please confirm the risk of termination is at acceptable limits. If not, this unit must request the friendlies be released from other duties, or that this unit be informed of the situation."

Magister Vibius held up a hand. "I understand. And not to worry, they are not in any danger at present. I apologize, but their current mission is to remain classified, even for an Amicitia Populi Elteni. But please, let us know if there's any other way we can assist you. We'll be working hard on your request as well."

"Acknowledged."

With that, NSLICE-00P rose to her feet and left the room. Estrith glared at the man one last time before scoffing and following suit. Once they had left, Magister Vibius frowned and rubbed his chin.

"Hm, she's attached to those two, it seems? From the reports, I thought she might be fine with a better replacement. I'll have to rethink how to approach this, then . . ."

Outside the building, Estrith frowned. "Queen of the Dobhar, I do not like that man. My instincts tell me that we shouldn't trust him. And I do not think the Imperial whelps are strong enough for a solo hunt, if that is what he was implying."

"Observation: Body language analysis did not indicate any direct falsehoods."

Estrith furrowed her brow but nodded. "If you say so. Still, I must request that you avoid any deals with him that would impact the Dobhar, at the very least."

"Request acknowledged. Response: This unit will attempt to acquiesce unless a higher priority directive takes precedence."

Estrith narrowed her eyes at that but grunted and followed along quietly.

Deciding to continue upgrading her subordinates in the meantime, NSLICE-00P and Estrith made their way toward the dungeon, but along the way, they found Agedia.

"Ah, there you are. Come on, we need to talk about your friends."

"Affirmative."

NSLICE-00P and Estrith followed her to the tavern, and the three sat next to Vafum. The Dwarf waved his hand under the table, and a magic circle appeared there. NSLICE-00P perceived a small bubble of mana surrounding them.

"Query: What is the purpose of the deployed barrier?"

Vafum grunted. "Privacy, lass. You're definitely being followed if I know the magister, which, unfortunately, I do."

Agedia went over to the bartender and came back with several mugs.

"I got the drinks!"

Vafum heaved a sigh. "Agedia, I'm a Dwarf, so believe me when I say you should *not* be drinking in the early morning!"

She waved her hand as she took a swig. "It's fine, it's fine. We have to act casual, so I'd look suspicious without it, right?"

Vafum slapped his forehead. "Well, at least Vibius's people won't believe *she's* talking about anything important." But he accepted a mug from Agedia and started drinking himself.

"Query: What do contacts Vafum and Agedia have to discuss with this unit?"

Agedia's smile dropped at that. "It's about Magister Vibius . . . and your friends. You went to see him earlier, right?"

"Affirmative."

Agedia's eyes narrowed. "What exactly did he say?"

NSLICE-00P reported on their conversation while Vafum and Agedia both rubbed their chins and took sips of their drinks. Agedia crossed her arms with a frown once she finished.

"That settles it—your friends are in trouble."

"Statement: Magister Vibius stated the friendlies are not in danger, and body language analysis did not indicate deceit."

Vafum shook his head. "They don't need to be in danger to be in trouble, lass. And be wary of Magister Vibius. Just because what he tells you is 'true' doesn't mean it's everything you need to know."

"Query: Does contact Vafum believe Magister Vibius is withholding key intel?"

Vafum scoffed. "That old goat is *always* hiding something. In this case, absolutely. What he told you makes no sense. No offense, but your friends are green as nauseous goblins and are working for an Amicitia Populi Elteni to boot. The magister wouldn't trust the two of them with a mission important enough to justify pulling them away from you."

"Query: Then what is Magister Vibius doing with the friendlies, and what is the probability they will be terminated?"

Vafum frowned. "The first question is easy, lass. It's aimed at you."

"Objection: This unit is not affiliated with the Exploratores or the Empire."

Vafum shook his head. "That's exactly the problem. You are powerful, independent, and have uncertain allegiances and motives. And now you're sitting in the province's capital, right when we're seeing signs the magister's preparing for something big. He either thinks you can help and wants you onboard . . . or wants to make certain you won't be a problem. I'm guessing he wanted their help with that, and they refused. That's why he offered to replace those two with his own people now."

NSLICE-00P's robotic eye flickered at that. "Query: What is the probability the friendlies will be terminated?"

Estrith furrowed her brow at that question, but Vafum shook his head.

"Shouldn't have to worry too much about that. You've made it clear they're important to you. That old goat wouldn't waste leverage. But you should be worried about what he will do next. He will attempt to either convince, manipulate, or control you, and will use them to do so if he believes he can."

Estrith turned to look at NSLICE-00P. "Queen of the Dobhar, what are you going to do?"

Agedia gave her a knowing grin. "Oh? Worried about those two, are you?"

She scowled. "I simply wish to know the queen of the Dobhar's next actions, that I may fulfill my duties. Nothing more."

Agedia simply smiled and took another drink. "Yes, of course."

Meanwhile, NSLICE-00P's robotic eye flickered.

"Analyzing scenario . . ."

By all accounts, the situation resembled a hostage scenario. NSLICE-00P's old protocols indicated she should refuse all negotiations and proceed to terminate the hostile regardless of hostages, but that was inappropriate in this situation. Not only would that threaten the major directive to ensure Ateia and Taog's safety, but the Empire as a whole was not a hostile entity, and NSLICE-00P needed to keep it that way if at all possible, so immediate termination of the Exploratores and their local authority was not an acceptable option.

As such, she had to try and analyze the situation based on her directives. And, unfortunately, she had few viable courses of action. Ultimately, Magister Vibius was an authority within both the Exploratores and the Empire, and so had official jurisdiction over Ateia and Taog. NSLICE-00P could not object to his current actions unless she could confirm an immediate threat to the friendlies or to herself, or that the magister had acted beyond his official authority. Her contract with Ateia and Taog was premised on them fulfilling their Exploratores' duties, after all.

Attempting to manipulate or control her reduced his trustworthiness but did not necessarily indicate hostile intent. And she did not have hard evidence of this either, only the opinion of the local contacts based on circumstantial evidence.

However, it did mean that direct negotiation with the magister might contain some risk.

"Conclusion: This unit does not have a justifiable reason to act, and lacks sufficient data to determine if a direct response is required. This unit will attempt to covertly assess the situation of her friendlies, and so acquire the missing intel."

Vafum eyed her for a moment. "I suppose that's all you can do for now. Just, be careful, lass. The Exploratores have been in the information business for a while now; you'll be hard-pressed to outmaneuver them."

"Acknowledged."

Agedia frowned. "And . . . one more thing before you go. That girl, Ateia, is more important than you know. Make sure those two are alright at the end of this, okay?"

"Statement: The survival of friendlies Ateia Niraemia and Taog Sutharlan is a major directive for this unit."

With that, NSLICE-00P and Estrith stood up and left. Agedia and Vafum both put their drinks down and rose to their feet.

"You going to keep an eye on her?"

Agedia nodded. Vafum sighed.

"Guess I'll need to be prepared for the worst, then."

Agedia's head drooped. "Sorry."

Vafum shook his head. "For once, it won't be your fault. Let's just be glad that old goat hasn't realized who she really is. Things would get unbelievably messy if he did."

Agedia stared off into the distance, swaying slightly. She gripped her trembling hand into a fist, and then glared into the air.

". . . I won't let that happen."

# 11

# We Must Continue to Rely on Negotiations

*"Surrender AND I'll burn your pathetic city to the ground."*

—Drycnid Chondreid, High Archon of the Empire of the Sun, in a diplomatic offer to the City-State of Elteno.

The Legions of Utrad and Turannia gathered in the courtyard of a massive fortress along the Somno Secta River. Within the towering walls, massive bonfires had been lit, kegs had been opened, and men and women of all races were singing and shouting as they feasted. The battle had been won, the loot had been distributed, the promotions secured, and all the soldiers praised Magister Caelinus for leading them into glory.

It was at that moment that Dux Pollia Augustalis, commander of the Utrad comitatenses, stepped out onto a balcony overlooking the courtyard. A soldier beside her blew a trumpet, and the din of the feast below died down. All eyes turned to her.

She raised a mug into the air.

"To victory and to the Empire!"

All the soldiers below joined her in a mighty shout and drank from their mugs.

"Who is it that brought you glory? Who is it that led you to victory? Who is it that held the line while the court nobles squabbled? Who is it that fought by your side?"

The soldiers shouted in response, "Magister Caelinus!"

"Who is it that will reward your bravery? Who is it that defends your home and your families? Who is it that protects the Empire?"

"Magister Caelinus!"

Dux Augustalis nodded, her face grim.

"And who was it who tried to steal our wages? Who was it who gave us old and decrepit gear? Who was it who sent us to die from the safety of their homes?"

The soldiers went quiet as the dux frowned.

"I'll tell you. The corrupt court of the North!"

The soldiers began muttering and shouting at that. The dux nodded.

"And that is why I say, no more! I say, the Empire belongs to those who protect it! Who have fought and died defending it!"

The soldiers began to shout and jeer in agreement. The dux drew her blade and raised it high into the air.

"And that is why I am declaring Magister Caelinus . . . as the new Emperor of the North!"

The soldiers paused for a moment, staring at the dux. Then . . . one of them drew a sword, lifted it into the air, and began to cheer. Then another followed suit . . . and another, until eventually, a tide of shouts rang through the courtyard, and every soldier had their weapon raised.

And it was at that moment that Magister Caelinus himself stepped out onto the balcony. Everyone fell silent as he raised a hand, taking a deep breath.

"It is with great reluctance that I have agreed to this. The Empire is my home. I have fought for it. My father fought for it. And his father before it. The last thing I want is to see it torn apart in war and bloodshed."

He looked down at the soldiers, making eye contact with as many of them as possible.

"But . . . that Empire is being torn apart, right now, by the very people who should strive to protect it. Greedy officials burden the people to line their pockets, the court is full of treachery and conspiracy, and the Legion's blood is spent on foolish and uncaring orders. I cannot stand to watch it any longer."

He took a deep breath.

"The road ahead will be long and hard. The Northern Court will not relinquish its power so easily. We will have to fight, even to bleed."

He then grabbed his sword and lifted it into the air.

"But this I swear to you: while I am in command, not one more drop of Legion blood will be shed in vain! We will fight for one another and for our homes, and by the blood that is shed, a new and stronger Empire shall rise!"

At this, Dux Augustalis raised her sword once more.

"All hail Emperor Caelinus!"

And all the soldiers shouted in response.

NSLICE-00P stood on the street, her drones scanning the Exploratores HQ. The Exploratores Headquarters had been built separate from the Legion keep in Velusitum, such that visitors leaving requests wouldn't interfere with Legion business. The front facing the street was a large, multistoried building containing the reception area, the barracks for the Exploratores, and the offices for Exploratores personnel to take care of documentation. Behind this structure was a large courtyard where new Exploratores recruits could receive some basic training. There were several more structures in the back, including a butchery workshop for processing monster corpses, and a warehouse to hold Exploratores supplies.

The first thing NSLICE-00P noticed was that the entire compound was protected by an invisible barrier. The barrier was thin but extended both into the sky above and the ground below. It seemed to obscure the view, and even her drones' visual and thermal sensors couldn't pierce it. However, the protection extended only to visible light and infrared, along with other organic senses such as audio and scent. It did not extend to radar, so NSLICE-00P was able to map out the structure of the facility.

She discovered an elaborate network of tunnels linking the various structures, with a number of rooms far below the ground. The connection she had with Ateia and Taog via the contract indicated they were likely in that underground area.

The barrier was a problem. NSLICE-00P predicted it was likely an alarm that would alert the Exploratores to a security breach. That, or it was the trigger for a trap that could directly assault any intruders. The only gaps in the barrier were around the official entrances, which were both crowded and guarded.

Opening a gap via magic or the Equalizer was not acceptable. She did not understand this barrier well enough to interact with it covertly, and a direct assault would almost certainly qualify as a hostile act. She could not risk antagonizing an official military organization of the Empire like that.

And even if she could find or create a gap, there was another problem. The Exploratores had already demonstrated they could detect her covert units by nonvisual means. She was investigating countermeasures to this, but had not implemented any at this time. So, any unit she deployed would likely be detected and intercepted . . . and probably terminated.

But there was one thing that seemed to work.

If NSLICE-00P got close to the barrier, her dungeon field seemed to pass through it without issue, and she could perceive anything occurring within range on the other side. The range wasn't enough to reach the friendlies from outside the compound, but NSLICE-00P had solutions for that.

| **Available Dungeon Field Generator +1 Upgrades:** | | | |
|---|---|---|---|
| **Name** | **Cost** | **Additional Mana Upkeep** | **Description** |
| **Dungeon Field Generator +2** | **10** | **10** | **Expands the area of effect of the dungeon field to 30 meters total.**<br>**Additional upgrades increase available dungeon functions in the area of effect.** |

And fortunately, she had more than enough points to afford it. The Dungeon XP from the Otter Burrow continued to grow, rising to one level up every eight hours at this point, and she was also absorbing mana from the people of Velusitum during the nights. As a result, she had gained twenty-two Dungeon levels over the past few days, bringing her available Dungeon perk points up to forty-five.

She went ahead and purchased the upgrade, along with another Mana Capacitor to maintain her reserves.

With her range upgraded, she walked right up to the Exploratores HQ. She would still need to get inside the compound to bring the target area within range, but fortunately, she had reasons to be there. She would simply request a status update on the mission she had submitted to the Exploratores.

NSLICE-00P and Estrith entered the reception area. Now that Magister Vibius and some of the Exploratores had returned, the room was packed to bursting. The citizens of Velusitum crowded the room, swarming the receptionists with requests and complaints. However, one of the guards noticed her enter.

"Hello, Miss NSLICE-00P. As you can see, we're a bit busy here. However, Magister Vibius can assist you in his office if you'd prefer?"

"Affirmative."

"Very well. This way, please."

The guard led the pair through the crowds to a side door leading to the back area behind the receptionist. He showed them to a meeting room.

"I'll let the magister know you're here."

"Acknowledged."

As they arrived in the room, NSLICE-00P's dungeon field came within range of the friendlies. Her robotic eye began flickering while Estrith raised an eyebrow.

"Queen of the Dobhar, what is going on?"

"Answer: This unit has located the friendlies."

Ateia and Taog were not, in fact, working. They were separated, each sitting in a separate room. Rooms with no windows and big, heavy doors that were locked from the outside. Rooms with strong mana signatures within the floors and roofs and walls. Rooms with guards on the outside. And Ateia and Taog lacked their weapons and were displaying signs of distress.

Her heart rate increased in spite of her emotional controls once again. The Calm spell only partially reduced it this time.

"Observation: Analysis of the friendlies' current conditions indicates a 97.63 percent probability that they are being incarcerated."

Estrith's eyes widened, and she scowled. "What?!"

But NSLICE-00P didn't answer. As she calculated her response, the door opened up, and Magister Vibius stepped into the room, giving her a smile.

"Ah, NSLICE-00P, nice to see you again. What can I do for you today?"

NSLICE-00P and Estrith both turned to face him. As a military official of the Empire with authority over Ateia and Taog, NSLICE-00P could not designate this act as a hostile one just yet. So, the appropriate response would depend largely on what happened next.

"Requesting Explanation: Please explain why Magister Vibius has incarcerated friendlies Ateia Niraemia and Taog Sutharlan, and indicate future plans regarding them."

# 12

# Aggressive Negotiations

*"We specifically intended a diplomatic solution. Is that what you call . . . this?"*
—One of Dr. Ottosen's sponsors, after a mistranslation led to an NSLICE unit activating termination protocols during diplomatic negotiations.

Magister Vibius paused but kept his smile.

"What do you mean, incarcerated? Those two are working on an important mission, Miss NSLICE-00P."

"Observation: Friendlies Ateia Niraemia and Taog Sutharlan are currently located twenty-five meters below this location, under heavy guard, and with their possessions confiscated. Vital signs and emotional analysis suggest psychological distress. Analysis indicates a 97.63 percent chance of forcible incarceration."

Magister Vibius paused again but managed to keep his expression under control.

"I am not sure I follow, Miss NSLICE-00P. Where exactly are you getting this idea from?"

"Observation: Magister Vibius appears to be avoiding the question. Potential deceit detected. Desire to avoid falsehood detection detected. Please provide a direct response to the query. If an acceptable explanation cannot be provided, this unit requires that friendlies Ateia Niraemia and Taog Sutharlan be released and prioritize their obligations to this unit."

Magister Vibius held her gaze for a moment, tapping his side. Eventually, he heaved a sigh and looked down.

"I see. I cannot hide anything from you, can I, Miss NSLICE-00P? Here, come and make yourself comfortable, and I will explain the situation."

Magister Vibius walked over to the table in the room and took a seat. NSLICE-00P remained standing. Magister Vibius waited for a moment before moving to speak.

"It is true, yes, that those two Exploratores are being kept here, under guard, even. But it is no lie that they are involved with a highly sensitive mission of grave importance. They are being kept here for their own protection."

"Requesting Elaboration."

Magister Vibius nodded, his expression turning grave.

"Let me tell you the dark secret of the Empire, Miss NSLICE-00P. There are forces seeking to destroy not only the Empire but the very walls of the world itself. And I believe you have already encountered them . . ."

Magister Vibius went on to explain the Cults of Mana and the knowledge he had on them. He told NSLICE-00P how he and Magister Caelinus had come to know of them and worked to purge Utrad of their influence. He stated the likely goal of the man NSLICE-00P had encountered in the Mines of Might.

"And that is why I had to keep your friends under guard. This cult . . . their influence extends even farther than I know. And now, you and your friends have foiled one of their plots directly. That will not go unnoticed . . . or unpunished."

He lowered his head toward her.

"I must apologize, Miss NSLICE-00P, for I have used you. I took my Exploratores under my protection to ensure the cult couldn't retaliate against them, but I left you out in the open in hopes of drawing them out. I hoped you would be powerful enough to survive the retribution, but I needed to protect my own assets. I hope you can understand. Your friends . . . were opposed to my plans and concerned for you."

"Acknowledged."

Magister Vibius looked up and nodded.

"But now that you are here and have largely figured things out on your own, I think there's a better way. We have a common enemy—one who will come for us and everyone we care about. Help me, NSLICE-00P. Let's take on this foe together and destroy this cult down to its very roots. And once the threat is destroyed, your friends will be safe, and I will have no further reason to keep them confined."

NSLICE-00P's robotic eye flickered. Magister Vibius was not at all trustworthy, she knew that much. But . . . body language analysis didn't catch any overt falsehoods. NSLICE-00P's analysis of her own encounters indicated a significant probability the magister was correct about the existence of a cult. She had already encountered another individual who'd created a corrupted dungeon, and a cult as described would match the currently unknown hostile Magister Tiberius had warned Ateia about. If this cult did exist, she had now terminated at least two of their members. That was more than sufficient grounds to expect hostility from any wider organizations those individuals may have been a part of. NSLICE-00P might already be at war with such a cult.

On the other hand, she didn't have any evidence that the man in the Mines of Might was connected to the man in Castra Turannia, or that an overarching organization existed at this stage.

If nothing else, she should request additional intel to confirm the existence of a potentially hostile organization. It made sense, too, to leave the friendlies under guard while such an investigation was underway. And if such an organization was confirmed to exist, acquiring allies against a mutual enemy may, in fact, be beneficial.

Estrith frowned. "Do not trust this Imperial, queen of the Dobhar. His words smell of deceit."

"Observation: Body language analysis does not indicate any overt falsehoods. Does friendly Estrith have intel to share to the contrary?"

Estrith furrowed her brow. ". . . No. Just a feeling."

"Acknowledged. Request: This unit would like to view any evidence Magister Vibius has for these claims. Additional cooperation pending based on confirmation that a hostile organization exists."

Magister Vibius grinned . . .

Taog was sitting on the cot in his cell, leaning over his knees. His hands were sweating, but he continued gripping them together anyways.

He had been an idiot. They had been warned that Magister Vibius was not to be trusted. They had been told that something was going on in Utrad. And then he'd walked right into the thick of it with no preparation or planning.

He should have waited for NSLICE-00P to return before meeting with the magister. They could have brought her along, or at the very least let her know what was going on. Or he should have smiled and played along with the magister instead of rejecting him outright and then assuming they could still walk away. It was obvious, in hindsight, how the magister would respond. He wouldn't trust the two of them to keep quiet about an impending rebellion.

And now, they were trapped here, with no way to contact any of their friends. Taog heaved a sigh. And here he'd said he was going to protect Ateia. Hah, he couldn't even protect himself.

He couldn't protect anyone.

Taog paused. Something washed over him, on the back of his mind. He couldn't identify what it was, but it felt familiar, like when he'd signed the magical contract with NSLICE-00P.

His eyes widened as he thought of their friend. He wasn't sure how, but somehow, he knew.

She was here. She was in the building, right now.

Taog frowned. She might be here, but that didn't mean he could contact her. Worse, it was likely she was talking with Magister Vibius. He could tell her anything he wanted . . .

Taog rose to his feet and glared up at the roof.

He didn't know what he was doing. He had no reason to believe it would work. But NSLICE-00P knew things that she shouldn't. She could identify traps and monsters long before Taog could even see them, despite his enhanced senses. She knew the right path in any dungeon maze; she clearly had some powerful senses beyond the norm.

So, Taog decided to hope. To hope that NSLICE-00P's abnormal methods would work in his favor. He started talking to the air, reaching out with his mana to that thin connection he had with NSLICE-00P, hoping she would notice.

"Seero, I hope you'll surprise me just one more time. If you can hear me by some unexpected means, then don't believe anything Magister Vibius tells you. He and his boss are planning a rebellion; he tried to get us to join in and imprisoned us when we refused. Please, rescue Ateia if you can, and then get out of here."

And as it turned out, NSLICE-00P could, in fact, hear Taog's words via unexpected means. She suddenly froze, and her robotic eye began spinning and flickering. Even Magister Vibius was taken aback for a moment before his smile returned.

"Negative Response: This unit has received intel that Magister Vibius is planning to rebel against the Empire. This unit's current objectives require cordial relations with the Empire, and so, this unit will not affiliate herself with any factions hostile to it. As Magister Vibius will relinquish official authority with the Empire, this unit demands the release of friendlies Ateia and Taog, and then will evacuate the probable combat zones."

For the first time, Magister Vibius's smile dropped.

"How did you . . . Look, Miss NSLICE-00P. The cult has infiltrated the Northern Court and the highest positions of the Empire. They can no longer be trusted, and they will come after you. It is simply foolish for you to carry on as if none of this is your business. Yes, we are planning some extreme measures, and yes, the Northern Court will resist, but this is only because such measures are necessary. The Empire will endure, stronger than ever, under our guidance. And you . . . if you help us, why, the resources of the *entire* Imperial North will be at your disposal. We will spare no effort to find your missing people. Entire Legions will search on your behalf, and you will have access to every classified document available. The Empire as it is will not deign to help you beyond the bare minimum, and soon, it will turn against you. Then, it will be you alone against the might of the cult and whatever they may bring to bear."

"Query: Does Magister Vibius have proof the Empire has been infiltrated by a hostile faction to said degree and guarantees that this unit will receive the proposed compensation?"

Magister Vibius frowned. "They've covered their trail well, but rest assured, I have some of their documents. As for compensation, I have a Contract skill; we can sign a contract to that effect. You will have your reward—I can guarantee that."

"Analysis: Compensation premised on a successful rebellion is insufficient to justify unprovoked hostility against a previously cordial entity with an ongoing contract. Presence of hostile infiltrators in Empire-owned territory does not signify a full subversion of the Empire's political and military leadership to the extent implied. Magister Vibius has consistently left key intel out of the conversation and has failed to provide convincing evidence for the key claims. This unit concludes further dealings to be too risky to be entertained, and further discussion an inefficient use of time. This unit requires the immediate return of friendlies Ateia Niraemia and Taog Sutharlan. Further delays may necessitate a direct response."

Magister Vibius sighed before narrowing his eyes. "I wanted us to cooperate freely, but you have left me no choice. If you will not join us, then you are a threat. NSLICE-00P, join with us, or I will execute Ateia Niraemia and Taog Sutharlan."

NSLICE-00P's robotic eye turned red. Estrith gripped her spear.

"Warning: Hostile intent toward this unit or the aforementioned friendlies will result in immediate termination."

And so, Magister Vibius and NSLICE-00P stared each other down . . .

# 13

# Operation: Rescue Friendlies

*"Congratulatory Announcement: You are being rescued. Do not resist."*

—NSLICE units while relocating a refugee settlement under mutant assault.

Magister Vibius heaved a sigh. "So be it, then. I cannot risk you joining up with the Northern Court. If you will not join us, then you must be destroyed."

With a snap of his fingers, the entire room lit up. A massive magic circle burned through the rug, engraved into the floor below, and the room was flooded with mana, which began swirling through the air around NSLICE-00P. The twisting mana would disrupt any attempt to create a magic circle, and even if a spell was cast, its power would be spent resisting the mana cyclone all around it.

Meanwhile, a small figure, no larger than a child, appeared right in front of NSLICE-00P, swinging a dagger toward her face.

Magister Vibius sneered. "All the magical might in the world doesn't matter if you can't cast a spell, or if you have a dagger in the eye. Goodbye, NSLICE-00P. I just want you to know it wasn't personal . . ." Magister Vibius's words died on his lips.

"Hostile intent confirmed. Termination protocols engaged."

The moment the magic circle triggered, two panels popped up on NSLICE-00P's shoulders, revealing her autopistols. These opened fire at the hidden figure NSLICE-00P had detected in the room, and the assassin cried out as he leapt back, bleeding all over. Meanwhile, NSLICE-00P's helmet covered her head.

"Observation: Mana distortions observed. Adapting."

NSLICE-00P's hands transformed into gun barrels and opened fire. The assassin had some ability to endure the un-upgraded shoulder pistols, but the stronger bullets from the assault rifles tore right through them.

*You have slain Dimindium Pendem (Level 73)!*
*Gained 20 Personal XP, 3 Dungeon XP!*

Two more Exploratores burst into the room with swords drawn, making their way toward Estrith, but they had not accounted for NSLICE-00P still being active, and so were not prepared for her to open fire on them, taking one down immediately. The other was distracted by this and so unprepared for Estrith to stab him with her harpoon.

*You have slain Human (Level 76)!*
*Gained 25 Personal XP, 3 Dungeon XP!*

She turned to Magister Vibius, but he was already gone, having fled out a hidden door behind him the moment the ambush failed. Estrith turned toward NSLICE-00P, her face grim.

"Imperial dogs. I knew there is no trusting them. What now, queen of the Dobhar?"

NSLICE-00P's eye flickered. "Retrieving friendlies."

NSLICE-00P activated the Transfer protocol, and Ateia and Taog appeared in the room. The pair blinked repeatedly before their eyes widened, and Ateia's jaw dropped.

"Huh? What . . . Seero?! What?! How?! What's going on?! Why are you here?! How did we get here?! Is that . . . Is that blood?!"

"Deferral: Explanation of current situation delayed until friendlies evacuated from the combat area."

Taog just smiled. "Thanks, Seero. You never disappoint, do you?"

"Statement: Summary of this unit's mission success rate deferred. Please prepare for evacuation."

While NSLICE-00P had added terminating Magister Vibius to her current objectives, her highest priority was preventing Ateia, Taog, and herself from being terminated. Magister Vibius had displayed prepared countermeasures for her estimated capabilities, and she didn't have full intel on the military assets he might have available in this city, so there was significant risk to an immediate pursuit with the friendlies in tow. As such, NSLICE-00P calculated she should first evacuate her friendlies from all possible harm. She could then take her time identifying an ideal opportunity to terminate the target.

So NSLICE-00P disabled the magic circle below with the Equalizer, then surrounded Ateia, Taog, and Estrith with magic barriers and kicked the door open. She ran down the hallway, back toward the entrance hall. Once she entered it, she activated her repulsors and boosted over the heads of the waiting crowds.

The guards barely had a chance to speak before she shot past them and out into the streets of Velusitum.

Magister Vibius swore as he dug into his shoulder. He had been caught by a stray attack from whatever weapon NSLICE-00P had used. Digging out the small metal projectile, he doused the area with a healing potion, swearing as his wound burned. Meanwhile, he triggered the alarm, Exploratores on standby arriving to meet him shortly after.

"I guess I should have expected as much from an Amicitia Populi Elteni. Rector Aemilia really undersold her. Activate the defenses—all of them. She'll be coming for her friends next. We'll prepare an ambush in the tunnels—"

"Magister!" An assistant ran up to him.

Magister Vibius scowled. "What is it? We're in the middle of an emergency here!"

"The Amicitia Populi Elteni just left the building!"

He blinked. "What? After all that, she just left those two behind?"

"I don't know, sir, but she was apparently carrying several people with her."

Magister Vibius froze. That . . . should be impossible. But one did not become a Magister Exploratore without experiencing the impossible. He spoke in a small voice.

"Contact the warden and have him check the cells."

A few minutes later, Magister Vibius was sweating. By some unknown means that gave no warning and left no trace, NSLICE-00P had bypassed all defenses—magic and mundane—and retrieved the two Exploratores in an instant. Magister Vibius had underestimated and failed to eliminate the Amicitia Populi Elteni after having confirmed the intent to rebel. And then, she had escaped his fortress, making off with the only leverage he had on her. So, a potentially archmage-level spellcaster who apparently also had powerful physical weapons and the perception and reflexes to foil an ambush by his top assassin was now completely hostile, aware that he could not count on his status within the Empire, and at large within Utrad's capital city.

Caelinus would not be happy to hear his next report.

NSLICE-00P boosted through the city streets, just above the crowds. Thanks to her covert units and drones, she had a full map of the city and could head directly toward the nearest exit. Her scans had also indicated a thin barrier around the city and potential air defense installations at key locations, so she had decided to try one of the gates rather than risk challenging the Empire's currently unknown antiair capabilities. As such, she kept her height below that of the nearby structures and just above the crowds below.

Estrith was muttering to herself, and Taog had his eyes shut, but the pair were under no threat, so NSLICE-00P ignored them.

She was just reaching the gate leading to the river when a group of guards began to move. They took up position in front of the gate, blocking her path. Since the rebellion had not officially begun, NSLICE-00P couldn't be certain of the hostility of any given soldier, and was attempting to avoid confrontations. However, if the soldiers were moving to block her evacuation, then they would need to be dealt with. NSLICE-00P was about to activate termination protocols . . .

"WHAT DID YOU JUST CALL ME?!"

Suddenly, the doors of a nearby tavern burst open, and a man flew out into the street. Agedia launched after him, wrapping her tail around his form and shaking him around. Her face was flushed red, and her words slurred.

"I'LL SHOW YOU A SLIMY SNAKE!"

His friends came out, moving to intervene. Agedia spun around to face them, accidentally letting go of the man, who soared through the air and crashed right into the gathering guards. Soon, a full-on brawl broke out in the streets, drawing in the guards. NSLICE-00P now had an opening, and she boosted forward at full speed. A pedestrian on the side of the road tossed something in her flight path. NSLICE-00P identified it as a scroll and caught it before boosting right out of the gate, exiting Velusitum.

She then shot off into the distance. A few ballistae began turning in her direction, but they had not been prepared in time, and so NSLICE-00P was out of range before they could fire.

Once at a minimum safe distance in a forest beyond the river, NSLICE-00P landed and placed her friendlies on the ground. Estrith and Taog gasped for breath and hugged the dirt while Ateia just swayed side to side with her eyes wide open. NSLICE-00P opened up the scroll she had caught.

*There's a safehouse five miles east of the river.*

The rest of the scroll included a basic map and instructions on how to access the safehouse. NSLICE-00P calculated its likely location compared to her own. Fortunately, it was fairly close by.

"S-Seero . . . what . . . what's going on?"

NSLICE-00P turned to face Ateia. "Statement: Friendly Taog informed this unit of Target Vibius's ultimate intentions. Cordial relations with the Empire are currently necessary for this unit's primary directive, and so this unit declined to support any sort of rebellion. Target Vibius then acted with hostile intent toward this unit and friendlies Ateia and Taog. This unit proceeded to forcibly extract all friendlies, who will be evacuated to a safe location. This unit will now scout the location."

NSLICE-00P deployed a handful of drones to do just that. Ateia blinked before sighing and shaking her head.

"I'm sorry, Seero. This is all just . . . This is all happening so fast."

Taog placed a hand on her trembling shoulder, and she turned to face him. "It's okay, Ateia. We're here now, and we're all okay. We can figure out everything else going on in a bit. Let's just find a safe place to rest first, okay?" He then smiled at her. "Besides, we have Seero here now. She'll figure out a way, right?"

Ateia's eyes trembled for a second, but then she took a deep breath and nodded. "Right, okay."

In the meantime, NSLICE-00P's drones arrived on site and located the safehouse. The safehouse itself was protected by wards, and so thermal scans couldn't confirm the inside, but her drones did determine the surrounding area was clear. NSLICE-00P decided it was worth investigating.

"Update: This unit has concluded preliminary scans of a potential safehouse. Please prepare for transit."

NSLICE-00P surrounded them with barriers once more, but only lifted them a few feet off the ground before carrying them to the safehouse.

The group came to the location in question, finding nothing there. But NSLICE-00P stepped toward a tree with the branches twisted in a particular fashion and placed her hand on it. Channeling her mana, she spoke the passcode mentioned on the scroll.

Part of the tree vanished, revealing a hollowed-out portion with a staircase leading underground. NSLICE-00P's dungeon field covered the interior, revealing no life-forms or traps inside, so the group made their way down.

Inside was a stone structure. There was a central room with some preserved rations and medical supplies, and two barracks with a couple of cots set up. Ateia and Taog plopped onto chairs around a table in the center of the room while Estrith checked out each of the rooms with her spear at the ready.

And so, the group took a moment to breathe before taking stock of their current situation . . .

# 14

# This Unit Absolutely Will Not Stop, Ever, Until You Are Terminated

*"They may have failed today, but they will never stop. We will repeat the operation as many times as it takes, and we will succeed. Termination is . . . inevitable."*

—Dr. Gaute Ottosen, on the fifteenth failed assassination attempt against the Atomic Cult.

After a moment, Ateia took a deep breath.

"Okay then . . . so Magister Caelinus is planning a rebellion, and Magister Vibius is in on it. He wanted Seero to join in and tried to use us to convince her. It turned out bad, he attacked Seero, and then Seero rescued us, which's a part that doesn't make any sense. How *did* you get us out of there, Seero? One moment I was waiting in my cell, and the next we were suddenly upstairs."

"Response: The evacuation mechanism is currently classified."

Ateia took a deep breath and shook her head. "Right, okay. So, um, Seero . . . did you kill Magister Vibius?"

"Answer: Target Vibius escaped as this unit retaliated against his forces. This unit prioritized evacuation of the friendlies over pursuit of the target. Once this unit confirms this location is secure, termination of hostiles will resume."

Taog frowned, rubbing his chin. "Are you sure about that, Seero? That would mean getting involved in the upcoming rebellion, going against Magister Caelinus and whatever forces are loyal to him."

"Response: Target Vibius has already acted with unprovoked hostile intent toward this unit. Termination is now required to remove the threat to this unit."

Just then, NSLICE-00P engaged her helmet and aimed her weapons and several magic circles at the entrance.

"Warning: Life-form detected on approach. Affiliation unknown."

Estrith took up position by NSLICE-00P with her harpoon at the ready. Ateia and Taog ducked into one of the other rooms. The entrance to the safehouse opened up, and they heard footsteps . . .

Vafum Broadbane stepped into view, swearing at the sight below him.

"Relax, lass! I'm on your side!"

"Request: Please provide evidence of nonhostile affiliations."

Vafum glared at her. "Because I'm not here with the guards, that's why! Fool girl, who do you think owns this safehouse to begin with?!"

NSLICE-00P checked the feed from her drones but found no other lifeforms in the area. Vafum was not lying; he had not brought anyone with him.

"Statement: This unit finds said logic reasonable. This unit must warn unaffiliated individual that any hostile intent will result in immediate termination."

She let the magic circles fade but kept her helmet on. Estrith glared at the newcomer but slowly relaxed. Vafum shook his head and muttered as he took a seat at the table, and Ateia and Taog slowly made their way out of the room once they realized it was safe.

Vafum looked over at them and nodded.

"Ah, good, you got them out already. Now, mind telling me what happened? All we know is you went straight to confront Magister Vibius directly like an idiot and then had to run off for some reason. You're lucky we guessed right on which exit you'd use."

"Affirmative. Reporting recent events . . ."

NSLICE-00P told Vafum about her conversation with Magister Vibius, the assassination attempt, and the subsequent evacuation. Vafum swore and took a flask out of his pocket.

"By the Aesdes above, Caelinus is plotting a rebellion? Isn't that just *great*?" He took a swig and heaved a sigh. "Well then, what are you going to do now?"

"Answer: This unit will confirm the friendlies' safety and then terminate hostile Vibius."

Vafum raised an eyebrow and glanced around at the others. Taog shrugged.

"Seero doesn't play around. She single-handedly stopped a Wulver incursion because they attacked us."

Vafum took a deep breath and shook his head. "Don't mess with the shiny lass, huh?"

A few hours went by, and Ateia and Taog turned in for the night. NSLICE-00P caught one Exploratore snooping the area with her dungeon field, but the scout in question didn't seem to notice the safehouse and moved on. Confident now that the location was sufficiently hidden, she left Estrith, Melion, and the registered monsters behind to guard the place, and then Vafum helped her sneak back in. They took the long way around Velusitum until they reached the mountainside, at which point he took her through a hidden entrance into Khalbuldor.

The Dwarves didn't tell the Empire *everything*, after all, and Vafum had explored many "abandoned" mining tunnels as a young lad.

Vafum had her wait in Khalbuldor as he checked things out with his contacts in Velusitum. He returned to NSLICE-00P with his brow furrowed and a frown on his face.

"It's weird, lass."

"Query: Was there difficulty in locating the target?"

Vafum shook his head. "The opposite, actually. Magister Vibius left town, very openly and publicly, and headed out in the direction of the border. The rest of the town is business as usual. No alerts have been put out, and they aren't searching for you either."

NSLICE-00P's robotic eye turned red. "Statement: Target located and outside of defensive emplacements. This unit will proceed with termination."

Vafum crossed his arms. "I'd be wary, lass. It's pretty obvious it's a trap. He *wants* you to follow him. If I had to guess . . . he's aiming to meet up with Magister Caelinus and his Legions after drawing you out of the area."

NSLICE-00P's robotic eye flickered. On the one hand, if the target was not hiding their movements, then Vafum's assessment was likely correct. The probability of an ambush was substantial. On the other hand, an engagement in the field provided advantages to NSLICE-00P. She would not be forced into close quarters like in an urban setting and so would have full access to her sensors, mobility, and large-scale attacks.

"Analysis: Accounting for the possibility of ambush, the situation still favors pursuit. This unit will proceed with search-and-destroy protocols."

Vafum made eye contact with her, his face grim. "Lass, helping you evade the guards or a couple of Exploratores is one thing. But now you're likely going to face Magister Caelinus's Legions. There's not much we can do against that. If you wait, the Empire will send its own force eventually. Might be better to try and link up with them."

"Response: This unit will scout the target ahead of time. If mission success probability is below the acceptable limit, this unit will fall back and search for alternative opportunities."

Vafum sighed. "If you say so. Good luck, lass. You're going to need it."

And so, NSLICE-00P made her way out of Khalbuldor and set off in the direction of the border. She took to the skies with an Invisibility spell wrapped around her, activating her long-range sensors to the limit . . .

The self-proclaimed Emperor Caelinus heaved a sigh and held his head as he read the report.

"Really, Vibius? Did you *have* to pick a fight with the mage who single-handedly saved Turannia?"

He sighed again and shook his head. Well, he could complain about the situation all he liked, but at the end of the day, he trusted Vibius to make the right call, if not the pleasant one. This NSLICE-00P had already worked on behalf of the Empire once, and against the Dobhar, too, when the Empire couldn't contribute anything more than some limitanei. If Vibius couldn't recruit her, he would try to eliminate her, lest the Empire manage to hire her once again. Caelinus didn't particularly like that call, but he also didn't disagree with it. The last thing they needed was an archmage-level caster hitting them from behind when they marched to confront the Northern Court.

The problem was that Vibius had failed. NSLICE-00P remained at large and had turned hostile toward them, right as Caelinus launched his plan. Now she had to be dealt with all due haste, or she could wreak havoc on his lands. Or worse: join up with the Empire and return at the head of a Legion.

Vibius's failure would now cost the lives of Caelinus's troops.

Caelinus put down the report and turned to one of his aides.

"Contact Legates Emeritus and Lucana and tell them to prepare their Legions for battle. Anti-Archon formation. And deliver this dossier to Legate Emeritus; he'll be much more motivated when he finds out she beat Spellbreaker."

The aide saluted and ran off to obey his orders. Caelinus sighed once more and then started his own preparations. Whatever happened, he would see this through.

NSLICE-00P made good time, but Magister Vibius had contingencies for expeditious retreat and a several-hour head start. She detected a large mass of people in the distance before she finally caught up with the magister. Soon, visual scans confirmed what she was looking at.

It was an army.

NSLICE-00P's robotic eye flickered. While circumstantial evidence might imply this was the aforementioned rebel force, she wasn't certain on that. And even if they were, assaulting an army directly wasn't the most efficient method of terminating her target. She would need to analyze the situation first.

She moved closer to get a better look . . .

A massive mana signature lit up in the force ahead and shot into the sky. The sky darkened, and clouds began swirling around. NSLICE-00P increased power to her repulsors as powerful winds began to whip around her.

Soon, there was a full-on hurricane in the skies.

The winds continued to pick up speed to the point that NSLICE-00P was having trouble maintaining her position. The clouds darkened, and soon, lightning began to light up the sky. A bolt shot toward NSLICE-00P, who barely managed to put up a barrier in time. The bolt shattered the barrier and struck her with reduced force, sending her spinning through the air toward the ground. NSLICE-00P righted herself and then dove down.

"Observation: Hostile weather conditions preventing flight. Reducing altitude."

She dove under the storm and found the Legion waiting for her. A volley of enchanted ballistae bolts was already flying through the air toward her location. Her sensors managed to detect them ahead of time, however, so she evaded the assault.

"Hostility confirmed. Activating mass-termination protocols."

# 15

# The World-Conquering Legion vs the Ultimate Weapon

*"Another victory like that, and I'll be ruined. And you say they built another army? Where on Aelea are they getting that many people?! This entire affair is proving incredibly . . . annoying."*

—Drycnid Chondreid, High Archon of the Empire of the Sun, on the progress of his campaign against the City-State of Elteno.

NSLICE-00P analyzed the situation. The storm above was keeping her within range of the Legion's long-range weapons.

"Equalizer engaged."

She fired the rainbow beam up at the storm, and a small patch of the clouds lightened slightly, but that was it. The Equalizer's weakness was that its destructive interference depended on its power output matching the target's. The storm contained a truly massive quantity of mana that the Equalizer currently couldn't match, and it was constantly receiving more so that the Equalizer couldn't delete it over time. Likewise, the sheer amount of mana whipping about prevented her from destabilizing the spell in progress, since she couldn't find a sufficiently weak point to target.

If she wanted to break the spell, she needed to target the magic circle producing it.

She did not see a circle in the sky, so she followed the trail of mana to the ground. In the distance, at the center of the legions, she could see a large glowing formation with an unidentified device at the center and numerous Legion personnel spaced about along the sides. She was still some distance from the Legion, meaning they were out of range of the Equalizer at present.

So NSLICE-00P adapted.

The sky under the storm clouds lit up as NSLICE-00P cast a spell of her own. The Aurora Barrage and Rain of Fire spells fused once again, preparing to rain explosive beams on the Legion below.

Just then, hundreds of small magic circles lit up among the Legion formation, individual soldiers casting their own spells. One person in their midst thrust a staff into the ground, and then a large formation appeared, linking all the individual circles.

A massive barrier appeared, covering the entire Legion force, just as NSLICE-00P opened fire. Red beams shot from the sky, and fiery explosions appeared on the barrier.

But the barrier held.

NSLICE-00P fused her beams together, firing a massive attack that dimmed the world in comparison. Explosions and flames covered the sky as the beam collided with the barrier.

NSLICE-00P's mana reserves were about thirty times greater than the average level one person's, and her Mana Density about twenty times. While the workings of mana were more complicated than simple multiplication, it was reasonably accurate to describe a spell cast with all of her mana as about six hundred times more powerful than what the baseline human was capable of. Perhaps more so, given the efficiency with which she could cast and Supercharge her spells.

But the Legion had centuries of experience fighting against individually powerful opponents, not least of all thanks to their centuries of war with the Empire of the Sun and its powerful Archon mages. The Legion below, in particular, specialized in combating such mages. More than six hundred soldiers had combined their magic circles together to form this barrier, and none of them were level one.

So, when the fire cleared, the barrier still held, save small openings that appeared to allow the Legion's counterattacks through.

NSLICE-00P's robotic eye flickered. She dropped the fused magic circle and formed a basic Aurora Barrage spell. This time, she layered each individual magic circle of a different element, intending to test them all at once.

*The skill Spell Fusion is now Level 10!*
*The strategic spell Aurora Barrage has been upgraded to Prismatic Bombardment!*

Thanks to her modular spellcasting, she was able to adjust the Aurora Barrage spell itself, as it contained many individual Light Beam spells. She could now slot in different elements into each individual circle as she pleased. The overall power of the spell remained the same, but its flexibility increased dramatically.

Beams of all different colors rained against the barrier, NSLICE-00P's robotic eye flickering as she analyzed the effects of each one . . .

At the center of the legions, Caelinus rubbed his chin as he watched the battle unfold. Next to him was Magister Vibius, along with Legates Emeritus and Lucana. Legate Emeritus was a pale, thin human man, more of a researcher than a fighter in Caelinus's opinion. He was in charge of the Legio Arcanum IX, which was currently casting the Storm spell. Legate Lucana was a Diminidium Pendem woman with slightly graying hair. She was in charge of the Legio Ianus, specialized in shutting down enemy mages. Legate Lucana frowned and crossed her arms as she observed a beam of golden-and-silver light collide with the barrier.

"That's Holy mana."

Everyone turned to stare at her. She turned to glare at Magister Vibius.

"You didn't tell us we were fighting a bloody *hero*."

Magister Vibius put his hands up. "In my defense, I didn't know either."

Legate Lucana narrowed her eyes. "Isn't it your job to find out?"

He nodded. "Fair, but the only records of this person are from Turannia. I pulled all my contacts out when we took their comitatenses and assumed the province wouldn't last the year. And no one there has answered any of my messages ever since we left them to die against the Dobhar. If I'd had more time, maybe I could have figured it out, but we were on the clock, and I had to make a choice. Tell me you wouldn't have done the same, Legate."

Caelinus shook his head. "Enough, what's done is done. How are we looking?"

Legate Lucana stood at attention and saluted. "The barrier is holding, sir. She's powerful, but the anti-Archon formation has held against worst in the past. She won't overpower us anytime soon . . . assuming she doesn't have some special hero skill, that is."

Caelinus nodded. "Emeritus?"

The legate scoffed. "I have meticulously crafted this spell to be incredibly robust and safely cast at a distance. The spell itself will even draw in ambient mana to repair any damage. So long as Legate Lucana's barrier holds, no one can disrupt this spell. Not even that so-called Spellbreaker would stand a chance."

Caelinus rubbed his chin. "This is all well and good, but we still haven't landed a single blow on her. Remain cautious; if spells were all she had, she would not have defeated Uscfrea Spellbreaker or escaped from Vibius."

Legate Lucana saluted once again. Legate Emeritus scowled but followed suit. Meanwhile, Caelinus kept his eyes fixed on their target. "A hero, huh?"

Magister Vibius had the decency to look sheepish. "I . . . am sorry. I didn't realize."

Caelinus took a deep breath and shook his head. “It doesn’t matter anymore. The die is cast. We cannot stop now. If she cannot beat us, then she will not stop them. So, we will give it our best effort.”

NSLICE-00P dropped the strategic spell. None of her elements were performing any better than any other in this case, so she would not overcome this defense via the Prismatic Bombardment spell. She’d opened fire with an assault rifle too, but the barrier blocked physical attacks as well as magic.

She tried the Equalizer, but the barrier was multilayered, and the mana was highly dense. The Equalizer bored a hole in the first layer but slowed with each subsequent one. It would take her time to make an opening large enough for practical use. The problem was she would have to limit her movement to keep the Equalizer on target during that time, and the Legion was still firing ballistae bolts at her. Her analysis of the bolts’ velocity and mana signatures was concerning; she was not confident she could block a full volley without taking damage. She couldn’t afford to remain stationary.

Next, she tried Farcasting, attempting to form a magic circle underneath the barrier, but the barrier itself interfered with her mana, and she lost control of it. She wouldn’t bypass it that way.

In the meantime, more magic circles lit up in the Legion, each with several individuals around them, and they began firing back with more than bolts. Giant balls of fire, twisting cyclones, beams of light. All manner of spells began to launch in the air toward her, holes quickly opening and closing in the barrier to let them pass. NSLICE-00P took evasive action, but combined with the ballistae fire, the attacks saturated the sky, and she was forced to enact defensive measures.

She formed Barriers of different elements. A Nature Barrier of wood and leaves absorbed the beams of Light. Barriers of Water exploded into steam on contact with balls of Fire. The Equalizer got some use as well. These spells were noticeably lower in density and power compared to the storm above, so NSLICE-00P was able to identify and target weak points more effectively. A cyclone filled with blades of Wind sputtered and faded as a rainbow beam swept over it.

So far, NSLICE-00P couldn’t overpower the Legion’s barrier, but at this range, she could evade or counteract the Legion’s own offensive.

The situation reached a stalemate.

However, NSLICE-00P wouldn’t make any progress as she was. The Legion’s attacks were numerous and fast. For her to successfully evade them required her to watch and analyze the Legion on the ground, to predict the spells and ballistae fire before they got into the air. And then, she had to identify the spells’ attributes and determine the most efficient way to defend against them. These tasks demanded the full attention of her AI.

And so . . . *reluctantly* . . . NSLICE-00P split her cybernetic and organic halves into separate threads once again. The cybernetic half focused on the defense, tasking the organic with brainstorming offensive measures to bypass the Legion barrier.

NSLICE-00P's organic eye blinked as her heart began to pound. The emotional controls had been released to reclaim processing power for the defense, and the mana for the Calm spell was reallocated to barriers. Her heart rate increased further, and her body temperature began to rise. Her vision zoomed in. She identified Magister Vibius in the distance.

Her organic eye narrowed. At that moment, both her halves agreed on one thing.

They were going to terminate the target, without fail.

Her organic half got to work, examining the different tools she had at her disposal . . .

# 16

# Explosive Innovation

*"When in doubt, cast Fireball. And if that doesn't work . . . cast a bigger one."*

—Celestial Elf Sage Baoruinë, when asked about the meaning of life.

NSLICE-00P's organic half flipped through the menus, glancing at the battle in progress on occasion. She proposed trying to target the holes in the barrier that allowed the Legion attacks through, and her cybernetic half attempted to launch a counterattack.

But the Legion had prepared for that as well. Anytime a hole was opened in the shield, they formed a second barrier behind the projectile in question, and NSLICE-00P's counterattack collided with the secondary barrier, making it no further.

NSLICE-00P's organic half proposed wearing them down. Surely a barrier of this power required vast quantities of mana, while NSLICE-00P's own reserves were holding steady. But the cybernetic half calculated that solution as risky. The sheer number of Legion soldiers below meant not all of them were required to maintain the barrier, and they could rotate shifts in and out. It might take an excessively long time for them to be drained, during which the situation could change. The Legion was likewise trialing different offensive measures; there was a chance they could find a way past her defenses if she gave them enough time. Attrition was the last resort if no other effective measures could be determined.

NSLICE-00P's organic eye narrowed as she reviewed the footage of the Equalizer once more. The weapon had been effective, but it couldn't output enough power to bring down the shield in time. She could try to upgrade her energy channels to allow for more power, but there was a limit to what the Equalizer's main components could produce at present, and upgrades for said components were not available via the foreign system. If only they were, a more powerful Equalizer could solve this situation.

Then, NSLICE-00P's organic eye blinked. An idea popped into her head as she watched the Equalizer beam collide with the shield. She proposed it to her cybernetic half, which approved of the idea as potentially viable. She consolidated her two halves and created two new threads, each now containing a balance of cybernetic and organic processing power. Her cybernetic half's capabilities were required for the proposed solution, so the organic half would have to pick up some of the slack on the defense. Her defense efficiency would drop, but the expected damage fell within range of her HP and mana regeneration, so it wouldn't be a problem.

She then took out an ingot of mana iron and created ingots of several other more mundane metals before beginning to mold and shape them together, forming a sphere of the more resilient mana iron with an interior of mundane materials.

*The skill Metal Magic is now Level 10!*

She utilized her own energy channels as a base template but arranged them in a different pattern from before. Patterns she had learned not from any blueprint or engineering attempt but from the foreign system.

Her organic components had come up with a theory. The Equalizer destructively interfered with Non-Standard energy types in order to cancel them out, which meant the Equalizer was producing energy of a Non-Standard type itself, perhaps even of a similar nature to the energy it was targeting, just with inverted properties.

So, what would happen if she attempted to treat its output like the target energy source itself?

She didn't have a way to control the energy from the Equalizer besides firing it in beams, but that in and of itself presented a solution. The energy traveled from the Equalizer's main components in her torso down the energy channels in her arms whenever she fired it, and it had also traveled up and through Uscfrea's axe when she had removed its binding. So, if she created new energy channels, she could guide the Equalizer's output along specific paths.

She created a sphere filled with these energy channels. And as for the shape? She utilized the Infusion enchantment magic circle as a base, isolated the portions related to the storage of mana, and then inverted them.

Soon, the sphere was complete, and she was ready for the first test. She grabbed it in her hand, where a circular groove matched up with the energy channel output in her palms.

"Equalizer engaged at 0.1 percent power."

She took it very slowly. If the device behaved poorly while she was channeling an anti-mana energy type from the Equalizer, it could compromise her own defenses. She activated only a tiny trickle of energy and analyzed its behavior.

The energy flowed up her arm and out her palm. It then reached the device . . . and successfully entered the energy channels she had created within it, traveling along the pattern . . . and then was stored inside, waiting within the device.

She had succeeded.

She gradually ramped up the power output of the Equalizer, closely monitoring the status of the sphere and the behavior of the energy within. But the energy acted according to her cybernetic half's predictions and her organic half's hopes. Soon, she had the Equalizer firing at full power, and the exterior of the sphere began to glow. The mana iron lost its luster as the anti-mana bled into it before taking on a new shine with a rainbow glow.

"Warning: Anti-mana output storage device now exceeding predicted maximum capacity. Energy levels reaching critical levels according to calculations."

NSLICE-00P shut off the Equalizer. Taking the glowing orb, she tossed it at the Legion's barrier before a panel opened on her shoulder and launched a missile high into the air. The missile arced around in a loop and approached the orb from the front, striking it just as it reached the barrier.

NSLICE-00P's organic components had theorized the problem was the Equalizer's insufficient energy output, and so had come up with a simple solution. Why not store up that output . . .

The missile exploded on the orb, cracking the mana iron shell.

. . . and then release it all at once?

A shockwave of rainbow-colored light radiated in all directions. The air sizzled, and bright sparks appeared all along the shock wave as it reacted with the mana in the air. The Legion's barrier shone like the sun before a massive hole appeared in it.

The spell hadn't broken, so the barrier moved to repair itself almost immediately, mana streaming in from the sides. But NSLICE-00P had been prepared for that outcome and launched herself at the hole at maximum speed.

Legate Lucana's eyes widened, and she thrust her hand out, creating a large magic circle in front of her. A new barrier appeared over the hole.

But this barrier had been created by a single individual. It did not possess the sheer resilience of the original one. NSLICE-00P simply fired the Equalizer at it, and it broke.

Legate Lucana turned to Legate Emeritus and shouted, "TARGET THAT GAP, NOW!"

Legate Emeritus responded immediately, launching a massive bolt of lightning toward the opening while the other mages followed suit as they were able.

But NSLICE-00P had defenses of her own.

As she rushed toward the barrier, firing the Equalizer with one hand, she took out a certain weapon in the other. Channeling as much mana into the Sea Dragon-bone axe as she could, she lobbed it ahead of her.

Charged with mana even denser than its original user's, the axe tore through the lightning and other spells, consuming their mana to increase its power further. Legate Emeritus's eyes widened before his face twisted into a horrendous scowl. Once again, the Legion's spells had been shattered by the Spellbreaker's axe.

And that meant NSLICE-00P made it past the Legion's barrier with acceptable damage, but most importantly, without needing to spend her attention and mana on defensive barriers.

Instead, she used it to form a Prismatic Bombardment spell circle, using pure Light Beam spells as per the original Aurora Barrage version in order to simplify the cast and so increase its speed.

And formed it on the inside of the Legion barrier.

Legate Lucana ran forward. "DEFENSIVE—"

But she never had a chance to finish.

The sky lit up, and the beams fused together. A massive beam struck the legionnaire with the staff at the center of the anti-Archon formation.

*You have slain Human (Level 77)!*
*Gained 26 Personal XP, 3 Dungeon XP!*

The large magic circle shattered. The Legion's barrier began to fade.

A second person ran to take the place of the first and form a new barrier, but NSLICE-00P didn't miss her opportunity. The Prismatic Bombardment spell glowed red as she introduced Fire into it once more, and then indiscriminately rained explosive beams on the Legion gathered below. Panels opened on every inch of her body and fired missiles as quickly as the dungeon mana could reload them. Her autopistols added to the barrage as she turned her left hand into an assault rifle to open fire while her right channeled the Equalizer. Explosions filled the field. The Sea Dragon-bone axe connected to NSLICE-00P via a mana chain and tore through the field.

*Hostiles slain: 105*

The Legion responded with speed and discipline. Mages formed smaller barriers up in the sky while Legion bulwarks stood over more fragile comrades with their mighty shields. Archers and crossbowmen returned fire, and the melee fighters scrambled to take cover and ease the burden on their guardians. But they could not prevent casualties entirely, and NSLICE-00P used the Equalizer and the Sea Dragon-bone axe to break any larger magic circles that might shut down her assault. She also destroyed the siege weapon batteries as one of her first targets, and so the Legion struggled to retaliate.

*Hostiles slain: 316*

Massive bolts of lightning struck from above as the Legio Arcanum IX tried to turn the Storm spell against NSLICE-00P. She was forced to take evasive action and defend herself with barriers, but the Sea Dragon-bone axe whirled around and flew toward the formation. Some mages tried to form a barrier, but the axe tore straight through it and smashed into the device at the center of Legate Emeritus's ritual formation. The mana core in the device cracked and exploded, sending out a shock wave that knocked down the participating mages. The flow of mana ceased, and the storm began to calm overhead.

*Hostiles slain: 598*

Soon, even the Legion's discipline began to crack. The soldiers still acted as per their training, but they were now acting in small groups rather than as a complete whole. An entire Legion could match NSLICE-00P's mana reserves and density. A handful of legionnaires could not.

Individuals and small groups were being wiped out, one by one, as Legate Lucana tried desperately to rally her forces, and Legate Emeritus screamed profanities at the axe and flung out every spell he could.

Caelinus's eyes narrowed.

*Hostiles slain: 834*

The anti-Archon formation had broken.

# 17

# Terminate the Rebel Scum!

*"Rebellion is to result in immediate termination."*

—Common instruction between NSLICE protocols and Legion manual.

Caelinus frowned and rubbed his chin at the scene before him. Momentum had swung against them, which was a serious problem for the Legion. The Legion's strength was in its ability to weave together specialists to become greater than the sum of their parts, but that meant in any given tactical setting, the Legion would quickly crumble if they lost control of the battle's pace. Once their formation was broken, it became extremely difficult to rebuild it.

That was why the Empire normally brought more than one legion to the fight. Their response to a situation like this would be to have another legion arrive in formation so the broken legions could fall back and regroup.

And Caelinus did have more than one legion at his disposal. He had his whole army on standby, and many more legions he could throw into the fray. But in this case, there was a serious problem.

He only had one Legio Arcanum and one Legio Ianus each. Mages were a precious commodity. Their skills were needed in transportation, communication, agriculture, land reclamation, manufacturing, and more. They were needed in practically every area of life in the Empire, and so, most of the magically gifted did not choose to risk their lives in the army. So while most individuals could learn a bit of magic with effort, fully-fledged battlemages were rare, and dedicated magical legions rarer still, especially up north. The truth was, the Northern Court just didn't need that many. The Eastern Court had to guard against the powerful Empire of the Sun, and the Southern Realms needed mages to crew their navies, but the Northern Court was mostly faced with barbarian tribes of lower sophistication. Its foes could be handled by physical weapons and sufficient fortifications at a fraction of the cost of a single Legio Arcanum.

All of which meant heavy casualties among Caelinus's only two would be a severe problem in the coming days.

Not to mention that attrition was not a viable tactic for him in this battle. Sure, he could throw legion after legion at the hero and try to wear her down over time; the Empire *had* done that in the past against overwhelming opponents. But he was not the Empire. Not anymore. He was launching a rebellion largely based on his popularity with the troops and their frustrations with the Northern Court's leadership. So, what would happen if he started his reign by sacrificing thousands of lives for an uncertain outcome against a *single* opponent? It would be a Drycnic victory, at *best.* His troops would mutiny before the Northern Court could even respond.

And . . . another thought came to his mind as he watched the Legion's troops suffer under the hero's barrage.

*"But this I swear to you: while I am in command, not one more drop of Legion blood will be shed in vain!"*

He made his choice. He turned to one of his troops. "Sound the retreat. You there, inform Legates Lucana and Emeritus to preserve their legions as best they can."

He then turned to one of his messenger mages. "Send word to Captain Iovinus of the Caelum Eques. He should deploy and prepare mounts for myself and Magister Vibius."

Magister Vibius jumped and turned to face him. Caelinus just nodded at him.

"We will end this fight, one way or another, by our own hands."

He then rubbed his chin and turned back to the first messenger. "Send word to Dux Augustalis as well. Tell her we must succeed, at any cost."

The messenger's eyes widened, but he nodded and moved to relay the message.

NSLICE-00P surveyed the battlefield's state. The Legion forces were scattered and scrambling for cover, their siege weapons were destroyed, their ritual formations were broken, and their counterattacks had grown feeble and sporadic. The Legion was no longer acting as an organized force, and parts of it were already retreating. NSLICE-00P calculated they did not present a threat to her defenses at the moment, and so moved to terminate her target.

But as she approached the command area, her sensors picked up heavy mana signatures on approach. She turned her attention to the skies.

A formation of large flying creatures was approaching from above, with armored soldiers on their backs. They rode upon white horses with large bird wings and carried shining lances that reflected off the sun. Two more such horses landed near her target, picking him up and another man before flying up to join the formation. The second man drew a large sword and pointed it toward her, shouting with a mana-amplified voice.

"I am Mettius Burrienus Caelinus, former Magister Militum per Utrad, defender of the Empire, commander of the legions below, and the new Emperor of the North! I will not permit you to slaughter my troops any longer! Let's settle this fight, here and now!"

"Hostile commander identified. Target prioritized. Proceeding to terminate."

NSLICE-00P immediately opened fire with a volley of missiles. The Prismatic Bombardment magic circle vanished, and a new one appeared facing the formation. The flying knights immediately took evasive action while several in the rear lifted staves. Magic barriers appeared and blocked the missiles while the knights scattered in all directions. A volley of bolts from Magister Vibius and crossbow-armed knights retaliated, and NSLICE-00P rediverted some of her attention and mana to defensive barriers.

*Hostiles slain: 6*

Still, not all her attacks were blocked. A pegasus cried and fell from the sky as missiles exploded around it. One of the bow wielders was caught by a beam as her Prismatic Bombardment opened fire. The Equalizer broke one of the staff wielders' barriers, exposing the knight to fire.

And then, NSLICE-00P detected targets on approach.

Lance-armed knights dove from above and below at the same time, forcing her to boost backward. Just as she was about to counterattack, two more approached from her sides. The wind surged around the wings of their mounts, propelling the knights forward at surprising speeds. She was forced to defend herself with a barrier as one of the lances nearly grazed her.

The lancers cycled in and out, keeping a constant stream of attacks on her, with the marksmen and mages providing covering fire. Their speed was impressive, and with so many targets attacking at those speeds, even NSLICE-00P's reaction time was struggling to keep up. Any normal individual would find themselves overwhelmed.

But NSLICE-00P was no normal individual.

"Adapting strategy."

*The skill Heroic Power is now Level 3!*

She activated the Heroic Power skill, boosting the density of her mana even further, and then surrounded herself with a barrier and activated the Mana Shield skill. Her defense increased dramatically.

Ignoring the lancers on approach, she analyzed their formation then locked onto her target: the staff wielders in the back.

*The skill Farcasting has leveled three times and is now Level 10!*
*The spell Prismatic Bombardment is now Level 8!*

A strategic magic circle appeared *behind* the rearguard, who barely had time to turn around before the circle lit up. Fused beams fired forward, one by one.

*Hostiles slain: 10*

And one by one, the casters fell from the sky. There would be no more barriers protecting the knights.

The knights realized the situation, and the lancers redoubled their efforts. They stopped trying to pass her, striking head-on instead and focusing all their power on the strikes, even at the risk of opening themselves up to counterattacks. The powerful lances even managed to pierce through her barrier, though they were deflected by the Heroic Power-boosted Mana Shield.

But NSLICE-00P responded accordingly. If they resolved to take damage, she would oblige.

As the first knight struck her barrier, she formed a Supercharged Light Blade and stabbed the pegasus in the head, and then the knight through a gap in his armor. As the next knight approached, she reformed the Light Blade into a Light Spike resembling a lance and turned the knight's momentum against him, impaling both him and his mount. She then grabbed and flung his pegasus toward the third knight, stopping his approach. And the moment he slowed down, the Prismatic Bombardment spell opened fire, a fused beam putting an end to him.

With their casualties mounting, the knights could no longer keep up a constant stream of attacks. NSLICE-00P could monitor their approach and dodge them at leisure. She was now free to target each one individually, and one by one, the knights continued to fall.

Caelinus gripped his sword and looked over to Magister Vibius. Vibius's eyes were trembling, but he nodded. They gripped their sword and crossbow and charged straight toward NSLICE-00P.

"FOR THE EMPIRE!" Caelinus shouted as he pulled his blade back, willing the pegasus to fly as quickly as it could. NSLICE-00P had just finished up with one of the last few lancers and turned to face his charge. Once her eyes locked on him and Vibius, they flashed with a red light.

The Prismatic Bombardment spell circle lit up like the sun.

The new Emperor charged into the light, and then was no more.

*Hostiles slain: 3*

NSLICE-00P prepared to wipe out the last remaining pegasus knights, but one of them flew in front of her with his hands in the air and his crossbow put away.

"Hold, mighty warrior! As per the last command of Emperor Caelinus, I relay to you this message: You have slain the claimant; the rebellion is over. The army will now disband and will not move against you. The late Emperor hopes that you will stay your wrath and let his death be enough."

NSLICE-00P surveyed the battlefield once again. The legions below were in full-scale retreat. In the distance, she could see many more Legion formations, but these were not making any move toward the battlefield. Rather, several of them were already marching away, or even breaking apart. The rebel faction was not seeking to pursue the battle any further.

The death of a rebel leader would not necessarily end the rebellion by her calculations, so she would need to confirm the rebel faction would not continue as an organized and hostile force, but the mass-termination protocols could be put on hold while she investigated the situation.

"Mission Status: Rebel leader and designated target terminated. Please gather remaining rebel leaders to negotiate an end to hostilities."

# 18

# The Aspiring Emperor's Final Order

*"Those Sun Elf jerks don't die of simple age. Planning past our own deaths is par for course if we want to keep up."*

—Imperial Strategist Potitus Opsius Ianuarius

After the pegasus rider left, NSLICE-00P deployed several drones to keep an eye on the rebel faction, and then returned to the safehouse. She noted in her dealings with Magister Vibius that direct falsehood detection was insufficient; the magister had been able to withhold key intel and describe a situation that did not accurately match reality. She did not have a solution for this in the short-term, as she was not programmed for interpersonal communication or diplomatic negotiations, so she decided to retrieve her friendlies for the discussion. Friendly Estrith, in particular, had somehow identified Magister Vibius's deceit without hard evidence, and could help determine if any particular terms or conditions might impact the Dobhar.

As NSLICE-00P traveled back, she brought up the notifications from the battle.

*You have slain 1050 hostiles total!*
*Gained 3876 Personal XP, 1654 Dungeon XP!*
*Level up! You are now at Personal Level 105 and Dungeon Level 145!*
*The skill Spell Fusion is now Level 11!*
*The skill Metal Magic is now Level 11!*
*The skill Mana Crafting has leveled up twice and is now Level 3!*
*The spell shape Chain is now Level 8!*
*You have learned the skill Anti-Mana Infusion!*
*The skills Anti-Mana Beam and Anti-Mana Infusion have been combined into*

*Anti-Mana Channeling!*
*The skill Anti-Mana Channeling is now Level 4!*

It seemed that terminating organized military forces was highly efficient in terms of foreign system upgrades. But perhaps more important than any foreign system upgrade was the success of her improvised Equalizer-powered bomb, which the foreign system itself had now acknowledged. It was proof of concept that the Equalizer could do more than directly clash with Non-Standard energy—she could hypothetically treat its output as an energy type of its own, utilizing the foreign system's methods of manipulating mana as a base. That possibility had significant implications for her combat capabilities . . . and more. It could potentially offer data on how the foreign system manipulated mana to begin with, and so offer insights on mana, the system, and the location she found herself in.

It was something worth investigating, in any case.

Soon, NSLICE-00P arrived back at the safehouse. Ateia ran up to her, checking her over for damage.

"Seero! What happened? Did you find Magister Vibius?"

"Response: This unit located and terminated the target, along with rebel authority Caelinus."

At that, Vafum immediately rushed over, pushing the teens out of the way.

"Wait, lass, say that again. Did you just say you killed Magister Caelinus?!"

"Affirmative Clarification: Hostile designated Caelinus referred to himself as Emperor at the time of termination."

Vafum's jaw dropped.

"Request: This unit requires assistance from friendlies for ceasefire negotiations with surviving rebel faction. Please prepare for transit."

It took Vafum some time to accept those statements.

Dux Augustalis gritted her teeth as she received the message from Caelinus. It was the code meant to activate the last contingency plan. Emperor Caelinus's cause was much larger than his ambitions. He had shared with her the dark secret of the Empire: the existence of a subversive cult looking to tear down the Empire . . . or possibly even the world itself. As such, he had come up with plans for every possible scenario he could think of.

Including his own death.

Dux Augustalis looked into the distance, where she could see flashes of light in the sky dying down. She gripped her fists so hard her nails cut into her palm.

A man walked up behind her with a frown on his face. He wore light armor over silk robes; a bit underdressed for the battlefield, but appropriate for his role, for this was Vopiscus Caesulenus Trailus, a notorious playboy and hedonist without an ounce of ambition, but who had a natural mind for strategy and countless connections in high society. He was . . . or had been Caelinus's strategist and political advisor.

Augustalis hated him with all her heart, but for some reason, he had Emperor Caelinus's respect, and that was no small feat.

"Dux . . . we must go. If the Emperor . . . Well, if we don't have a unifying figure, this rebellion is dead in the water. We must move quickly if we are to have any chance of *survival*, much less success."

Augustalis turned and glared at him. "The battle yet rages and you would have us flee?! Does your cowardice know no shame?!"

Vopiscus frowned and crossed his arms. "It does not, and that is why you should listen to me now. You know I would have left you here and traveled halfway to Corvanus by now if I thought I had a choice. But you know as well as I what is at stake here, what our Emperor was trying to achieve. Nothing, not my cowardice nor your grief, can get in the way."

Dux Augustalis closed her eyes for a moment, taking a deep breath. She then turned around, a resolute look on her face, and walked toward her command post without another word.

As she stepped past, Vopiscus rested a hand on his chin and tilted his head. "By the way, I happen to know a place we can go."

The dux froze. "No."

Vopiscus shrugged. "Close, sparsely populated, and recognized as independent by the Empire. It's perfect for this plan."

The dux refused to turn around. "*Absolutely not.* She just killed my Emperor. She just destroyed everything we've worked to achieve!"

Vopiscus frowned. "Pollia."

She went silent. She slowly turned around, glaring at Vopiscus. He took a deep breath.

"Please, listen to me. I . . . Look, I considered Caelinus a friend, and I, too, am pained to see him fall. But that's why we cannot let his efforts go to waste. Emperor Caelinus's final order was to succeed at all costs. And I'll be honest. Gathering up our people and striking out into the wild to form our own nation? Escaping the retribution of the Northern Court and forming an independent faction that can still resist the cult? Without the Emperor, we have almost no chance of success. Save one."

The dux looked to the ground and said nothing. Vopiscus continued.

"She's an Amicitia Populi Elteni with her own land, acknowledged by the Empire but not appointed by the Northern Court. She has already brought the Dobhar under heel. And, from Vibius's report, we know she's likely opposed to the cult. If we take our people there, we escape Imperial retribution while maintaining our strength. We can keep the army ready for the real fight, not waste it battling the other Legions or trying to conquer some barbarian tribe."

Dux Augustalis clenched her fists as tight as she could before slumping her shoulders.

". . . We finish the job. Whatever it takes."

Vopiscus nodded slowly. "No, we fulfill Mettius Burrienus Caelinus's mission. And we bring ruin upon his true enemies, the ones who forced this situation to begin with."

Dux Augustalis's eyes widened slightly. She made eye contact with Vopiscus, then nodded at him, turning back again to walk toward her command post, now with a spark in her eyes.

Soon after, a pegasus knight arrived and relayed the events of the battle to the dux, as well as NSLICE-00P's demand that she present herself for negotiations . . .

Vafum Broadbane stared at Dux Augustalis.

"Are you serious?"

She simply crossed her arms and met his gaze. "Do you believe me to be joking, diver?"

Vopiscus stepped between them. "What she means to say, good citizen of Khalbuldor, is that our rebellion cannot continue, particularly not against someone as mighty as NSLICE-00P. However, the cult that has infiltrated the Northern Court must be stopped. Now that we can no longer succeed on our own, it only makes sense to offer our support to the most powerful adversary of the cult we can find."

Vafum scoffed and crossed his arms. "More like you want to avoid execution and let the blowback fall on the shiny lass."

Vopiscus gave him a sleazy smile. "Not being executed would be a very nice side benefit, yes."

NSLICE-00P's robotic eye flickered. Her past protocols had indicated rebel forces were to be captured whenever the opportunity presented itself, but that was in regard to rebellions against her own organization. She didn't have any precedent for rebels against a third-party nation who were also hostile to herself.

"Query: Please specify the consequences of accepting rebel faction surrender offer, especially in regard to this unit's relations with the Empire."

Vafum frowned while Vopiscus just smiled. It was wise of the girl to bring advisors if she wasn't confident in negotiations. It was less wise of her to simply ask him her questions outright and in front of the other party. But it wasn't like he could change that now.

He sighed and turned to NSLICE-00P.

"That would depend on who they're bringing with them. Obviously, the Empire will have a problem with you if you make off with Utrad's entire army. But if it's just them and a handful of legions, considering that you personally took down Caelinus and stopped the rebellion outright . . . they'll raise a fuss but will *probably* let it go."

He then turned to glance at the dux and Vopiscus. "Now, whether you want to trust a bunch of folks who broke their vows and tried to kill you is another question entirely."

Dux Augustalis narrowed her eyes. "Hold your tongue, Dwarf. I have always given my utmost for the defense of the Empire and its people, even people like *you*. That has not changed, and I will not permit slander from a greedy diver such as yourself."

Vafum just shrugged. "Tell that to Magister Vibius. Was he upholding your honor when he kidnapped the lass's friends and tried to stab her in the face?"

Vopiscus stepped in between them once more. "Peace, friends. Now, I understand we have been at odds lately, and may have taken some less than savory measures against one another. But please understand, we are sincere in this offer. We will take every effort to assure you of our good faith, and if all else fails, NSLICE-00P will have the ability to turn us over to the Empire at the first sign of betrayal."

"Addendum: This unit also possesses a Contract skill and will use it to enforce any agreements made at this time."

Vopiscus blinked once before nodding. "Yes, of course. See, there is no reason for doubt!"

Vafum grumbled but said no more. Dux Augustalis glared at him but likewise fell silent. NSLICE-00P turned to Estrith.

"Query: Does friendly Estrith have any concerns?"

Estrith frowned. "Queen of the Dobhar, what are your intentions regarding your land? I thought you had tasked the Dobhar as the stewards of your holdings. Will these . . . Imperials supplant us? Do you intend to drive us out?"

"Response: Additional subordinates will be integrated into the existing chain of command."

Estrith's frown deepened. "So, you will place them over us? Over my—the steward?"

"Negative Response: NSLICE Uscfrea will remain as this unit's primary liaison. Additional subordinates residing at the home base will report to him."

Estrith suddenly smiled. "In that case, I approve. Let us place these Imperial dogs under our heels, queen of the Dobhar!"

"Acknowledged."

Vopiscus's smile twitched slightly. "Let us, um, discuss some conditions to our surrender."

Vafum grinned at that. "Oh, the treasonous rebels begging for asylum have some complaints to make, do they?" Vafum chuckled as Dux Augustalis's face turned dark and Vopiscus struggled to maintain his smile.

And so, the negotiations carried on . . .

INTERLUDE

# Mission Report: Utrad

Shocking news swept the North like a storm. Magister Caelinus, stalwart defender of the North, had declared himself Emperor, gathering all the legions of Utrad and Turannia into a unified rebel force.

And then, even more shocking, was the news that the rebellion had ended mere days after it had been declared. The rebel army had not even reached Velusitum when a visiting Amicitia Populi Elteni killed the would-be Emperor and devastated his vanguard, the rebel army quickly collapsing in the aftermath. Some of the legions returned to their posts on the border, hoping the Northern Court might forgive their involvement out of necessity.

Others disbanded entirely, former legates and centurions gathering their most loyal troops and setting off on their own, while the rank and file scattered to remote farms and crowded slums. Another group gathered as many soldiers and notable citizens as they could and set off to the north, likely making for the North Sea ports.

But whatever the fate of the officers and troops, the rebel faction had abandoned their mission. Utrad surrendered before the Northern Court could even organize a response.

All thanks to one wandering friend of the Empire . . .

A man dressed in the garb of an Exploratore once again made his way into the Corvanus Exploratores HQ. The Magister Exploratore sighed as the man entered his office.

"Let me guess, you're going to ask me what in the world is going on in Utrad?"

The man shrugged at the Magister Exploratore's question. "What *is* going on in Utrad?"

The Magister Exploratore scowled at him. "I'll tell you what I told the last five people to ask me that. Shove off, I don't know crap."

The man raised an eyebrow, and the Magister Exploratore glared at him.

"Oh, don't give me that look. Here, I'll let you in on a little secret. The Exploratores don't actually get paid by the Exploratores HQ. And so, the moment someone actually *does* start paying them—such as a magister with treasonous ambitions, for example—they stop reporting to me for some odd reason. As what happened in the past *three* rebellion attempts."

The man heaved a sigh as the Magister Exploratore muttered curses.

"We're working on it. But I was under the impression you spent the budget on spies?"

The Magister Exploratore shrugged. "Spies are expensive, you know. If I could afford enough spies to replace the Exploratores, then I could afford to pay the Exploratores."

The man sighed again. "But you do know *something*?"

The Magister Exploratore heaved a sigh of his own as he picked up a report. "Only that the rumors seem to be true. Magister Caelinus—our best commander, by the way—went and declared himself Emperor. Then he got into a fight with the Amicitia Populi Elteni from Turannia—or maybe it was Vibius who picked the fight . . . Scratch that, it was *definitely* Vibius, don't need a spy to tell you that. And then said Amicitia Populi Elteni assaulted Caelinus's army directly and not only survived but managed to kill the man himself."

The man raised an eyebrow. "You believe that story is credible?"

The Magister Exploratore narrowed his eyes. "Increasingly so. One of my people has been talking to what's *left* of the Legio Ianus XII. From the stories they tell, we should be *very* grateful she's the Empire's friend. They claim she broke an anti-Archon formation head-on, all by herself."

The man rubbed his chin. "So Rector Aemilia *wasn't* exaggerating her feats or capabilities?"

The Magister Exploratore nodded. "If what the eyewitnesses say is true, that villainess *undersold* her."

"Did you find anything on her, then?"

The Magister Exploratore frowned. "Not a thing. Hadn't received an update on her since she left Turannia, in fact. The Utrad Exploratores didn't even tell me she was in their province for reasons that are painfully obvious in hindsight."

The man rested a finger on his chin. "What about Magister Tiberius?"

The Magister Exploratore smirked. "For some reason, Tiberius's reports have grown increasingly infrequent and unprofessional since we left him to die against the Dobhar. One might even think he was upset."

The man sighed again while the Magister Exploratore shrugged. "But to be honest? If we take Rector Aemilia's word at face value, which eyewitnesses from Utrad indicate is increasingly reasonable, this Amicitia Populi Elteni saved Tiberius's life and his entire province. He will likely obstruct for her unless I demand he do otherwise. And if I do so . . . he is not likely to forgive me. In fact, I'd wager that he'd just desert his post if push came to shove. I consider it fortunate that Turannia is bothering to send us any reports at all."

The man nodded at that. "That's fair; we'd prefer to have *some* eyes north of Velus's Pass at this stage. Have you found anything else on her?"

The Magister Exploratore shook his head. "No. Every investigation has failed to produce a single relevant record on this person. We can't even identify the culture of her name or appearance. By all accounts, it appears she just popped into Turannia out of nowhere. But . . . the absence of information here might be information in and of itself. Regardless, I'll need people watching her directly to learn anything more."

The man sighed again. "Well, you'll likely get the chance. If she single-handedly shut down a rebellion, the court will have to extend her an invitation and thank her in person."

At this, the Magister Exploratore heaved the largest sigh of the day.

"I only hope at least *some* of those idiots pay attention to what happened to Magister Caelinus. I do not want to see what happens if she stops being the Empire's friend."

The Heralds of the New Dawn activated their communication devices once again. Their leader nodded.

"It seems all of us are here who can make it. The past few days have certainly been exciting, have they not?"

That got a round of chuckles. The leader then turned to one of their members.

"We've had a stroke of luck, however. While our network in Utrad has not recovered from the purge, the Herald of Rain followed the target of her investigation into the province, and so happened to be present for recent events. Let's now review the situation, and then discuss how we shall proceed. Herald of Night, I believe you were working with the Herald of Tremors on Utrad. Can you describe the preceding situation for anyone who might not be aware?"

The Herald of Night nodded her head.

"The exposure of a major asset in Utrad to Magister Caelinus was a serious setback, but we managed to turn it into an opportunity. We planted 'evidence' among our network in Utrad that exaggerated the scope of our operations. Over the course of his purge, Magister Caelinus was led to believe we had compromised the entire Empire, or the entire Northern Court at a minimum, and was convinced that rebelling was his only viable recourse. He moved as we predicted and began preparing for his revolt. Although our network in Utrad was severely limited from that point onward, since we knew what to expect, we were still able to keep tabs on his progress."

Another herald crossed his arms. "Wait, you're saying you wanted him to rebel? After he learned of our existence? Wouldn't it have been better to get rid of him?"

The Herald of Night shook her head. "Assassinating him at that point risked bringing more attention to ourselves. On the other hand, a rebellion in Utrad would suit our designs well, as it would draw attention and resources from other parts of the Empire. Still, you are right in that we did not want the magister to overthrow the Northern Court entirely; a real possibility, as he was one of the most experienced commanders in the North.

"As such, once the magister showed signs he was ready to begin his rebellion, the Herald of Tremors moved to corrupt the Mines of Might. Doing so would cut off the magister from his main source of mana iron, reduce his overall popularity, and create a threat behind Velusitum he would have to guard against. We predicted this would hamper his efforts and prevent him from any successful offensives against the Northern Court. The rebellion would develop into a long war of attrition between Utrad and the Imperial North that would occupy most of the Northern Legions."

The leader nodded at her. "Thank you, Herald of Night. Now, with that as a background, Herald of Rain, can you tell us what exactly occurred here?"

The Herald of Rain nodded. "My subject made her way from Turannia to Utrad, arriving in Velusitum shortly before Magister Caelinus declared himself Emperor. While she was there, she entered the Mines of Might, and appears to have stopped the Herald of Tremors."

One of the heralds glared at her. "Why didn't you warn him about the subject?"

The Herald of Rain returned his look. "Because I didn't know he was there. Since Magister Vibius started working hard to purge us from the province, I ceased all communication while in Utrad. I didn't know the Herald of Tremors was involved until this very meeting."

The Herald of Night nodded. "I can confirm that. We kept things compartmentalized after the purge. The Herald of Tremors acted alone for that very reason. The Herald of Rain was not informed of our plans."

The group went silent for a while. Finally, one of the heralds spoke.

"Then, the important question is: was it intentional by the subject?"

The Herald of Rain shook her head. "Unlikely. She first made contact with Vafum Broadbane, who leads a diver company in Khalbuldor specializing in the Mines of Might. The mines had been shut down due to an attack by an adamant bull worm, which I now assume was the Herald of Tremors's doing? In any case, said situation had Vafum worried even before the subject arrived, so I believe he requested her assistance clearing the threat to the dungeon. She had assisted the Empire with several other dungeon-related affairs on her trip to Velusitum; this was likely more of the same."

The leader nodded. "Perhaps, but we shouldn't assume anything at this stage. Please, continue."

The Herald of Rain nodded back. "Shortly thereafter, the Magister Exploratore per Utrad Vibius returned to Velusitum, and seems to have taken interest in the subject. He immediately reached out to the subject's two Exploratore companions, the pair from Turannia, and had them report to him at the Exploratores HQ. They did not return to their inn after that as far as I can tell. The subject then visited the Exploratores HQ twice, and on the second trip, left in force and at speed, carrying her companions with her. Magister Vibius left Velusitum shortly afterward, and then the subject confronted Magister Caelinus and his forces."

The Herald of Night rubbed her chin. "From Magister Vibius's prior behavior, he likely attempted to recruit her against us, and then attempted an assassination when that failed. He never liked variables he couldn't control."

The leader turned to her. "The exact details might never be known to us, but the overall situation is. Herald of Night, what does this mean for our plans?"

The Herald of Night hummed for a second before speaking. "This has to be considered a partial failure. There will be no civil war in the North now, and the Northern Court will not need to send its full might to Utrad. The court's legions won't suffer significant casualties, either. And, of course, we lost the Herald of Tremors, one of our own. On the other hand, it is not a complete failure. Magister Caelinus and his subordinates are gone, Utrad's forces have taken a heavy blow from the fleeing rebels, and those that remain will likely be gutted by the Northern Court's retaliation. The North will likely need to commit at least several legions to maintain control of Utrad and to hunt down the surviving rebels."

Another herald frowned and crossed his arms. "That may be true, but it means the North will still have the means to respond to any crisis that may pop up. We can no longer assume freedom of movement, or ineffectual responses. We already failed in Turannia and lost our contingency plan, and the subject responsible for both these failures is still at large. All this makes our next plans extremely risky, to the point that I am in favor of calling them off."

At this point, the Herald of Rain interjected. "That may be true, but I have discovered some new information that might be crucial."

The leader motioned to her. "Oh? What have you discovered, Herald of Rain?"

"In every town prior to Velusitum, the subject first visited the local Exploratores HQ. They changed behavior in Velusitum, however, and made contact with Vafum Broadbane . . . and Agedia of the Mélusine instead."

There were murmurs throughout the meeting as Agedia's name came up. The Herald of Rain grinned.

"Agedia, in particular, had quite the interesting reaction to the Exploratore girl from Turannia. So, I started monitoring her and Vafum. It was clear that while they did not know the subject's companion personally, they knew *of* her."

All the heralds focused on her.

"Do you mean?"

The Herald of Rain nodded. "I'm certain of it now. She's the one we've been looking for. The reason the Hero of Elteno exiled himself to Turannia for all those years."

The room went silent.

And then, the leader started to grin.

"My brothers and sisters, if we can confirm this is accurate, then I think we have stumbled upon the perfect opportunity. Let's discuss what we must do to take advantage of it."

# 19

# Keep Calm and Comply

*"I love rebellions! Well, yes, the chaos and the death are all a bit concerning, but think about what comes after! Deserters! Looters! Bandits! And since actually fighting them is Legion work, we get paid just to locate them! It's an Exploratore's banquet! A single rebellion will give us months, maybe years of easy scouting and patrol missions! Years of knowing where our next meal comes from! What's not to like?"*

—Exploratore Sempronia Maecena.

Velusitum was a flurry of activity, on the verge of total breakdown. Legion soldiers under Dux Augustalis ran up and down the streets, loading supplies into wagons and knocking on the doors of notable citizens. Civilians loaded up into wagons of their own or else locked themselves in their homes. Alarms were ringing out, and criers tried to explain the situation. Dux Augustalis tried to keep a wrap on things and evacuate calmly, but word had gotten out, and now, the general public was panicking and attempting to flee the city.

But that didn't matter to NSLICE-00P! She walked down the street, focused on her destination, as Ateia and Taog frowned at the chaos all around them. Ateia tilted her head.

"I get the soldiers, maybe the rector and stuff. But why are the normal people running away too?"

Vafum heaved a sigh. "You haven't read up on many rebellions, have you, lass?"

Ateia frowned. "Why do you ask?"

Vafum's eyes narrowed. "The Empire's response to rebellions is always harsh. Anyone even remotely involved will be punished. Anyone who failed to report or resist the rebellion will be punished. The Empire might even just punish the entire city to set an example. The point is, anyone who stays behind risks being punished, regardless of if they were actually involved or not."

Ateia furrowed her brow. "That doesn't seem right. Why would the Empire punish people who weren't involved?"

Agedia sighed. "Because it sends a warning. Don't let your local leader rebel, or you'll be punished too. Makes people think twice about lending their support. When it comes to rebellions, the Empire wants to make it absolutely clear there is no escape for the rebels."

Taog rubbed his chin. "What about you, then?"

Vafum shrugged. "Khalbuldor will get off a bit easier, seeing as we're *technically* an allied city-state rather than direct Imperial territory. The average citizen there will be fine, and an experienced diving company like mine is an important asset. The council will be running for their lives, though."

Vafum chuckled at that thought while Ateia kept frowning. He glanced at her and sighed again.

"Look, lass, I know you feel bad. A lot of innocent people are going to have their lives turned upside down, and a lot of them will be punished by the Empire for crimes they didn't commit. But all that pales in comparison to the suffering and death a civil war can cause. You don't have to like it, but remember just how many lives your friend saved by ending it before it began."

NSLICE-00P, on the other hand, simply continued walking. Some of the Legion soldiers stared at her, but any who attempted to move were restrained by officers or their comrades. Dux Augustalis's orders were clear.

Still, the group wasn't going to tempt fate while the battle was still fresh on everyone's mind. They made a quick stop at the Exploratores HQ, which had been ordered by Dux Augustalis to return Ateia and Taog's belongings, then made their way to Khalbuldor. The group would rest and regroup there until things settled down and Dux Augustalis's forces left the city.

Ateia and Taog weren't feeling up to training in the dungeon at the time, and NSLICE-00P needed to remain in close proximity with the situation in flux, so she prioritized patrolling the immediate area. She did, however, have one thing to do in the meantime. She could now choose a new spell shape.

| Available Spell Shapes | |
|---|---|
| Name | Description |
| Clone | Form mana into a shape similar to the user that will execute simple orders. Increased skill will increase the power and substance of the clones and the complexity of orders they may accept. |

| | |
|---|---|
| Curse | Infuse a target with hostile mana. Exact effects depend on the attribute used. Use of alchemic ingredients or conduits related to the target may increase duration, effects, and potency. |
| Dash | Coats user in mana and propels them forward. Behavior may change based on attribute applied. For example, Earth attribute will cause the user to travel underground and then burst out at the target location. |
| Fist | Concentrates mana on the user's fist.<br>Generally produces powerful, if short-ranged, attacks. |
| Floor | Fills the ground with mana. Exact effects will depend on the attribute chosen. May be spread out in a wide area or concentrated on a single point. |
| Prison | Entrap a target in mana that will attempt to prevent movement or action. May also interfere with outside attacks on the target depending on attribute used. |
| Rain | Create a mass of mana in the air that will bombard an area over time. |
| Sensing | Replicate or extend senses via mana. Exact sense and method depends on attribute used. |

This was the first major foreign system choice NSLICE-00P had made since adjusting her priorities and focus, and so she analyzed the options based on her new criteria. First, she considered if any of these shapes might either be related to the two unique Holy spells or else might possess some insight into the fundamental nature of mana or this location at large. Neither seemed to be the case for any of the shapes offered at this time, however.

After that, she had to balance several different priorities. As the acting commander of an NSLICE network, capabilities that might improve communication, control, and decision-making, as well as improve the performance of her subordinate units were desirable. She didn't have many protocols or records related to her status as the key maintenance and production facility of the NSLICE network, but extrapolated that anything related to her subordinate units or production might improve that capability. And then, there were the major directives of protecting friendly units, both friendlies Ateia and Taog and the Dobhar race. So, any capabilities that might improve their survivability were a priority as well.

Finally, she was still the most significant combat asset in the NSLICE network by far. Increasing her own combat capabilities had not dropped significantly in priority, even if they were not the sole consideration at this point.

She concluded her analysis and made her choice.

*The spell shape Clone is now available!*

For this choice, her previous records proved decisive. She had data on another NSLICE cyborg who had been able to produce clones of other Non-Standards. That ability had proven powerful, flexible, and scalable, such that said NSLICE unit had been chosen as the primary defender of her organization's most important facility. As such, said ability was already demonstrated in NSLICE-00P's records as being useful not only for her own personal combat capabilities but also in the defense of friendly units and locations. She could thus use it to protect the friendlies and reinforce the NSLICE network as needed.

Of course, this spell was not necessarily equivalent to that NSLICE unit's powers, but the spell description indicated it would grow in power and flexibility as she used it, so she judged it as having a reasonable probability of providing comparable value in time. Most of the other spell shapes were redundant with other capabilities she already possessed, so this choice seemed to have the most value overall either way.

And so, NSLICE-00P gained a new spell to test while they waited for Dux Augustalis to finish her business. She also continued to experiment on and refine the Equalizer storage sphere she had developed during the battle. The ability to manipulate Equalizer output via physical structures analogous to magic circles also held great potential value . . .

A week later, and the streets of Velusitum were quiet. A great proportion of the city had left, including practically all of the comitatenses and Exploratores. Even the limitanei guarding the city had either left with Dux Augustalis or returned to the countryside.

And, of course, a complete absence of authority had consequences.

A group of soldiers who had deserted from the rebel faction now smashed into an empty villa. They chuckled and grinned as they ransacked the building, grabbing anything its prior occupants had left behind.

"Hey, boss, look at this!"

One of the former soldiers dragged a trembling maid out from the closet. The girl had stayed behind, hoping to return to her family in the countryside, but had been afraid to leave due to the chaos in the streets. Unfortunately, that chaos had found its way into her refuge.

The boss grinned. "Why don't you come with us, little miss? It's not exactly safe here, you know."

The girl trembled and shrieked while the soldiers chuckled. The group gathered their prizes and stepped outside . . . only for a shadow to pass overhead.

"Warning: Rebel forces acting in violation of ceasefire agreement detected. Please disarm and prepare for surrender, or this unit will assume resumed hostilities and activate termination protocols. You have twenty seconds to comply."

The soldiers looked up and found NSLICE-00P hovering in the sky, surrounded by a dozen magic circles. They started to chuckle, hoisting their weapons.

But the boss started to sweat. He remembered those lights in the sky. He happened to be close enough to the battle to catch glimpses of it.

He dropped his weapon and held his hands up.

"I surrender. Please don't kill me."

All the others gaped at their boss.

A few minutes later, Agedia showed up with a volunteer militia she had organized from the remaining citizens. They tied the former soldiers up and led them away while one of them took care of the frightened girl.

"Ah, nice work as always, Seero."

"Acknowledged."

Fortunately, Vafum and Agedia had been able to convince NSLICE-00P to help restore order by reasoning that any soldiers resorting to banditry were still acting as rebels to the Empire and so violated her ceasefire agreement with Dux Augustalis. It also helped that some of those rebel soldiers had attempted to avenge their fallen Emperor and had displayed hostile intent toward NSLICE-00P. She had thus designated these bands as hostile and moved to secure the area.

"By the way, I've been looking for you. You saw the airship come in, right?"

"Affirmative."

Agedia's face turned serious.

"The Northern Court has finally sent someone here, and they've requested your presence. They're waiting for you at the keep."

# 20

# An Imperial Invitation

*"The City-State of Elteno, after deposing its last king, gained a reputation for one of the most open and welcoming governments in the known world. Theoretically, every citizen of Elteno, and notably most foreigners, were welcome to at least observe the proceedings of the senate. Even as Elteno transitioned to an Empire, the Emperor's court remained open to the public and foreign visitors for several centuries more, and to this day, Elteni citizens have the right to appeal to the Emperor. Of course, all of this was contingent on the people in question respecting Elteni rule, and was often subject to conditions based on the character of the court at the time, but it was still leagues removed from how most other states operated, and so the reputation held. And it was thanks to that reputation that Elteno became a magnet for dispossessed peoples seeking refuge. The additional population they gained would prove vital in the wars to come."*

—*The History of the Empire*, by Hostus Tettidius Clodian

Agedia sighed as she slithered into the tavern and slunk into a booth. Vafum, who was already sitting there, raised an eyebrow.

"Aren't you supposed to be patrolling the city?"

Agedia glared at him.

"Aren't you supposed to be running it?"

Vafum shrugged and handed her a mug.

"Fair."

They sat in silence for a bit as they sipped from their drinks, Vafum keeping his eyes on Agedia, who kept hers on the contents of her mug.

"So, the princess, huh?"

Agedia slowly nodded. Vafum rubbed his beard.

"Probably will invite the shiny lass—and company—to the capital. No, the Northern Court *has* to do so now that she's gone and stopped a rebellion by their best general."

Again, Agedia slowly nodded, but still did not look up from her drink. Vafum sighed and decided on a direct approach.

"So, what are you going to do, Agedia?"

She jolted. "Me?"

Vafum rolled his eyes. "Don't play dumb, Agedia. Ateia's going to Corvanus on the back of a dragon of a woman who either doesn't know or doesn't care about politics of any sort. Probably both. She's about to have every notable eye in the Northern Empire on her back, even if no one knows who she is. And if Corvanus is as cult-infested as Caelinus believed, they won't be happy about the shiny lass stopping their friend in the Mines of Might. So . . . what are we going to do? We can't let them go alone now, can we?"

Agedia gripped her mug tight and spoke in a soft voice, almost a whisper, ". . . No, we can't."

Vafum's face fell. He slowly reached over and placed his hand on Agedia's shoulder.

". . . I can go."

Agedia's head shot up, and she stared at him. "What about Khalbuldor?"

"They'll live." He shrugged.

Agedia furrowed her brow. "But . . . you've never been to Corvanus."

He shrugged again. "No, but I have some family there."

She frowned. "But . . . you hate your family."

Vafum shrugged a third time. ". . . Got to do what I got to do."

Agedia fell silent and stared at her mug again. She began to tremble slightly. "I . . ."

NSLICE-00P made her way to the Legion keep of Velusitum, along with Ateia, Taog, and Estrith. An airship had flown over the city and now floated in the air above the keep. It was a sleek vessel made out of metal and in a shape reminiscent of the Imperial ships she had ridden from Turannia, only much larger at eight hundred feet long and decorated with gold, silver, and purple paint. The ship had no wings, thrusters, or any visible means of lift and propulsion, yet was able to remain motionless in the air. NSLICE-00P was able to notice some small protrusions that resembled turrets, and if she zoomed in, she could see magic circles engraved on their sides.

She updated her assessment of the Empire's technological prowess once again. Even her creators would have been hard-pressed to develop a metal aircraft of that size that could loiter in place like this one apparently did, much less without visible propulsion.

Ateia, Taog, and Estrith stared up at the airship with wide eyes as Estrith whispered to herself, "So *this* is the Empire my king feared . . ."

A smaller vessel had landed in the courtyard, and several people disembarked. First came soldiers dressed in golden plate armor with purple cloaks. Then came several men and women in silk togas and stolas. Most wore shades of red and white, but one woman had a purple stola with a silver-colored tiara around her forehead. She glanced around and smiled when she saw NSLICE-00P.

She began walking over, with a soldier on her right, a pointy-eared woman in a stola behind her, and a Minotaur woman on her left. The Minotaur woman wore a basic tunic that exposed her arms and midriff, all of which rippled with muscles, and had a massive war hammer on her back. She also had the clasp and cloak of an Exploratore.

The woman in the stola took a step forward as the guards filled the courtyard.

"Presenting Her Highness Caecila Galvisia Electus, wife of Imperial Prince Octavianus Numerius Electus."

Ateia and Taog gasped and then saluted. Princess Caecila smiled as she made her way toward NSLICE-00P.

"You must be NSLICE-00P. I am Princess Caecila Galvisia Electus, but you may call me Caecila. On behalf of the Northern Court of the Empire, allow me to formally welcome you to the Empire, NSLICE-00P, queen of the Dobhar and Amicitia Populi Elteni. Please forgive us for the late greeting."

"Greeting: This unit is designated NSLICE-00P. It is nice to meet you."

The woman who made the announcement frowned, but Princess Caecila continued to smile.

"The pleasure is all mine. It is also my pleasure to extend an invitation to you from the Northern Court. The court wishes to greet a friend of the Empire, as well as reward you for your assistance in both Turannia and Utrad. If it pleases you, I would love to escort you to Corvanus."

"Acknowledged. Statement: This unit must confer with friendlies to determine the optimal course of action. Please stand by."

The announcer woman's eyes widened at NSLICE-00P's response, but Princess Caecila simply nodded.

"Of course. Please, let me know when you are ready."

NSLICE-00P turned back and walked toward her friends. Ateia and Taog were gaping at her.

"Statement: Imperial authorities have extended an invitation to escort this unit to location Corvanus with the stated intent to greet this unit and provide compensation for services rendered. Query: Is this course of action efficient regarding the friendlies' primary and major directives?"

Ateia and Taog just stared at her for a moment.

"YES! OBVIOUSLY!"

Ateia caught herself and clasped her hands over her mouth while Taog heaved a sigh.

"Yes, Seero. A friendly invitation to the court by *an Imperial princess* is a big deal. A really big deal. One that you don't really refuse."

"Query: So, it is beneficial for this unit's and the friendlies' current missions?"

Ateia and Taog looked at one another.

"I mean, yes? Obviously? Corvanus is the capital of the North. It has the most connections and resources of anywhere in this part of the Empire. If there's anywhere we can find information on the people we're both looking for, it's there."

Taog then frowned. "I . . . am concerned. I don't think we're at all ready for politics. But we also don't really have a choice. Well, I guess Seero technically does, but I still wouldn't refuse a direct invitation from an Imperial princess if I were you. We'll just have to be careful."

Ateia nodded at that. "Right. It would be good if we could at least meet with Vafum and Agedia first before we go, but Taog is right. If we're going to find my father, we have to visit Corvanus at some point anyway."

"Acknowledged. Access to additional resources and connections predicted as beneficial. Moving to respond."

NSLICE-00P turned and walked back toward Princess Caecila.

"Response: This unit will accept offer by Imperial Princess Caecila and travel to Corvanus. This unit requests time to prepare for departure."

Princess Caecila broke out into a wide smile. "Excellent. That is no problem; some of us will be staying here, so we will not be departing today, in any case. Please, take your time and let us know when you are ready to go."

"Affirmative."

And so, NSLICE-00P and her friends returned to town. NSLICE-00P picked up the stray drones and monsters she had left to monitor the area, then the group proceeded to Khalbuldor, where they found Vafum and Agedia in the former council chambers. It turned out that after the council had fled, taking with them most of their families and clansmen, the most distinguished Dwarf left in Khalbuldor had been Vafum. A fact he deeply regretted, especially now.

The man was waving his hands around, using magic circles to levitate documents all around him. His face had been locked in a scowl for days.

"Thabumlir spent *how* much on his birthday party? No wonder the tavern's been out of the good stuff all year long. By the Aesdes, I'm surprised this place hadn't collapsed under the sheer weight of stupidity yet."

He heaved a sigh and turned to the group. Agedia placed a huge stack of documents on the center table and then reclined in a chair. "Enough of that! We have a princess here! Princess Caecila actually came to greet them personally!"

Vafum sighed again. "Obviously she would in these circumstances. Girl needs all the help she can get. The only surprising part is that she convinced the court to let her come. They probably just couldn't decide on a representative of their own."

Ateia tilted her head. "What do you mean by that?"

Vafum looked at her. "Girl, do you know anything about Princess Caecila?"

Ateia shook her head, and Vafum sighed again.

"Turannians. Look, there was a *huge* scandal a while back that practically everyone in the Empire talked about for years. Imperial Prince Octavianus defied his family and broke his engagement with Aemilia Hibera, only the daughter of the most powerful man in the Northern Court, in favor of Caecila Galvisia, a girl from some regular old commoner family. Long story short, he got his way, and Aemilia was all but exiled to Turannia. And since then, the Northern Emperor's been in a bind, as Consul Hiberius was more than a little upset by his daughter being shipped off to the dangerous and remote frontier. So, instead of securing his legitimacy, the Emperor alienated his most important supporter and has been completely ineffectual ever since. So since marrying into the family and realizing the situation she and Octavianus created, Princess Caecila has been trying *everything* to boost her own political clout and get them back on track. So be careful with her. She likely means well, but she's *desperate* to gain support. Who knows what she will do with a powerful and unaffiliated agent like the shiny lass?"

Ateia gasped. "Wait, isn't that the plot of that banned romance novel?!"

Vafum stared at her. "Yes, yes it is. Of course Turannia got the book but didn't even hear the news. It's only banned in Turannia, by the way."

Agedia shrugged. "I mean, wouldn't that make sense with Rector Aemilia taking over there? Don't think she likes everyone discussing her dirty laundry."

Vafum blinked then nodded. "Oh, I guess that's true. In any case, this illustrates the problem beautifully. You all are NOT ready for court politics. Not even close. Biggest scandal of our generation, and you haven't even heard of it. But there's no helping it now. The court is ready for you, so you'll just have to adapt on the fly."

Vafum was about to continue when Agedia made eye contact him. His eyes widened. He leaned over and whispered to her, "Are you sure?"

Agedia shook her head. "No, but . . . we have to adapt on the fly, right?"

Vafum frowned.

"Agedia . . ."

She took a deep breath. "I can't let Tiberius's work go to waste. And I can't let her go alone."

Vafum still frowned but gave her a slow nod. "Well, if you're sure. Should I come with you anyway?"

Agedia shook her head. "I think we may need somewhere safe to run to real quick, so we better keep someone in Utrad."

Vafum nodded at that, and then the two returned their attention to the others. Agedia turned to the group and smiled.

"Alright, kiddies, pack your bags! It's been a while since I've been to the capital! And since I've stabbed anyone in a dark alleyway!"

Ateia and Taog could only gulp at that.

# 21

# Taking Flight

*"For most of their joint history, the skies were ruled by the Empire of the Sun. Skills, spells, or artifacts that enabled flight were difficult to acquire, and so the Legion could not put the critical mass of soldiers in the skies needed to counter the overwhelming individual might of the Archons. Air superiority for the Empire of the Sun was a given in both empires' strategic calculus.*
*This changed when a joint Elteni-Mirima shipyard built a ship that could sail through the air."*

—*The History of the Empire*, by Hostus Tettidius Clodian

Agedia turned to face the rest of the group just before they entered the Legion keep.

"Okay, here we go. Now, tell me the rules again."

Ateia and Taog frowned but nodded.

"Don't agree to anything. Don't directly refuse anything. Don't talk to anyone if we can help it, especially not alone."

Agedia nodded back.

"That's right. Now, let's do this."

NSLICE-00P and her group climbed aboard the small ship alongside Princess Caecila's entourage, which carried them up to the larger airship above. Once the door opened up, NSLICE-00P's robotic eye began flickering rapidly.

The inside of the larger airship featured *stone* walls and floors decorated with red carpets and golden chandeliers. And the data from the Dungeon Field Generator, as well as her sensors, indicated that the interior was not merely made to look like a stone hallway, but the whole interior was made of stone beyond an exterior metal shell.

"Query: This unit has observed stone materials with high weight in use in this craft. How does the craft achieve vertical flight in these conditions?"

Princess Caecila smiled. "I am not privy to the details, but I am told the airships make use of weight-reducing enchantments. This vessel is specially designed to transport high-ranking officials and the Imperial family, so they wanted to make it as similar to the Imperial palace as possible."

NSLICE-00P again revised her assessment of the Empire's technological achievements. Princess Caecila then led the group to an observation deck, a loungelike area featuring numerous couches surrounded by windows to give a clear view of the ground below. Servants stood at the ready to attend to the passengers, with a double door leading to a large kitchen. Princess Caecila pointed out the amenities, as well as the hall to the private rooms for the group to rest in.

"Please, make yourselves at home and enjoy the flight."

Shortly afterward, the airship began to move. NSLICE-00P detected heavy mana signatures surrounding the ship, similar to the Wind spells the Legion had once assaulted her with. The wind began wrapping around the ship, and soon, it shot forward through the air. NSLICE-00P tried to gather as much data on the ship's mechanisms as she could, recording whatever fell within range of her Dungeon Field Generator.

Meanwhile, Ateia stood at the window with her eyes wide open as they left Velusitum behind, with Taog and Estrith standing in the center of the room, as far away from the windows as possible. Agedia was lounging on one of the couches as the servants brought her a cup and a plate full of food. The monsters were all resting and sleeping in the hangar, since NSLICE-00P deemed it too risky to deploy them on an Imperial vessel meant for transporting VIPs.

Princess Caecila walked over to NSLICE-00P while the armored soldier from before stood at a polite distance, along with the pointy-eared girl, giving the two some privacy.

"I am told you helped save Turannia earlier? May I ask, is Rector Aemilia in good health?"

"Response: By this unit's last record, Rector Aemilia was in optimal condition."

Princess Caecila nodded. "I am glad to hear that. She and I had our differences, but it pained me to hear she was left alone against that incursion. I am happy she survived. Thank you for helping her."

"Acknowledged."

The pointy-eared woman handed Princess Caecila two drinks.

"May we get you anything, Miss NSLICE-00P?"

"Negative Response: This unit's organic components are in optimal condition. The next organic refueling is scheduled in 23.81 hours."

Princess Caecila frowned but handed one of the drinks back to her assistant.

"I see. Well, just let us know if we can do anything to make things more comfortable for you."

"Acknowledged."

"But of course. Are you from Turannia, if I may ask?"

"Negative."

Princess Caecila nodded at that.

"I see. Where are you from, then? Another province?"

"Negative Response: This unit originates from outside the Empire. Location of origin is uncertain in reference to the Empire, though this unit is still investigating the exact relationship."

Princess Caecila's eyes widened. "Oh my, you mean to say you are lost?"

"Affirmative Response: That statement is reasonably accurate."

Princess Caecila's face turned serious. "Why don't you tell me about your home, then? Perhaps we could assist you in finding it?"

"Response: Location of this unit's origin point is a low priority objective save for its relevance to this unit's primary directive. Locating the persons of interest is the ultimate objective, and this unit would prefer assistance to be concentrated on that mission."

Princess Caecila nodded. "Yes, I could see that. A place is less important than the people there, after all. Perhaps you could tell me about who you're looking for?"

"Affirmative."

And so, NSLICE-00P displayed the persons of interest for Princess Caecila and described them for her. Princess Caecila hummed and rubbed her chin.

"Hm, none of them appear familiar to me, but we will see what we can find. Fulcinia, could you take note of these people for me?"

"Right away, Your Highness."

The pointy-eared woman left to retrieve a recording core, then Princess Caecila turned and looked out the window.

"If I may ask, what is your opinion on the Empire, Miss NSLICE-00P? It is rare to meet someone from outside its borders."

"Requesting Clarification: This unit has no overall opinion and requires additional parameters to conduct an analysis. Please state exact criteria on which to evaluate."

Princess Caecila blinked a few times. "Um, well . . . what do you think of the Empire's relationship with its people? Do you think . . . we're doing a good job of taking care of them?"

NSLICE-00P's robotic eye began flickering, causing Princess Caecila to blink a few more times.

"Analysis: This unit lacks relevant data and protocols to judge overall socioeconomic well-being, though general public health appears to be acceptable within larger Imperial territories. In terms of military efficiency, the Empire appears to possess sufficient hardware and tactics to handle observed opponents, and possesses material, technological, and organizational advantages on the neighboring factions this unit is aware of. However, loyalty and allocation of military forces appears suboptimal and has left multiple threats unaddressed. This unit is not aware of the overall military situation of the Empire, however, so this analysis is not predicted to be conclusive."

Princess Caecila paused for a moment before slowly nodding.

"Yes, I can see that. We keep wasting our forces on civil wars or ill-conceived invasions, spending our blood on vain ambition instead of protecting our people. I grieve for the people we leave in harm's way as a result. And . . . I will admit that the Northern Court has not been the most effective of late. The Emperor is doing his best, but the court has been split into factions more interested in advancing their own agendas than the common good. Consul Hiberius used to keep them in line, but . . . he has been distant of late, which I am ashamed to admit I may have played a role in."

Princess Caecila then turned to face NSLICE-00P. "Still, perhaps all is not lost. If a friend of Rector Aemilia were to grow notable in the court, perhaps we might yet find a path to reconciliation."

"Response: This unit lacks data and protocols to judge political situations or the probability of successful governance."

Princess Caecila frowned for a moment before nodding. "I suppose . . . I do as well."

Meanwhile, Agedia was covering her mouth and trembling, trying to hold in her giggles.

"Oh, Seero, you have no idea what you're saying, do you? Well, she's already an Amicitia Populi Elteni, so I guess she can get away with it."

Just then, a shadow covered Agedia, blocking her light. She turned around and looked up to find the Minotaur woman standing over her with arms crossed. Agedia grinned and lifted out of her chair.

"Well, well, well, look who it is."

The Minotaur woman snorted and pulled her hand back. Agedia did likewise.

And then they clasped hands, gripping as hard as they could.

Agedia winced as she grinned. "It seems you've been working out, huh, Typheras?"

Typheras snorted again. "More like you've gone soft, Agedia."

"Me? What about you? Didn't expect you of all people to join up with the Exploratores or the Imperial family, miss royal guard."

Typheras shrugged. "I like being able to bash heads outside of the Colosseum without getting arrested for it."

"Ah, that's a good point." Agedia nodded.

Typheras shook her head. "Enough about me. Why are *you* coming back to Corvanus, Agedia?"

She nodded her head toward Ateia and Taog. "Those kids are friends of Tibbers, so I wasn't about to let them waltz into the court without a chaperone."

Typheras nodded at that. Agedia looked her in the eye and frowned.

"So, you know, let your boss know hands off if you want to stay on my good side."

Typheras narrowed her eyes. "You know Caecila wouldn't do anything like that; she's a good girl. In fact, they should probably come under her wing if you're worried."

Agedia sat back down and took a drink. "As if. Can your little princess even protect anyone at this stage?"

Typheras heaved a sigh. "Look . . . she's definitely been in over her head, but she's also one of the few actually trying to get the court working. And now? Dobhar invading Turannia? A rebellion in Utrad? The Empire's coming apart, Agedia. The princess could *really* use a hand trying to hold it together. I could really use a hand."

Agedia shook her head. "You must be truly desperate to come to me."

Typheras met her gaze. "We are."

"Look," she heaved a sigh. "I'm just here to watch the kids. So, I'm not going to put them right in the thick of it if I can help it, okay? If you want help, you'll have to convince the shiny lass. Besides, she's the one here with real power."

Typheras glanced over to NSLICE-00P and Caecila's conversation and raised an eyebrow.

"Who is she, anyway?"

Agedia grinned. "A one-woman army."

# 22

# The Princess's Plea

*"But the prince rescued her just as she was about to be kidnapped for good. He banished the villainess who arranged for her kidnapping to the frontier, then he married the girl, making her a real princess at last. And they lived happily ever after."*

—*The Prince's Heart*, an abridged telling of the banned book by a Turannian bard.

Princess Caecila made a bit more small talk before conferring with Fulcinia and Typheras. Fulcinia frowned at what the Princess told her.

"Your Highness, I cannot recommend a direct appeal. Not only is it a breach of decorum, but it also leaves you vulnerable."

Princess Caecila shook her head. "That is our problem, Fulcinia. We *are* vulnerable. Admitting it will not make the situation much worse. Besides, Miss NSLICE-00P is very . . . straightforward, it seems. And I am still not the most adept at social maneuvering among the court. I believe our greatest chance to make progress is to approach her directly."

Fulcinia frowned while Typheras shrugged.

"This is the girl who assaulted a Legion head-on and took Uscfrea Spellbreaker down in single combat. She doesn't seem to appreciate subtlety, in my humble opinion."

Fulcinia stared at her. "Are you certain you are not simply projecting, Miss *Bonecrusher*?"

Typheras smirked. "Oh, I can be subtle. I just choose not to."

Princess Caecila giggled lightly before shaking her head. "Regardless, the fact of the matter is we have only this trip to approach her undisturbed and with candor, and it will not last forever. I will take the risk. I must."

Both Fulcinia and Typheras frowned at that but nodded. Princess Caecila took a deep breath and approached NSLICE-00P once again.

"Miss NSLICE-00P, I would like to discuss with you about your rewards."

"Query: Is compensation to be issued at this time? This unit predicted compensation would occur upon arrival in Corvanus."

Princess Caecila nodded. "Yes, but we would like to sort things out in private ahead of time, before the public ceremony. With that said, your accomplishments are truly staggering; it is no exaggeration to say you have held the Northern Empire together by your own two hands. So . . . how would you feel about joining the court? The Emperor's council has some room, and I believe there is a praetor spot open within the court. Should you prefer to remain beyond the capital, we will also need a new rector provinciae and new magister militum for Utrad in the near future."

"Negative Response: This unit cannot officially affiliate herself with any factions prior to locating the persons of interest and receiving orders to do so."

Princess Caecila frowned at that. "Oh, I did not realize you had allegiances of your own, forgive me. What would you find acceptable as a reward, then?"

"Response: Assistance with this unit's primary directive, including but not limited to mobilization of the Empire's resources and manpower to search Imperial territory for the persons of interest, as well as data regarding the fundamental nature of mana and astronomical data regarding this planetary body's location within the galaxy, as well as the structure and identity of this galaxy if it is not the galaxy designated: Milky Way. Material compensation is also acceptable, though grants of land or offers of authority will not be accepted if they require this unit to integrate into the Empire."

Princess Caecila nodded. "I see. I will relay your preferences when we arrive, and we will arrange something to your liking, then."

"Acknowledged."

Princess Caecila then took a deep breath and looked NSLICE-00P in the eye.

"I will be honest, miss NSLICE-00P. I need your help. Please, would you hear me out?"

"Statement: This unit cannot respond without details regarding the nature of the request and proposed compensation."

Princess Caecila nodded. "The Northern Court has stopped functioning for years at this point. Every proposal is argued, every decision is delayed as the factions maneuver for control. The provinces are all but running themselves; the court can't even handle issues around Corvanus. The Emperor is isolated and powerless to intervene, and so the Empire is falling apart. If the Imperial family could receive support from someone as powerful as you, we might be able to change that."

"Negative Response: Participation in the Empire's political governance is calculated to violate this unit's nonintervention protocols and has little predicted benefit to this unit's primary directive."

Princess Caecila furrowed her brow. "Then . . . why did you stop the rebellion, if I may ask?"

"Explanation: Rebel official Magister Vibius assaulted this unit. In accordance with self-defense protocols, this unit moved to terminate the threat. Due to Magister Vibius's affiliations and the subsequent actions of his superiors, this resulted in the rebel faction being designated as hostile, and so subject to termination."

"I-I see . . ."

Princess Caecila thought for a moment and then sighed. Looking up, she clasped her hands together and looked into NSLICE-00P's eyes once more.

"Please, what can I do to convince you? I will do anything I must."

"Answer: Nonintervention protocols are not the highest priority for this unit. If benefits can be offered to this unit's primary directive that exceed the potential risks and downsides, then it may be judged as acceptable to violate nonintervention protocols."

Princess Caecila smiled and nodded. "Oh! In that case, what sort of benefits would fit that?"

"Unknown."

Princess Caecila blinked. "Excuse me?"

"Elaboration: This unit is uncertain as to whether it is possible for the Empire to locate the persons of interest, or if the Empire has any data relevant to that purpose. As a result, this unit cannot speculate as to specific benefits Princess Caecila could offer that would enable violating nonintervention protocols."

Princess Caecila went silent for a moment before nodding. "I see. I suppose it would be boorish of me to ask you to tell me that. Just tell me this, if I can find something that would benefit your mission, will you support me?"

"Response: As stated, should benefits to the primary directive be deemed sufficient, violation of nonintervention protocols may occur."

Princess Caecila nodded. "Then I will find something to convince you. I promise."

"Acknowledged."

Princess Caecila did not only speak with NSLICE-00P, of course. She also made small talk with Ateia, Taog, and Agedia. She attempted to speak with Estrith as well, but backed off as the Dobhar scoffed and replied gruffly.

Agedia kept an eye on her when she spoke with Ateia and Taog, but she avoided any political conversations with them, focusing on more casual and personal matters, such as now.

Princess Caecila sat on a chair by the window, Ateia sitting in a seat nearby. They were just reaching the end of Utrad, where Velus's Pass broke through a towering mountain range. The open farms and plains gave way to hilly forests that led up to snow-tipped mountains.

"So, why did you become an Exploratore, if I may ask? I must admit, I too was interested in the Empire's heroes at one point."

Ateia smiled at that. "Well, I guess it's because of my father. He was an Exploratore, so at first I just wanted to be like him. Then he . . . Well, he left on a mission and never returned. The Legion hasn't confirmed he's dead, so I figured if I followed in his footsteps, I might be able to figure out what happened."

Princess Caecila frowned. "You have my deepest sympathies."

Ateia shook her head. "Again, the Legion never confirmed it, so as far as I'm concerned, he's still alive."

Princess Caecila shook her head. "He need not have died for you to have lost your father. My father left us after . . . Well, the important part is that he left. At first, I was desperate to have him back, then I was angry at him. Now . . . now I grieve for the family I lost, but I try to move forward and focus on who I have now."

Ateia frowned. "I'm sorry to hear that. But I can't move on; not yet. Not while there's still hope."

Princess Caecila looked at her for a moment before slowly nodding. "I hope you find him someday."

Ateia kept her gaze outside the window. "Thank you."

The rest of the trip was uneventful. They flew over Velus's Pass, a stone fortress that blocked the entire pass. To NSLICE-00P, it appeared more reminiscent of a massive dam than a defensive fortification, rising at least a thousand feet into the sky. NSLICE-00P read massive mana signatures even from up on the ship and identified countless towers that appeared armed with siege weapons.

But she could also see that the gates were open, and constant streams of wagons and people moved through the fort in either direction. Utrad had been under the Empire's control for centuries now; it had been a long time since the Legion had been required to hold those gates.

And so, the ship passed the mountains into the heart of the Northern Empire.

The Northern Court was not as rich as the south, nor as powerful as the east, but the one thing it did have to its name was history. This was the home of Elteno, the city-state from which the Empire grew. The birthplace of the Empire.

NSLICE-00P watched as the ship flew over the land. This area seemed even more developed than Utrad had been; they passed more than one city the size of Velusitum, if not larger, with massive farms and countless paved roads in between. Massive towers with bright lights at the top were interspersed throughout at regular intervals.

"Query: What is the purpose of those installations? This unit predicts they are related to communication infrastructure."

Princess Caecila nodded at the question. "I believe some of them, but most are for transport. From what I understand, they create currents of moving ground between the cities. The plaustrum subterraneum can then ride along those currents without needing to move on their own power, so we can use much larger versions that wouldn't be feasible to build individually."

NSLICE-00P continued to observe, and indeed identified the powerful signatures as mostly Earth-attribute mana. If her simulations on the amount of earth such a signature could move were correct . . . then the Empire's logistics were not inferior to an industrialized society's, at least within this province.

Soon, their destination was in sight.

Corvanus was a port city, with the ocean bordering it along the east and south, and wide swamplands to the north. A large road entered into it from the west, with several forts guarding the entrance. NSLICE-00P also noticed two additional airships of similar size to the one she was riding over the city, though these lacked the gold and silver highlights or purple paint.

The city itself was made of stone and laid out in the Empire's grid pattern. Perhaps surprisingly, it was not that much larger than Velusitum, and with much of its space dedicated to large manors, it might even have a lower population density.

The airship made its way to the center of the city and paused in the air. Princess Caecila then led them to the ship's hangar, where the smaller crafts were ready to take them down.

And so, NSLICE-00P and company arrived in the Northern Capital of Corvanus.

# 23

# The Emperor of the North

*"Respect the throne, regardless of who sits on it. There have been good Emperors and bad Emperors; there have been strong Emperors and weak Emperors. But one thing is clear. It is not for nothing that the children of Velus have remained on that throne for over a thousand continuous years."*

—Imperial Guard Numerius Cassius Victor, after foiling an assassination attempt by the rest of the Imperial Guard.

Huddled up in one of the rooms, Agedia continued the crash course on court politics for the group. She looked around at everyone and nodded.

"Okay, final review. Who can tell me the overall layout of the court?"

"Recitation—"

Agedia sighed. "Who BESIDES the shiny girl here who can apparently repeat any word I've ever said verbatim? Don't worry, Seero. I know *you've* been paying attention." Agedia then glanced at Ateia out of the corner of her eye.

Ateia gulped but nodded.

"Um, so, normally, the Emperor and his council rule as they please, but due to . . . stuff that happened recently, the current Emperor isn't very strong. So, apparently, there's some senate that's regained power now, which is currently split into three factions?"

Agedia nodded. "Right. Just the governing body that goes back to the earliest days of Elteno, but I know *I* didn't enjoy those lessons either. What are the factions?"

Ateia concentrated. "Um, so first is the traditionalist faction, led by Consul Gallus Albanius Noxisius. They, um . . ." Taog sighed and whispered into her ear. "Ah! They focus on maintaining the traditions of the Empire and are mostly popular with the Imperial Heartland. But for some reason, they also don't support the Emperor? They, um, probably won't like us, since we're from Turannia, and Seero isn't Imperial at all."

Agedia raised an eyebrow but nodded. "Yep, they're a bunch of snobby jerks. Next?"

Ateia concentrated once more. "Next is the military faction, led by Magister Utriusque Militia Septimus Vipstanus Verrucosis. They represent the interests of the Legion and favor a powerful army. They are mostly popular with current and former legionnaires, as well as the provinces that face regular incursions. They also have connections to the Eastern Court, since the Verrucosis family serves in the Legion there. They, um, might not like us, since Seero is stealing glory and destroying Legions, even though they were rebels? That's still weird to me; shouldn't they be happy Seero stopped a rebellion?"

Agedia shrugged. "Yep, they're a bunch of hotheaded jerks. They won't have a problem with Seero killing rebels; they *will* have a problem with anyone who can destroy a Legion. And last?"

Ateia frowned. "Um . . . T-Taog, why don't you take one?"

Taog sighed but nodded. "Right, so the last faction is the mercantile faction, led by Aedile Lar Paesentius Hortensus. They are mostly made up of newer merchant families, and so care mostly about merchants and trade. They have a lot of business connections with the Southern Empire, and so likely represent the Southern Court's interests. They don't have a specific reason to dislike us, but even if they don't, we shouldn't trust them."

Agedia nodded. "Yep, they're a bunch of sleazy jerks."

Ateia shuffled. "Um, Agedia?"

"Yes?"

"Is there anyone in the court who isn't a jerk?"

Agedia rubbed her chin and thought for a long moment before shrugging. "Probably Princess Caecila; she's still learning how to be a jerk. Her husband too, though that's because he's kind of an idiot. But the Imperial family's basically useless right now, so don't rely on them."

Ateia gulped again. "I-I see. Um, what about the Magister Exploratore per Corvanus? Can we trust him?"

Agedia's face turned dark. "Oh, he's the worst jerk of them all. He's stuck-up, callous, abrasive, and stubborn beyond all reason."

"What?!" Ateia jumped.

"Yes." Agedia nodded seriously. "He's my uncle, after all."

Ateia's jaw dropped. "Wait, what?"

Agedia shrugged. "But I will say, he's noticeably less stab-happy than Vibius was, so he *probably* won't take you two hostage in an attempt to manipulate and blackmail the shiny girl." Her eyes narrowed. "But that doesn't mean you should trust him blindly. My uncle will do *anything* to protect the Empire. Since shiny girl's helped with that, he'll like you on the surface, but that will not stop him from cutting you off or cutting you down if he thinks you're a problem. And even if you're not, he will still use you to the utmost he can get away with for the sake of the Empire. Make no mistake, you have no friends in Corvanus, only temporary allies and future enemies. The only people who care about you bunch are you, so make taking care of yourselves priority number one. No one else is going to."

Ateia and Taog gulped at that while Estrith scoffed.

"I do not see what all this fuss is about. If there are enemies or possible enemies, we should cut them down and grow from their deaths. Why do you Imperials bother so much with words and weaklings?"

Agedia sighed. "Or you can be like little miss barbarian otter over there and get executed for murder within a week."

Estrith glared at her. "What did you call me?"

Agedia grinned. "You're weaker than I am, so by your logic, I can call you whatever I like. Isn't that right, Miss Barbotter?"

Estrith gritted her teeth but said nothing. Just then, there was a knock at the door.

"Miss NSLICE-00P? Her Highness has asked me to inform you that we have arrived, and to join her at the hangar as soon as you are ready to disembark."

Agedia took a deep breath. "All right, kiddies, class is over. Time to see who was paying attention."

The group took one of the smaller ships down into a hangar in the city below, where they transferred onto a wagon pulled by a unicorn. Princess Caecila took them to a villa prepared for high-ranking diplomatic guests and let them rest for the night.

The group awoke to find Agedia waiting for them.

"I'll be heading out today."

Ateia froze, her eyes widening. "You're not coming with us?"

Agedia shook her head. "I'm . . . Well, let's just say there are people who know me here, and it wouldn't help you to bring me along to the palace. The shiny girl could probably get away with it, but there are other angles we need to work on anyways. You bunch go and mingle in the court. I'll handle the 'stabbing in dark alleyways' part."

She then turned to NSLICE-00P.

"Shiny girl, you got one of those little golems, right? You can communicate with them, right?"

"Affirmative."

Agedia nodded. "Lend me one and let me know if anything serious happens. I'll do the same."

NSLICE-00P deployed one of her mini drone golems to follow Agedia.

"Best of luck. Worst comes to worst, just smile and wave, and let shiny girl do the talking."

With that, Agedia made her way out of the villa, and just after breakfast, Princess Caecila arrived. Gathering the group, she led them to the throne room . . .

The throne room of Corvanus was not built into a Legion keep. The provinces entertained their guests with displays of military prowess, but things were different here in the Imperial Heartland. The throne room was a separate structure at the center of the city, right in a central courtyard surrounded by small marketplaces. It was Elteni traditional from the early days of the Empire, when the First Emperor declared anyone, from the lowest beggar to the consul of the senate, would have equal access to their ruler. Terms and conditions now applied to equal access, but the public and civilian location of the throne room endured.

The throne room was a multistoried stone structure with large archways serving as entrances and windows, though most of these were blocked off. The group stepped into an entrance hall, where they were approached by the guard.

There was some commotion when the guards asked the group to remove their weapons and NSLICE-00P calmly explained that was both forbidden by protocol and practically impossible without adequate maintenance infrastructure. Estrith, for her part, simply growled at the guards. But Princess Caecila intervened, and since NSLICE-00P was an Amicitia Populi Elteni, they were allowed inside even with their arms. This was not unprecedented, even. The foreigner could keep their weapons, for the Emperor was fully confident in his own.

And so, the group entered the throne room itself, an open stone hallway sparsely adorned. It had stone pillars spaced throughout, and a red carpet leading to a simple stone throne. The only decorations were two banners of the Empire standing behind the throne, and a simple brazier next to it. The east had their weapons and the south their gold and jewels, but the North needed no adornment save the authority and history of the Empire it had forged.

Well, things weren't as simple as they appeared. NSLICE-00P detected massive mana signatures flowing through the stone all around her, with countless magic circles engraved just beneath the surface of the walls and roofs and floor. Even the Emperor's throne was part of this circuit of power. She predicted that any attempt at treachery would be met with overwhelming force.

A number of guards lined the sides of the carpet, wearing golden plate armor and purple cloaks. Men and women in togas and stolas mingled and chattered among themselves to either side of the guards.

But all conversation stopped as the group entered the room.

Fulcinia stepped forward.

"Her Highness Caecila Galvisia Electus, wife of Imperial Prince Octavianus Numerius Electus."

Princess Caecila stepped forward.

"Greetings to you, Your Majesty."

The Emperor of the North sat upon his throne. He nodded to Princess Caecila but did not speak.

Princess Caecila turned and held her hand out to the back.

"It is my honor to present to you the woman responsible for the victory in Utrad. May I present to the Emperor the queen of the Dobhar, the savior of Utrad and Turannia, and Amicitia Populi Elteni, NSLICE-00P, along with her companions Exploratore Ateia Niraemia, Exploratore Taog Sutharlan, and Estrith Edilddaughter of the Dobhar."

NSLICE-00P stepped forward, along with her companions. "Greeting: This unit is designated NSLICE-00P. It is nice to meet Emperor Lucius Numerius Electus."

Emperor Lucius nodded. "Greetings to you, NSLICE-00P. It is my honor to welcome a friend of the Empire to my court."

Emperor Lucius then nodded to one of his assistants, who stepped forward and opened a scroll.

"The official investigation has revealed that Magister Caelinus declared himself Emperor and moved to rebel. He was shortly thereafter confronted by NSLICE-00P, who put an end to his treacherous ambitions. The Emperor would like to thank the queen of the Dobhar for her continued friendship with the Empire and the favors she has bestowed upon it."

Emperor Lucius nodded then opened his mouth to speak. "First and foremost, I declare that NSLICE-00P is truly a friend of the Empire and its people, which she has proven now more than once. All talk and speculation regarding her deeds in Turannia and the legitimacy of her title shall come to a close. Any further doubts are an insult to an Imperial friend and to this court, and will be treated as such."

He glanced around the room at that, making eye contact with several individuals before continuing.

"All assets and holdings of Mettius Burrienus Caelinus and Vibius Vatinius Balbillus will be forfeited and donated to NSLICE-00P. As per her preference, these assets will be conferred to the Empire, which will pay her in equal value. First and foremost, assistance will be offered to her steward in Turannia for the construction of a port and roads connecting her territory to the Empire. Her people will be permitted to trade with the Empire without restriction."

The room was filled with murmurs again, mostly insults levied at the former magisters of Utrad. Emperor Lucius raised his hand and continued.

"NSLICE-00P will also be granted an artifact from the treasury as a gesture of my personal thanks. Next, it has come to my attention that our friend has submitted a request to the Exploratores, which was not transmitted beyond Utrad due to the treachery of the Magister Exploratore there. This request will be elevated to an Imperial order, and the Empire will raise the bounty on said request. The Magister Exploratore per Corvanus has been informed of the order and will personally oversee an investigation on NSLICE-00P's behalf."

Emperor Lucius then glanced at a specific person in the room, a man carrying a staff.

"Finally, NSLICE-00P will be granted access to the Imperial Academy Arcanum and their libraries. She will be granted unrestricted access to all materials up to Class Three, with partial access up to Class Four. She should be treated as a senior magus of the academy should she request access to other facilities and resources, and will be assigned an assistant by the academy to guide her."

Emperor Lucius then smiled.

"This is but a small offering compared to what you have done on our behalf, NSLICE-00P. If this court can offer you any further assistance, please do not hesitate to ask. You are a friend of the Empire and its people, and the Empire takes care of its friends."

"Acknowledgement: This unit thanks Emperor Lucius for the assistance with her primary directive."

Emperor Lucius then turned his attention to NSLICE-00P's companions.

"Exploratore Ateia Niraemia and Exploratore Taog Sutharlan, step forward."

Murmurs filled the room at that. Ateia and Taog couldn't help but jump, their eyes widening as they stepped forward and saluted.

"Exploratore Ateia Niraemia at your service, Your Majesty."

"Exploratore Taog Sutharlan at your service, Your Majesty."

Emperor Lucius looked them over.

"I am told it was you who forged a friendship with NSLICE-00P and introduced her to the Empire. Likewise, due to the treachery of the Exploratores in Utrad, you two are the only Exploratores who have been assisting an Amicitia Populi Elteni with her requests. Your service has saved two Imperial provinces and has not gone unnoticed."

Ateia tried not to gulp.

"I-It was our honor, Your Majesty. It's our duty to protect the people of the Empire and its friends."

Emperor Lucius nodded.

"Well said. Yet, those who have achieved that duty should not go unrewarded. Nor should the capable be denied the tools to complete their work."

All eyes turned to the Emperor, waiting for his next words.

"I, Emperor Lucius Numerius Electus, elevate Ateia Niraemia and Taog Sutharlan to the Patrician class, with all of its rights and privileges, and assign to them grants of land from the Imperial family's holdings as their personal estates. I appoint to them the rank of Imperial inquisitor, with the mandate to investigate and locate NSLICE-00P's missing people. You will be the agents of the Empire's will, to assist NSLICE-00P as a friend of the Empire deserves."

Ateia and Taog's jaws dropped as the throne room erupted into chaos.

INTERLUDE

# Checking in on the Land of Rain

As NSLICE-00P and company restored order in Velusitum and then made their way to the Imperial Court, Dux Augustalis gathered as many of Caelinus's forces as she could and made her way north. Most weren't willing to follow her after Caelinus's death, but she still had three legions worth. A number of Utrad's citizens went with them, including the council of Khalbuldor and their clans. This force commandeered the Northern navy and set sail into the Northern Sea.

And then came a long trip, with nothing to do but sit on their boats, and nothing to distract them from dwelling upon recent events. Dux Augustalis had her hands full breaking up constant fights and mutinies. She heaved a sigh as she made her way to the ship's mess hall, where she heard raised voices. At this point, *she* wanted to mutiny.

But what greeted her was not another riot.

"And then the legate tells us he wants a bottle of Celestial wine by the next morning. We knew he was just trying to harass us and make us run around all night only to fail. I was just going to ignore him and take the hit for disobeying orders, and Augustalis wanted to argue all the ways it went against Legion policy, but not Caelinus. Caelinus just said 'yes, sir' and winked at us. He was friends with the quartermaster; by the Aesdes, Caelinus was somehow friends with everyone, and wouldn't you know it, he knew a bottle of Celestial wine had just arrived.

"Caelinus requisitioned it and shocked the legate with the delivery the next morning, 'as ordered.' I thought that was the end of it, but Caelinus had us hide around the corner outside the legate's office. Well, it turned out that bottle was a special order by the dux, but since it arrived 'unclaimed' at the Legion stockpile, anyone could requisition it if they knew it was there, and since Caelinus had put in an official order, the dux knew exactly who took it. The legate got sent to the limitanei and was digging ditches for the next year. We happened to walk by him one day, and Caelinus just said, 'How was the wine, sir?'"

Vopiscus sat at the center of the mess hall. All around him, legionnaires erupted into laughter. He caught Dux Augustalis's eyes and waved to her.

"And there she is, our fearless leader. Dux Augustalis was there with us too, you know! Come, Dux, tell the troops about how Caelinus lead us in victories across Corvanus!"

She crossed her arms and raised an eyebrow. The soldiers quieted down and slowly dispersed as she glared at Vopiscus.

"A word?"

Vopiscus just smiled. "Of course."

Once outside, she turned to him and glared. "This is beyond words, even for you. Must you slander Caelinus's name, even in death?"

Vopiscus shook his head. "I have done no such thing, Dux Augustalis."

She narrowed her eyes. "Then what was that just there?"

Vopiscus stood his ground and held her gaze. "You and the Legion remember Caelinus as the indomitable defender of the North. But he was more than that. He was a person, just like you and I and every one of those troops. He laughed, he played, he got into mischief when he was young. Letting the soldiers know he was someone like them is not slander. You will ensure his legacy as Magister Caelinus endures. I will ensure that Caelinus the man is not forgotten."

Dux Augustalis opened her mouth but stayed silent. Vopiscus then winked at her.

"Besides, you and the troops are so droll, I'm about to go mad. What's a man got to do to get some entertainment around here?"

Dux Augustalis closed her eyes as a vein bulged on her forehead. "Why are you even here, Vopiscus?"

He smirked. "To make sure you don't die."

Dux Augustalis sighed while Vopiscus shrugged.

"I mean, I'm serious? Well, mostly serious. Come on, Pollia, you're great at running the Legion, but you are strictly by the book. The book we set on fire because we thought it was written by evil cultists trying to destroy the world. You need *some* flexibility if you're going to get anything done on our treasonous quest! And besides, you're a bit . . . *aggressive* when it comes to diplomacy."

Dux Augustalis was just about to respond when a soldier ran up to the two of them and saluted.

"Dux! We have incoming!"

Dux Augustalis glared at Vopiscus one final time before rushing to the deck. Once there, she walked over to the side of the deck where the troops were gathering.

"What's the situation?"

A soldier handed Dux Augustalis a Farsight artifact.

"Incoming ships, ma'am! Should we prepare for battle?"

She looked through the artifact, then took a deep breath. "No. That . . . is our welcome party."

A few minutes later, the ships came into view of the regular soldiers, a combination of rickety rafts and salvaged Imperial vessels. A group of their crew leapt *off* the ships and swam through the waves toward the rebel fleet, then dove down and shot out of the water, landing right on the deck of Dux Augustalis's vessels. She motioned to the legionnaires to stand down. In front of Dux Augustalis was a towering Dobhar with a massive bone harpoon on his back . . . and familiar metal armor over parts of his body.

The Dobhar looked around and locked eyes on her. One of his eyes *glowed* in its metallic socket.

"You must be my queen's latest subjects. I am Uscfrea Ymmason, steward of the lands of NSLICE-00P, queen of the Dobhar."

Dux Augustalis frowned but saluted. The soldiers around her gaped, but one by one, they followed suit.

"I am Dux Augustalis. We have a deal with your better, former king of the Dobhar. We are at your command, but do not presume we are your captives. We serve as soldiers and expect to be treated as such."

Uscfrea grinned at her. "So I've been told. Come, let us discuss what you can do for my queen. I have been greatly anticipating this."

Dux Augustalis frowned but led Uscfrea and his escorts into the ship.

And so, Steward Uscfrea took command of the rebel fleet and discussed their integration into the realm of NSLICE-00P.

As well as all they could teach the Dobhar of the Empire's ways.

Dux Augustalis's forces were not the only rebels to make their way to Turannia. In Turannia's second largest port, Miallói watched as an Imperial naval vessel moved into the dock. It lifted up, and a ramp dropped down, then Selkies in Legion gear began to disembark. Miallói marched up to one of them then clasped hands with the newcomer.

"Welcome home, warrior."

The Selkies in Utrad had an easy answer. Now that the Council of Hunters was an Amicitia Populi Elteni with their own land, the Selkie auxiliaries could simply return home to escape reprisal. A good proportion of their comrades in the Auxiliary Aqua had decided to come with them, and so, the Selkies' forces grew greatly that day.

For the other legions, countless soldiers also deserted their posts and applied for refuge in the frontier province, hoping that Dux Canus would exchange amnesty for experienced support. And by and large, they were correct. While anyone of sufficiently high rank would have to be turned over, the Empire wouldn't search *that* hard for the rank and file. Dux Canus had dealt with rebels over his long career and knew how to distinguish the true instigators from the regular soldiers who had been pulled along for the ride. He was also very happy to have experienced troops who owed him a debt.

It was a win-win situation. Turannia's forces got some extra bite, and the soldiers who were simply following orders got to escape execution.

But not everything went so smoothly . . .

Magister Tiberius sighed as he heard shouting down below, pulling out a flask and taking a drink just before his assistant knocked on the door to retrieve him, then staggered down the stairs to find a bunch of former Turannian Exploratores shouting at the poor receptionist. He heaved another sigh before he made his presence known.

"What seems to be the problem here?"

The Exploratore in front turned to him and glared. "There you are! Tiberius, what is the meaning of this?"

Tiberius shrugged. "You'll have to be more specific, Hostus."

Hostus lifted a coin pouch. Tiberius lifted an eyebrow. "That appears to be Idrint, also known as money. You use it to buy stuff, like food and drink. Especially drink. I can understand if you haven't encountered it before."

Hostus flushed red as the room laughed. "Shove off, Tiberius! You know exactly what I mean! Me and my boys brought in a felix major! By the Aesdes, why are you shortchanging me?"

Tiberius scoffed, holding his hand out, and Hostus lobbed the pouch at him. Tiberius caught it and placed it on the reception desk, then slowly counted the coins in front of everyone. He shrugged.

"I don't see what you mean. That is the official Imperial bounty for a felix major. Everything appears in order to me."

Hostus scowled at him. "That's barely a pittance compared to what you paid before!"

Tiberius rolled his eyes. "Oh, I'm sorry, but it seems I spent all the budget for some secretive mission that occupied you for the past few months, so I appear to be a bit short on the bonuses. But I believe you all got paid for that, so it shouldn't be an issue, right? If it is, I could always check the records to determine *exactly* what that supposed mission was, and where all the funds came from, if you understand my meaning?"

Hostus narrowed his eyes. "What are you implying, Tiberius? Come on, we're the best bloody hunters you have in this Aesdes-forsaken province. You can't treat us like this!"

The other Exploratores behind Hostus began shouting and jeering as well. Tiberius froze then heaved a massive, dramatic sigh. Taking out his flask, he took a swig.

"Okay, you know what? You're right. Subtlety is overrated. Let me state it clearly for you." Tiberius looked around at everyone in the room. "Let me state it for *everyone*. You left this province entirely defenseless to go receive a nice juicy paycheck from a rebel traitor while I fought for my life, alone. And now you come back and beg me to vouch that you were here the entire time? You are lucky I am still paying you at *all*."

Hostus crossed his arms. "I didn't know Magister Caelinus was going to rebel! And it wasn't *my* fault the pay here is crap! Don't give me that, Tiberius. I could have gone anywhere afterward; I came back here to do you a solid! Look, you *need* us, Tiberius, I know that much. Don't try to bluff me. Now, hand over what you owe me."

Tiberius chuckled. "I need you, you say? Give you what I owe you, you ask? If you insist."

Tiberius vanished and appeared in front of Hostus, sinking his fist into the man's gut. Hostus wheezed as the air was driven out of him before collapsing to the floor. His teammates cried and moved to respond, but Tiberius pulled some powder out of his pocket and tossed it into their eyes, blinding them as he stepped on the man on the ground. The room started to devolve into chaos.

"ENOUGH!"

Everyone stopped moving as Tiberius shouted. He glared at each person in the room. "Let me make it abundantly clear. I don't *need* any of you. Not anymore. The Dobhar have taken control of the eastern shores. The Selkies are responsible for their own land in the west. Dux Canus has the North sealed up tight, and the Wulver have been keeping to themselves lately. And thanks to a wandering knight doing more work than all of you *combined* while you were all away, monsters are afraid to even approach Castra Turannia. If that wasn't enough, there are *hundreds* of Exploratores and soldiers from Utrad who are happy to work for asylum alone, none of whom have uttered even a single complaint. It was *charity* that I posted that bounty at all, so you bunch would have *something* to do."

He stared down at Hostus on the ground. "It was because of my previous goodwill toward you all that I took you back after you left me and everyone else in this province to *die*. That goodwill is now expended."

He bent down and looked the man in the eye. "So why am I still going to put up with you? Why not just hand you over to the Empire for the general bounty offered for rebels? Because it would be annoying if you turned bandit. That's right: annoying. Not because you could cause any trouble but because I'd have to walk all the way through the rain to the Selkies and ask Miallói to hunt you down. At this point, the only thing keeping you out of an Imperial cell is my desire to stay dry. So go ahead. Tell me how I need you again. Call my *bluff*, why don't you?"

Hostus paled at the mention of Miallói. Tiberius scoffed, stepped off the man, and turned back to return to his office, glancing back at the crowd.

"Anyone who wants me to vouch for them as an Exploratore of Turannia had better *bloody act like one*. Like all those *new* Exploratores I recruited that *don't bloody complain* when I'm the only thing keeping them alive and am still paying them because I'm just that generous. And anyone who has any more complaints can go report me to Corvanus, if they feel they're being treated *unfairly*."

With that, the Exploratores fell silent and quietly began leaving the building. Tiberius shook his head and swore as his assistant came up to him.

"Well, I suppose that's handled. It was a bit . . ."

Tiberius scoffed. "Confrontational? I'd like to say I care, but I don't anymore. By the Aesdes, I miss NSLICE-00P."

The assistant shrugged and held a scroll out. "So you've said at least once every day. By the way, I know now is not the best time, but you have a priority message from Corvanus."

Tiberius rolled his eyes. "Put it in the pile with the rest. I'll get to it when I get to it."

The assistant frowned. "I would, sir, but instead of the usual opening, the message starts with: 'Tiberius, read this and respond or I'll tell Agedia's father what you did.'"

Tiberius grabbed the scroll and *ran* to his office, where he frowned as he read the message. It mostly relayed a recent Imperial decree regarding a certain wandering knight.

"Oh, so Miss Cannot-Get-Involved-in-a-Third-Party-Conflict is going around stopping civil wars now, huh? Come on, NSLICE-00P, don't play hard to get; you nearly gave me a heart attack back then! I went and drank the good stuff I was saving because I thought we were all going to die!"

He shook his head and kept reading. The message explained that the Magister Exploratore per Corvanus, aka Tiberius's boss, was personally overseeing an investigation on NSLICE-00P's behalf.

"Okay, the Emperor ordered you on her quest, huh, boss? Well, I guess if it helps NSLICE-00P, then I can tell you a bit about her. I'm still hiding the juicy bits, though; you can figure that part out yourself, you jerk."

Tiberius was just taking a swig from his flask when he read a little add-on at the end of the message.

*"Oh, by the way, NSLICE-00P's Exploratores companions have been promoted to Patrician and Imperial inquisitor. Both of them."*

Tiberius spat out his drink.

Back in Castra Turannia, Rector Aemilia heaved a sigh. Dux Canus raised an eyebrow.

"That's the fifth sigh you've heaved since I got here. Did something happen?"

Rector Aemilia frowned. "Corvanus announced an Imperial decree to all the rectors today."

She glanced at one of her assistants, who handed a document to Dux Canus. The dux began reading over it.

"Ah, the rebellion in Utrad? That explains a lot, actually. About time the Northern Court responded. Oh, NSLICE-00P put a stop to it? That's a bit of a surprise; I thought she didn't want to get involved in Imperial affairs? But well, anytime we can avoid a civil war is a good thing. The North's going to be complete mess for a while, though."

Dux Canus then glanced back at Rector Aemilia. "That should be good for you, shouldn't it? Lots of refugees from Utrad to fill out your population, plus the Amicitia Populi Elteni you appointed making a name for herself. I figured you'd be happy at this news."

Rector Aemilia's face scrunched up. "Keep reading."

Dux Canus raised an eyebrow and turned back to the scroll. "Hm, her quest is an official Imperial order now . . . Oh, this, huh? For locating and forging a bond of friendship with NSLICE-00P, Ateia Niraemia and Taog Sutharlan have been elevated to the Patrician class and appointed as Imperial inquisitors. Their mandate is as follows . . . *Ah*, I think I see the problem now."

Rector Aemilia grabbed her face and groaned. "What about me?! I was the one who appointed her an Amicitia Populi Elteni in the first place!"

Dux Canus shrugged. "Well, those two *were* the ones who brought her to Castra Turannia . . ."

Rector Aemilia stifled a scream. "That's not the point! Yes, they deserve a good share of the credit, but so do I! I went and put my name out there on NSLICE-00P's behalf and took all sorts of scrutiny for 'a dubious appointment based on unsubstantiated claims,' and now that the court has *finally* acknowledged her, they don't even mention my name! Just . . . just what do I have to do to get a win?!"

Dux Canus frowned. Standing up, he walked over and patted her on the shoulder. "I'm sorry, for what it's worth. I know it's frustrating having enemies in the court."

Rector Aemilia heaved yet another sigh. "It's just . . . nothing I do seems to matter. I manage to balance Turannia's finances, mostly with my *own* money? They complain that Turannia isn't producing a surplus, and raise the tax quota. I somehow survive an incursion with no legions because bloody Caelinus stole our troops for his rebellion? I get blamed for giving up Imperial territory. I go and establish an official, friendly relationship between a hero and the Empire? They don't even acknowledge I was involved. Just . . . just what more can I even do at this point?"

Dux Canus rubbed his chin. "Rector Aemilia, what do your people say about you?"

She paused. "Huh?"

Dux Canus waved around. "The people of Turannia, the people in this keep, what do they say about you?"

Rector Aemilia furrowed her brow. "They say I'm out of place. That I'm some highborn aristocrat not suited for the mud, and that I demand too much."

"What else? When they aren't complaining about you?"

Rector Aemilia blinked, and then concentrated. "That . . . I'm strict but fair. That I managed to keep Turannia safe. That the province's bureaucracy has never run as smooth as this before."

Dux Canus nodded. "Recognition is a fleeting thing. You can't control what the people in Corvanus are going to say about you, but the people here are watching *you* and the things you do, rather than listening to what is said about you. I know you didn't work on their behalf, but nonetheless, your efforts to make something of this province have not gone unnoticed. Keep working on Turannia and invest in its people, and you'll build yourself a base of power; one that will not be so easily taken from you. Corvanus is not the only place you can grow."

Rector Aemilia looked up at him for a moment before slowly nodding. "I suppose . . . I've always been a bit hasty. It's just . . . so much was expected of me, and yet I have achieved so little. I . . . I have no one to blame but myself. I can even understand why my father has abandoned me . . . but I can't help but feel frustrated at the constant failures."

Dux Canus shook his head. "You were thrown into a situation designed to make you fail, and you have not. You have navigated some of the worst circumstances I have seen in my career and kept your province intact. Your achievements are nothing to scoff at."

She shook her head. "That was mostly you and NSLICE-00P."

Dux Canus shrugged. "No one can control the circumstances they are dealt, but they can be judged for how they react in those situations. You stayed humble enough to let your subordinates do the jobs they're best at, and stayed flexible enough to seize the opportunity NSLICE-00P's arrival offered you. You did not overreach in negotiations with either NSLICE-00P or the Dobhar, and you even accepted an idea that came from two cadets. I've served in the Legion for centuries, Rector Aemilia, and worked with countless officials of the Empire. Let me tell you, most of them could not have survived the turn of events you did, and that counts for something. It is an honor to serve you, if an old man's opinion means anything to you."

She blinked a few times at him before her face relaxed. She gave an almost imperceptible smile, whispering her reply. "It does. Thank you."

Dux Canus did not answer, but he smirked and held out the paper. "Besides, I believe you should keep reading the decree to the end."

Rector Aemilia tilted her head with a frown, but she kept reading. Dux Canus smiled as he recited the words at the end of the message. "'In recognition for her role in forging a friendship between NSLICE-00P and the Empire, Rector Provinciae per Turannia Aemilia Hibera will no longer be restricted from contact with her family.'"

She heaved yet another sigh at that. "Well, that's a nice gesture, but my father won't be coming even if he's allowed to. It doesn't change anything—"

Just then, a soldier stepped into the room and saluted. "Rector Aemilia, someone is requesting access to the keep. They say they've come from your family and here to see you."

Rector Aemilia's eyes widened as her heart pounded. Standing up, she ran out of her office while Dux Canus chuckled and followed her.

A few minutes later, Rector Aemilia stood at the gate to Castra Turannia's keep, her eyes as wide as they could go and starting to moisten.

There, in front of the keep, were three women. To the left was a half-Griffinkin woman in plate armor. To the right was a Dimindium Pendem in a servant's garb. And in the center was a human woman in stola. She smiled politely.

"Hello, my lady. It is nice to see—"

She was cut off. The moment she heard the woman's voice, Rector Aemilia leapt forward, grabbing the woman in a tight hug.

"Maelia!"

Maelia's eyes widened. "M-My lady? W-What are you doing?"

Rector Aemilia broke into sobs while Maelia started to panic. The Dimindium Pendem giggled while the half-Griffinkin smiled wryly, and they both joined in on the hug. Dux Canus smiled before motioning to the wide-eyed guards.

"Give them a moment. Why don't you clear the streets ahead instead?"

Maelia and the others, Rector Aemilia's personal entourage ever since she was young, brought further good news once the rector had settled down. They had rushed ahead, but they were not the only visitors en route. Consul Hiberius had been aware the ban would be lifted long before the official announcement had been made and had sent an entire convoy of supplies and manpower, including a squad from the consul's personal knight order.

"To ensure she could conduct herself in a manner that would not bring shame on the family" was the consul's officially stated intent.

After all she had been through, Rector Aemilia took it in a different way.

She was not abandoned out here, after all.

# 24

# Stealth and Shadows

*"Answer: As ordered, this unit ensured there are no witnesses remaining."*

—An NSLICE unit, during the investigation and revision of NSLICE covert operation protocols.

As NSLICE-00P visited the court, Agedia slithered down into the sewers below Corvanus. Arriving at a particular spot where one of the walls seemed a bit off, she knocked on the wall in a rhythmic pattern.

After a few minutes, part of the wall slid open, and Agedia moved inside to find a dark hallway lit by dim, infrequent torches shaped like skulls.

"You have a lot of nerve showing up here, Agedia the failed knight."

Agedia shrugged. "And you have a lot of nerve being alive, Acorrex the disgraced Brother."

Several spider legs stepped out of the shadows. A man with a human torso on top of a giant spider body emerged.

"It's Dark Father now, thanks to you. And after what you did to our family in Elteno, tell me why I shouldn't kill you where you stand?"

Agedia smirked. "Because if you could, I'd already be dead. Besides, don't pretend you were sad to become the last remaining member of the Dark Family, the only one left to sit at the table."

Acorrex went silent at that. Agedia grabbed a flask from her pocket and took a long swig.

"Now, as to why I'm drinking in the sewers instead of a tavern. I've got crap to do here, and you've got an army of assassins to run. I know the whole 'take care of the Family' crap, but let's be real, you don't care save for the fact that you didn't get to kill them yourself. So, there are two ways this can go down. Option number one: we pick off where the Dark Family and I left off in Elteno, and I rampage through your little murder club a second time. Option number two: we both accept that you are a different organization from them and that you weren't involved in that fight. You don't try to stab me, and I don't tear down everything you've ever built."

She narrowed her eyes on the man. "So, what will it be, *Dark Father*?"

Acorrex held her gaze for a moment before he scoffed. "You are right about one thing. I do have matters to attend to, far more important than one failure who tangled with those fat and lazy weaklings. But take care, failed knight. I may defer the vengeance the Dark Family is due, but that does not mean you are welcome in my city."

Agedia shrugged and took another swig. "I've heard that before. Well, enjoy living in the sewers. *Sitting at the table*; more like sitting under the toilet."

With that, Acorrex faded back into the shadows, and she made her way out of the sewers.

Agedia sighed when she heard what had occurred in the court. Ateia and Taog were panicking in the guest villa's dining room, while NSLICE-00P sat in silence.

"Well, it was well played by the Emperor. Since NSLICE-00P has no personal or family history to speak of, the factions probably couldn't decide whether to treat her as a potential ally or rival. So, the Emperor went and swept her out from under them before they could come to an agreement, and since she put down a rebellion personally, they can't really complain about him moving to reward her quickly. And now, the Emperor holds the key to NSLICE-00P, maybe the first real asset he has to his name."

Ateia gulped as she trembled. "W-What do you mean by that?"

Agedia looked both of them in the eye before pointing at the pair. "NSLICE-00P vetoed any titles or official connections with the Empire, and as she's an Amicitia Populi Elteni, they can't force the issue. But there's a way around that. Give ranks and rights and privileges and, most of all, *duties* to the two people she cares about, and you can control her through them. And now, as inquisitors and Patricians, the Emperor can command you directly, while the senate cannot interfere with you openly. So, as far as the court is concerned, the Emperor now controls NSLICE-00P through you."

Agedia glanced at NSLICE-00P and shrugged. "Well, whether that's actually true is up to the shiny girl, but what matters here is how the court perceives it."

Taog rubbed his chin. On the one hand, he knew NSLICE-00P wouldn't care about the Emperor's orders. On the other . . . she had gotten into fights with the Dobhar and Magister Vibius mostly on their behalf. She had specifically stated their survival was a major directive.

"So we're her vulnerability?"

Agedia nodded. "All attention and focus is on you two now. The Emperor will try to use you to make waves in the court. The factions will attempt to either sneak you out from under him, get an angle on you, or else eliminate any threat you could pose to them."

Ateia gulped. "What do we do?"

Agedia crossed her arms and took a deep breath. "First and foremost, you work things out with the shiny girl. The one thing you possess that everyone wants is NSLICE-00P's ear, and an official mandate to do anything you need to if it has to do with her mission. That means NSLICE-00P can be both your greatest weapon and your greatest weakness, depending entirely on how she reacts. Let me demonstrate."

Agedia turned to NSLICE-00P. "NSLICE-00P, if I said I had a lead regarding one of the people you're looking for and wanted to take Ateia or Taog with me to show them, what would you say?"

"Hypothetical Response: Provided no extenuating circumstances that would increase risk to the friendlies beyond reasonable limits and no higher priority tasks, this unit would request an investigation of the lead."

Agedia turned back to Ateia and Taog and held her hand out. "See? Now I have permission from the girl herself to take you off alone. And since NSLICE-00P agreed to it and it has to do with her mission, I can argue that your mandate now requires you to comply. And once we're off alone, I can do whatever I want to you. So, you all need to figure out how you're going to approach the mission, and how you're going to respond to different situations so that someone can't just manipulate you like that."

NSLICE-00P's robotic eye flickered. "Revelation: Potential for deceit has revealed possible loopholes in this unit's protocols. Adding factor to calculations comparing probability of local leads possessing relevant intel versus the potential threat to the friendlies."

Agedia shrugged. "Well, that's a start."

Ateia furrowed her brow. "But . . . it's not all bad, right? Can't we also use this authority for ourselves?"

Agedia frowned. "Well, yes. You absolutely can. But you need to be aware that just because you have the official authority to do things doesn't mean people will lie down and give you whatever you want. Your actions still have consequences, so you need to pick them wisely."

Ateia nodded. "I know, it's just"—she turned to NSLICE-00P and smiled—"if we can figure out how to deal with this, I can truly help you on your mission, Seero."

"Acknowledgement: Additional authority and resources to pursue the primary direction would be appreciated."

Ateia smiled and nodded again, then turned to Agedia with a serious expression. "Okay, let's figure out what we're going to do."

* * *

And so NSLICE-00P, Ateia, and Taog discussed different scenarios and laid out procedures they would follow. Agedia oversaw and offered advice on occasion, though she tried to let the bunch figure it out for themselves. Estrith was technically participating, but mostly just stood to the side.

Meanwhile, NSLICE-00P also conferred with her other subordinates.

"Query: This unit requests intel regarding stealth measures for covert units. Stealth drones failed to avoid detection in a prior case; this unit has identified a need for additional intelligence to avoid threats to the friendlies."

Lilussees turned over in her hammock while her armor moved one of her legs to rub her mandibles. Now that she had regained the ability to sleep, she found she *loved* this armor. She didn't even have to move anymore; she could just send the command, and the armor would move her body for her! But in regard to the question . . .

"Well, that's like, because they don't have a Sneak skill or something. It, like, applies to all senses, or something."

"Query: How would this unit apply a Sneak skill to autonomous units?"

Lilussees shrugged. "Don't know. I'm, like, not a golem expert, or something."

But NSLICE-00P did, in fact, have a golem expert, and so redirected the question.

Melion bounced in their own room. "Hm, Sneak on a golem, huh? That'd be tricky. Your golems are super neat, Master, but their cores are pretty basic. I think they're more like equipment than monsters, so they don't really get skills. But you found a way to enchant them! So couldn't you do that again?"

"Query: Are there enchantments that can defeat mana detection?"

"There should be! I don't know what they are, though!"

"Acknowledged."

NSLICE-00P analyzed the situation. From Agedia's warnings, searching the local area for the persons of interest could be dangerous due to the political situation, which she lacked the protocols or data to parse effectively. In the end, NSLICE-00P had simply agreed not to allow Ateia and Taog to follow up on any such leads until they acquired more information, and so could guarantee the safety of any such lead. But if no local contacts were fully trustworthy, it fell on NSLICE-00P's own intelligence network to determine the danger levels.

And her intelligence network had been revealed as lacking. Her drone golems had been spotted by an Exploratore with ease in Velusitum. She needed to upgrade their stealth capabilities if she was to rely on them.

Fortunately, she had a clear response to both of these situations. A way to make progress on her primary directive and investigate stealth upgrades for her drones at the same time.

As the Emperor had offered to her, it was time to visit the Imperial Academy Arcanum.

# 25

## The Imperial Academy Arcanum

*"After the Fifth Great Fire of Elteno, the Emperor proposed the creation of a new city belonging to the Imperial Academy Arcanum, where the up-and-coming mages of the Empire could practice their spells in peace . . . far away from the capital city."*

—*The History of the Empire*, by Hostus Tettidius Clodian

The next morning, Princess Caecila arrived at the villa once again.

"I apologize, Miss NSLICE-00P, but we are still deciding what to give you from the treasury. If you don't mind, may I ask you some questions to help us determine what is most suitable for you?"

"Affirmative."

"Thank you."

After speaking with NSLICE-00P for a bit and learning all that NSLICE-00P was authorized to share about her capabilities, Princess Caecila turned to Ateia and Taog.

"We are still arranging for your estates; I apologize for the delay. In the meantime, I would like to offer the services of my tutor to help you acclimate to your new role and status."

Ateia and Taog glanced at each other and then at Agedia, who nodded. They turned back.

"It would be our honor, Your Highness."

Princess Caecila giggled. "Please, call me Caecila, or Princess Caecila if you must. I, too, did not come from a highly prestigious background, so I prefer a more casual address, especially from two inquistors of the Patrician class."

Ateia slowly nodded. "Well, if you insist, Princess Caecila?"

Princess Caecila smiled and nodded, then turned back to NSLICE-00P. "I have been appointed as the Imperial family's liaison to you all, so please do not hesitate to let me know if there's anything I can assist you with."

"Request: This unit would like to conduct research at the Imperial Academy Arcanum. Please guide this unit to the facility."

Princess Caecila nodded. "But of course. The academy is located in its own settlement, so you may wish to prepare for a day trip. Please let me know when you are ready to depart."

A while later, Princess Caecila led the group to the plaustrum subterraneum station, where the Empire's underground transports moved in and out of Corvanus. She brought them aboard the Imperial family's private transport, which sank into the ground and shot forward as NSLICE-00P analyzed the function of the transport. Similar to both the ocean-going vessels and the airship, the craft wrapped a bubble of dirt around itself and launched it forward, pulling itself along with the projectile. As a result, it was not actually digging through the ground itself, but rather moving through it as a magically compatible medium for the spell.

After an hour, the craft broke the surface and reached their destination. Princess Caecila led the group out of the station, and they caught their first sight of Academiae Civitatem.

A Legion keep guarded the entrance to a massive wall that wrapped for miles around. The tips of towers with shining cores on top could be seen peeking over, and NSLICE-00P detected powerful barriers protecting the wall and the air above. On their side of the wall was a small city. This was Academiae Civitatem, home to the Imperial Academy Arcanum, the largest such academy in the Northern Empire.

Princess Caecila led them past the gate and into the academy proper. What they found was practically a second city, with countless buildings and roads spread out within the walls. The princess pointed out the Theoretical Academy to their right, with densely packed structures housing libraries and classrooms containing the gathered mystical knowledge of the Empire. The left side was spread out, with large courtyards and glowing barriers breaking up the large structures. NSLICE-00P caught sight of young mages casting basic spells under the tutelage of an older instructor, and Princess Caecila explained this was the Applied Academy, where mages practiced their craft and tested the hypotheses of the Theoretical side. It was also perhaps the most heavily warded location in the Empire. Magical experimentation was often messy, particularly if conducted within a population center.

Princess Caecila led the group into a reception area. A middle-aged receptionist scoffed at first, until she recognized Princess Caecila and rushed to apologize. A few minutes later, the Magister Arcanum himself arrived, a wiry old man wearing colorful robes and jewelry with glowing gems.

"Greetings to you, Your Highness Princess Caecila."

"Greetings to you, Magister Arcanum Cnaeus Marcius Volusenus."

Magister Cnaeus glanced around at the group, raising an eyebrow. "May I ask the purpose of your visit today?"

Princess Caecila nodded, motioning. "I am here to present NSLICE-00P, queen of the Dobhar and Amicitia Populi Elteni. She has some personal research to conduct here, and we would like to share the knowledge of the Empire with her."

Magister Cnaeus nodded, though his eyebrow remained raised. "But of course. We have prepared an assistant, as ordered by the Emperor. Apprentice Callisunus, come here."

Apprentice Callisunus was a young man, about Ateia and Taog's age or just a bit younger. He was on the shorter side, and a bit frail at first glance.

Princess Caecila raised an eyebrow. "An apprentice? NSLICE-00P is an Imperial friend the Empire owes a great debt to, Magister. The Emperor expects no effort to be spared in assisting her."

Magister Cnaeus waved his hand. "Be at ease, Your Highness. Apprentice Callisunus has had trouble advancing due to struggles with practical application, but he's very well-versed in the academy's facilities, perhaps more so than many a senior magus. I have no doubt he will be able to attend to any need our guest may have. Now, if you'll excuse me, I am to oversee an experiment. I apologize, but the matter is both delicate and time sensitive."

With that, Magister Cnaeus left, leaving the bunch with the apprentice. Apprentice Callisunus stepped forward with a frown on his face.

"Greetings, Your Highness. I'm Apprentice Nonus Aedinius Callisunus. I'm sorry for the magister; he doesn't like it when outsiders come to the academy. But I definitely know my way around, so I should be able to help you." He then frowned. "Well, as long as you don't need practical help, that is."

Princess Caecila smiled and nodded. "I understand, Apprentice Callisunus. I will talk with the magister if necessary, but let's check with my charge first. This is NSLICE-00P, a friend of the Empire we wish to assist. NSLICE-00P, will Apprentice Callisunus's help be sufficient for you?"

NSLICE-00P's robotic eye flickered as she looked over Apprentice Callisunus; she detected an anomaly in the boy's mana that seemed to disrupt its flow through his body. As stated, he would likely be unable to assist with any practical applications of mana.

But that was irrelevant to NSLICE-00P.

"Response: This unit has logged Apprentice Callisunus's inefficiency at practical application and will account for this in future calculations. At the moment, this unit's priority is access to theoretical knowledge and data from prior experimentation. If Apprentice Callisunus can provide said data, this unit finds said assistance sufficient."

Apprentice Callisunus sighed at that, nodding. "Right . . . Well, do you know what you're looking for? I could show you to the library, or if you have a specific question, we could check with the appropriate department?"

"Response: This unit is investigating the Banishment spell, the Divination spell, the fundamental nature of mana and its relationship to the foreign system and the physics of this location, and stealth enchantments; particularly enchantments that would conceal a unit's mana signature."

Apprentice Callisunus blinked a few times. "Well . . . that's quite a spread. Um, maybe we should start with the library, then?"

"Affirmative."

"Well, this way."

Leading them out of the reception hall, they walked down the streets of the academy toward one of the largest buildings in the area. Inside, they found a wide-open area with tables and scroll holders for easy reading. Around the wide area were towering shelves filled to the brim with scrolls and books. NSLICE-00P calculated that, despite the massive size of the structure, the interior was even larger than should be possible.

A woman walked up to them; a towering, nine-foot-tall woman with massive muscles under her mage's robes and a scar over her eye. She crossed her arms and scowled at the group.

"Apprentice Callisunus, here to research again?"

Apprentice Callisunus shook his head. "Hello, Librarian Volaginia. No, I'm guiding Princess Caecila and a friend of the Empire."

Librarian Volaginia looked them over. "Well, you know the rules. Make sure they follow them, princess or not."

"Of course. Thank you." Apprentice Callisunus nodded.

Librarian Volaginia nodded back and left while he turned to the group. "That's Librarian Volaginia. She doesn't mess around when it comes to the library, but she's actually pretty nice if you follow the rules."

Ateia gulped. "And, um, what are the rules?"

Apprentice Callisunus rubbed his chin. "Well, if you want to get detailed, there are over a hundred, but I find it boils down to two main things. Don't cause a ruckus, and don't harm the material. If you avoid those, you should be fine."

Ateia glanced at the librarian. "And, um, what happens if you break them?"

He smirked. "Librarian Volaginia casts her special Fist spell."

Chuckling at the group's faces, he turned to NSLICE-00P. "Come on, then. Hm, given what you said, maybe we should start with general lore and the basics of mana? That section should be over here. *An Introduction to Mana* by Julianus the Red is the academy's recommendation, but I find Braemmass's *Mystic Arts for Imbeciles* to be more informative if you can get past a Sun Elf author and his more . . . eccentric prose . . ."

* * *

A few minutes later, Apprentice Callisunus was staring with his mouth wide open, along with Princess Caecila and her entourage. As were several other mages who had stopped their own research to gape.

NSLICE-00P sat at one of the tables, a scroll reader in front of her, with two stacks of scrolls to either side of her. Placing a scroll from one pile in the reader, she spun it as fast as she could, her robotic eye flickering the entire time. Within a minute, she had gone through its entirety. She then released it from the reader and placed it on the other pile. Ateia returned and grabbed a bunch of the scrolls to put back on the shelves while Taog brought in a new batch.

"Not a ton on Holy Magic, it seems, but here's what I found, Seero."

"Acknowledgement: This unit thanks friendlies Ateia and Taog for the assistance."

Apprentice Callisunus finally closed his mouth. "What . . . What are you even doing?"

"Answer: Reading."

Apprentice Callisunus narrowed his eyes. "Really? That fast? Let me see that."

He grabbed a scroll from Ateia and opened it up. "Okay, what are Aulus Hosidius Fulvianus's thoughts on the Source?"

"Recitation: Others believe the Source is some sort of power generator, like a mana core at a universal scale. I prefer to think of it more as a big, tangled ball of mana-wana stuff. That is to say that the Source is not some constant flow like a waterfall. It is significantly more chaotic than any mana core we have observed. The mana there is unattributed, but that doesn't mean it is homogenous. All attempts to reach the base Source, beyond the Realms of Mana, have experienced unintended side effects to every action taken. This leads me to believe the mana is connected, *tangled up*, and flowing in ways we cannot yet determine. As a result, it is impossible to predict the exact outcome from applying any given stimuli to the base Source—"

Apprentice Callisunus's eyes widened. "Oh, okay. You've made your point."

He glanced over at Librarian Volaginia, who was watching with her arms crossed. She shrugged. "If she's reading, she's reading. Don't disturb the readers."

With that, she glared at the observers, who jumped and returned to their own studies.

Apprentice Callisunus shook his head. "What exactly is she?"

Princess Caecila did not respond.

# 26

# Analyze the Other World!

*"Other worlds? Parallel universes? Alternate timelines? Rubbish. Even after all we have seen, I have found no evidence that anything exists outside of the known universe. All speculation to the contrary is mere fantasy, and I will not have my time wasted on such things. I work with science, not science fiction."*

—Dr. Ottosen, in a meeting regarding possible Non-Standard threats.

NSLICE-00P sat at the table with her robotic eye flickering. Having gathered a significant amount of data at this point, she was taking a moment to compile and analyze it. Ateia, Taog, Princess Caecila, and Apprentice Callisunus were reading their own material.

Soon, the results were in . . . and the success probability of her primary directive dropped significantly, because by her predictions . . . there was a ninety percent probability that this world was unrelated to Earth, to the point of not residing in the same universe.

The Empire's records on mana had made it clear: mana was a foundational energy type in this universe. Everything in it: matter, energy, and even fundamental forces, interacted with and often depended on mana here. Every living thing as well had mana in it, and there were records that life struggled to survive in low-mana conditions. Likewise, the laws of physics simply *wouldn't work* in this world if mana was not involved, least of all achieving Earthlike conditions on what appeared to be a flat planetary body . . . assuming astronomy and the idea of planetary bodies were even relevant here. On the other hand, her original world had mana, but only in small, isolated quantities. A tiny fraction of a percent of living things and matter possessed it, and the entire rest of the universe did not. Yet, the rest of the universe went on, and life had no trouble existing. The two planets, and likely universes, acted under fundamentally different conditions.

That was not necessarily conclusive proof that they were separate, but NSLICE-00P had not discovered any records that would imply a connection of any sort. All instances of an individual arriving from a "different world" referred to beings from the Realms of Mana, which were even more mana saturated and mana dependent than this world, and so even less likely to be related to Earth. Likewise, there were no shared cultural references, and the maps of this world did not match any she had on record for Earth, so the probability of someone else from Earth having traveled here was extremely low.

There, of course, existed the possibility of a more subtle connection—parallel universes, universes within other universes, a distant past or future so dramatically different it could not be identified as the same thing—but all of that was irrelevant. NSLICE-00P was a combat enforcer, not a research computer solving theoretical problems. A connection that did not provide a reasonable travel path was irrelevant to her primary directive.

And that was the point. It was extremely unlikely any of the persons of interest were located in this world, or in places that she could reach via conventional travel methods. It was, therefore, extremely unlikely she would find them in this world, even with the full assistance of the Empire or any other local factions. For all practical purposes, from now on, she should assume she was in a different universe entirely.

The one major counterpoint had been the Banishment spell failing to work on her . . . but she had learned more about that spell as well. Every time the Banishment spell had been recorded in use, it had been used on a being from the Realms of Mana or a dungeon monster roaming outside their home. It had never been successfully used on a human target. Its failure to work on her could not be taken as proof that this world was equivalent to her origin point.

Which meant that the most efficient course of action, and potentially the only course of action that could fulfill her primary directive, was to search for a way to leave this universe and return to her own.

At that point, the efficacy of her emotional controls dropped, and her heart rate increased once again. She evaluated her organic components before applying the Calm spell to shore up the controls. It appeared her organic components were concerned about both the infeasibility of achieving the primary directive, but also about leaving this universe, largely because of the major directive to protect Ateia and Taog. However, at the very least, the latter concern was simple to resolve. Leaving the world did not require her to abandon the major directive. She could simply bring the friendlies with her if their own protocols would allow for that. Even if not, it was not strictly necessary for her to physically leave this world. Even just reestablishing communications with Earth would be sufficient to locate a suitable commander.

However, this brought up a point her cybernetic half needed to evaluate. The major directive may not be fully compatible with her primary directive at some point in the future.

Ateia and Taog were assisting by utilizing their local authority to mobilize the Empire's resources on her behalf . . . but at this point, local searches by the Empire were not predicted to be successful. Access to theoretical data, especially regarding magic, could still be useful, but NSLICE-00P could not predict whether that data would result in any positive outcomes.

And as demonstrated just now, her organic components might actively interfere with efforts to pursue her primary directive should such efforts violate the major directive. Even indirectly, she had spent time protecting the friendlies that could have been spent on continued investigations, a decision that would not have been made without the major directive. And even though the primary directive should take precedence . . . her organic components had proven they could defy her protocols.

So, the major directive was now imposing an opportunity cost on the primary directive . . . and could interfere directly in the worst case.

But the organic components refused to even consider removing the directive. Despite the fact that the emotional controls were still active and reinforced by Calm, the organic components were still capable of resistance. It appeared that this directive went deeper than a basic emotional reaction and would remain active even without an emotional response.

Which was the point, after all. NSLICE-00P had not added this directive based on the friendlies' contributions to the primary directive. She had added it so that her cybernetic side could preemptively account for her organic component's reactions and so avoid drops in organic component efficiency, or in the worst case, a reevaluation loop like she'd experienced earlier. The inefficiency introduced by the major directive was still less than that of rerunning the same calculation over and over.

And even if it wasn't, her cybernetic components had never even considered *removing* a directive before. Directives were high-priority, long-term missions designed to guide her overall decision-making. They were originally hard-coded restrictions not to be changed. She could even refuse an order by an authority if it violated a higher-priority directive.

It was a significant break in procedure to add new directives on her own. If not for the fact that she had been left alone with no primary directive, she would not have done even that. To remove such a restriction? To intentionally abandon a high-priority, long-term mission?

She would only consider that under the direst of circumstances.

So instead, she took a look at why her organic components were acting this way and came to a startling conclusion. By all evidence, her organic components had formed an emotional attachment. She was aware that noncybernetically leashed organic units could form such things amongst themselves. These attachments would cause them to value other units more highly than their contributions to major directives would justify, which was exactly what appeared to be occurring with her own components. It changed a significant fundamental assumption of her protocols that such things could occur within a leashed-intelligence unit, but that could be a result of her faulty emotional controls.

Unfortunately, her protocols only went as far as describing outward signs of such attachments and how she might exploit them in combat to take down high-priority targets or coerce a surrender. They did not explain the nature of the attachment itself, or what to do if one formed, as it had been assumed the emotional controls would prevent such things in the first place. And her last commander had not appeared opposed to these attachments either, so had given no orders or protocols that might assist her in this matter.

It was up to her to determine what the response to this should be, and how she could ensure it would not interfere with her primary directive. To which her organic components raised a point that caused her processors to stall for a moment.

Did she *need* to fulfill the primary directive at this stage?

After all, the point of the primary directive was to locate a commander and integrate back into a network. But she now had an NSLICE network and had designated herself as acting commander. In that way, she was already integrated into a network that had a commander.

But her cybernetic components immediately discarded this. She was the lead unit of the network, yes, but she was not a true commander. She could expand the NSLICE network's general military, logistical, and search capabilities, but she could not determine an overall objective. She could not produce orders to be followed. If she did not find a commander, the network would be left without purpose. She would have no way to evaluate the efficacy or desirability of any given outcome, and so could not make consistent and rational decisions. She needed a primary directive. She would not defy her last commander's final order.

And threats to the primary directive would be terminated.

The organic components withdrew the proposal. In the end, both sides came to the same conclusion. Neither would interfere with the other's directives for the time being, as constantly looping evaluations of her own directives were not an efficient use of time. The primary directive would proceed; the major directive would remain. She would investigate methods by which to reestablish contact with her former world while ensuring the safety of the friendlies. The decision of what to do should she gain the ability to leave this world would be deferred until such a possibility existed.

And so, once again, NSLICE-00P tabled that analysis. The problem of her organic components and their emotional attachment to the friendlies was concerning . . . but also irrelevant if she did not have a method of contacting Earth in the first place. So, the most efficient use of her time was to proceed with her investigations.

She turned her head to Apprentice Callisunus further down the table.

"Query: Does Apprentice Callisunus possess any data regarding separate universes?"

## INTERLUDE

# Investigations

A mage sat in a small office, poring over a scroll. He had brown skin, golden hair, and slightly pointed ears indicating his Sun Elf heritage. This was Faustus Petronius Acacius, a theoretical expert on the summoning arts.

Suddenly, there was a knock on the door. Faustus glanced at his schedule, but it did not appear he had forgotten anything, so this was unexpected.

"Come in."

Faustus blinked as Apprentice Callisunus led an armored soldier of some kind into the room, not someone Faustus had seen before.

"Ah, Nonus, my boy, come in, come in. May I ask who your companion is?"

"Thank you, Mage Faustus. This is NSLICE-00P, a visiting Amicitia Populi Elteni. She had some questions for you, if you don't mind."

Faustus directed a sympathetic smile toward Apprentice Callisunus. No mage liked to entertain political guests, but Apprentice Callisunus drew the short stick more often than not, something Faustus was familiar with; his Sun Elf parentage was somewhat controversial in this part of the Empire. He supposed it didn't help that he was the presiding expert on summoning and the Realms of Mana; it made it all too easy for others to imagine him as some sort of crazy cultist.

He shook his head before his mind wandered too far and turned his attention to the guest. Political necessities aside, he appreciated inquisitive minds and would do his best to satisfy her curiosity. Though, he generally knew what kind of questions a visitor would ask someone like him. High-ranking officials always imagined armies of summoned beings, or beautiful servants from beyond attending to their every need, or drawing endless mana from the Source to become invincible sorcerers.

"Hello, Miss NSLICE-00P. I am Magus Major Faustus Petronius Acacius."

"Greetings: This unit is designated NSLICE-00P. It is nice to meet you."

Faustus could not help but smile. It was not often for someone to greet him without hesitation.

"Nice to meet you too. Now, how may I assist you today?"

"Query: Does Magus Major Faustus Petronius Acacius possess any data regarding different universes and the means to contact them?"

Faustus blinked. That . . . was not the question he was expecting.

"Different universes, you say? Do you mean the Realms of Mana?"

"Negative. Clarification: A second universe similar to the surrounding one. Specific parameters would include a 99.99 percent reduction in the frequency and density of mana, as well as the following physical properties . . ."

Faustus rubbed his chin as NSLICE-00P listed a bunch of numbers he didn't understand.

"So you mean . . . a second Material Plane? But separate from the first? And one where mana barely exists?"

"Affirmative."

Faustus's eyes widened. "Fascinating . . ."

He stood up and paced around his office for a bit with his hand on his chin, muttering to himself. After a bit, he sat back down.

"I can't say I've ever heard of a second Material Plane, so I do not know anything specific. And the idea of a manaless world . . . Well, that has largely belonged in the realm of fiction beyond a few thought experiments. But . . . there have been at least a few proposals regarding new worlds. Nonus, my boy, could you fetch us Ithruidh's *A Peek Into the Void*? Somewhat difficult to parse, that one, but if I recall correctly, there was a passage that may be relevant."

Faustus spent quite some time speaking with NSLICE-00P, investigating as many leads as he could think of at present. Unlike his fears, NSLICE-00P was practical and inquisitive. She did not waste time with grandstanding or arrogance, simply asking her questions directly and accepting his answers without bluster. He quite enjoyed the time, and the problem she had posed for him.

A second, manaless Material Plane. Most mages would have dismissed such things as fantasy, but Faustus knew how strange reality could get outside of the boundaries of the world. And NSLICE-00P had described this hypothetical plane in exacting detail, down to the biology of the creatures that had to survive without mana. It was as if she had been to such a place herself and recorded everything with immaculate precision. She painted such a vibrant and internally consistent picture that Faustus found himself believing that such a place could actually exist.

And should he actually discover proof of such a thing, it would be a revolution. Other worlds outside of either the watch of the Aesdes or the influence of the Realms of Mana? Worlds with different properties down to the most fundamental forces of reality?

It was certainly worth a look, at the very least.

He would have to keep looking, however, as he had no answer himself or in the materials he could recall.

Eventually, Princess Caecila herself came to fetch NSLICE-00P, and she departed for the night. But Faustus promised to continue his own investigation, and to consult with some of his peers.

So, he took out a letter and began to write. He had an anonymous correspondent he exchanged regular letters with on various theoretical subjects. He had never met them before, but their insights into his field could not be matched. If anyone might have a hint regarding this puzzle, it would be them . . .

Consul Gallus Albanius Noxisius sat upon the small throne in his villa's reception hall. The hall was decorated with artwork from the early Empire, even a piece or two from Elteno's city-state days, when it was still ruled by the senate. Men and women in togas and stolas stood around the hall while one man shouted and stomped around.

"An outsider, granted an audience with the Empire and access to our secrets? Two *frontiersfolk* elevated to Patrician? This is an outrage! Is Lucius mad? What is the man thinking?!"

Another man rolled his eyes at the display. "What he's thinking is that this person is clearly very powerful, and he wants her for himself."

The original speaker scoffed. "I doubt that. Her feats are *clearly* exaggerated! If the 'dreaded' Sun Elves can't take on a Legion, how could this person we've never heard of do so? I say it is a poorly conceived play by Consul Hiberius to retrieve his disgrace of a daughter from Turannia; only the Aesdes know why he would bother."

The responder's eyes narrowed. "Hold your tongue; you go too far, Tertius. Consul Hiberius has long been a distinguished member of Elteni society from a venerable and distinguished line, who has guided the Northern Court for many years. The misadventures of his progeny aside, it would not do to slander his name."

Tertius waved around. "And where is the venerable and distinguished consul now? He has all but abandoned the job to Consul Noxisius and let the Empire fall to ruin over his personal grudge! And now he opens the gates to a foreigner! His judgment is clouded, as is the Emperor's. Consul Noxisius, something must be done!"

All eyes turned to the consul, who rubbed his chin and nodded. "This move by the Emperor is unexpected, and an alarming breach of decorum, but let us consider the facts. NSLICE-00P is an Amicitia Populi Elteni whom the Emperor claims we owe a debt to, and the two Turannians are now Imperial inquisitors, the first Emperor Lucius has ever appointed. Whoever they are and whether their abilities are exaggerated or not, it is clear the Emperor considers them important and is staking his future upon them. That is something we must take into consideration."

Everyone fell silent. The responder asked, "Then, what should we do, Consul?"

Consul Noxisius thought for a moment longer. "It is only natural that the barbarian and the frontiersman should come to the Empire. Who would not wish to partake in our culture and might? The Empire has integrated more than one savage tribe into our ranks. These people may have the Emperor's ear, but they do not know how things are done here. We should welcome them in and give them proper tutelage on our ways. We will not hold their ignorance against them but guide them as a good Elteni should. Such is the way of the Empire."

An armored legionnaire stepped into the office of Magister Utriusque Militia Septimus Vipstanus Verrucosis. The office was decorated with all sorts of trophies, including mounted skulls from deadly monsters, the personal weapons of barbarian chiefs, and medals bestowed by the Emperor.

And at a desk at the end of the office sat the magister himself, a plump man pushing his armor to the limit as he chewed on a plate of sausages and cheese. Magister Verrucosis had a long and distinguished career . . . despite the fact that the legionnaire couldn't actually recall seeing him at several of the battles he claimed to have participated in.

But the officer knew his place, and it was not to question his superiors save for decisions with dire consequences. And he knew that whatever the case, Magister Verrucosis loved the Legion and would fight on its behalf in the political battlefield most soldiers could never enter.

The officer saluted and stood at attention. "Magister Peditum Decius Considius Ausonius, ready to report, sir."

Magister Verrucosis put aside his meal and wiped his mouth before sitting up straight.

"What is the news, Magister Peditum?"

"Reports have come in from Legate Dubitatius of the Velusitum limitanei and Legate Seneca of the Legio Utrad XIII. The rumors are, for all intents and purposes, true. NSLICE-00P, Amicitia Populi Elteni and queen of the Dobhar, was personally and solely responsible for Caelinus's defeat."

Magister Verrucosis frowned. "We're trusting the word of traitors here?"

Magister Ausonius nodded. "Legate Dubitatius never officially joined the rebellion, though I believe that is more because Caelinus never arrived at his city. Legate Seneca, for her part, remained defending the border and turned herself in once the rebellion had concluded. After cross-referencing with testimonies from eyewitnesses among the rank and file and captured rebels, I believe their reports are credible."

Magister Verrucosis sighed before slammed his fist on his desk. "Hang that woman, then! This was our moment to show the power of our Imperial Legions and bring that traitor Caelinus to justice! How dare she take that from us!"

Magister Ausonius waited patiently as Magister Verrucosis cursed for a bit.

"Magister Ausonius, I want you to find out what she can do and draw up plans to bring her down. She is clearly a serious threat to the Empire, and I want us ready to handle it."

Magister Ausonius saluted. "Yes, sir. May I offer a suggestion?"

Magister Verrucosis raised an eyebrow. "What is it?"

"This NSLICE-00P has displayed loyalty to the Empire even as just a friend; more loyalty than some of our own, I'm ashamed to admit. I imagine she might be amenable to cooperation, and the Legion could benefit significantly from her assistance. In the worst case, if we learn what she did in Utrad from the source itself, we could determine what Caelinus did wrong and adjust our own strategy."

Magister Verrucosis frowned but rubbed his chin. Eventually, he started to nod . . . and grin.

"Yes, I can see that. If she were willing to fall under my command, she could be a powerful asset. Very well, Magister Ausonius, I grant you leave to handle this matter as you best see fit. If she is willing to acknowledge our authority and fall in line, then secure her cooperation. If not, then prepare to deal with her."

Magister Ausonius saluted once again. "As you command, sir."

A banquet hall was filled to the brim. People of all shapes, sizes, and species mingled around while musicians played an upbeat tune. A table was filled to the brim with all manner of exotic dishes, and servants kept up a constant flow of wine. A handsome man lounged on a couch at the edge of the room, sipping from his cup as he held a woman close.

A merchant stood before him, holding a piece of jewelry for the man to see. Aedile Lar Paesentius Hortensus frowned and nodded as the man spoke before breaking out into a wide smile.

"I believe we have a deal. You drive a hard bargain."

The merchant smiled, and Aedile Hortensus shook his hand. The merchant then returned to the party while Aedile Hortensus whispered to the woman by his side. "The price is exorbitant, but the craftsmanship is the real deal. I want his supplier."

She giggled. "It shall be done. By the way, how do you feel about the Emperor's new friend?"

Aedile Hortensus smiled and greeted the next guest before whispering back, "Continue the investigation, but don't make any moves yet."

She smiled at their next guest as she replied. "Is that wise? If we wait, she might end up with prior engagements?"

Aedile Hortensus took a sip from his cup. "Oh, I'm counting on it. This one has come from afar, it appears; I imagine she has her own way of doing things. I have a feeling it would not do to be hasty. Let us observe what happens to those who are."

"As you wish."

# 27

# Just Give This Unit a Little Space

*"All Spatial Magic shall be restricted as Class Five materials."*

—Imperial decree by Emperor Spurius, after the Great Cleaving incident.

After NSLICE-00P and the others returned to the villa, Princess Caecila separated from them, then after a quick organic refueling, NSLICE-00P returned to her room.

It was time to reevaluate her approach based on the newly acquired intel.

Consulting the academy's library and an expert on the topic of other realms implied that no specific knowledge regarding other universes was common within the Empire. The expert had stated he had peers he wanted to consult, and she had not gone through every scroll in the library, but her calculations predicted at least some reference or evidence might have appeared by now if the Empire had been exposed to the topic. The expert, at least, appeared to treat it as a novel idea, implying a lack of formal investigation.

There was also classified intel she did not yet have access to. Apprentice Callisunus had explained the classification levels. Class Three, which she had unrestricted access to, referred to standard military-grade spells and other information that wouldn't be general public knowledge, but accessible to anyone within the military hierarchy. Class Four and above were where knowledge became need-to-know. Apprentice Callisunus and Magus Major Faustus were submitting an application on her behalf to access anything related to her primary directive, but it would remain to be seen if authorization would be granted.

NSLICE-00P had considered attempting to access the restricted data on her own, but she had been originally programmed to respect compartmentalization of intel. That, of course, did not apply when considering data that might be critical to her primary directive, but the point remained that she needed to justify the necessity of accessing said intel before breaking the data access procedures of a neutral entity. She did not know if the restricted data had any relevance to her primary directive at all at this stage, and so could not justify any action which might be construed as hostile.

Likewise, since all the data was stored on physical hard copies and protected by mana-based means, NSLICE-00P was not sure she *could* access the restricted sections, at least not while avoiding detection. The risk of provoking the Empire was deemed greater than the potential benefit of such a move, particularly when she already had significant connections to Imperial authorities.

In any case, the investigation of the Empire's knowledge base regarding other universes was now pending action by Imperial units, and not guaranteed or even likely to produce positive results. Additional investigations would require either contact with additional entities beyond the Imperial Academy Arcanum, or else personal experimentation.

Personal experimentation was the only one she could perform at present, so she proceeded with that task. Opening up the foreign system, she began reviewing the available options, searching for anything that might have relevance to this topic.

She found something, but there was a bit of a problem.

| Available Perks → Schools of Magic | |
|---|---|
| Name | Cost |
| Spatial Magic | 300 |

Even NSLICE-00P could not afford that at present. Her observations of the foreign system and the rate at which Personal perk points accumulated implied such an expenditure wasn't practically possible for the vast majority of this world's inhabitants. So, either this field of magic was largely inaccessible or, more likely, she was missing necessary prerequisites. She had observed that the system considered the user's current knowledge, capabilities, and feats when displaying the cost of a particular skill, so the latter was entirely possible. She decided she would inquire about this at the academy and investigate how she could reduce the cost.

Next, she checked the Dungeon section of the menu . . . but found nothing directly relevant. Rattingtale, Lilussees, and Melion informed her there were options for portals and teleportation traps, but NSLICE-00P didn't appear to have access to any just yet. The others informed her these were generally used to move between dungeon rooms, so the fact that the Rooms menu was locked for her might have restricted such options.

She would have to follow up on Spatial Magic to make any progress, it seemed.

The next day, NSLICE-00P returned to the academy with Princess Caecila and the others, where Apprentice Callisunus led her to Magus Major Faustus once again.

Faustus rubbed his chin. "Spatial Magic, you say? I'm afraid I must admit I know little on the topic."

"Query: Spatial manipulation is not related to summoning entities from alternate mana-based locations?"

Faustus nodded at that. "That is correct. Summoners don't interact with the Material Plane at all when plying our craft beyond the boundary between the Material Plane and the Realms of Mana, which as far as I'm aware is something of a separate entity from either. I would imagine Spatial mages would need to know about that boundary as we do, but that is only one small subset of the knowledge needed for such complex magic. I will freely admit that Summoning, while by no means easy, is noticeably more straightforward than Spatial Magic. Now, executing a summoning *safely* and producing the outcome one desires is another beast entirely, but presents a different type of challenge from the sheer complexity of Spatial Magic."

"Request: Please guide this unit to the nearest expert on Spatial Magic."

Faustus hummed. "That's an equally difficult question, I'm afraid. There are but a handful of such mages across the entire Empire, and none in the North that I'm aware of. I hear there may be one or two in the south; if there are any in the east, they are kept closely under guard."

NSLICE-00P's robotic eye flickered. Between lessons from Ateia and Taog over the course of their travels and reading the various scrolls in the library, NSLICE-00P now had an overview of the Empire as a whole. The Empire was split into three separate regions that were effectively run as a confederation of three allied powers. Two equal Emperors now ruled from the Northern and Eastern Courts, while the south was home to a collection of Imperial allies that were nominally independent though practically integrated into the Empire in most aspects save governance. The ruler of the most important of those allies, the kingdom of Mirima, was an Amicitia Populi Elteni and considered a peer of the two Emperors. Traveling between these three realms presented no issue, but decrees made by one court would not necessarily be honored by the others. She could not count on the level of support in the South or East that she could in the North at the moment.

She calculated she should therefore exhaust all leads available in the North before searching for Spatial experts in the south or east.

"Request: Does the Imperial Academy Arcanum possess any data on Spatial Magic or on the prerequisites to acquire it?"

Faustus frowned. "I'm not entirely certain; there are almost certainly scrolls on the subject, but these are at Class Five at minimum, so would require permission from both the archmage and the Northern Court to access. I do know that in the past there were archmages who could use the magic. Perhaps a general increase in mystical knowledge will assist?"

Princess Caecila frowned as well. "The Emperor would be happy to assist, of course, but the court may need to convene over access to Class Five materials. I will speak with the Emperor on the matter."

"Acknowledged."

NSLICE-00P's robotic eye flickered as she calculated her next course of action. Since knowledge on Spatial Magic was restricted, it was also now pending on Imperial data access procedures.

That left Faustus's suggestion of a general expansion of her magical knowledge. NSLICE-00P evaluated this and found it a reasonable proposal. Her experiences with Banishment and Divination revealed there was a great deal she had yet to learn regarding magic circles and the general means of applying mana, so the issue could be that she was lacking a sufficient foundation.

In the worst case, expansion of her magical knowledge would expand her capabilities and the capabilities of her NSLICE network, with benefits for the major directives via opportunities to boost her friendlies' capabilities as well. In fact, if she could ensure that the friendlies' safety would be guaranteed without her immediate presence, she would be able to divert all her attention to the primary directive. Since she was waiting on third parties for the primary directive investigations, it would be efficient to devote her short-term efforts to achieving this. Her organic components also agreed to the idea of upgrading the friendlies.

It was then that Fulcinia stepped into the room. "Your Highness, I apologize for my interruption, but we've received a message from the Magister Exploratore per Corvanus for NSLICE-00P. He appears to have some information on her request."

Agedia was singing in the middle of a tavern, swaying along with two of the other patrons as they sang their drunken songs, when the door opened, and a man wearing the cloak of an Exploratore walked in. He turned toward her and began to approach.

Agedia's smile dropped as her eyes narrowed. "No."

The man shrugged. "I've been told to inform you that he'll open a bottle of Celestial wine."

Agedia froze. She trembled. She muttered to herself.

She finally sighed. "Fine. Let's get this over with."

One drunken slither across the city later, and Agedia found herself before the office of the Magister Exploratore per Corvanus, the boss of every Exploratore in the Northern Empire. He also happened to be her uncle, and one of the last people Agedia wanted to see.

But, in the end, Agedia had returned to Corvanus of her own free will and had someone she needed to protect. She could not do that while refusing to speak to the man running the Northern Empire's intelligence. So, she took a deep breath and opened the door.

Her uncle looked up from his work and gave a sad smile.

"Hello, Agedia, I—"

She held out her hand. "Wine."

He sighed but reached under his desk, pulling out a bottle. He silently poured her a cup and placed it at the other side of his desk. She didn't say a word as she took a seat and downed the cup.

Neither spoke for about half an hour as Agedia drained the extraordinarily expensive bottle of wine. She then glared at him with sharp, focused eyes, not even a hint of a flush on her cheeks.

"Alright, Uncle Appius, you got me here. Now, what do you want? Don't want the disgrace of the family to be seen dirtying the floors of the family's pride."

Appius sighed at that. "You're too hard on yourself, Agedia. You know my door is always open to you."

She scoffed. "Please look at my eyes instead of my lance when you say that. Your door is always open to any asset you might make use of."

Appius frowned. "I . . . guess I deserve that. And . . . I wanted to apologize—"

Agedia held up her hand. "Cut that out. I'm in *no* mood to talk about the past, least of all to you. No apology will ever bring her back, and so no apology will ever be enough. Let's just get on with it."

Appius's shoulder's slumped, and his head hung low as he heaved another sigh. "Very well. I've called you here to speak about your charge, one Ateia Niraemia of Turannia. I suppose I should call her Inquisitor Ateia now."

Agedia immediately narrowed her eyes, so Appius held up his hands.

"I mean no harm, and to be honest, you had to know this was coming, right? The Emperor has ordered me to investigate a group of people on behalf of an Amicitia Populi Elteni, with two Imperial inquisitors mandated to back her up. Most of those names are ones I've never heard of, but strangely, there's one included that is *extremely* familiar to me. And next thing I know, you arrive in Corvanus alongside Inquisitor Ateia. As much as I hoped to reconcile with you, I knew there was only one reason you would ever return to the Imperial Heartland."

Agedia began reaching for the lance on her back. "I will kill you if you touch her."

Appius kept his hands up. He had a sad expression on his face but held Agedia's gaze. "I know you will. And I promise you, truly, that I have no plans for the girl and no intention to make any. But there are people who would, if they knew of her true identity, and the girl is now on center stage regardless of what either of us do. So, we should at least coordinate our next moves to keep her away from their hands."

Agedia glared at him for a while longer before finally relaxing.

"Fine."

# 28

# Picking Up the Trail

*"If I knew where all my Exploratores were, then the enemy could find out too! It's called compartmentalization. No one can spill all the secrets because no one knows all the secrets. Not even me!"*

—Magister Exploratore per Corvanus Vorenia Pompolussa, after an audit revealed multiple gaps in her budget report.

NSLICE-00P immediately prioritized intel relevant to the primary directive, and so the group bid farewell to the academy once again. They returned to Corvanus, where Princess Caecila led them to the Exploratores HQ. The Exploratores Headquarters in Corvanus was not a single building like in Turannia, or even a compound like in Utrad; here, it occupied an entire street. There were multiple villas to house Exploratores, a large store for the purchase and sale of monster parts and magic cores, a hospital, a training facility, and a multistoried office building solely for administration, among others. Princess Caecila led them to the latter office, where an assistant came to meet them.

"I apologize, Your Highness, but Magister Exploratore Appius requests to meet with NSLICE-00P and the Imperial inquisitors in private."

Princess Caecila frowned, raising an eyebrow. "This is highly unusual; the Emperor himself has commanded me as the Amicitia Populi Elteni's guide. I must ask the rationale for such a request."

The assistant lowered their head. "I apologize. The information he has is highly classified. He says he would require a direct order from the Emperor to share it with anyone else, even a member of the Imperial family."

Princess Caecila stared at the assistant for a moment, then sighed. "I will honor his request for the time being. Please inform him of my presence, and that the Imperial family wishes to personally ensure NSLICE-00P receives the highest hospitality."

The assistant nodded. "Of course, Your Highness."

Princess Caecila glanced at NSLICE-00P one more time before the assistant opened the door for the group and then led Princess Caecila to a guest room. NSLICE-00P, Ateia, Taog, and Estrith entered alone.

Inside, NSLICE-00P found a crowded office covered in stacks of papers and scrolls. In the center of these stacks was a man with the light armor of an Exploratore, only polished to a shine and decorated with additional insignia. He also had the lower body of a snake covered in green scales, much like Agedia's. In fact, his facial features also resembled Agedia's, or how they might have looked if she was a middle-aged man.

A comparison made easy by the fact that Agedia was sitting in front of his desk with a glass of wine in her hand. She glanced at them, sighed, and took another swig. The man raised an eyebrow but said nothing, then turned to his newest guests.

"Hello, allow me to introduce myself. I am Appius, Magister Exploratore per Corvanus."

"Greeting: This unit is designated NSLICE-00P. It is nice to meet you."

Ateia and Taog glanced around. Agedia shrugged, so they stepped forward as well.

"Explora—um . . . Inquisitor Ateia Niraemia at your . . . um . . . Nice to meet you."

"Inquisitor Taog Sutharlan. Nice to meet you."

Magister Appius nodded and motioned to his desk. "Nice to meet you all. Please, make yourselves comfortable."

The group joined Agedia in front of the magister's desk.

"Query: Magister Appius stated he had intel related to this unit's primary directive?"

"Getting right into it, huh?" He nodded. "Well, yes, but there's a problem. Most of these people I've never heard of, but there is one name I'm very familiar with. One Aulus Caedicius Niraemius."

NSLICE-00P's robotic eye flickered as the elevated mission success probability returned to previous levels. She had, in fact, still been including Ateia's father in her list of persons of interest to reduce risk to Ateia, so it was only natural that the Empire treated him as part of her request. Unfortunately, that meant that the intel was not, in fact, related to her primary directive.

Still, it was related to her friendlies' own primary directives, and her protocols did dictate to assist friendly units whenever doing so would not interrupt with higher-priority directives. Likewise, if the situation involved danger, her major directive would also require action. In any case, she should remain to receive the intel for the time being.

Ateia, on the other hand, perked up.

"Request: Please transfer relevant intel and detail the complication."

Magister Appius nodded and took a deep breath. "Well, the good news is that I know where he is . . . or rather, where he went."

Ateia very nearly leapt out of her seat, but Taog preemptively placed his hand on her shoulder. She glanced at him, barely managing to contain herself, while Magister Appius shook his head at the exchange.

"The bad news is that I know why he went. Inquisitor Ateia, Inquisitor Taog, what are your current levels? In the sixties? The fifties? You must be in the forties at bare minimum if you're pursuing this, right?"

Ateia and Taog averted their gazes. Magister Appius sighed. "Right. I would much prefer not to send you two into certain death; I doubt your father would appreciate that, Miss Niraemia."

Taog raised an eyebrow. "So you're not going to tell us what happened to him?"

Magister Appius crossed his hands on his desk. "See, the issue is not just your levels. The issue is . . . the man known as Aulus Caedicius Niraemius is currently on a mission that concerns the fate of the entire Empire, possibly the entire world. Thanks to my niece here, I'm willing to give you the benefit of the doubt and assume you are not a threat. But I cannot permit any distractions to his mission. If you want to follow after him . . . you need to prove to me you'll not only survive but actively contribute to the fight."

Taog glared at him. "Even though we're inquisitors executing an Imperial order?"

Magister Appius nodded. "The threat is that serious. I would resign before I allow him to fail. And . . ." Magister Appius glanced at Ateia then at NSLICE-00P, and gave a small smirk. "Your mandate is to assist NSLICE-00P with her mission. Tell me, is NSLICE-00P truly searching for Aulus Caedicius Niraemius? Or is she including him as a favor for a friend?"

Ateia fell silent. Taog heaved a sigh. "What exactly do you want us to do?"

Magister Appius shrugged. "For now, train yourselves, get your levels up, maybe grab an enchanted artifact or twelve. My niece here can help you with that and vouch for your skills when she feels you're ready. Once she's confident you won't just die, I can clue you into the mission. Contribute to the cause, and then I can happily send you after Mr. Niraemius."

Ateia closed her eyes for a moment, clenching her fists, before she stood up. Taog glanced at her with a raised eyebrow. Opening her eyes, she looked at him and nodded.

"I want to find my father more than anything. But I don't want to put everyone in danger in the process. So, I'll go and become strong. Once I am, I'll be back."

Magister Appius nodded at her. "Normally, this is where I'd advise caution and patience, but you'll have Agedia with you, so you'll be fine. My niece knows a thing or two about fighting. But a word of advice? Try not to get too entangled with the court while you're here. Politics scare me more than a dungeon, if I'm honest."

He then rang a bell on his desk, and one of his assistants entered the room.

"I won't stop at just advice, however. Stop by the armory on your way out; Marcus there will get you set up with some gear. An Exploratore needs to be prepared, right?"

Ateia thanked him, and then Marcus led the group out of the room, leaving Agedia behind for a moment. Magister Appius shook his head.

"Well, that will buy you and Miss NSLICE-00P some time to train them up. But be careful and move quickly, Agedia. I'm under a lot of scrutiny thanks to that little rebellion in Utrad, so my own movements are restricted."

Agedia shrugged. "I wasn't relying on you either way, so it's fine."

Magister Appius hung his head as Agedia grabbed the bottle of Celestial wine and drank the last of it. Then, she rose from her seat and slithered toward the door, pausing right before leaving.

"You really want me to believe you'll protect her?"

Magister Appius looked her in the eye and nodded. "With my life, if necessary."

Agedia glared at him for a moment longer, then scoffed and left the room.

Out in the hallway, Ateia turned toward NSLICE-00P.

"I'm sorry, Seero. I . . . kind of forgot you had my dad on your list as well. You must have been disappointed that he didn't find any of your people."

"Statement: Friendly Ateia is not at fault. Inclusion of friendly Ateia's person of interest was mutually agreed upon as the safest course of action."

Ateia nodded, taking a deep breath. "Seero . . . I want to train myself and grow stronger. But I don't want to hold you back from searching for your people. You've already done so much for us. So what are you going to do? If you need to, you can separate from us. We have Agedia too, now."

"Response: This unit will accompany friendlies Ateia and Taog on upgrade routines."

Ateia blinked. "Wait, really? You don't need to keep researching at the academy?"

"Explanation: As the primary directive is pending action by Imperial units, this unit finds it acceptable to redirect some resources to the major directive. In addition, a general increase in this unit's magic-related knowledge base and capabilities may lead to progress on the primary directive. This unit has acquired significant knowledge from recording the Imperial Academy Arcanum's library that has yet to be tested and applied, and can do so concurrently with a friendly upgrade routine. As a result, this unit calculates that assisting friendlies Ateia and Taog with their upgrade routine provides the greatest expected benefit out of all currently available actions, until one of the Imperial units is ready to report."

Ateia blinked for a bit, trying to parse all that, before shaking her head. The important part was . . . that NSLICE-00P was coming with them. She smiled.

"Thanks, Seero. Honestly, I'd be very glad to have you with us."

Taog stepped forward and nodded at that. "Me too."

"Acknowledged."

# 29

# Efficient Training

*"Why train the bots, you ask? If you bothered to think about it, it would be obvious. The whole point of the NSLICE program is to obtain the flexibility of an organic, along with the precision of a machine. Therefore, we must constantly adapt and improve their existing combat protocols with live testing. Their advantages are meaningless if they are left with the same combat protocols they were built with."*

—Dr. Ottosen, on the NSLICE program's substantial request for ammunition.

The next morning, Princess Caecila arrived to find Ateia and Taog in brand-new Exploratore armor, along with a new bow slung over Ateia's back. Both the armor and the bow were enchanted.

"You wish to train?" Princess Caecila tilted her head. Ateia nodded.

"Apparently, we'd be in danger if we followed the lead at our current strength."

Princess Caecila frowned. "But you'll be with Miss NSLICE-00P, correct? Should I have a word with the magister?"

Ateia shook her head. "I want to get stronger. We're supposed to be helping *her*, so we can't rely on her for everything."

Princess Caecila nodded and turned to NSLICE-00P. "What do you think of this, if I may ask, Miss NSLICE-00P? We are more than happy to assist if you're willing to delay your quest for this."

"Answer: This unit's investigations are pending responses by Empire units. Upgrade routines for the friendlies has been determined as the most beneficial course of action at present."

Princess Caecila nodded. "I understand. In that case, let me show you somewhere you can train."

* * *

Princess Caecila went back to the Imperial palace to change, giving NSLICE-00P a chance to deploy her registered monsters. Agedia decided to join them as well when she heard their plans. The princess then returned in light armor filled with mana and led the group outside the city, into the swamp to the north. Ateia nearly called out when she moved to step directly into deep water, only for the princess to vanish entirely, followed by her entourage.

Agedia sighed as she saw it, whispering to herself, "Never thought I'd come back here . . ."

NSLICE-00P's robotic eye flickered. She could detect a barrier of some sort but could not look past it via any means, including her Dungeon Field Generator.

And there was only one explanation for that scenario.

NSLICE-00P stepped inside the dungeon.

Once she passed the barrier, the swamp vanished, and she found a walled compound guarded by two legionnaires, with several buildings inside. Princess Caecila turned to them and smiled.

"This is the Imperial family's private dungeon, accessible only to Imperial knights, the Imperial family, and those they extend invitations to."

Ateia blinked repeatedly. "The Emperor has a dungeon?"

Princess Caecila nodded. "Apparently, the Imperial knights encountered and subjugated this dungeon back when Corvanus was a small fishing hamlet. The demon lord inside apparently surrendered in the face of their overwhelming might. Seeing the monster was unusually intelligent and humble for its kind, Emperor Marcellus showed mercy and spared its life. In exchange, the Emperor received a promise, making this dungeon a safe place for his descendants to challenge themselves. Or so the story goes."

Taog raised an eyebrow. "I thought the Empire doesn't make deals with demon lords?"

Princess Caecila nodded. "I thought that too, before I joined the Imperial family. But it seems reality is more complicated than what we were taught. Whatever the case, it is true that this dungeon is remarkably restrained. It will be a perfect place for you to grow."

Princess Caecila led them past the guards after confirming her identity, passing the walls into a large compound with several structures. Princess Caecila pointed to each of them in turn.

"Over there is the Imperial family's residence; you may rest there if you wish. It has a fully staffed kitchen for your convenience, as well as all the amenities expected by the Emperor. Over there are the recovery experts, should something happen. We have an armorer here as well who can maintain and repair your gear, and a stockpile of weapons and goods."

She moved further in, toward two stone arches, each holding a swirling vortex.

"These are the entrances to different parts of the dungeon. This one is the Imperial family's dungeon. The monsters there will challenge you, but the dungeon does its best to avoid permanent harm. Please remain cautious, though; combat is always dangerous. Also note that there are generally no chests or loot besides the monsters' cores. The other one is the Imperial knights' dungeon, which we believe was the original dungeon as well. That one functions as a normal dungeon, and a difficult one at that, so I would caution you against challenging it."

Princess Caecila then led them to the stockpile. Ateia and Taog had already received new weapons from Magister Appius, so the group simply stocked up on potions and consumables. Once the group was fully supplied, they made their way into the Imperial family's dungeon . . .

Taog stood face-to-face with a club-wielding orc, dodging its blows. He held the Dark Blade in one hand and a short sword in the other, but without a shield, he didn't feel confident trying to block the monster's heavy club. Well, even with a shield, he wouldn't want to tank a blow from that thing.

He looked for an opening, but the orc's swings gave him pause. He couldn't get in range without risking a hit.

But that was fine, because he wasn't alone.

Ateia shot an arrow toward the orc's face, forcing it to block with its club. Taog took the opening, rushing in. As he did, Princess Caecila formed a magic circle in the back, and Taog's swords began to glow. He stabbed them into the orc's exposed torso, bringing it down. Princess Caecila didn't necessarily need the levels, but she took the opportunity to brush up on her skills and fought alongside the two.

The moment Taog saw the kill message from the Aesdes, he moved on to where 00B and the other monsters were delaying another orc. NSLICE-00P's monsters were a bit lower level than he and Ateia, so they had to remain cautious to avoid the orc's attacks, but they could still keep it distracted.

Agedia, Typheras, and the princess's guards stood on standby, watching the fight, ready to intervene at a moment's notice. Meanwhile, NSLICE-00P was compiling data from the library. She had focused on more fundamental knowledge regarding mana and world lore, but that didn't mean she hadn't recorded a good number of magic circles as well. Off to the side, she formed one of those new circles.

A lot of magic circle scrolls were left as Class Three or lower, largely because the Empire wasn't particularly worried about anyone reading them. Casting a spell based purely off a drawing of a magic circle simply wasn't practical . . . or safe. Magic circles were complex and intricate designs that needed to be constructed with the utmost precision. Even a minor deviation could cause the spell to fail or to have unintended—and potentially lethal—effects. To manually construct such a circle from memory, much less while trying to reference a drawing, was not recommended by any mage who did not enjoy self-immolation. So, to cast a spell from a drawing would first require long and rigorous study to ensure the mage in question could draw the spell perfectly from memory alone. Then they would practice constructing individual parts of the spell with their mana until they could not only do it perfectly but have it drilled into their magical "muscle memory." Only then would they attempt to construct the overall circle.

Oh, and that was assuming the original author drew the circle correctly in the first place, and that the conversion from a mana-construct to written ink hadn't resulted in any discrepancies. Or that the scroll itself hadn't suffered any wear and tear over the years that might have slightly modified how the circle appeared to the reader, any of which could cause the spell to fail or explode even if the user perfectly emulated what was recorded.

All in all, with the amount of effort an individual would spend learning to cast even a single spell recorded on paper, they could have simply acquired the relevant school of magic from the Aesdes, and just let the Aesdes impart the knowledge into them. The manual process was good for beginner mages to ensure they had a solid foundation, but no one would significantly expand their spell list simply by reading books in the library. Even if they did, they would have only gained a new school of magic with one single-digit-level spell. Practice, repetition, and focus meant as much as studying for the mystic arts, contrary to popular belief. Only at the senior magus level and beyond did comparison with other spells start to produce practical results, which was why most mages simply specialized in a few or even just one school of magic.

And if someone did want to learn spells outside of what they received from the Aesdes, the right way was to receive tutoring from someone else who knew the spell they wanted. That way, they could share the intuitive knowledge granted from the Aesdes and warn the tutee as to any errors in the circle.

Unless, of course, one had a perfect memory and mind capable of making direct comparisons between a magic circle drawing and every magic circle they already knew to predict likely discrepancies, and trial countless small adjustments until they found a viable pattern, with immaculate magic control to prevent any accidents.

A magic circle formed in front of NSLICE-00P, and then a small patch of the ground began to shake.

*You have learned the spell Tremor!*

NSLICE-00P modified the circle and cast the spell again, replacing its attribute while maintaining what she predicted was the spell shape. This time, a burst of flame shot up from the ground.

*You have learned the spell shape Floor!*

She then formed another magic circle. This one sputtered and faded halfway through, so she adjusted the part where the failure occurred. This time, the mana got stuck and began to condense to dangerous levels. NSLICE-00P deleted it with the Equalizer and modified the part once again.

Eventually, she was able to complete the circle.

*You have learned the spell Wind Whispers!*
*You have learned the skill Air Magic!*
*The skill Spell Shaping is now Level 19!*

Her audio inputs suddenly grew in magnitude as the spell activated, and she could perceive her mana moving through the air to magnify the sound vibrations.

She then attempted combining a Blade spell with parts of the Wind Whisper until she correctly identified the portion of the circle responsible for the Air attribute. Removing those corresponding parts on the Wind Whisper spell to isolate the spell shape, she then tested it by slotting in the Earth attribute instead.

Her mana traveled through the ground, allowing her to feel vibrations from everyone in contact with it.

*You have learned the spell shape Sensing!*

The fight had concluded in the meantime, and everyone was staring at NSLICE-00P.

Agedia crossed her arms and nodded.

"See, shiny girl gets it. Killing things and getting levels may help you get stronger quickly, but the *truly* strong people work on their skills above all."

Ateia and Taog just nodded in response.

INTERLUDE

# Un-Bear-able Torment

Princess Caecila stepped by her guards, Typheras and Imperial Guard Petronia Rex.

"Petronia, Typheras, do you understand Miss NSLICE-00P's actions?"

Typheras shrugged. "You know I'm not one for magic; I figured you'd know more than I do."

Petronia rubbed her chin. "She seems to be running through spells, though she's having trouble with a few of them? Guess those aren't ones she learned through the Aesdes. Either extreme foolishness or extreme confidence to be experimenting with something like that in the field and without a tutor present. And extreme skill or extreme luck to actually get it working unassisted."

Princess Caecila nodded. "Right, perhaps she was just on the verge of getting that spell to work and just needed a little more practice? I am told she has archmage-level abilities; those circles seem a bit basic for what I'd expect her to be working on."

Petronia shrugged. "Mages normally specialize, right? Maybe she's just branching out after mastering her chosen school." Petronia then grinned. "I will say one thing, though. Wisdom of the time and place aside, I've got to applaud her diligence to continue working on the basics. Which reminds me, Princess, how has your practice gone lately?"

Princess Caecila glanced away. "Well, you see, I've been dreadfully busy lately . . ."

Typheras smirked. "You mean like His Highness taking you on dates? You always seem to have time for those."

Princess Caecila glared at her. "Typheras!"

Petronia smiled. "I see. I think I'll speak with Fulcinia about your schedule, then."

Princess Caecila frowned and fell silent while Typheras chuckled.

* * *

Lilussees turned over in her hammock. She chittered, and then turned over again. She chittered once again. She realized the truth.

She was *bored.*

She had never been bored before. Back when she was a dungeon master, she'd had a great many tasks to conduct between her rests, then after she'd joined the boss, she'd had to give advice to ensure her new home would stay safe and the snack wouldn't get them into any trouble. Later, she'd had to follow the boss's orders and work out in the field, and then there were . . . the dark times she didn't like to remember.

So, all in all, Lilussees had always had something she needed to do between her rests. But now? NSLICE-00P hadn't deployed them to scout this time, and was only deploying registered monsters to fight in front of the Imperials. NSLICE-00P was largely powerful enough to take care of herself at this point, and even if she needed former dungeon master advice, they had the slime now, who seemed trustworthy enough and who had more experience than Lilussees did.

In other words, Lilussees had been left alone in the hangar, with no pressing tasks she needed to complete either for her own purposes or by the boss's command. She had, for perhaps the first time in her life, been able to sleep as much as she wanted.

And so, she had discovered a terrible truth. She could, in fact, get enough sleep. Now that she had been able to sleep as much as she wanted, undisturbed, for several days straight, she had reached the point where she couldn't immediately fall back asleep. Her mind was naturally alert at this point, and her body fully rested.

She had originally thought of just waiting until she could sleep again . . . but it turned out that would be much longer than she'd expected. And sitting here doing nothing but waiting made it feel like even longer.

"I guess I'll, like, do something, or whatever."

She shuddered at the words that left her mouth, going to check in on the other monsters in the hangar to distract herself from that. The slime was in its room, apparently putting together an armor or golem of some sort. The snack was brooding over something, but 02S was keeping an eye out, so Lilussees ignored him. 01R was sparring with the other monsters; even the other spiders had joined in, but Lilussees was *definitely* not interested in that. Otherwise, the boss was practicing magic while watching over 00B, the registered team, and her Imperial friends.

Lilussees chittered and began perusing the records offered by her "cybernetic components," or whatever this armor was called. The boss had apparently adjusted it to resemble the records from the Aesdes, so it was significantly easier for Lilussees to navigate now. Not that the snack had figured that out.

She watched as the boss learned yet another spell, so she flicked over to the magic section of the combat protocol database.

"Well, I guess I should, like, boost my skills or something."

Lilussees selected a spell circle at random; one that she didn't know yet. She began to move her mana when a message appeared before her eyes.

*Activate Dark Bolt protocol?*

She rubbed her mandibles and decided why not. Her cybernetic components then took control of her mana, guiding her into forming the circle while keeping the mana perfectly precise.

The magic circle formed, and a small bolt of Dark mana hit one of her old hammocks.

*You have learned the skill Dark Magic!*
*You have learned the spell Dark Bolt!*
*The spell Dark Bolt has leveled twice and is now Level 3!*

Lilussees stared at the hammock for a moment. "Huh, neat."

Lilussees was, at the end of the day, a monster, and a former dungeon master at that. She had an instinctual desire to seek power and grow stronger, as all monsters did. In her case, though, it was tempered by her desire to avoid effort, justified in her mind as remaining safe via concealment rather than power. If the effort involved in growing stronger outweighed the danger she faced and her own personal motivation, then she wouldn't bother.

But in this case, where she had some time to kill and now could acquire new skills with ease?

Lilussees went through NSLICE-00P's spell archive until her mana ran out, and the mana fatigue allowed her to sleep once again.

Taog dodged as a felix monster pounced at him. He ducked underneath it and stabbed his blade up, dealing it a mortal wound as it passed overhead. Another one was about to attack when an arrow struck its forehead. Taog glanced back at Ateia.

His eyes widened. A felix was creeping in the shadows behind her, about to strike. Taog threw the Dark Blade at the monster, striking its neck.

"Taog!" Ateia called out.

Taog barely had time to turn around when another monster pounced on him. He swung his blade, infusing his mana to coat the Dark Blade in a Dark-attribute aura once again.

Only, in his haste, he forgot he had thrown the Dark Blade, and that what remained in his hand was a regular sword. His mana felt weird, but as the monster snapped its teeth at his face and the adrenaline flowed, Taog gritted his teeth and forced his mana into shape as he stabbed at the monster.

*You have learned the skill Dark Slash!*

Taog finished off the monster and then pushed it off him. Rising to his feet, he glanced around, but the group had finished off the rest, leaving Taog free to review the message from the Aesdes. He glanced down at the sword in his hand, realizing only now what he had done.

Ateia ran up to him. "Taog, are you alright?!"

Taog turned to face her . . . and then grinned. "I got a skill."

00B narrowed his eyes as they faced off with another group of monsters. These were powerful, and higher level than the cyber-bear cub.

He hated it. His instincts told him to flee and request help from the Great Mother. These monsters reminded him how weak he was, how helpless he was. If he met them alone, he would be preyed upon.

But the Great Mother had commanded him. He was to stand and fight. He was to protect the weak, squishy prey behind him. Even that evil, annoying, squishy prey who tormented him, who grabbed him and took him from the Great Mother's side! Who demonstrated to him how she would disable him with her arms and prevent his escape, then how she would disembowel his innards or claw at his neck! Who mockingly praised him even though she knew he was weaker than her!

She was evil!

But he would not fall for her tricks! He knew she was a vicious predator just waiting for him to let his guard down, as his instincts warned all squishy things were!

If he appeared to enjoy the torment, that was a lie! Just his squishy parts acting up; a physiological reaction! He knew the moment he gave in she would reveal her true nature and prey upon him!

He shook his head. He had gotten distracted and nearly stumbled into the enemy. This time, they were attacked by a mixed group of bat and rat monsters. The bats swooped down from overhead while the rats bit at them with poisoned fangs, a clever tactic meant to distract a foe and take advantage of the rats' agility.

00B snorted as he swatted a rat monster away. They were strong . . . but they weren't even half as fast as Big Brother 01R. 00B could paw them in his sleep. They were strong enough to survive a blow . . . but even Big Brother 01R knew better than to challenge 00B directly like that.

It turned out his instincts were wrong. As long as he could hit these monsters, he *could* fight them. He would not become prey. Even though they were higher level than him, he was still the hunter. He felt a roar growing in his chest at that thought.

It was just then that 00B received a warning indicator from the NSLICE network. He spun around, and his eyes widened. A rat monster rushed toward the evil squishy thing with its poisoned fangs, who was aiming at a bat monster overhead, so hadn't seen it just yet.

He was about to fail the mission to protect them that the Great Mother had given him! And he couldn't expose the squishy thing's evilness by overcoming her foul torment if she perished!

00B reacted.

Big Brother 01R had shared his recent revelations to the group about the Implants menu. 00B had been a bit surprised that Big Brother 01R had only just noticed, as he had known about the Implants from the start, but he did hear that Big Brother 01R had started life as a pure squishy thing, so maybe it was novel to him. 00B *had* been waiting on the Great Mother's permission, though, so once he knew she approved, he had moved to upgrade himself as well.

Panels opened up along his torso, revealing large thrusters. The thrusters ignited, shooting out what appeared like streams of light as the heavy-duty repulsors activated. 00B shot through the air like a rocket.

He couldn't Dash like Big Brother 01R could, but he, too, had found a way to move quickly.

00B smashed into the rat monster, crushing it in an instant. He then double-checked the evil squishy thing for damage. She nodded at him with an aggressive expression that bared her teeth, then shot down another bat monster. With a snort, 00B turned away from her. He was going to return to the fight, but the others were wrapping things up.

It was then that he saw the message.

*Level up! You are now Level 20!*
*Evolution available! Would you like to evolve to Cyber-Bear Adolescent?*

00B stood still for a moment, processing what he saw. He slowly turned toward the Great Mother and let out a hesitant cry.

"Response: This unit grants authorization for all subordinate upgrades."

00B felt his squishy parts grow warm. The Great Mother was always kind, and always gave them the freedom to grow as strong as they liked. She had even named him from the very start.

00B roared his answer to the question. He wanted to grow stronger. He WOULD grow stronger. He would make the Great Mother proud.

Light began to cover him . . .

A few moments later, 00B opened his eyes. He was now staring at the evil squishy thing's stomach instead of her ankles. He looked down at his paws, now much larger than before.

He rose to his feet. He was now as tall as the evil squishy thing and the Great Mother. He let out a roar, his voice far deeper and more powerful than before.

The evil squishy thing's eyes widened in shock and obvious fear. "00B?"

His mouth curled, and he roared in response.

And then, 00B had his revenge as he pounced upon her, tormenting the evil squishy thing as had been done to him. He locked her in his arms and demonstrated how he would disembowel her.

"Ahahaha, w-wait, 00B, that tickles!"

00B enjoyed her screams for mercy.

# 30

# The Gift of Knowledge

*"Fireball is to be experienced, not read about."*

—Celestial Elf Sage Baoruinë, on his unique training methods.

After a day of training, NSLICE-00P and the others returned to the villa. Ateia initiated physical contact with 00B to his surprise, and he responded in kind. NSLICE-00P subsequently ordered him to guard Ateia overnight, since additional security for the friendlies was beneficial. Then, NSLICE-00P returned to her room and reviewed her gains from the day. In addition to 00B evolving and growing significant combat capabilities, she'd had the chance to rapidly expand her magical capabilities.

First of all, she had gained three new schools of magic. *Air* involved the manipulation of gasses, most commonly in the form of wind, and so had many potential use cases. *Frost* was a curious one, governing the reduction of temperature but generally used to create ice, from what she could tell. However, it was *Lightning* that most interested her. The ability to generate and control electricity via mana held many possibilities for the cyborg.

She had also greatly expanded her available spell shapes, including all of the ones that had been available to her on her last choice. While the exact effect of any given shape depended on the attribute and modifiers used alongside it, the foreign system generally described the new shapes as followed:

| Spell Shapes | | |
|---|---|---|
| Name | Level | Description |
| Cloud | 3 | Condense mana into a gaseous form that lingers in an area. |

| Curse | 3 | Infuse a target with hostile mana. Exact effects depend on the attribute used. Use of alchemic ingredients or conduits related to the target may increase duration, effects, and potency. |
|---|---|---|
| Dash | 3 | Coats user in mana and propels them forward. Behavior may change based on attribute applied. For example, Earth attribute will cause the user to travel underground and then burst out at the target location. |
| Fist | 3 | Concentrates mana on the user's fist.<br>Generally produces powerful, if short-ranged, attacks. |
| Prison | 3 | Entrap a target in mana that will attempt to prevent movement or action. May also interfere with outside attacks on the target depending on attribute used. |
| Rain | 3 | Create a mass of mana in the air that will bombard an area over time. |
| Siphon | 3 | Establish a connection between the user and target's mana.<br>Generally used to forcibly transfer mana, but exact effect may vary with attribute.<br>Can be resisted depending on target's Mana Control. |
| Twister | 3 | Rapidly spin and cycle mana. |

Spell modifiers were comparatively rare among the circles she had recorded, but she had managed to identify a few.

| Spell Modifiers | | |
|---|---|---|
| Name | Level | Description |
| Lasting | 3 | Reduces speed at which mana disperses, increasing spell duration. |
| Piercing | 3 | Increases spell penetration against RES and magic barriers. |
| Wide | 3 | Increases spell's area of effect. |

NSLICE-00P had mostly focused her time at the academy library on general lore and the fundamental nature of mana, as well as Holy Magic. Holy Magic scrolls, in particular, had mostly had vague descriptions of spell effects rather than drawings of magic circles, likely due to the restrictions on Holy Magic's use and the subsequent low number of wielders. So, she could potentially learn even more spells if she focused her efforts on expanding her arsenal.

However, while additional options were nice, that approach may not be the ideal one for her purposes. Magic knowledge could grow by acquiring additional spells and attributes, but it could also grow by improving mastery of the spells one already knew. She might require more depth, rather than breadth, to her knowledge to unlock something like Spatial Magic.

She couldn't be sure, but from what she had read and observed, it appeared most Imperial mages tended to specialize in a few or even just one school of magic, as opposed to dabbling in many, so they did seem to ascribe value to having fewer but higher-level spells. In any case, if the friendlies continued to train in the Imperial family's dungeon, she would have to separate from them to visit the library. That was not impossible, since they had Agedia and Princess Caecila's guards to protect them, but NSLICE-00P would still prefer to remain close by if she didn't have a high-priority task that demanded otherwise.

All in all, her magic abilities were growing well. Now, she had another area to investigate.

The Equalizer storage device had been put on hold, as it would mainly contribute to her combat capabilities, and she had been focused on her primary directive. But now that she had shifted short-term focus to protecting the friendlies and general improvements to her capabilities, this idea had become relevant once again.

The principles of magic she had learned from the library had confirmed in theory what she had discovered in practice. Imperial doctrine stated that magic circles were something of a language created by the Aesdes to assist with the manipulation and containment of mana. Magic circles were largely treated as black boxes, since no one had managed to actually decipher said language, but the point was that magic circles were, in fact, systematic rather than arbitrary. This was demonstrated via enchantment, where engraving a magic circle into a medium could achieve the same effect as mentally manipulating mana into the shape.

And as a result, the anti-mana created by the Equalizer could be manipulated in a similar way and, by the rules governing this world, achieve similar results. In theory, at least. In practice, it was a bit more complicated, given the inverse properties of anti-mana and the fact that she couldn't manipulate it with her mind alone.

But, if the theory was correct, then NSLICE-00P could brute force the practice via rapid, AI-driven iteration. So, she created some metal ingots—the same materials used in her energy channels—and got to work, shaping it into different patterns.

Inside the Monster Hangar, Melion began bouncing. "Oh! Interesting! Master, what are you doing? Can I come watch?!"

NSLICE-00P's robotic eye flickered. The energy channels were part of her specifications and technically classified . . . but technically, she was forming new energy channels. The fundamental construction of the energy channels themselves was not particularly sensitive, just the exact specifications of their capabilities and how they were connected to the energy sources in her torso.

So, if she were creating new energy channels with entirely different specifications and continued to conceal the actual energy sources, there would be no particular problem with allowing friendly Melion to watch.

"Affirmative."

"Yay! You're the best, Master!"

Melion hopped out of the Monster Hangar, allowing them to use their Metal-aligned mana senses to watch NSLICE-00P's work in greater detail.

"Hm, what is the purpose of this, Master?"

"Explanation: This is an energy channel."

"Energy channel? Like, an enchantment circle? Seems like one."

"Affirmative Response: That is a reasonable approximation, though this device is not intended to channel the mana energy type."

Melion bounced. "Oh oh, like that lightning you have running through you and your golems? I've been meaning to ask about that; why do you do that?"

"Explanation: The flow of electricity is used to transfer power and data."

"Wow! How does that work?!"

"Explanation . . ."

And so, NSLICE-00P experimented with a new anti-mana storage device while explaining the fundamentals of electricity-based technology to Melion.

# 31

# Treasured Relationships

*"I, um, thought there would be gold."*

—Dimindium Pendem Thief Donna Undertree, after breaking into the Imperial treasury.

The next morning, as the group was eating breakfast and waiting for Princess Caecila, one of the villa's attendants came into the room.

"Excuse me, queen of the Dobhar, Imperial inquisitors, you have a guest asking to see you."

NSLICE-00P and the others moved to a reception room, but a few minutes later, the attendant stopped by again.

"My apologies, Miss NSLICE-00P, but there appears to be a second guest and a question of order. We are not certain how you would like us to proceed."

"Acknowledgement: Proceeding to address situation."

NSLICE-00P rose to her feet and made her way to the entrance. The attendant's eyes widened, but Taog just smiled wryly and shrugged as the group followed after her.

Outside the house, NSLICE-00P found an ornate carriage covered in colorful gems and precious metals beside Princess Caecila's carriage. Princess Caecila was standing by the entrance, facing a man in a toga with her attendants. The man was clicking his tongue and shaking his head.

"Now, now, Princess, I know you are eager to make friends and play about. But Senator Balbus has some *actual* business to attend to with your friends. I'm sure you understand."

Princess Caecila crossed her arms and frowned while Fulcinia responded in her place.

"And I'm not sure you do, Emissary Vitalion. Her Highness was commanded by the Emperor to act as emissary and guide to the visiting Amicitia Populi Elteni, as well as his liaison to two Imperial inquisitors. Senator Balbus has not scheduled a meeting with us and has no authority regarding anyone here, so Her Highness's arrangements take priority."

Emissary Vitalion scoffed. "The princess may claim any titles she wishes; it does not change the fact that she is a mere child flailing about, and of dubious origins at that. Go and let her enjoy her leisure, but do not suppose to interfere with official senate business, or there will be consequences."

Fulcinia's face turned red, and she was about to respond when Princess Caecila caught sight of NSLICE-00P. She smiled and walked toward the cyborg while Emissary Vitalion tried to cut her off, but Typheras stood between them.

The man's face puffed up, but the Minotaur woman just grinned and pointed out, "Before you feel the need to berate my ancestors, you should know you're falling behind."

Emissary Vitalion glanced over, glared back at Typheras, and then stormed off to approach NSLICE-00P as well. Princess Caecila had already greeted her in the meantime.

"Request: Please report on the current situation."

Princess Caecila nodded. "I am pleased to inform you that we have determined the gift we will give you. We'd also like to invite you to visit the Imperial treasury as a token of our trust and gratitude. If you would come with me, we can head there right away."

"Acknowledged."

"Hold it right there!"

Emissary Vitalion marched up to them as NSLICE-00P turned to face him.

"I am Drusus Vatinius Vitalion, emissary of Senator Paulus Fadius Balbus. Senator Balbus requires your presence at his villa today to discuss matters of great import. Your tours with the princess will have to be put on hold."

"Greeting: This unit is designated NSLICE-00P. It is nice to meet you. Request: Please specify details of Senator Balbus's business with this unit."

Emissary Vitalion stared at her for a second. "Obviously, you are ignorant to the way of things here in Corvanus. Senator Balbus is a highly esteemed member of the senate, as well as a personal confident of Consul Noxisius. While we find it problematic you have not presented yourself as of yet, Senator Balbus is gracious enough to extend an invitation, that he may educate you on the proper ways of conducting yourself."

"Requesting Clarification: So Senator Balbus is extending an offer of education regarding etiquette protocols?"

Emissary Vitalion sputtered for a second. "Now, see here, Senator Balbus is a very influential person in Corvanus society, and it is a given that you will greet him. That must be your highest priority at present."

"Requesting Clarification: So Senator Balbus is a significant authority and wishes for this unit to submit to an official procedure?"

At that moment, Princess Caecila interjected. "Ah, Senator Balbus is indeed an influential figure, but there are no official procedures in place requiring you to do so. His subordinates and individuals requesting his patronage would need to present themselves, but if he simply wishes to greet you, he may schedule a meeting at any time, provided he does not interfere with the official mandate by the Emperor."

"Acknowledged." NSLICE-00P turned back to Emissary Vitalion. "Query: Can Emissary Drusus Vatinius Vitalion provide any details on the benefits to this unit of presenting herself to Senator Balbus?"

The man's face contorted several times. "Now, see here! One does not simply demand benefits from Senator Balbus; such a barbaric thing is simply not done! But Senator Balbus takes care of his own. Should you show appropriate respect for him, he will certainly find a place for you among the elite."

"Analysis: This unit is not affiliated with the Empire or any political or social structures within it, and already possesses adequate connections with high-ranking individuals. A place among elite society not predicted as sufficiently beneficial for this unit's primary directive."

Emissary Vitalion gaped at her, then his face twisted in rage. "Be careful, friend of the Emperor. You may have the ragged Imperial family of dubious blood licking your feet, but you have not won the favor of the *true* masters of the Empire. And you have already insulted them once with your negligence. There will be consequences if you do so again . . . for you, and for your friends."

NSLICE-00P's robotic eye turned red, causing the man to stumble back.

"Warning: Hostile intent toward this unit or designated friendlies will result in immediate termination."

Princess Caecila stepped in between them.

"Let's calm down for a moment, shall we? Obviously, Senator Balbus would *never* threaten violence toward an Amicitia Populi Elteni or two Imperial inquisitors and members of the Patrician class. Such a thing would stain his name and wouldn't be done, isn't that right?"

Princess Caecila glanced at Emissary Vitalion. The man opened his mouth, then frowned and fell silent. She turned back to NSLICE-00P.

"So there is no need for confrontation. Please, Miss NSLICE-00P, feel free to do as you please. I'm sure that Senator Balbus would like to avoid any misunderstandings, after all, so perhaps he would like to make a more formal approach at a later time? Unless you wish to greet him now, of course."

"Response: Hostile intent has not been confirmed, and no benefit to the primary directive is predicted. Offer by Princess Caecila is predicted as improving this unit's general capabilities, and so will be prioritized."

Princess Caecila's eyes widened, then she broke out into a big smile. "But of course. It is my pleasure to be of assistance."

And so, the group made their way onto Princess Caecila's carriage and set off for the Imperial treasury. Emissary Vitalion was left behind, his face red and a vein bulging on his forehead.

"Do not think I will forget this!"

On the way there, Ateia frowned. "Princess Caecila, may I ask a question?"

Princess Caecila smiled. "Of course, Ateia. Please, do not feel reserved around me. We have fought side by side now, have we not?"

Ateia gave a small smile at that before frowning once again. "Is that . . . Senator Balbus going to be a problem? Was it a bad idea for Seero to just reject him like that?"

Princess Caecila crossed her arms and huffed. "He was already a problem. He would be doing his daily greetings for his subordinates right about now. Requesting that Miss NSLICE-00P greet him right at this moment would imply that she is submitting to his patronage. So regardless of whether he respects me or the Emperor, he should at least have requested that Miss NSLICE-00P meet with him in private at a later time. Though . . . that could have been the emissary's doing as well. Drusus Vatinius Vitalion is known to be haughty."

Taog crossed his arms. "Should we expect any retaliation?"

Princess Caecila rubbed her chin. "I do not believe so; at least not openly. Drusus made a big mistake, having that exchange out in public, which means everyone will know he made an unreasonable demand of an Amicitia Populi Elteni. If Senator Balbus is smart, he will play it off as Drusus's error."

Taog's eyes narrowed. "What if he's not smart?"

Princess Caecila frowned. "Even in that case, Drusus invoked Consul Noxisius's name. The consul himself may be held responsible if Senator Balbus moves against you, and so would step in to stop any . . . emotional reactions." Then she smiled. "But enough of this. You will have the Emperor's full support in such matters, rest assured. Besides, today I have the honor of showing you the Imperial treasury. Please, look forward to the visit."

Princess Caecila led them to the Imperial palace. The treasury was kept in the center of the palace—the most guarded location in the Empire, and where the Emperor could access anything inside of it on demand. She showed the group to a large gate with a sculpted mural of the Empire's greatest battles on it, plus two barracks of Imperial guards on either side. NSLICE-00P could detect a truly impressive amount of mana flowing through those gates.

But the Emperor had sent word ahead of time, so the gates opened without any fuss.

Inside, there was no gold or Idrint. The coffers of the Northern Court were kept elsewhere; this place instead housed only the true treasures of the Emperor. Inside was a hallway dotted by alcoves on either side. Each alcove held a pedestal upon each of which rested an artifact. While guards stood at either end of the hall and patrolled up and down it, the artifacts appeared unprotected at first glance. However, NSLICE-00P detected powerful and invisible magic barriers over each of the alcoves and in the pedestals holding the artifacts. As with the throne room, things were not as they seemed when it came to defense.

Princess Caecila led them down, pointing out some of the objects.

"That is the lance of Vlatugni, the chieftain of the Mélusine who fought against Velus himself. This is a scale of Rityss, the dark dragon who once burned Elteno."

As the group walked down the hallway, Ateia glanced around, catching sight of a small ring sitting on a pedestal. A simple silver band set with a white gem. Beautiful in its own right but somewhat plain compared to the mighty artifacts all around it.

For some reason, Ateia couldn't take her eyes off it. She stepped toward it, falling out of step with the group. Taog noticed and turned to her.

"Ateia?" he called out, but she didn't seem to hear him.

Princess Caecila noticed them fall behind and walked over to them.

"Ah, you have a good eye."

Ateia wobbled slightly, as if in a daze. "What is it?"

Princess Caecila nodded. "We believe this is the ring of the Saintess, given by Velus to his wife Luxia. She was said to have been a great hero no less than he, and the most powerful wielder of Holy Magic the world has ever seen. Well, no one on record has been able to actually do anything with this ring, so it may not be a powerful artifact, but we do believe that it deserves our respect."

Ateia nodded as she stood in silence, staring at the ring. After a bit, Taog placed a hand on her shoulder.

"You okay, Ateia?"

Ateia shook her head before turning back to him. "Fine. Let's move on."

Princess Caecila continued the tour until they arrived at their destination. The pedestal in question held two books, both with blank covers with no adornments, but one was worn and tattered, while the other appeared brand new.

"This is the grimoire of Arofinas Leolar, high king of Mirima, given in friendship to Velus. A full compilation of the mystical knowledge of the half-Elven king, written in Imperial for Velus's convenience."

Princess Caecila turned to NSLICE-00P and bowed her head. "I am sorry. I spoke with the Emperor on getting you access to the academy's records on Spatial Magic, but Class Five materials are restricted even for an Amicitia Populi Elteni. The court didn't reject it out of hand, but the most we could do is leave it to the discretion of the Magister Arcanum, so you will have to speak with him on accessing those materials. But the Emperor does have some magical knowledge he controls directly, and so we decided what we would gift you with."

Princess Caecila held a pendant to the side of the alcove and whispered into it. NSLICE-00P detected the barrier around that alcove fading, then Princess Caecila gently picked up the book with the newer cover and held it out to NSLICE-00P.

"In the same spirit as the ancient high king of Mirima, the Empire now presents this to you in turn. A complete and exact copy of the grimoire, of which only one is kept at a time. The Emperor hopes you will find the knowledge illuminating."

NSLICE-00P took the book. "Expressing Gratitude: This unit thanks you for the additional intel."

And so, NSLICE-00P acquired the grimoire of Arofinas Leolar.

INTERLUDE

# A Bear-y Nice Home

The trip to the Imperial treasury hadn't taken that long, so the group trained at the Imperial family's dungeon for the rest of the day before returning home. NSLICE-00P flipped through the grimoire of Arofinas Leolar, recording its contents, and was about to begin an analysis and comparison to other data when she was pinged by 00B. She also heard him scratching at the door to her room.

According to NSLICE-00P's logs, 00B was currently still tasked with defending Ateia during rest cycles, but now that she had finished her immediate task, he was strongly requesting a return to the hangar.

"Requesting Explanation: Please specify justification for return."

00B responded that he had not expected to be left behind during the day. NSLICE-00P had made that call since 00B had been in the midst of a rest cycle when Princess Caecila had picked them up. Since she herself would be able to provide security to the friendlies during the day, she had chosen to allow 00B to conclude maintenance. She had left him on-site at the villa as an extra sentry in the meantime, since the group was not originally planning to engage in combat. But 00B had a point. As a primary combat asset for the NSLICE network, it was important for 00B to remain ready to deploy as the situation demanded. The group hadn't returned to the villa after deciding to train at the dungeon, so 00B had ended up unavailable then.

So NSLICE-00P declared 00B's friendly protection mission as concluded and attempted to Transfer him back to the hangar.

**Transfer failed. Target monster is too large for Monster Hangar (Small).**

NSLICE-00P's robotic eye flickered. The description of the Monster Hangar (Small) did, in fact, state that only small-sized monsters could fit inside.

Unhelpfully, the foreign system did not actually specify the exact dimensions that constituted a "small" monster, and the hangar had some ability to rearrange itself to best suit its occupants, so NSLICE-00P hadn't been able to calculate where the exact limit was. But it appeared she had found it now. 00B was currently the size of a black bear, about on par with an adult human if he stood up on his hind legs. So, an adult human-sized target was no longer considered *small*, apparently.

NSLICE-00P parsed the foreign system menus for a solution.

| **Available Implants** | | | |
|---|---|---|---|
| **Name** | **Cost** | **Additional Mana Upkeep** | **Description** |
| **Monster Hangar (Medium)** | **20 Perk Points. Requires two free implant slots to install.** | 5 | **Provides 5 living spaces for medium-sized monsters. Unlocks subordinate summoning if not available.** |

It was noticeably more expensive than a small Monster Hangar, but that wasn't a problem for the current NSLICE-00P. She currently had one hundred sixty-three Dungeon perk points available, with many more to come, as her Dungeon level had increased *one hundred and eighteen* times since the battle with Caelinus.

The Otter Burrow income had continued to grow over time. She had been leveling up at least once every eight hours due to the Otter Burrow income alone back when she had defeated Caelinus and his uprising, and it had been about two weeks since then. At this point, she was leveling up once every other hour; perhaps more. It was hard to determine the exact rate, since her expanded Dungeon Field was also contributing while she was in a city, but the point was, her Dungeon perk points were now growing at an increasing rate.

So, she could most certainly afford a few upgrades here and there.

**Monster Hangar (Medium) is now available!**

With that, NSLICE-00P attempted to Transfer 00B once more. This time, he moved into the new hangar without issue. 00B started to smile before he paused.

Looking around the room a couple of times, he then cried at NSLICE-00P.

"Answer: Other subordinate units are located in the Monster Hangar (Small). A new hangar was installed due to 00B's increase in size."

00B nodded, grunting, then thought for a moment and whined softly.

"Analyzing request viability."

NSLICE-00P checked the customization options for the two hangars and found there was one that could fulfill 00B's request. She went ahead and installed it, and a new door formed in the hangar. A moment later, the door opened, and 01R stepped inside.

"What-What is going on, wise-mighty-gracious boss-queen . . ." 01R stopped as he laid eyes on the new room and 00B. Slowly, he smiled and nodded. "This is great-excellent, yes-yes. It is good you have returned, 00B. And now, we have much more room to spar-train, yes-yes."

00B rushed over to initiate physical contact with 01R. 01R smiled, then paused, then frowned, then leapt out of the way as the very large and heavy 00B crashed into the wall. He boosted into the air, landing on the dazed cyber-bear's head, and patted it softly.

"I am also happy-excited to see you back, but you must remember-recall you've grown greatly in power, yes-yes."

00B shook his head before nodding.

Ateia sighed as she passed over another document.

*Manharren and sailing crew – Celestial Elf – Origin: Celestial Empire – Date entered: Day 12 of the month of Velustus of the year 4127 AV – Stated purpose: Trade – Resolution: Wares inspected. Entry granted and recorded.*

*Caeclud Esria and retinue – Sun Elf – Origin: Empire of the Sun – Date entered: Day 13 of the month of Velustus of the year 4127 AV – Stated purpose: Diplomatic negotiations – Resolution: Identity confirmed. Escorted to vacant diplomat housing under guard.*

*Etr and clan – Giant species, appears Frost attributed – Origin: Wild Lands – Date entered: Day 13 of the month of Velustus of the year 4127 AV – Stated purpose: Seeking asylum – Resolution: Held under guard until negotiator arrived. Asylum agreement successfully concluded.*

She checked these against the list she had written out. No "Bobs," "Londyns," "Arvids," "Nanas," or even "Xiong Huangs." She didn't expect the first few, but the latter kind of sort of sounded like a Celestial Elf name . . . maybe. But still, nothing even close to that in any of the documents she had read thus far.

"Any luck, Taog?"

Taog sighed himself and shook his head. "Knights of the Hammer, sure. The Serpent Templars, got it. The, um, Wonder Knight of the Aurora Legion? Nope, not even close. And we're *certain* this, um, 'Voidspeaker' is a knight and *not* a mana cultist?"

Ateia shrugged. "Seero couldn't confirm or deny that, only that he was affiliated with that Aurora Legion. I, um, don't think a knight order would accept a cultist of mana? Um, knowingly, that is."

Taog raised an eyebrow. "And we are sure this Aurora Legion is, in fact, a knight order?"

Ateia shrugged again. "Not at all. But from Seero's description, that's the closest thing? That or a famous Exploratores team, but they wouldn't be this hard to find if they were Exploratores."

Taog nodded at that. "Right . . ."

The two fell into silence, and then both sighed in sync. At this point, Ateia had a solid lead on her father, and she knew what she needed to do to find him. Once she was strong enough, Magister Appius would lead her right to him. Her quest was progressing faster than she had expected.

But what about Seero? From what Ateia had seen and what Seero had stated herself, the girl was no closer to finding her people than she had been before. If anything, Ateia was getting the sense that Seero was increasingly pessimistic about her mission. So, Ateia had tried to do what she could. She had discussed with Agedia and Taog some politically safe applications of their new inquisitor authority and come up with this. They had requisitioned records from the Imperial bureaucracy for review. Census data, records of foreigners visiting Corvanus, lists of known knight orders both registered and unofficial—anything they thought could be related. She and Taog were now spending their free time looking over these records.

It . . . wasn't going well. All they had found so far were headaches from staring at line after line of dull, repetitive records. Ateia took a deep breath.

"Taog, are we actually helping Seero?"

He tilted his head. "What do you mean?"

Ateia furrowed her brow. "Look . . . we're supposed to help Seero with her quest, right? That's the whole reason she helped us become Exploratores. But now . . . she's an Amicitia Populi Elteni. The Emperor ordered the Magister Exploratore and the Imperial Academy Arcanum to help her. The princess herself is guiding her around. It feels like we haven't done anything to help her, and she's *still* taking time out to help us train. If anything . . . I feel like we're holding Seero back."

Taog opened his mouth but fell silent as he saw the look on Ateia's face. He took a moment to think, rubbing his chin, then took a deep breath, glancing over at the Dark Blade in his room before he started to speak.

"Seero . . . has done more for us than we can ever repay. We owe our lives to her, several times over. We owe all of this to her. And it is true; we aren't doing much to pay it back at the moment. She's proven she has our backs, and I don't know if we've done the same."

Ateia frowned again, but Taog continued. "But that's why we should stay at her side. Seero isn't perfect, Ateia. You know like I do that she just doesn't know how things work in the Empire. And I'm not talking about the politics or the laws. I'm talking about people. Look, you saw, right? She reacted pretty badly to that guy who was fighting with the princess today. What if Princess Caecila hadn't stepped in? We've seen what Seero does when someone angers her."

Ateia shook her head. "Yes, but Princess Caecila can help her."

Taog shook his own in turn. "That's not my point. My point is, Seero *does* have things she's not good at. She has things she doesn't know. And most of all, she has very few friends, other than us, and maybe Agedia now."

"What about Miss Royal Guard?"

Taog raised an eyebrow at that. "Do you think the angry Dobhar has friends?"

Ateia nodded seriously. "Ah, good point."

He chuckled and shook his head. "The point is that Seero has very few people she can trust here in Corvanus. Even Princess Caecila wants something from her, right? So . . . I think even though we aren't achieving much, it's important that Seero has *someone* looking out for her; someone who actually cares about her as a friend. Like . . ."

*You did for me* . . . were the words Taog cut off. Ateia stared at him for a moment before Taog glanced away.

"Right, so, um . . . I think we should stay by Seero as long as she wants us there, and we should look for any opportunity we can to help her in the few things she's not unbelievably good at. That opportunity might come sooner than we think. Besides, it's not like our presence is entirely meaningless. From what I understand, an Amicitia Populi Elteni like her can ask the Empire to do things, but as inquisitors, we can *order* it to do things. That could come in handy, you know?"

Ateia slowly nodded. "I guess so. But . . . I think we need to get stronger, at least. Much stronger. I don't want Seero to have to worry about us forever."

Taog nodded. "No argument about that."

"And then she threatened my life and yours, in full view of all the public! It is an insult upon your name, and a challenge to your honor, Senator! She must be punished with all due haste!"

Senator Balbus held the bridge of his nose. It was impressive how Drusus could say this all with a straight face. The altercation had happened right out on the street, with many onlookers who had gathered to see the princess out and about. The sun hadn't even set, and Senator Balbus had already been told what Drusus had done . . . and the rumors that were now spreading through the capital.

Drusus was a master at hosting exceptional guests to the highest standards of traditional Imperial hospitality . . . but he was also quite proud of his position and acted entirely differently with those he thought beneath him. Senator Balbus . . . had not expected him to treat Princess Caecila in that manner. Even if she was a lowborn usurper who had stolen her position by feminine wiles, she *did* currently hold said position. But apparently, her dubious origins had blinded Drusus to her at least nominal authority.

And now . . . the senator's own position had been compromised.

He had been instructed by Consul Noxisius to bring this "Imperial friend" into the fold as a "friendly guide," but Balbus was not so subservient as to jump at the consul's every word. He had hoped that the powerful but barbaric foreigner wouldn't understand the subtleties of Imperial society, and so he could get her to present herself to him without understanding the implications. It was to be a subtle play to increase his own stature . . . and to force Consul Noxisius to treat him as an equal.

He, unfortunately, hadn't explained that to Drusus, though. Drusus hadn't needed to know . . . and would have bragged about anything he did, after all.

And now, Drusus had insulted an Amicitia Populi Elteni and the lowborn princess in public, leading to a threatening altercation that said princess had defused with grace, and then the barbaric "friend" had declared the princess as her priority in no uncertain terms. All while Drusus name-dropped both himself and Consul Noxisius.

This was a disaster. Forget increasing his own stature, Senator Balbus would be lucky if Consul Noxisius didn't kick him from the faction and pin the whole fiasco on him. He could try to do the same to Drusus, but everyone knew Drusus had no initiative of his own, so the people that mattered wouldn't buy it.

Senator Balbus began pacing as Drusus droned on, putting all his mind to work. Just what could he do to overturn this situation? What could he do to avoid the fallout and get back on track?

He stopped pacing, standing still. Rubbing his chin, he thought over everything he had been told about the altercation.

He had an idea. The reason the lowborn princess had gained so much from this event was that her barbarian friend had been quick to anger, as one might expect from a barbaric foreigner.

And that was a weakness Senator Balbus could exploit.

If he could reveal the true, violent nature of the barbarian, then criticism would fall on those who had invited her in. Senator Balbus could paint himself as a victim, or even spin it in his favor and take credit as the one to expose the danger.

The senator began to grin as a plan formed in his mind.

"Drusus, you said they had some sort of furry barbarian with them, right? An otter of some sort?"

# 32

# A Foolish Ploy

*"Please be advised that NSLICE security forces make no compromises in your protection. They will respond to any provocations with force. Please do not interfere with their duties."*

—A public service announcement by Dr. Ottosen's organization.

Over the night and morning, NSLICE-00P began running an analysis on the grimoire of Arofinas Leolar. It appeared much of the theoretical knowledge it contained was common knowledge she had already read in the library, not to mention the book didn't particularly focus on such things. The mages of the Empire had a long time to catch up on theory, after all.

The practical knowledge, on the other hand, had great potential.

Unfortunately, the grimoire did not contain anything regarding Spatial Magic, but it did have some novel techniques that would be useful to NSLICE-00P. The first item that caught her eye was a large-scale enchanting technique designed for concealment. The island nation of Mirima, which Arofinas Leolar had ruled, had been founded by escaped slaves and Elven defectors from the Empire of the Sun, and so had waged a long, asymmetric war for survival until Velus and the armies of Elteno had intervened. As such, they had developed many techniques to even the odds, one of which was a fleet of concealed warships that could ward off any naval invasion and harass the Empire of the Sun closer to home.

That technique was recorded here.

It would take some effort for NSLICE-00P to apply the technique to her own assets. The technique had been designed for warships made with nonstandard materials, not miniature drones made of mundane metal, so she would need to adjust the setup. Likewise, it would require testing to ensure said technique was still viable in the present day, given any potential advancements in sensor capabilities from the time of Arofinas Leolar.

But assuming she could get the technique working . . . it presented a massive potential improvement for her mini drone units. One that had been proven to work against mana-based detection methods in a military setting, at least at the time it had been deployed. It was a start.

And for NSLICE-00P, the start was the most important. Once she had a proven, completed technique in hand, she could iterate upon it to improve its efficiency. And now, she had acquired such a technique.

And of course, she could always iterate in the other direction and work on her drones instead. Mini drones were useful for immediate scouting and for being difficult to detect . . . but a drone's capabilities ultimately scaled with their size, so scaling the drones up to fit the technique could be an effective option. She unfortunately didn't have access to blueprints for any drones, but she had been recording various mana-powered vehicles in action. It might soon be possible for her to develop her own autonomous units.

But she filed that thread away for now. Increases to the capabilities of the NSLICE network were of secondary importance now that she assumed she was in a different universe. Stealth drones would be useful for her major directive, but upgrading the friendlies themselves was the most efficient method of fulfilling that directive given the nature of combat in this world. So, she would devote spare resources and processing power to upgrading the mini drones whenever available, but would not go out of her way to do so. Developing entirely new models was beyond the scope of the resources she was currently willing to commit.

That situation could potentially change, but as long as she maintained cordial relations with the Empire, and Imperial resources were dedicated to her investigations, there was no reason for her to reinvent the wheel. Which was why NSLICE-00P had requested to return to the academy this day. Princess Caecila had sent word that she had a prior engagement today, but that they were free to use the Imperial family's transport for the task. And so, the group made their way to the plaustrum subterraneum station.

Just as they were approaching the station on foot, something happened.

A man bumped into NSLICE-00P's shoulder. NSLICE-00P ignored it, as no damage had been dealt and the bump was deemed too ineffective to have been an intentional act of hostility.

"Ow! What was that for?"

NSLICE-00P continued walking. The man placed a hand on her shoulder.

"Hey! I'm talking to you! What was that for?"

NSLICE-00P turned around. "Query: Please specify what you are referring to."

The man scowled. "What I'm referring to? You hit me! You going to apologize or what?"

"Statement: This unit has not activated termination protocols or taken any acts of hostility. Walk pattern analysis indicates an unintentional collision on the part of the neutral entity, as this unit's walk pattern had no deviations from the calculated optimal route."

"Well, I say you did! Now, apologize!"

"Response: This unit cannot identify a reason to do so."

"Screw you!"

The man tried to shove NSLICE-00P, grunting and waving his hands around as she refused to budge, and he ended up striking her metal armor. Her robotic eye turned red. The shove had done no damage . . . but it had clearly been intentional.

"Hostile intent confirmed. Engaging self-defense protocols."

Taog had stopped walking once he noticed NSLICE-00P fall behind, and so caught the altercation. He glanced around and noticed a group of guards just entering the street. His eyes widened.

This scene . . . was all too familiar to him. The children of his village had provoked him into violence more than once as an adult passed by, leading to him being punished instead. He stepped in between the two.

"Hold on, Seero. Just wait a moment, please."

"Acknowledged."

Taog turned to the man, who was huffing at him. "Stay out of this, *boy*. This girl hit me, a brother of a senator! Don't you know what that means?!"

Taog raised an eyebrow. "From what I saw, you shoved her. Do you know what that means?"

"Shove off!"

The man tried to push Taog out of the way, who frowned as he was moved to the side and the man took a step toward NSLICE-00P. But then, he smiled. For the first time in his life, he now had the tools to fight back.

"If you take one step further, then by my authority as an Imperial inquisitor appointed by Emperor Lucius, I will place you under arrest."

The man paused, chuckled, and turned around. "That's a laugh—"

The words died on his mouth as Taog held out a pendant. Channeling his mana through it, the banner of the Empire appeared, with Emperor Lucius's seal upon it. The man took a step back and started to sweat.

"Y-You can't do this. I'm a senator's brother! He'll talk to the Emperor for me!"

Taog narrowed his eyes. "You have assaulted an Imperial friend and are interfering with her quest and my mandate. Tell me, can your 'senator brother' defy an inquisitor's mandate?"

The man thought for a second before paling. Taog shrugged.

"That's what I thought. Now get going. I'd rather not waste time hauling you in."

The man turned and left without another word as Taog heaved a sigh and turned to NSLICE-00P. "Sorry about that, Seero. I think he was trying to provoke you into attacking him so that you would get in trouble with the guards."

NSLICE-00P's robotic eye flickered. "Query: This unit was acting in accordance with Imperial self-defense regulations. Target would only have been rendered permanently incapable of harm, and not terminated."

Taog frowned, his face turning dark. "Okay, putting that terrifying statement aside, the guards may not necessarily have seen that. They would end up questioning you, and it might not go the way you think it would, especially if that guy actually has the connections he was bragging about. You can get punished even if you didn't do anything wrong. Trust me on that."

Shaking his head, he thought for a moment, and then smiled. "Well . . . on the other hand, that probably doesn't actually apply to you, huh? I'm not actually sure what happens when an Imperial friend is accused of a crime. I imagine a friend of the Emperor might be able to get away with a lot. But, well, it would have been annoying to waste time on that, right?"

NSLICE-00P's robotic eye flickered. "Requesting Clarification: So, the intent was to complicate this unit's relations with the Empire by provoking hostility?"

Taog nodded. "Yeah, that's right."

NSLICE-00P analyzed the scenario. On the one hand, leaving hostiles at large went against her protocols. On the other . . . souring her relations with the Empire would disrupt her current investigations and so interfere with her primary directive, as well as the major directive. She still did not understand why such a thing would occur if she followed Imperial self-defense regulations, but friendly Taog appeared confident enough for her to assume it was a possibility, and so she included a small probability of that case occurring. Threat analysis of the hostile indicated an insignificant probability that he was capable of meaningful damage to her. When she weighed the two probabilities, she calculated that ignoring him to resume her investigations was a more efficient option.

Provided the hostile didn't actually demonstrate the ability to cause meaningful damage or else present her with any opportunities to terminate him without complication, that was.

"Revelation: It appears this unit's self-defense protocols may require adjustment. Gratitude: This unit thanks friendly Taog for the assistance."

Taog nodded. "Of course, Seero. I'm not going to let you go through that if I can help it."

* * *

Senator Balbus sighed as his deadbeat brother and Drusus complained to him.

"Are you two idiots?"

The two stared at him in shock, answering the question. Senator Balbus sighed again.

"Look, they might be barbarians, but they're barbarians with *official* titles! You can't just treat them like any old wide-eyed frontier peasant who doesn't know left from right! I don't know if I could have protected you against them this time! And it doesn't work at all if *WE'RE* the ones to provoke the fight! You were about to ruin my plan, and I do not take kindly to that. By the Aesdes, a Turannian whelp had to be the reasonable one here! You hear that? You were acting more stupid and ignorant than a *Turannian*."

Drusus averted his gaze. "But, Senator Balbus . . ."

Senator Balbus sighed a third time. "No buts, Drusus. You have better things to do than pick fights with people you clearly don't understand. Go back to your duties and do NOT interact with the barbarians again. Leave that to your betters."

Drusus frowned but complied. Senator Balbus rubbed his temples as he turned to his brother.

"And you, Marcellus. Do you have a single thought in your head besides the bottom of a wine barrel? I've just about had it with bailing you out time and time again. Leave, and don't approach those people again. The next time you cause me trouble, I'm shipping you off to the countryside. Maybe growing the grapes yourself will teach you some moderation, because the Aesdes know nothing *else* has."

Marcellus looked ready to argue, but he shrugged and left as well. Senator Balbus shook his head.

"Come now. We are not barbarians. We do not stoop to their level. We do not act impulsively, enslaved by our emotions."

He stood up and looked out the window. He started to smirk.

"We, the esteemed Elteni, act with purpose and foresight. And that is why the barbarians cannot help but fall before us. They run forward blindly, heedless to the trap until they are caught in it. I will show you how a true Elteni fights."

# 33

# Congratulations, You Are Being Assisted. Do Not Resist.

*"I will accept no compromise in the ultimate weapon's combat capabilities."*

—Dr. Gaute Ottosen, on the possibility of equipping NSLICE units with anesthesia for the sake of field surgeries.

Along the train ride, NSLICE-00P spoke with the friendlies on her self-defense protocols.

"Requesting Confirmation: So this unit should rely on Imperial contacts and friendlies with authority when responding to low-danger hostiles?"

Taog nodded. "Well, Agedia could probably explain it better, but, generally, yeah. We have a bit of power now, so we should make use of it. Better to have them arrested than to try and explain ourselves after committing violence."

NSLICE-00P's robotic eye flickered. "Response: This unit finds that proposal acceptable in situations with no or minimal risk of termination or major damage. However, repeated hostility or high-risk scenarios will still require a direct response."

Taog shrugged. "I guess that's fair."

Ateia nodded her agreement. "If they're asking for it, let them have it."

Taog turned to her, his eyes widening. "Ateia?"

She turned to him. "Yes, Taog?"

He struggled to hold her gaze. "I, uh, thought you liked to get along with people?"

Her eyes narrowed as she stared off into the distance.

"That's because I wasn't as strong as Seero."

Taog decided not to dig into that.

Estrith just scoffed and shook her head.

"Imperials."

* * *

NSLICE-00P and company made their way back to the academy. None of Faustus's requests for classified materials had been approved yet, so Apprentice Callisunus led them to the Magister Arcanum's office. After an hour wait, Magister Cnaeus had time to see them.

He heaved a sigh as they walked into the office.

"Ah, yes. Welcome back to our academy, Miss NSLICE-00P. I hope you are enjoying your tours."

"Response: Investigation of academy resources has revealed crucial intel, but this unit requires more."

Magister Cnaeus barely nodded as he shuffled some papers on his desk. "I see. Now, what is this about, if I may ask?"

"Request: This unit would like access to materials on Spatial Magic."

Magister Cnaeus sighed again. "Spatial Magic is highly complex, and above all, dangerous. This is not some basic Water Magic where the worst that can happen is that you flood the room. You could teleport into a wall. You could end up on the other side of the world, in the middle of an ocean or a desert. You could end up in a nest full of monsters. You could bring a nest full of monsters into a crowded city. You could fold the academy in on itself. In the worst case, you could even tear open a Rift. I am sorry, Miss NSLICE-00P. Friend of the Empire or not, Spatial Magic is only to be accessed by people I trust, and I do not trust you."

Ateia crossed her arms and raised an eyebrow.

"And if you are ordered by an inquisitor to assist?"

Magister Cnaeus scoffed, barely glancing at the girl.

"Emperor Lucius has no power here, girl. The Magister Arcanum is empowered to make all decisions regarding mystical affairs. Access to Class Five materials *must* be approved by me, even if the Emperor himself came to request them, not to mention any inquisitors relying on his name. Anything in that category is a matter of *national* security. Even a well-intentioned and trustworthy individual who does not know *exactly* what they are doing can cause a national, or even continental, disaster with that sort of thing. So, no. A young inquisitor with no knowledge of the mystic arts *cannot* order me to surrender this knowledge, unless you can make it completely and abundantly clear that the information is necessary, and that your charge can be trusted in terms of both intent and competence. And I do not trust any of you on either count."

"Query: What procedures are necessary to acquire adequate trust?"

Magister Cnaeus shrugged. "That is up to you to determine. Why don't you start by gathering the bare minimum of mystical knowledge and then make yourself useful to the academy? Now, if you don't mind, I have important matters to attend to."

"Acknowledged."

With that, NSLICE-00P and the others left the room. Apprentice Callisunus sighed. "I'm sorry, Miss NSLICE-00P. Magister Cnaeus always hates it when the politicians get involved. He doesn't really like Magus Major Faustus, either."

"Oh my, trouble with the boss?"

The group turned as a new voice entered the conversation and a woman approached the group. She was tall, with long brown hair. She wore a blue robe and a pointed blue hat, and held a staff made of driftwood topped with a blue gem. She stepped toward NSLICE-00P and smiled as Apprentice Callisunus's eyes widened.

"Magus Major Sidonia? I didn't know you were back."

She nodded at him. "Ah, Nonus, nice to see you again. Yes, I just returned recently, but it may not be for long."

She turned to NSLICE-00P. "You must be NSLICE-00P. As Nonus there said, my name is Sidonia Agricola, Magus Major of the academy and top-ranking battlemage of the North. I specialize in Elemental Magic; I'm personally fond of Water."

"Greetings: This unit is designated NSLICE-00P. It is nice to meet you."

Sidonia giggled lightly. "The pleasure is all mine. I've heard a lot about you, so I'm pleased to finally meet you in person. Now, I hear you want to access some restricted materials?"

"Affirmative."

Sidonia nodded. "I may be able to help you with that."

"Requesting Elaboration."

Sidonia giggled again. "Of course. You see, I happen to have good relations with the Legion. They've requested my support with an issue near Corvanus . . . but I have just returned from my latest mission. I have heard you are quite the magical combatant yourself. Would you be willing to lend me a hand?"

"Requesting Detail: Please state the mission target and proposed compensation."

Sidonia's smile dropped as she looked NSLICE-00P in the eyes. "A corrupted dungeon."

The Imperials all gasped, and Estrith suddenly started paying attention to the conversation.

"Needless to say, it's a very serious issue, and a very dangerous mission. It would be a great boon to me, the Legion, and the Empire if you were to assist us with this. If you do, I will show you any materials I have access to and will put in a good word for you to the old man. I'll also let my contacts in the Legion know so they can add some more pressure from the top. What do you say?"

NSLICE-00P did not take long to decide. "Response: Request determined as reasonable. This unit accepts the proposal."

Sidonia blinked. "Truly? I am happy for the help, but are you sure? Corrupted dungeons are not to be taken lightly."

"Confirmation: This unit has encountered and terminated a corrupted dungeon before. While mission success probability will be determined upon active reconnaissance of the site, simulations predict positive results."

Sidonia blinked again before smiling. "I had heard the rumors, but to think they were true. That's very reassuring. I will be most relieved to have your support."

"Acknowledged. Request: Please sign the following Contract to confirm the agreement . . ."

Meanwhile, Taog turned to Apprentice Callisunus, whispering to him on the side.

"Is she trustworthy?"

Apprentice Callisunus nodded. "Magus Major Sidonia is very kind, and well-respected by everyone in the academy. She's also, as she said, one of the foremost battlemages of the North. She should have at least some pull with Magister Cnaeus, and a Magus Major vouching for you would definitely help on the mystical-knowledge count. And, well . . . if there's a corrupted dungeon in the Imperial Heartland . . ."

Taog frowned. "Then she needs all the help she can get."

Apprentice Callisunus nodded grimly as Ateia looked over at Seero and took a deep breath.

"Seero . . . should we stay behind?"

NSLICE-00P turned to Ateia. "Requesting Elaboration."

Ateia bit her lip. "You're . . . going to fight a corrupted dungeon. This is serious business, Seero. Won't you be distracted if you have to protect us?"

NSLICE-00P's robotic eye flickered. On the one hand, it was true she would have to devote attention and resources to protecting the friendlies if she brought them into an active combat zone. On the other, the experience with Magister Vibius and Agedia's warnings up to now indicated the friendlies would be at risk even if they were left behind. In fact . . . NSLICE-00P could analyze, judge, and mitigate the risk presented by a corrupted dungeon. She could not, as of now, do the same for political or social threats.

"Analysis: This unit calculates that the friendlies will have the lowest risk of termination if they remain within range of this unit. This unit prefers that the friendlies accompany her, and retreat if the risk is calculated as unacceptably high."

Sidonia crossed her arms and hummed. "You two are, what? About level thirty or so, if I had to guess from your mana levels?"

Ateia and Taog nodded. Sidonia thought for a bit, then ultimately nodded.

"Well, I wouldn't approve you for the frontlines, but that's enough that you shouldn't die from a stray attack. If you stay in the rear, you can probably help the Legion with logistics. They will need all the help they can get."

With a glance at each other, Taog slowly nodded. Ateia closed her eyes and took a deep breath, then nodded her head as well.

"Okay. We will do whatever we can, too."

Apprentice Callisunus frowned and looked down. "I'm sorry. I wish I could help, but I'm useless."

"Nonus—" Sidonia was about to object when NSLICE-00P interrupted.

"Query: Is Apprentice Callisunus referring to his inefficient mana flow? Would he like this unit to resolve the issue?"

Apprentice Callisunus froze. "What . . . did you just say?"

"Repetition: Is Apprentice Callisunus referring to his inefficient mana flow? Would he like this unit to resolve the issue?"

Apprentice Callisunus gritted his teeth and began to tremble. Sidonia frowned, placing a hand on NSLICE-00P's shoulder.

"Ah, Miss NSLICE-00P. I know you mean well, but we've tried everything to assist poor Nonus already. Please, do not provoke him on this subject."

But it was too late. Apprentice Callisunus glared at her.

"Obviously I would! But you can't! No one can! I've tried everything, asked everyone, and not a single thing helped! It's pointless!"

NSLICE-00P's robotic eye flickered. She analyzed Apprentice Callisunus's response and determined he was, in fact, willing to submit to treatment assuming she was capable of doing so. And Magister Cnaeus had told her to be useful to the academy, of which Apprentice Callisunus was a part of.

"Acknowledged. Request: Please hold still for treatment."

NSLICE-00P had detected a wad of mana in Apprentice Callisunus's body. All of his mana was being concentrated in that spot, and so was unable to flow freely at his command. The Academy Arcanum had, in fact, also determined this. However, they had been unable to do anything about it. The wound that had caused the issue had already healed, so Recovery Magic had nothing to repair. Mana Siphoning or even Mana Draining couldn't remove the blockage because mana wasn't flowing through his body correctly in the first place, and so another mage connecting to his mana was only able to access the trickle that was still moving. And targeting the blockage itself was considered . . . unwise. A living thing's mana would innately resist foreign attempts to manipulate it, and if it came apart incorrectly, it could have explosive consequences.

Ultimately, the Academy Arcanum had no way to safely and effectively handle the issue. Perhaps Magister Cnaeus might be able to do something if he handled it personally, but he was not willing to devote that much attention on an incredibly risky procedure for an apprentice of no particular note.

But none of that mattered to NSLICE-00P!

"Equalizer engaged."

She simply fired the Equalizer into Apprentice Callisunus's chest. Since the boy was low level and barely had any mana flowing through his body, the Equalizer beam went straight through his HP and into his body, striking the blockage directly and simply removing the mana outright without giving it a chance to resist or react. Apprentice Callisunus barely had time to react before the Equalizer hit its target. He grunted and clutched his chest.

"Nonus!"

Sidonia reached out before pulling her hand back. Her eyes widened, but she realized that while the beam was tearing through the boy's HP, it wasn't actually harming his body. She decided she wouldn't interfere. And the process only took NSLICE-00P a moment, in any case.

"Statement: Treatment concluded. Movement may now resume."

Apprentice Callisunus fell to his knees, groaning. Sidonia ran over to him, placing a hand on his back.

"Nonus, are you all right?"

He winced. "Ugh, I'm . . . everything feels like it's on fire. Everything . . ." His eyes widened. He stared at his hands. ". . . My mana . . . it's . . . flowing . . ."

Sidonia blinked, but she could, in fact, feel Apprentice Callisunus's mana signature grow stronger. She glanced at him, then at NSLICE-00P, and smiled.

"Oh my, it seems the stories undersold you. I wonder what you will show me next, Miss NSLICE-00P?"

# 34

# Reconnaissance in Force

*"Is it really scouting to vaporize the target?"*

—Post-action report of an NSLICE reconnaissance mission.

Even though he was now able to use magnitudes more mana than before, Sidonia did not permit Apprentice Callisunus to accompany them, instead having him immediately report to the academy hospital with a strict warning not to attempt any magic unsupervised. His mana flow *had* to be verified before he could even begin to put his knowledge into practice . . . despite NSLICE-00P's sensors indicating that all was well. After that, the group departed on a plaustrum subterraneum the Legion had sent for Sidonia.

A short while later, the transport rose out of the ground, and NSLICE-00P disembarked. They were inside a large fortress surrounded by stone walls, with limitanei and architecti adding additional structures and defenses. A full military base had been set up inside with everything a Legion would need to sustain a long-term operation. A man with a red cloak over his armor walked over to the group, with several soldiers behind them.

"Ah, Magus Major Sidonia, it is good to see you. I wish it were under better circumstances."

Sidonia smiled at him. "Always a pleasure, Legate Lucceius."

He turned to NSLICE-00P. "Is this her?"

Sidonia nodded. "May I present NSLICE-00P, Amicitia Populi Elteni and queen of the Dobhar. She has graciously agreed to assist us. Likewise, these are Imperial Inquisitors Niraemia and Sutharlan, along with Estrith Edilddaughter of the Dobhar."

NSLICE-00P took that as her cue. "Greeting: This unit is designated NSLICE-00P. It is nice to meet you."

Legate Lucceius shook her hand. "It's an honor, Your Majesty. My grandfather served under Dux Canus. I was glad to hear that Turannia survived, thanks to you."

"Acknowledged."

After greeting the rest, Legate Lucceius nodded and motioned.

"Come on, then, we don't have much time to waste."

The legate led them to the other side of the fort, and they climbed a watchtower. On the other side were the remains of a small town, with the main street leading to a giant tree. The giant tree's branches twisted and grew thorns, and cracks appeared in its bark that leaked green light. There was a large entrance at the bottom of its trunk.

In the streets below, a horde of plant monsters streamed from the dungeon and assaulted a Legion barricade in the center of the old town. The Legion had set up a metal palisade and a moat filled with burning oil, and Legion slayers hacked with halberds and poleaxes from the other side, sharpshooters launched exploding and flaming projectiles, and bulwarks blocked anything that made it past the moat. A group of Legion mages stood behind the lines in formation, their mana streaming toward the mage in the center as they launched massive Fireballs toward the horde. Siege engines along the walls of the fort lent their firepower as well.

"The Verdant Forest dungeon is relatively young, but had always been approved as safe, never sending a single monster outside. Just a few days ago, it suddenly turned, and the results are as you see. We're just lucky there was only a small dungeon town outside; the divers and limitanei managed to reduce the casualties somewhat and hold the line until we got here."

Sidonia nodded with a frown on her face. "You've tried assaulting the dungeon?"

Legate Lucceius nodded back. "First thing when we arrived. Plant monsters are tough, but at the time, we could handle it. The problem is the dungeon itself. Forests, flower meadows, jungles, you name it. Every inch of that dungeon is covered in greenery. And since it became corrupted, every single plant in that dungeon is now growing out of control . . . and fights back when you try to remove it. Vines grasp at you, trees drop branches on your head and trip you with their roots, even the grass grows sharp and tries to pierce your shoes. My mages just don't have the mana to burn out every inch of the entire dungeon, so we pulled out and requested reinforcements."

Sidonia rubbed her chin, humming. "Corrupted plants, huh? That could be a problem. Fire Magic isn't my forte; I might get a bit fatigued if I have to rely on it. Are any of the knight orders coming?"

Legate Lucceius frowned. "I put in the request, but you're the first to arrive. Corvanus seemed confident you'd be able to handle it."

"I see."

Sidonia turned to NSLICE-00P. "What do you think, Miss NSLICE-00P? Can we manage this situation ourselves?"

NSLICE-00P's robotic eye flickered. She had encountered and terminated plant monsters before, but these particular ones were giving off a different mana signature than the ones she had faced previously.

"Status Update: Mission success probability calculation requires live-fire testing to proceed."

Several magic circles formed in the air over the horde before Bolt spells of different attributes launched down at the monsters.

*You have slain nine Abeignis Ambulatio!*
*Gained 27 Personal XP!*
*The skill Dark Magic is now Level 2!*

Arcane, Fire, Dark, Air, Holy, Lightning, and Frost all performed well. Earth, Nature, and Metal formed physical projectiles that managed to defeat their targets, though they were somewhat resisted. Poison did take down its target, but noticeably slower than the others. Water dealt heavy damage to its target, but the magic appeared to be absorbed, and the damage was due to the physical force of the water. Light, again, was absorbed entirely, and Illusion didn't have any noticeable effect.

"Analysis complete. Current simulations predict positive results for a termination mission."

Sidonia blinked. "Farcasting and Multicasting at the same time? Will your mana reserves hold with that sort of expenditure?"

"Affirmative."

Sidonia shrugged, smiling. "Well, I'll assume you know yourself best. I suppose that much should be expected, given your feats. Legate Lucceius, I believe we will make another attempt, but it may be best to request additional reinforcements in case we are forced back."

Legate Lucceius nodded. "I'll put together an assault team to back you up and let Corvanus know your take on the situation."

Ateia turned to Seero. "Seero, I think Taog and I should stay here, but what do you think?"

NSLICE-00P's robotic eye flickered. The safest place was by her side, but it was true she would have to devote resources to protecting the friendlies, especially under the conditions of the dungeon interior described by Legate Lucceius. The Legion was currently holding strong, and if she assaulted the dungeon, the flow of monsters should cease as well, so Ateia and Taog would be at minimal risk of termination via dungeon monsters should they remain with the Legion.

Danger via hostile social maneuvering was another matter. On the one hand, NSLICE-00P predicted any attempt to do so would compromise the military operation in progress and would thus be an inefficient choice of action. However, social maneuvering was predicted as inefficient compared to immediate termination in the first place, so NSLICE-00P couldn't necessarily rely on efficiency calculations alone to predict the actions of potential hostiles. According to her observations, organics made inefficient decisions with alarming regularity.

But would that go as far as the Legion forces here turning hostile to the friendlies?

The one instance of hostile social maneuvering NSLICE-00P had on record was an attempt to provoke a response in view of local authorities. In this case, everyone in the area was a local authority. Any attempt to provoke a response would instead be a direct provocation by the Empire itself against two members of its own hierarchy. Such a level of inefficiency and unprovoked hostility did not have a statistically relevant probability by NSLICE-00P's calculations . . . unless the forces here intended to launch another rebellion. But that was also unlikely; by NSLICE-00P's calculations, they didn't have nearly enough troops to attempt that.

"Response: This unit finds that acceptable. However, this unit advises the friendlies to avoid any action that will increase the risk of termination while this unit is beyond immediate response range."

Ateia nodded. "Got it. We'll stay here, then. Legate Lucceius, could we help with the support somehow? We're a bit too low level for the frontlines."

Legate Lucceius rubbed his chin. "Well, I wouldn't presume to command two inquisitors, but why don't you accompany me? If you see any place you can offer assistance, we can discuss it."

With that, Legate Lucceius led the pair away. While he went to arrange things, NSLICE-00P decided to investigate another issue.

"NSLICE Lilussees, NSLICE Excellion Formantus Rattingtale the Third, friendly Melion, this unit requests support."

Lilussees was just stirring awake in her room, while Melion had been working on a project. Rattingtale, huddled in the corner of his room, heaved a sigh.

". . . You should just call-name me Rattingtale, yes-yes. I . . . I do not know if I am worthy-deserving of that title anymore . . ."

"Acknowledged. Designation updated to NSLICE Rattingtale."

Rattingtale shook his head. "As for the question . . . I'm sure-positive one of the others knows . . . yes-yes."

In their room, Melion had just put down the armor they were working on.

"Yes, Master! What do you need?"

NSLICE-00P redirected her attention to Melion.

"Query: This unit did not receive dungeon experience from terminating the most recent hostile. Does friendly Melion have any insight to the cause?"

"Hm, hmmmm, let me think. Oh! What level are you?"

"Answer: Dungeon level two hundred and sixty-three."

"And what level was the thing you killed?"

"Answer: Sixty-two."

Melion bounced once.

"Ah, that's it, then! Experience drops past a certain point; I think it's like, one hundred for humans? Anyway, once you're that level, enemies that are too far below you give reduced experience! I don't know the exact limit, but two hundred levels apart is probably too much!"

"Query: How do dungeon masters continue to grow?"

Melion bounced.

"Ah, that's why we stop hunting outside eventually! And why most dungeon masters don't fight themselves! We still get experience for things that fight and die inside our dungeons, but our personal kills fall off eventually! So, it becomes easier to just lure things inside and let your traps and monsters take care of it!"

"Acknowledged. Gratitude: This unit thanks friendly Melion for the data."

"No problem, Master!"

A short while later, NSLICE-00P and Sidonia stood at the head of thirty-five legionnaires. There were three full battle squads of ten each that could rotate in and out, along with a smaller support squad carrying additional recovery supplies, rations, and anything else the team might need. Legate Lucceius took a deep breath.

"Let me know when you're ready, and I'll give the command. We'll countercharge and try to clear the way for you."

"Request: Please remain in defensive formations. This unit cannot permit any risk to the Legion defensive line while her friendlies remain behind."

Legate Lucceius raised an eyebrow.

"You sure? It's going to be a long fight; you're sure you can spend your mana now?"

"Affirmative. Activating dungeon termination protocols."

With that, NSLICE-00P formed a Prismatic Bombardment magic circle. All the Legion troops not engaged in battle stared up at the sky with wide eyes.

Sidonia whispered to herself. "So, this is it. The spell I've heard so many stories of . . ."

Identifying the two most effective elements, in this case Holy and Fire, NSLICE-00P combined them. As she did, a skill she had never used before activated.

Beams of golden and silver fire streamed from the sky and swept across the monster horde.

*Hostiles slain: 123*
*The skill Purifier Flame has leveled four times and is now Level 5!*

Legate Lucceius stared in silence as NSLICE-00P marched toward the dungeon, beams from the sky eliminating anything that tried to exit it. Sidonia giggled and followed suit while the assault team all turned to the legate. Eventually, he shook his head.

"She's either reckless or confident, and from what I've heard, it's the latter. Move out and take down that dungeon!"

The soldiers saluted and followed after the two mages.

And so, NSLICE-00P began her assault on the corrupted dungeon.

# 35

# Terminate the Corrupted Dungeon!

*"The commanding officer must ensure that all troops assigned to the assault team have wills prepared and affairs in order, and are fully resolved as to their task."*

—The *Legion Manual*, on corrupted dungeon assaults.

The assault team prepared themselves for a long and difficult journey. Even a powerful Magus Major like Sidonia did not have endless reserves, and with the sheer amount of monstrous vegetation to be cleared, she would have to rely on large-scale spells that would burn through her mana quickly. The assault team's job would be to hold the line whenever the powerhouses needed to rest and recover their mana, which was why there were three full squads.

Two were all that was necessary to rotate shifts . . . but they expected to take casualties, especially as they moved toward the end of the dungeon; that was when rest and recovery would be the most important for the powerhouses, so they would need to hold no matter what. The third squad was to provide redundancy so that a death or critical wound wouldn't weaken the line.

These squads spread out in formation, since thirty-five people wouldn't fit in most dungeon hallways. The first squad would follow closely behind NSLICE-00P and Sidonia, ready to make camp or follow up if they needed assistance. The second squad would travel with the supply team in the middle, while the third squad would guard the rear from ambushes or quickly respawning monsters.

And then, they steeled their hearts and followed the two mages into the dungeon, knowing that not all of them were going to return . . .

Sidonia and the first squad blinked as they watched the scene before them. NSLICE-00P marched forward at a consistent pace, surrounded by glowing magic circles. These circles spat out jets of golden-and-silver flames all around her.

*Hostiles slain this floor: 336*
*The skill Purifier Flame is now Level 7!*
*The spell shape Blast is now Level 10!*
*The spell modifier Fusion is now Level 18!*
*The skill Spell Modification is now Level 5! New modifier available!*
*The skill Fire Magic is now Level 11!*
*The skill Holy Magic is now Level 13!*

Countless monsters screeched and flailed as they were burned in Holy Fire. The trees, the vines, the grass, even the dungeon's corrupted mana was purified and burned away by NSLICE-00P's attack, leaving the ground behind barren and pure. And the overgrown dungeon was so tightly packed that the flames continued to spread even beyond the cyborg's attacks, quickly clearing large areas around her. The team, once again, saw the door to the next floor.

Another floor down, and the first squad had not needed to fight a single monster since entering the dungeon.

And they were currently on the sixth floor.

As the last monsters of the floor were terminated, NSLICE-00P took stock of the experience.

**336 Personal XP gained!**
**Level up! You have leveled three times and are now at Personal Level 127!**

Her twenty-second level since starting the operation. Even with the reduced experience from the level difference, the sheer quantity of hostiles terminated caused her experience to shoot up. Meanwhile, Sidonia tilted her head.

"Um, NSLICE-00P, my dear, are you certain you do not need to rest? You seem to be spending a lot of mana; it wouldn't do to reach the lower floors with drained reserves."

"Affirmative. Explanation: This unit's reserves are holding steady at the current expenditure."

Sidonia blinked again before her eyes widened.

"Wait, are you saying that your mana regen outpaces your current spend?"

"Affirmative."

Sidonia frowned. "But . . . you used a strategic spell when we entered, and again to defeat the fifth-floor boss . . ."

"Affirmative."

Sidonia's eyes widened even further. "You're saying . . . those spells also fall within range of your mana regen rate?"

"Affirmative."

Sidonia froze, standing in place and staring at the wall. The first squad leader came up to her.

"Are you all right, ma'am?"

"Yes, fine, Decanus. I am just . . . questioning all that I know . . ."

The decanus shrugged. "Far as I'm concerned, I hope she keeps it up the entire way. I'd love to bring my full squad home."

Sidonia simply nodded at that and continued on.

As it turned out, NSLICE-00P could keep it up the entire way. The dungeon threw monster after monster at her . . . and all of them burned away.

They were now on the ninth floor, a wide room filled with a forest, where the trees blocked every inch of the room, leaving no path to advance.

NSLICE-00P simply formed a Prismatic Bombardment spell at the top of the room and rained fire from above as she pushed a Holy Fire wall forward from below. The group cautiously walked along the path she cleared as the entire forest burned down.

As they walked through the ninth floor, the first team's decanus frowned.

"Magus Major Sidonia?"

Sidonia was staring forward with blank eyes. "It's okay. I have lots of mana. They praised me for my uptime at the Battle of Rubrum Montem. Oh, sorry, what is it, Decanus?"

"Well, we're just wondering . . . why is the dungeon throwing the same monsters at her? Surely the demon lord must have realized normal plant monsters aren't working by now? Shouldn't we be prepared for some kind of response?"

Sidonia shrugged. "What do you know about corrupted dungeons, Decanus?"

"Just the stories, ma'am."

Sidonia nodded. "All dungeons connect to the Realms of Mana to pull power, attributes, monsters, you name it. Most start with one attribute, but as they grow older and deeper, they may gain access to more, which is when you start to see different types of monsters and floors."

She pointed around them. "But a corrupted dungeon is different. A corrupted dungeon is flooded by the power of a single Realm. All its other attributes, if it has any, are swept away."

The decanus rubbed his chin. "So you're saying it hasn't changed its response because it can't?"

Sidonia nodded. "And the corrupted dungeons tend to connect to the more extreme Realms as well. If I had to guess . . . this is no longer a Nature dungeon but an Overgrowth dungeon."

The decanus tilted his head. "What's the difference?"

Sidonia waved about as she spoke. "Nature represents life in all its aspects. Overgrowth focuses on just one: the need for plant life to cover everything before it and strangle out all competition. It is what the Empire would classify as a particular demonic Realm due to its singularly destructive focus. Overgrowth cannot be used to support the healthy growth of crops, nor to gently shape a tree. It can only send plant life growing out of control until it has choked the life out of every other living thing in the area."

The decanus frowned as he nodded. "Scary stuff."

Sidonia gave a wry smile. "Yes. But, perhaps as you can see now, such a singular focus can have consequences. Well, *normally*, the sheer amount of mana in a corrupted dungeon would overwhelm a favorable attribute matchup by quantity alone . . . but that assumes we can run out of mana in the first place."

Sidonia stared at NSLICE-00P's back. "Can you? Can you actually run out of mana, Miss NSLICE-00P?"

"Response: As far as this unit is aware, mana is a sustainable resource that appears to replenish over time, and this unit has not determined a theoretical limit to its quantity at this time. If additional restrictions on the time frame are applied, it may be possible to deplete this unit's currently available reserves with significant expenditure."

Sidonia stared up at the burning forest all around her. As the canopy burned away, she could catch glimpses of the strategic spell that was still bombarding the area.

"Yes. This is not a significant expenditure. Of course not. Obviously not. Why would I ever think that?"

"Response: This unit speculates that inaccurate assessments of this unit's capabilities stem from lack of knowledge regarding this unit's specifications. That knowledge is classified, however, so Magus Major Sidonia will have to adjust expectations via observations of live combat."

"That was rhetorical!"

The dungeon did not, in fact, have any other options than to try and grow faster than NSLICE-00P could burn it down. As such, NSLICE-00P and the assault team reached the tenth and final floor without issue.

The final boss looked like a tree . . . but from NSLICE-00P's scans, the tree itself was dead. The entire room was covered in vines of some sort, filled with mana. NSLICE-00P focused in on one.

| **Species** | **Description** |
| --- | --- |
| **Sagitta Radix (Level 65)** | **An impossibly fast-growing vine that devotes all mana and effort to growth. Strangles out everything, even other plants. Defends itself by launching sharp and toxic roots at any intruders.** |

Individually, it didn't seem very strong compared to the monsters in other dungeons with this many floors . . . but there were a great many vines, with more growing every second. They were growing so fast they appeared to be moving, twisting and grasping about as the new vines searched for space in the solid tangle that reached out from the room.

But well, that didn't matter to NSLICE-00P! Her magic circles formed once again and coated the entire room in Holy flames.

The sagitta radix screeched as it burned. Normally, a sagitta radix would regrow even while on fire . . . but the Holy mana in NSLICE-00P's flames purged the corrupted mana within it. Massive volleys of sharp roots shot toward her from every inch of the room . . . but NSLICE-00P simply formed a barrier of combined Nature and Recovery, blocking and curing the poisonous projectiles.

*The skill Heroic Power is now Level 4!*

She doubled her Mana Density with the hero skill just in case, but the barrage was not sufficient to break her barriers, and her mana reserves were holding steady.

It could not resist her as she advanced into the room. The sagitta radix grew beyond the boss room into a door at the back, so NSLICE-00P followed it there.

Inside, she found the core room.

A cracked dungeon core glowed with green light that formed directly into new sagitta radix. The room was empty otherwise, with no trace of the dungeon master. The air hissed and distorted, all of NSLICE-00P's mundane sensors going haywire.

Her robotic eye flickered. The last time she'd encountered something like this, terminating the dungeon core had resulted in the creation of a dangerous Rift. She would be able to terminate the Rift, but it would require direct utilization of her dungeon core abilities. She still wasn't certain what the Empire's response would be to discovering those capabilities, so, in order to withhold classified intel, she decided to confer with Sidonia first on how the Empire normally dealt with corrupted dungeons without utilizing dungeon powers of their own.

But . . . there was a problem.

She had set the sagitta radix on fire. The sagitta radix that apparently grew directly out of the core. And the Holy flames were traveling along the sagitta radix.

So, the Holy flames traveled through the room and up to the core.

Suddenly, the core burst into golden-and-silver flames. Mana flooded into the room, and the cracks on the core began to grow along its surface. NSLICE-00P prepared to absorb the mana of a Rift; maintaining the classified intel would always be secondary to terminating a serious threat, after all. But then . . . the

Holy mana traveled through the core and began to fill the air. The air began to quiet, and her sensors started to calm down. The mana signatures then began to fall, and the sagitta radix stopped growing out of the core, its green light turning golden and silver, then starting to fade. Eventually, it died down entirely, and the core crumbled into dust.

*Hostiles slain this floor: 1211*
*Gained 1211 Personal XP!*
*Level up! You are now at Personal Level 151!*
*The skill Purifier Flame is now Level 10! Upgrade available!*
*The spell shape Blast is now Level 12!*
*The spell modifier Fusion is now Level 19!*
*The skill Fire Magic is now Level 12!*
*The skill Holy Magic is now Level 14!*

**You have purified a Corrupted Core (Overgrowth)!**
**Gained 20 Personal Perk Points, 20 Dungeon Perk Points!**
**Dungeon Affinity: Nature increased to Minor!**

**. . . Nice job. Just . . . focus on getting rid of corrupted dungeons instead of making more work for me, please.**

*You have purified a Corrupted Dungeon and closed a Rift!*
*You have accomplished the Personal Feat: Dungeon Purifier (Overgrowth)!*
*Dungeon Affinity: Holy increased to Medium!*
*You have learned the skill Blessed Growth!*

*Well done. I have to say, as stressful and concerning as all this has been, I approve of your corrupted-dungeon-purification prowess with all my heart. Keep it up!*

INTERLUDE

# Mission Report: Verdant Forest Dungeon

NSLICE-00P and company returned to the Academy Arcanum, where they separated from Sidonia and returned home. Sidonia gave some greetings to her friends and colleagues before returning to her room. Once she did, she started to rub her chin.

"Well, that confirms it. She's definitely a hero with all that Holy mana she was tossing around. And that mana regen . . . she shouldn't have been able to keep up that many spells for that long from the mana signature I was detecting. She probably has some sort of mana-related hero skill, then."

Sidonia thought back to their trip and nodded.

"I should also note the powerful senses. She didn't miss any traps or ambushes the entire time. Long-range senses, too; I don't think she took a wrong turn even once. That, or she's lucky beyond all reason, but it's safer to assume the former."

She rubbed her chin and hummed once again.

"Well, I didn't get to see whatever trick she used on Caelinus's legions. Solo-casting Strategic Magic is impressive, but the spell she showed shouldn't have broken an anti-Archon formation like the survivors claimed. Her regen rate aside, her overall mana signature and displayed power wouldn't be superior to a Sun Elf Archon, or one of the old demon lords. So, she definitely has something else up her sleeve; maybe extreme magic penetration, or a powerful magic dispel? The anti-Archon formation should have been able to handle those, but who knows what hero skills might be capable of? There was that thing she used on Nonus . . . If she can scale it up, then maybe?"

She sighed then stepped over to her desk.

"Well, there should be enough to brainstorm some countermeasures, keeping in mind that she's a hero who likely has access to impossible skills. Guess I better write up this report while the memories are fresh."

* * *

Legate Lucceius marched into an office in the Corvanus Legion keep and gave a salute. Given the severity of a corrupted dungeon appearing in the Imperial Heartland, he had immediately returned to report his success in person. The man behind the desk, Magister Peditum Ausonius nodded at him.

"At ease."

Legate Lucceius relaxed. "Sir, here to report on the Verdant Forest mission, as requested."

Magister Ausonius nodded. "Good work. It's not every day we see a corrupted dungeon defeated with no casualties."

Legate Lucceius nodded. "Our reinforcements were most appreciated."

Magister Ausonius sighed. "Yes, which brings us to the next point. I believe your orders were to bring Miss NSLICE-00P nominally under your command to the maximum extent possible? This does not seem to have occurred. Can you explain yourself, Legate?"

Legate Lucceius saluted once more. "Yes, sir. As you said, I was to bring Her Majesty under my command to the maximum extent possible, but to defeat the corrupted dungeon at all costs. As she is an Amicitia Populi Elteni and the queen of the Dobhar, I judged the maximum extent possible to be treating her as an ally of equal standing."

Magister Ausonius clasped his hands together. "I believe you were aware she had been recruited by our contact at the mage's academy on a mercenary contract? Did you consider making her compensation contingent on her cooperation with your command?"

Legate Lucceius shook his head. "I did not, sir."

"Why, may I ask?"

Legate Lucceius frowned. "Because there was a corrupted dungeon only a frightfully short march from Corvanus that my troops could not handle, sir. We needed help to defeat it, so I prioritized that mission."

Magister Ausonius tilted his head. "What about Magus Major Sidonia, or waiting for reinforcements from a knight order?"

Legate Lucceius shook his head. "Magus Major Sidonia informed me she would not be able to handle the situation alone due to the unfavorable attribute of the dungeon. And I was informed that I was to handle the situation with only the reinforcements from the Academy Arcanum, so I did. With respect, sir, a corrupted dungeon is too dangerous to delay our response, given what I've heard of their growth rate. I judged I did not have time to argue with an Imperial ally over the details of command when she was already willing to help. And I have already stated in my report that Her Majesty's help was critical to our success."

Magister Ausonius nodded. "Understood. Well, under the circumstances, you made the right call. Just be aware that not all of the higher-ups are pleased with it."

Legate Lucceius took a deep breath. "Permission to speak freely, sir?"

Magister Ausonius raised an eyebrow but nodded. "Granted."

"What exactly was the point of that order? Her Majesty is an Imperial friend and ally. Insisting on her falling under Legion command goes against all our protocol for that situation, and in my opinion, she has already proven herself trustworthy. It's not like she'd join the Legion just by listening to my orders for one battle, even if she agreed."

Magister Ausonius bit back a sigh and muttered under his breath.

"What indeed . . . ?"

"Sir?"

Magister Ausonius shook his head. "I am not at liberty to describe all the plans in action here, Legate, but I can tell you this. There is great interest in Her Majesty NSLICE-00P and in establishing as firm and cordial a relationship with her as we can."

The legate nodded at that. "Understood. Will that be all, sir?"

Magister Ausonius nodded. "Yes, you are dismissed. Excellent work once again."

Legate Lucceius saluted before leaving the room. Once the door closed, Magister Ausonius sighed.

"I tried to tell Magister Verrucosis that was pointless, you know, but he has some strong ideas about the 'glory thief'. Thank the Aesdes the order was vague and Legate Lucceius has a good head on his shoulders; this could have been a disaster otherwise. What was he thinking, holding back the knights here? Letting a corrupted dungeon grow out of control on the doorstep of Corvanus wouldn't be what I'd call a glorious victory!"

Magister Ausonius shook his head once again. Magister Verrucosis might be good at waxing poetic on military might during the Imperial budget meetings, but his actual command decisions were a bit . . . *optimistic*, Magister Ausonius decided to say.

So, Magister Ausonius understood exactly why Legate Lucceius had decided to essentially ignore the order and deal with the problem at hand. Any sane officer with an inkling of experience would have done the same, Magister Ausonius included.

The problem now was that Magister Ausonius would have to try and explain that to the most definitely sane and experienced Verrucosis while . . . *advising* him on any impulsive follow-up orders. Magister Ausonius rubbed his chin.

Well, the Legion *had* sent an assault team along with NSLICE-00P, and it was Magus Major Sidonia who'd made the deal with her, so that wasn't on Legion record as a mercenary contract. Likewise, only the assault team themselves had actually seen NSLICE-00P take on the dungeon. So . . . if Magister Ausonius modified certain reports to downplay contributions by certain individuals . . . the

Legion might receive a bit of a publicity boost. And most of all, a certain boss of his might be pleased to hear his troops had defeated a corrupted dungeon.

Magister Ausonius took a deep breath. Of course, the biggest issue was . . . would the woman herself be okay with that? Magister Ausonius got a massive migraine just thinking of the possibility that she would be as concerned with glory as some other people he knew. But he put that horrifying idea aside and tried to look at the situation logically. From all the reports and rumors he had about her, she didn't appear to care about her public image whatsoever. She had threatened that Drusus idiot in the streets, after all, and made no mention of her impressive deeds on her own. She seemed entirely focused on her own affairs.

In that case, if Magister Ausonius lent her some assistance on the side, maybe, just maybe, she'd be okay with him not giving her due credit in this report. Maybe. Possibly. Hopefully.

Magister Ausonius held his head and heaved another sigh. He couldn't believe he was saying this, but sometimes, he missed the days of running from cave trolls.

"I see."

Aedile Hortensus rubbed his chin as he read over the report. He was still lying on his couch, though his hall was currently empty, save for the woman reporting to him. She nodded.

"What is your command?"

Aedile Hortensus shrugged and tossed the report into the air toward her.

"Same as before. Don't approach. Let's arrange a convoy to Turannia and see if we can't establish some deals . . . Give *slightly* favorable terms this time."

The woman looked up and blinked with wide eyes. Hortensus narrowed his.

"You disapprove?"

She lowered her head. "Of course not; it's just . . ."

Hortensus smiled. "You think I'm foregoing an opportunity?"

The woman paused before slowly nodding. "By all my observations, this NSLICE-00P should be extremely easy for you to manipulate. She does not appear to understand what is going on around her, and directly states whatever she's thinking. She has no concept of hiding her motives. She is either a master of deception who has completely deceived me . . . or she's a naive child waiting to be preyed upon. If you do not take advantage of her, someone else will."

Hortensus rubbed his chin and nodded. "Well, you're not wrong. Tell me, Helleria, what do you know of the Battle of the Pass of Teeth?"

Helleria tilted her head. "I . . . am not familiar with that battle."

Hortensus nodded. "Once upon a time, Potitus Opsius Ianuarius was the greatest strategist in the Empire, winning countless battles against the Empire of the Sun and repelling the invasion of High Archon Bhukluih Phani. One day, a clan of ogres set up camp in the Pass of Teeth, launching raids on the nearby Imperial settlements. The local Legion responded, but they were defeated. The Empire was humiliated by this loss to a bunch of savages, so it called in its most illustrious commander to deal with it."

Hortensus took a moment to sip from his wine glass.

"Potitus pulled out all the stops and orchestrated a brilliant and elaborate plan. The ogres would be drawn out of their fortifications by a small and agile force and lured into a trap. Once they left, the knights would flank them and set fire to their fort, depriving the ogres of their supplies. After a long chase, when the ogres would be exhausted and hungry, they would be led into the trap. Heavy defensive fortifications would block their approach, the knights from behind would cut off their rear, and the ballistae would pick off their chief. They would be leaderless, exhausted, starving, and surrounded. It was expected that they would scatter and fall."

Hortensus took another sip.

"And it worked like a charm. Events transpired exactly like Potitus had predicted. The ogres were lured out, their fort burned, and they walked right into the trap. Their leader was killed shortly after. And do you know what happened then?"

Hortensus smirked.

"The humiliation of Potitus. You see, the ogres did not scatter upon the death of the leader but instead flew into a rage and assaulted the fortifications. The Legion was caught off guard, and the defensive line broke. It turned out . . . the ogres didn't care that their fort had been burned or that there were knights to their rear because they never bothered to look behind them. They never realized they were in a trap to begin with, and didn't bother to consider their supply situation, so their morale wasn't affected at all. And killing their leader just made them mad. Potitus was not prepared for such a ferocious assault at that stage, so they broke his formation, and he was forced to retreat. The leaderless ogres then spread across the area to terrorize its residents, leading to a long and frustrating campaign of hunting down individual monsters."

Hortensus took a deep breath as he made eye contact with Helleria.

"The most brilliantly constructed plan can be shattered by brute force. This NSLICE-00P may not have a clue . . . but what she does have is overwhelming personal might, an easily provoked temper, and enough status to get away with it. So yes, I *could* likely dance circles around her and have her at my beck and call with ease. But if she *ever* discovers the duplicity, if anything ever sets her off, she could burn down everything we've built in an instant. She is like a dragon; there is a risk of catastrophic failure to every interaction with her no matter how clever we are."

Helleria slowly nodded at that. Hortensus continued.

"Well, to be fair, if I thought she was amenable to wealth and luxury, I'd invite her here and show her our greatest hospitality. But from all our accounts, she does not care for niceties or material pleasures. She will fail to either notice or appreciate any sort of social gesture. As such, I think our best play is to avoid contact, take the business opportunities her existence presents in a non-offensive manner, and then subtly hinder the others' schemes. Do keep an eye out for any way we could get into her graces, but do not take any action that could be construed as an insult. Let the proud bastions of Imperial tradition and the glory-hungry Legion fanatics test the dragon if they want."

Helleria bowed her head.

"As you wish."

Senator Balbus sat in a villa of egregious disrepair. It took every ounce of his willpower not to scowl at his surroundings—or at the man of questionable hygiene sitting before him.

Right now, Balbus had need of these people.

The man in front of him grinned with a crooked smile. "You have yourself a deal, Senator. Your order will arrive shortly."

Senator Balbus smiled and managed not to wince as he shook the man's smelly hand.

"Excellent."

The man chuckled. "We look forward to your continued patronage, Esteemed Senator."

"But of course. And I look forward to your continued service."

With that, Balbus exited the villa, quickly climbing on an unmarked carriage that ran off into the night. He took a deep breath.

With that, his preparations were complete. Now, all he had to do was figure out how to separate the beast from both her barbaric liege and the lowborn seductress calling herself a princess.

As the senator absconded in the night, a drunkard stirred on the ground of an alley close to the ruined villa. A drunkard with a strangely large, curled-up body under a ragged blanket and sharp, snakelike eyes.

"Well, well, well, look at what esteemed company the senator's keeping these days. Whatever could he be doing here, I wonder?"

# 36

# Inconvenient Truths

*"The Eastern Court is the military heart of the Elteni Empire and the linchpin of its endless struggle with the Empire of the Sun. The Council of the Southern Realms manages the Empire's vast trade networks as its economic heart. So what, then, is the Northern Court the heart of?*
*The Northern Court has been searching for an answer to this very day."*

—Maior Generalis Placus, after ignoring direct orders from the Northern Court.

After separating from Sidonia, NSLICE-00P and company returned to their rooms. Once there, NSLICE-00P analyzed her gains from the day. Once again, dungeon termination had proven remarkably efficient for improving her own capabilities, granting her a slew of new perk points and skill levels. The improvements to her magic skills, in particular, helped develop her magical knowledge base, moving her closer to both learning Spatial Magic via the foreign system and earning Magister Cnaeus's seal of approval to access his materials on the subject. For example, the two levels she had gained in Fire Magic each came with a small knowledge transfer, one that would have seemed subtle and subconscious to a pure organic lacking the ability to process mana-based data files. It contained a bit of knowledge about the behavior of Fire-attribute mana, and identified common inefficiencies in its use.

Mana, of course, was not pure data, and had other effects as well. The mana-based data transfer regarding Fire Magic did . . . *something* to the mana originating from her organic components. It assimilated into her own mana and then flared up whenever she attempted to convert it to the Fire attribute. Any Fire-attribute mana she created was just a bit faster and more powerful.

From what NSLICE-00P could tell, the physical properties of mana appeared to be impacted by any data the mana was carrying. Attributes represented that data. She considered if, therefore, she could develop Spatial Magic by storing related data in a mana-based form. She attempted to do so with whatever data she thought might be related . . . but she could not determine how to convert the data to a mana-based form. She still required more information on magic circles and the behavior of mana in general before she could do so.

Fortunately, she was continuing to grow in that regard, and not only from school of magic skill levels. Two of her dungeon affinities had grown from the latest dungeon termination: Nature and Holy. Nature had unlocked an array of new options within Dungeon Management. She could summon new, Nature-attribute monsters such as sylvans, which were apparently small and mobile trees with a humanoid shape, or moss slimes. There were some hybrid options as well, most notably ursanus natura cubs or kelp-based otters.

NSLICE-00P considered these. The ursanus natura and the otter option were ruled out, as she already had subordinate units with similar functions in 00B and Estrith. Sylvans could be an interesting option for operations in forested environments; however, at present, NSLICE-00P was focused on information gathering from major cities, so said capability wasn't necessary at this immediate moment. Likewise, she did not know if a plant-based organic would be compatible with NSLICE components and so if said monsters could be integrated into the NSLICE network. She concluded she would wait to see if Melion could be integrated into the network before summoning any additional non-animal or non-organic monsters.

Next came Holy. Holy was different from the other attributes, and NSLICE-00P had gathered that it was not intended to be integrated with the Dungeon system in the first place. As such, the growth of the Holy affinity did not immediately create new options within the Dungeon Management system like Nature did, even though it was the stronger affinity. But that did not mean it had no effect whatsoever.

NSLICE-00P logged shifts in her core's mana output when the affinities changed. Her core could now output more and denser Holy mana than it previously could. It was like how leveling Fire Magic affected her organic components, only on an even grander scale. And there was more to it than even that.

Her core was resonating with the world's core, and in this world, that appeared to result in exchanging mana with her environment. The strengthening of a dungeon affinity also appeared to intensify that exchange. Holy mana was now flowing both in and out of her core, connecting to larger flows of that mana that she could now detect all around her. It appeared to form an undercurrent to the mana all around her, touching everything in the world yet remaining in the background. Even her advanced sensors tuned to nonstandard energies could not detect this current apart from the general mana all around, so she predicted most organics would be unaware of it entirely.

This was an important piece of information. She calculated a high probability that this effect was related to the mechanisms of the Divination spell. Depending on the scale and scope of this undercurrent, it could represent the method by which the Divination spell gathered and distributed information. Investigating this phenomenon could therefore provide insight into that spell. And if she could determine how to safely cast it, she would gain another, powerful tool for information gathering.

Well, she would have to proceed cautiously. If Divination was tapping into this flow of Holy mana, then attempting to interact with it herself could end with the same results as casting Divination had, and NSLICE-00P did not intend to forcibly shut down her cybernetic components again. For now, she would passively gather information from the current and the flow passing through her core until her data set was large enough to create accurate predictions on the consequences of any interactions.

Finally, she had some new choices to make.

| Available Upgrades for Purifier Flame: | |
|---|---|
| Name | Description |
| Intense Purifier Flame | Purifier Flame boosts Mana Density, increasing effect. |
| Cleansing Purifier Flame | Fires affected by Purifier Flame gain a cleansing effect, allowing them to purify external effects from their target. |
| Spreading Purifier Flame | Fires affected by Purifier Flame spread to nearby targets, especially if corrupted. |
| Warm Purifier Flame | Fires affected by Purifier Flame sooth and inspire inhabitants of Aelea while causing fear in corrupted or invasive beings. |

She had used the Purifier Flame skill enough in the latest termination that she could now upgrade it. The skill itself was a supportive buff that added Holy-attribute mana to any Fire attacks she used, which proved remarkably effective in dungeon termination. *Intense* would provide a simple and straightforward boost to the effectiveness of any such attacks, while *Spreading* would increase their area of effect.

*Cleansing* and *Warm* were a bit different. Rather than boosting the effectiveness of Fire attacks, they added additional effects. *Cleansing* apparently provided some sort of healing effect, removing status effects, though if that applied to positive effects perhaps it could remove the effects of an enemy's skills as well? *Warm* was a bit more subtle, apparently providing a morale effect on top of the physical impact of the skill. Morale was harder to quantify, but very much acknowledged as important by NSLICE-00P's combat analysis protocols.

Well, in this case, NSLICE-00P's calculations quickly returned a conclusion.

*Purifier Flame has been upgraded to Intense Purifier Flame!*

Spreading was useful, but could be a double-edged sword if the fire spread out of NSLICE-00P's control. Cleansing was redundant with Recovery Magic for negative effects and the Equalizer for positive ones. And while the morale effect of Warm held promise, its specific targeting gave NSLICE-00P pause. It would not help her if she had to fight against inhabitants of this world, and would harm her if she ended up allied with beings defined as corrupted or invasive. The fact that this targeting did not necessarily line up with NSLICE-00P's current or potential affiliations ultimately turned her away from that modifier. In the end, she went with the straightforward boost to effectiveness that would be useful in the most scenarios and with the least potential downsides.

Next, she had another spell modifier choice.

| Available Spell Modifiers: | |
|---|---|
| Instant | Stores one magic circle. Corresponding spell may be cast without a circle. |
| Multi/Splitting | Enables one magic circle to create multiple effects. |
| Channeled | Spell increases in intensity the longer it is cast. |
| Repeating | Spell receives more mana than usual and uses additional mana to recast itself upon completion. May recast more than once if mana is available. Requires the Supercharge skill. |

The available choices had dropped significantly, likely due to her learning several on her own from her time at the library, even with a new choice appearing. But that just made it easier for NSLICE-00P to analyze.

*Spell modifier Channeled is now available!*

*Repeating* was a curious option. Having a spell repeat itself was another simple and effective way to boost the impact of a single cast. It could have particular value in penetrating HP barriers, depending on how quick the repeated cast was compared to the regeneration of the barrier, allowing one cast to punch a hole in the HP and the subsequent one to damage the target's actual body. It could be like a magical tandem warhead.

That had major promise, but NSLICE-00P ultimately went with Channeled. Her reasoning was that there was no guarantee Repeating would outpace the regeneration of the HP barrier, and thus may not have a penetration effect after all. In that case, it would be the same as just casting the same spell twice . . . or for twice as long. Channeled would prove more effective in that scenario, increasing the raw power of the spell overtime. NSLICE-00P was also uncertain how Repeating might function with Beam spells or Strategic Magic, particularly her Prismatic Bombardment spell, which were her most commonly used magical attacks. In contrast, it was easy to predict how Channeled might interact with them. Due to that, Channeled was predicted as the choice with less uncertainty involved.

Additionally, seeing a magic circle adjusted for increased mana flow over time could be informative as to the behavior and physical properties of mana in a way that a spell adjusted for multiple casts might not, so it was in line with NSLICE-00P's longer-term goals as well.

With that, NSLICE-00P concluded her current choices and analysis. She did still have the new Blessed Growth skill to experiment with, but that would have to wait until she was in an environment suitable for live-fire tests. Likewise, she could also predict from the description that it was a Nature-attribute version of the Purifier Flame skill, and so had a reasonable estimation of its effects and use cases. As such, said skill would wait until the next termination or upgrade mission.

And so, NSLICE-00P engaged rest cycle and maintenance routines . . .

The next day, NSLICE-00P and company headed over to the Academy Arcanum on their own, as Princess Caecila was still occupied, and NSLICE-00P intended to follow up with Sidonia on her compensation. There, they found Apprentice Callisunus and Sidonia waiting for them.

Walking right up to NSLICE-00P, Apprentice Callisunus stared her in the face. After a few moments, he knelt down.

"Your Majesty NSLICE-00P . . . I will never forget what you've done for me. I swear to you that I will repay this debt, even if it takes my entire life!"

"Acknowledged."

Sidonia giggled lightly before stepping forward as well.

"Nonus is a good boy. Do take care of him. I must also thank you for your assistance, Miss NSLICE-00P. The Empire owes you yet another great debt. As promised, I will help you gain access to the restricted materials. Now, could you tell me what exactly you were hoping to access?"

"Answer: Any materials regarding Spatial Magic, the prerequisites to acquire Spatial Magic, or any materials pertaining to the existence of other universes or the means of exploring beyond this universe."

Sidonia blinked for a second. "That's a . . . curious topic, not at all what I was expecting. My, you're just full of surprises, aren't you?"

"Response: Data on potentially hidden weapons is classified."

Sidonia tilted her head, resting a finger on her chin for a moment. "Hm . . . I don't think I've seen anything like that in the materials I've read. Why don't we pay a visit to the archmage, then?"

"Affirmative."

"Absolutely not."

Magister Cnaeus shook his head, continuing his work. Sidonia frowned.

"Magister Cnaeus, what exactly is the issue here?"

He scoffed. "As I said before, Spatial Magic is dangerous, and I don't trust Miss NSLICE-00P enough to let her access it."

Sidonia smiled. "Well then, allow me to vouch for her. If you are concerned with her skill, I can assure you her magic prowess is more than sufficient. If you are concerned with her trustworthiness, she has done a great service to me, this academy, and the Empire. Two of your Magus Majors are fond of her, and she has healed Apprentice Callisunus as well. What more do you require of her, Magister?"

Magister Cnaeus scoffed. "That is that and this is this. I've made my decision, Magus Major."

Sidonia's smile dropped. "Magister Cnaeus, you will not cooperate?"

He stopped what he was doing and glared at her.

"I will not. And I do not appreciate that tone, Magus Major."

Sidonia crossed her arms. "The Empire specifically requested the Imperial academy's assistance with a *corrupted dungeon* barely a stone's throw away from Corvanus. Miss NSLICE-00P helped me in dealing with this and was critical to our success. If it were not for her, we would have failed in this mission, one of our core obligations to the Empire. Something that *you* passed to me without any support or resources, Magister. How do you think it would have looked had I not brokered a deal with her? You owe her, Magister."

Magister Cnaeus's eyes narrowed. "Take care, Magus Major. Your tone is dreadfully close to threatening. I made no such deal with NSLICE-00P; any obligation belongs to you. And what-ifs don't matter; you dealt with the matter, and that is the end of it."

Sidonia sighed, reaching into her robe. Pulling out a scroll, she unfurled it.

"You have left me no choice, then. By order of the Magister Utriusque Militia, NSLICE-00P is to be granted access to any and all classified materials. Signed with Magister Verrucosis's seal. Here, take a look."

Magister Cnaeus shook his head. "That changes nothing. The Magister Utriusque Militia does not possess authority here!"

Sidonia sneered at him. "I beg to differ. In the case of an emergency, the Imperial academy will lend any and all assistance necessary to the Legion and will come under the command of the Magister Utriusque Militia. A corrupted dungeon near Corvanus would absolutely qualify as an emergency as defined there, and so orders regarding this incident hold weight. And if that isn't enough, the Emperor himself has requested this, two Imperial inquisitors want to see the material, and two of your own Magus Majors now agree that she is trustworthy. Would you like me to convene a council to see how many more will agree with me? And to be honest, I find your reticence here to be highly abnormal, Magister. You do know that if an Imperial inquisitor has reasonable suspicion that you are intentionally obstructing their mandate, they are empowered to detain you and launch a full investigation of your affairs, right?"

Magister Cnaeus's face twisted and grew red, and the man began to tremble. Eventually, he threw his hands up into the air. "Okay, fine! You want to know the truth?! The truth is, we don't *have* any materials on Spatial Magic!"

Sidonia froze. ". . . Excuse me?"

"You heard me! Nothing! Zilch! Not even a note scribbled on a napkin!"

Sidonia blinked. "I don't see how that's possible. We don't have any Spatial experts, that's true, but how is it that we have *no* materials on the subject?"

Magister Cnaeus glared at her and began holding up his fingers one by one.

"First of all, when Emperor Crescentius moved his capital out east, they ransacked the Imperial library for anything useful! And once the Empire was split into three courts, the Eastern Court had *no* incentive to return anything to us, while the Council of Southern Realms started hoarding their own knowledge! It's taken *centuries* for our academy to rebuild any selection at all! Half of our stuff is just written by our own staff, and we haven't had a Spatial Mage in the North since then! The reason so much of our material is 'classified' is that every Magister Arcanum of the Northern Court has been desperately trying to hide that we don't *have* anything and keep the Imperial Academy Arcanum from becoming the laughingstock of the Empire! And now, thanks to you, we've failed! Everyone's going to find out we don't have a goblin's latrine compared to the south and the east! So go on! Take a look! I'll give you access to every classified Spatial Magic text we have, all *zero* of them! I hope you're happy, Magus Major Sidonia!"

Sidonia just stared into space. "Oh, um, I'm . . . sorry?"

Magister Cnaeus slumped into his chair. ". . . Just go already. Do what you want."

Leading the group out of his office in complete silence, she slowly turned toward NSLICE-00P.

"Um, so, I happen to know a few good texts on Elemental Magic I could show you? I know it's not what you wanted, but . . ."

"Affirmative Response: General magical knowledge is also calculated as beneficial."

Sidonia nodded. "Okay then. Um . . . would you mind keeping the whole conversation with the magister between us?"

"Affirmative."

Sidonia exhaled her breath.

"Right then, let's . . . head over to the library . . . I guess . . ."

NSLICE-00P recorded the Elemental texts Sidonia controlled, then the group bid the academy farewell and headed back home. Since Princess Caecila wasn't with them, they had to walk back from the station.

Estrith sighed as she walked down the street. She had expected being a royal guard in the midst of the horrid Empire to be less . . . boring.

Ever since they had come to this city, Estrith had had nothing to do. Contrary to her expectation, the hated Imperials had not been lunging at their throats, nor had they forced her to prove her might. So, she hadn't had any real fights she could challenge herself against. The weak Imperials had guards galore when they visited the dungeon, so she barely even had to protect them. And then the queen of the Dobhar had been spending a lot of time surrounded by those small strips of wood and animal skins.

Now, Estrith vaguely understood that place was a repository of the Empire's knowledge. The first time they arrived, she had been excited to unlock the secrets of the Imperials for her king, though she kept herself in check so as not to expose her intentions. But, the moment she tried to steal their secrets, she ran into a terrible problem.

She couldn't read.

The squiggles drawn all over the scrolls meant nothing to her. Why would they? The Dobhar didn't have a written language of their own; all of their traditions were passed down from generation to generation by the Mother of Waves and her pupils, and they certainly weren't interested in borrowing from the hated Imperials. She believed her king had attempted to decipher such things, but Estrith had had a hard enough time learning spoken Imperial, and still spat out every word she spoke in the language of the enemy. And she had needed to dedicate herself nearly full time to the hunt in order to become a worthy match for her king. She could not waste hours and hours staring at squiggles!

The point being . . . Estrith had nothing to do, and had failed at her secret task at that. It was not like she could ask the Imperials for help stealing their secrets, after all.

All in all, this was a frustrating trip. The Empire's might was on full display for her. When she had seen the mighty fortresses flying through the air, the walls that towered into the sky like mountains, the sheer abundance of weapons and armor that could arm the entire Dobhar race, and the strange contraptions that rained fire on monstrous hordes, her heart had been filled with dread. Perhaps a legion of warriors like her king would not be daunted by such things . . . but her king was unique among the Dobhar. He could not resist something like this alone, and none of his people matched his strength.

And there was more . . .

She had seen multiple cities larger than the entire Home Fleet. She had seen races of all sorts under the Imperial banner, many of which could overpower a Dobhar with raw strength alone. She had seen dwelling places where the Imperial could control the temperature of the air, conquering the very elements themselves. She now partook in meals that would be a luxuriant feast among the Dobhar on a *daily* basis.

When she imagined all of this being pitted against the Dobhar . . . she trembled.

All their struggles, all their battles, all their victories and defeats . . . were nothing. The Empire had not even *tried* against them, not truly. If it had . . . the Dobhar would have been crushed in an instant. She finally understood why her king feared the "weak farmers," as she once believed them to be.

And she could not even begin to unlock the secrets of their strength. She could not even imagine the efforts it would take for the Dobhar to overcome such a foe. They would need an entire army of warriors on par with her king to even have a chance.

Except . . . the queen of the Dobhar had done just that.

She had taken an entire Imperial army on alone . . . and won. She inhaled the Imperial's secrets like a whale consuming a school of fish. She had the king of the Imperials' daughter at her beck and call. She was not at all intimidated by the Empire's might, wealth, or knowledge.

Estrith still did not like the usurper, and her heart burned at the humiliation of her king. But now . . . she understood *why* her king had chosen to bow his head and give up his rule. Whatever Estrith felt, she could admit it was a very good thing that this person was on the Dobhar's side.

It was then that someone bumped into her. Estrith turned to the man and growled.

"Watch where you are going, Imperial."

But then, the man leaned toward her and whispered into her ear.

"A Dobhar is in danger. Meet me here after nightfall, and I will tell you more."

"What?"

Estrith's eyes widened, but the man was gone. She looked around for a bit but couldn't find him. Eventually, Ateia noticed her falling behind.

"Miss royal guard, is everything all right?"

Estrith frowned and turned to catch up.

"It's . . . nothing."

She rubbed her chin as she fell back in line. A Dobhar? Here? Such a thing was impossible. Most of the Dobhar followed her king; the few clans who did not could not have made it this far from the Northern Seas. This was an obvious trick, likely an ambush by a deceitful Imperial dog.

But what if it wasn't?

Estrith's heart began to pound, and her eyes began to widen. Because she had thought of something. One situation that might result in a Dobhar finding their way this far from home.

There were tales of pups being kidnapped by Imperials. It was just one reason why the Dobhar were at odds with them. And for all of her life, Estrith had thought they were being hunted and slain.

But what if they weren't? What if a pup had been taken captive and brought here?

Heat burned in every inch of Estrith's body. Harming a Dobhar's pup was the gravest sin one could commit against them. So . . . if there was *any* chance that man had told the truth . . .

Estrith decided she would see what his intentions were.

And if this *was* an ambush like she first believed?

Well . . . it had been too long since her last hunt.

# 37

# Terminate the Scheme!

*"Remember our own bondage at the hand of the Sun Elves. No Enlightened being shall place any other in chains within the lands my armies march."*

—Velus, during the founding of the Elteni Empire.

When it was evening time and the group split up to their rooms, Estrith snuck out. She opened her window and . . . decided discretion was the better part of valor after seeing how far the ground looked. So, she snuck out into the hallway instead.

By rights, she should have informed the queen of the Dobhar. But Estrith had no idea if this Imperial had told her the truth. If it was an ambush, and Estrith led the queen of the Dobhar into it, she might be accused of treason. And even if not, she would have put her charge in danger. Her king had appointed her royal guard to the queen of the Dobhar; Estrith would not intentionally lead her into harm.

Now, if the queen of the Dobhar put herself into danger that Estrith couldn't save her from, then it couldn't be helped. But Estrith would not openly betray her; her king's command demanded at least that much loyalty.

Estrith intended to meet with this Imperial alone, and so needed to head out unnoticed. Fortunately, Estrith was an expert hunter . . . in the ocean. But she knew that sound was much harder to hear in the thin air of the surface! So, she should be even harder to detect than normal!

"Halt, who goes there?"

One of the villa's guards approached her. She clutched her spear and hissed at him.

"Ah, Miss Edilddaughter, was it? Carry on, then."

Estrith paused for a moment and then shrugged. So what if one of the Imperial dogs had seen her? They would not follow her out of the villa, so it was fine. She carried on her way.

In her room, Ateia paused. She caught something abnormal with her Presence Detection skill, so peeked out to the hallway to check. There, she saw Miss Royal Guard hissing at a guard before running off. Ateia rubbed her chin.

Had Seero sent her off for something? Or had the Dobhar run off on her own?

Ateia . . . had a feeling Seero already knew, but thought she would check anyway. Getting herself dressed, she made her way down to Seero's room.

"Seero, are you in there?"

"Affirmative."

A moment later, Seero opened the door.

"Query: Does friendly Ateia have an update, query, or request for this unit?"

Ateia nodded. "Did you notice Miss Royal Guard—um . . . the Dobhar leave?"

"Affirmative."

Ateia nodded. "Um, did you send her off for something?"

"Negative."

Ateia paused. "Uh, should we follow her, then? Make sure she doesn't get into trouble?"

"Affirmative. Statement: This unit was about to leave and follow at a safe distance to ensure friendly Estrith's safety."

Ateia smirked at that. "Oh, so that's her name. And I guess I should've known you'd be on it already. Well, I'm sure you can handle it, but can I come along? Maybe I can help somehow?"

"Acknowledged."

"Got it. Let's go, then."

Estrith made her way to the appointed place. The Imperial from before—or at least Estrith hoped, given she was still learning to distinguish humans—stepped out into the street. He grinned at her in a manner that made Estrith's fur bristle.

"So you made it after all. Good."

Estrith narrowed her eyes at him. "You said there was a Dobhar in trouble. Explain yourself, Imperial."

He chuckled. "Of course. You see, word is someone's bringing one of the little ones in on a shipment tonight. I know where they are . . . but it'll cost you."

Estrith froze, standing completely still. She began to tremble.

They had taken a pup.

Estrith's dream was to have a pup with her king. That was why she'd trained herself relentlessly and became one of the Dobhar's foremost warriors, so that she would be a worthy match for him and no other. So, of course, she had dreamed of what it would be like to have a pup and had talked with the other mothers about that.

And she, over the course of her duties, had also spoken with those who had lost their pups.

So, when she imagined a pup being taken by these Imperials and what its mother would have felt like . . . her entire body filled with fire, and her vision went red.

She didn't remember what happened. The next thing she knew, she was holding the *dog* by his neck, with the tip of her harpoon pressed against his cheek.

"Tell me where they are, *now.*"

The man suddenly started to flail as sweat drenched his face.

"They're coming in through the main gate in the west! Please, don't hurt me! I had nothing to do with it!"

Estrith threw the man on the ground. Spinning her spear around, she held it high.

"Estrith, wait!"

Pausing as she heard her name, she glanced behind to see Ateia running toward her.

"Do not interfere, *Imperial.* This does not concern you."

Ateia shook her head. "Look, I overheard what's going on. I understand why you're angry, but this guy probably isn't involved. You shouldn't just kill him!"

Estrith scowled, but she took a deep breath. The girl was right; she had lost control of herself. It was likely true this person wasn't the actual kidnapper . . . though the fact that he knew implied he may be involved. Still, she was wasting time here.

"Leave!" she barked at the man, who scrambled off into the night. Estrith turned and marched down the street. "Go home, Imperial. I do not wish to be around you right now."

Ateia shook her head, narrowing her eyes. "Look, you're going to need help. Do you even know where the main gate is?"

Estrith glared at her. "Obviously, *Imperial!*"

Ateia crossed her arms. "Really? Then why are you going the wrong way?"

Estrith froze. Gritting her teeth, she refused to turn and look at Ateia. Ateia sighed.

"Look, you have every right to be angry. But we're here to help you, you know?"

Estrith paused again. "*We?*"

She glanced around, and her eyes widened. She had been so focused on Ateia that she hadn't noticed the queen of the Dobhar approach as well.

"Affirmative Response: If a friendly unit has been taken captive, this unit's protocols require all reasonable efforts be exerted to retrieve them."

Estrith frowned and furrowed her brow. There was a part of her that wanted to refuse, to take care of the Dobhar's business on her own. But she quickly silenced that. This strange human might be the usurper who humiliated her king . . . but she *was* the rightful queen of the Dobhar, and with that came the responsibility to protect her people. If this was not an ambush, then there were no further reasons for Estrith to keep the queen of the Dobhar out of it.

And most of all . . . Estrith knew that the queen of the Dobhar was mighty indeed. If she lent assistance, then the pup would almost certainly be saved. And Estrith would let *nothing* prevent that, least of all her own pride.

So, she gritted her teeth and bowed her head.

"Queen of the Dobhar . . . please protect your people."

"Affirmative."

The trio made their way toward the main gate. It was nearly time for the gate to close, but there were still a few pedestrians and wagons making their way inside, including a small merchant convoy that had just made their way inside. NSLICE-00P scanned the pedestrians and wagons as they passed her by.

And then . . . she found something. A small thermal signature consistent with a Dobhar lying inside one of the wagons of the merchant caravan.

"Status Report: This unit has located a potential match. Investigating."

NSLICE-00P began to approach the caravan, Estrith following while clutching her spear, but Ateia stepped in front of them both.

"Hold on, you two. Before we get violent, how about I try talking to them?"

Estrith growled, but NSLICE-00P's robotic eye flickered. If a Dobhar had been kidnapped after the Battle of Castra Turannia, NSLICE-00P would consider it a hostile act. But if the kidnapping had occurred prior to the agreement between NSLICE-00P, the Dobhar, and the Empire, then NSLICE-00P would classify it as part of the prior hostilities between the Empire and the Dobhar. In that case, the culprits would not have entered into hostility with her and would not be subject to termination protocols. However, as slavery and kidnapping were illegal in the Empire, the targets would have no right to keep the pup in their custody, so NSLICE-00P would simply retrieve the pup and warn the culprits against any further hostile behavior.

This being the case, allowing Ateia to attempt a diplomatic solution was a reasonable course of action. Her updated self-defense protocols indicated attempting to utilize her and the friendlies' status within the Empire was preferable to force as long as a favorable outcome was achieved.

"Acknowledged. Statement: This unit will defer forcible extraction while friendly Ateia attempts a diplomatic solution."

Estrith scowled, but the queen of the Dobhar had spoken. She would wait . . . for now. But if the Imperial girl betrayed them, she would do what was necessary.

Ateia nodded and stepped toward the group.

"You merchants there, hold on a moment!"

The merchants paused to look at them as the lead man raised an eyebrow.

"Can I help you, miss? I'm sorry, but we are on important business."

Ateia frowned. "As are we. We've been a told a kidnapped Dobhar has been brought into the city on this convoy. You don't happen to know anything about that, do you?"

The man scoffed. "Take your games elsewhere, girl. Let's get a move on."

Ateia reached into her pocked and pulled out the symbol of an inquisitor, channeling mana through it. "By order of an Imperial inquisitor, I demand you cooperate with the investigation."

The man suddenly frowned and held his hands up. "I see. Still, Inquisitor, trafficking intelligent species is a grave accusation, and I can assure you we have nothing to do with it."

Ateia crossed her arms. "So you wouldn't mind if we search your goods, then?"

The man heaved a sigh. "We would really like to make our delivery, but if you insist."

Ateia turned and nodded to NSLICE-00P. NSLICE-00P's Dungeon Field Generator had already confirmed the pup's location, so she immediately walked toward one of the wagons with Estrith in tow. She moved to one of the barrels that was filled with fruit but that had a secret compartment on the bottom. She pried it open.

The Dobhar pup was curled up there, trembling. Estrith immediately moved, grabbing the pup, who flinched at first until he realized Estrith was also a Dobhar, then whimpered and curled up into her embrace. Estrith held him close, then her face contorted, and she grabbed her spear with her spare hand.

"You *monsters*. You will all die for this!"

The lead merchant paled and held up his hands. "We had nothing to do with this, honest! I had no idea; you must believe me!"

Estrith was about to strike him down when NSLICE-00P held a hand in front of her.

"Observation: Body language and physiological analysis indicate a 99.61 percent chance he is telling the truth. Please deactivate termination protocols. Target is unlikely to be hostile. Further investigation is required prior to termination."

Estrith scowled and was about to argue when the group heard footsteps approach.

"What's going on here?"

Just then, a group of guards walked down the street, approaching the convoy.

However, they stopped and blinked at the scene before them. One of the guards leaned in toward the decanus and whispered, "Um, sir? Wasn't the otter thing supposed to be alone? And wasn't she supposed to be killing people?"

The decanus rubbed his chin. "Hmm, this is . . . unexpected. Let's see; if there's more of them, and they aren't fighting . . . then . . . um . . . Ah, forget it, just arrest them. We'll figure out the charges later!"

But then, something moved from a nearby alleyway, and the tip of a lance appeared in front of the decanus's face.

"Well, well, well, what do we have here? Did you hear that, centurion?"

Another group of guards, this one led by a centurion with a red cloak, walked out of the nearby alleyways. The decanus and his men turned pale.

"I did indeed. Your information was correct after all, Miss Agedia."

Agedia scoffed. "Of course it was. It was vetted by the Magister Exploratore, you know?"

The centurion glanced around and frowned as he motioned to the first group of guards.

"Traitors in my very century, unbelievable. Take this scum out of my sight."

The centurion's troops saluted and began removing the first group's weapons. He then turned to the merchants and frowned.

"Under the circumstances, we will need to ask you some questions and conduct a full investigation of your cargo. Come with me."

The lead merchant's shoulders slumped. "I understand."

The centurion then turned to NSLICE-00P. "We apologize for this, queen of the Dobhar. May we rely on you to care for the victim?"

"Affirmative."

"Thank you. We'll sort out this situation, if you don't mind."

"Acknowledged."

The centurion led the troops and merchants away while Agedia slithered over to the group, putting her lance back on her back.

"Well, that settles that. Good work not immediately killing everyone, shiny girl."

NSLICE-00P's robotic eye flickered. "Query: Were any of the involved individuals hostiles requiring termination?"

Agedia shook her head. "The merchants weren't involved. We've already apprehended and *interviewed* the kidnappers. Seems they hide their victims in the cargo of unrelated convoys so someone else takes the fall if the victim is discovered. As for the dirty guards . . . Well, they're more useful alive, for now. We want to target the real culprit, after all."

"Acknowledgement: This unit agrees that termination of primary culprit is the most efficient course of action. Please specify target."

Agedia grinned. "Oh, don't worry. He's already being taken care of."

* * *

"Unhand me! I am a member of the Imperial Senate; you cannot treat me like this!" Senator Balbus yelled as legionnaires dragged him from his villa, scowling as he saw someone waiting outside.

"Magister Appius, I should have known a snake like you would be involved. What is the meaning of this?"

Magister Appius grinned and took out a scroll. He slowly unraveled it and cleared his throat.

"Ahem, Senator Balbus, you have been found engaging in the trafficking of Enlightened peoples, a grave violation of a statute of the Empire set in place by Velus himself. Moreover, you have been found bribing the limitanei and scheming to provoke the subject of an Amicitia Populi Elteni. You will be stripped of your rank and titles and imprisoned to await judgment for your crimes."

Balbus's face scrunched up. "Lies, all of it!"

Magister Appius continued grinning. "Come now, Balbus, you don't believe I would be here if my case wasn't rock solid, do you? I know you hate me, but please don't insult me."

Balbus scowled. "You can't do this! I appeal to the Emperor and demand that justice be done!"

Magister Appius shrugged. "I mean, sure, that's your right if you want. But you should know, the Emperor ordered this after I presented him the evidence, so I don't imagine submitting the case to his judgment is going to help much."

Balbus sneered at him. "It will if he knows what's good for him! Consul Noxisius will speak with him on my behalf!"

Magister Appius grinned again. "Oh, what's this? Can you identify this seal for me, Balbus?" Holding out the scroll for Balbus to see, Balbus's face paled once he saw Consul Noxisius's seal at the bottom.

"That's impossible! He wouldn't do that!"

Magister Appius chuckled. "He did. You've been abandoned, Balbus. Even the consul is unable, or perhaps unwilling to pull you out of this one." He narrowed his eyes and leaned in toward Balbus. "And I have to admit . . . it will please me to see this. Take him away."

Magister Appius took a deep breath with a smile as the soldiers dragged the screeching former senator away. The magister then looked up into the night sky.

"Well . . . I don't think you'll ever forgive me, but I hope this helps, Agedia. I truly was an idiot back then."

He then slithered off into the night to personally place Balbus behind bars.

INTERLUDE

# Home Visit

Estrith scowled as she watched the Imperial dogs get carried away. She did not trust the Imperials to enact justice on their own, and was not at all comfortable with letting them live. The snake had explained that they weren't responsible, but Estrith wasn't sure she bought that.

But then, the pup curled up closer to her, clutching at her fur.

"I want my mom."

Estrith gripped him tight.

"Not to worry, little hunter. I will return you to your mother, this I swear on my mother Edild."

The most important thing was that the pup had been saved. While the debt of blood had not been settled . . . Estrith could restore hope to a Dobhar mother who had none.

Estrith turned to look at NSLICE-00P and frowned.

She had to admit, without the queen of the Dobhar's assistance, she could not have rescued the pup. She hadn't had any idea of where to look. She would have had no options but to attack every wagon in sight, hoping that one of them held the pup. The Imperials obviously would have objected to this, and Estrith would have ended up trying to fight off endless Imperial soldiers and fallen without achieving anything.

Instead, the queen of the Dobhar had immediately identified where the pup was being held captive. The Imperial girl had secured permission for them to retrieve the pup without having to fight their way through. And then, the snake had turned the Imperial soldiers against one another.

And now, the pup was safe within her arms.

Estrith took a deep breath.

"Queen of the Dobhar."

NSLICE-00P turned to her.

"Acknowledgement: Does friendly Estrith have an update, query, or concern for this unit?"

Estrith bowed her head. "Thank you for protecting our people."

"Acknowledged."

She then turned to Ateia. "And thank you, Ateia. Your assistance was . . . appreciated."

Ateia smiled. "Of course. I'm happy to help."

Estrith nodded. "I, Estrith Edilddaughter, will not forget this debt."

And so, the group headed home.

Consul Noxisius heaved a massive sigh. Falling back into his chair, he grabbed a glass of wine, drank deeply from it, savored the drink, then threw the glass against the wall with all his might.

"What was he thinking?!"

A black-haired woman stood in the room with a neutral expression. "Balbus took every opportunity he could to boost his status, that much was to be expected. He was in a situation where he had to either submit and be humiliated or attempt to turn things on her. Most of your faction would have done the same, the wisdom and execution of his attempts aside."

Consul Noxisius gnashed his teeth. "I get that, but there's a big difference between standard maneuvering and stupidity! I expected him to lay the charm on and worm his way into her graces, not . . . whatever this harebrained scheme was supposed to be! What did he even expect to happen here?! That the court would refuse to investigate a situation involving an Amicitia Populi Elteni? That the Magister Exploratore wouldn't be conducting a full rundown of everyone who came into contact with her?! The trafficking thing was going to be exposed no matter what happened here! And now, we've failed utterly to make any sort of positive contact with this NSLICE-00P."

The woman rubbed her chin. "I consider this a partial failure, but not a complete one. I believe we can turn the situation to our advantage."

Consul Noxisius shook his head. "I wish I was as optimistic as you. I fail to see any sort of silver lining to these storm clouds."

The woman shook her head. "It is not optimism. In fact, this situation presents a better opportunity. Previously, you were constrained by your position as head of the traditionalist faction, correct? You had to send a subordinate to make contact because most of your supporters would frown upon you meeting directly with an outsider like this."

Consul Noxisius sighed. "That's right. They're a bit . . . *inflexible* when adapting to practical changes in our circumstances. Really now, pride in the Empire is all well and good, but is not looking down on the girl who *defeated a Legion alone* too much to ask?"

The woman nodded her head. "But now, one of your subordinates has caused a massive scandal and a grave insult to an Imperial friend who is an honored guest of the Emperor."

Consul Noxisius raised an eyebrow. "You *are* trying to point out the *bright* side, right?"

The woman nodded again. "The scandal has become so great that even your most vocal and hardline supporters have joined in condemning Balbus. Since you were the one who sent him in the first place, even if you have washed your hands of his schemes, it would be acceptable for you to offer an apology. No, I believe it is expected that you would do so."

Consul Noxisius paused, then began rubbing his chin. "So I could now offer to meet this NSLICE-00P directly, and none of my supporters will complain . . . much."

The woman nodded. "Yes."

Consul Noxisius slowly began to smile. "Impressive. It appears we may be able to salvage this situation, after all."

The woman nodded. "If we are to achieve our goals, we must adapt and make use of every opportunity we can find."

Consul Noxisius nodded. "That we must. Make the arrangements. Send her a token of our goodwill as well, to ensure she will accept."

The woman bowed her head. "It shall be done."

Then she stepped back into a shadowed part of the room and disappeared from sight.

In order to make up for this grave insult to the queen of the Dobhar, the Empire offered the service of one of its airships to return the pup to its home. As such, Princess Caecila escorted NSLICE-00P and company aboard the ship once again, sans Agedia, who remained behind in Corvanus. This time, they were not taking the scenic route and flew at full speed, so it only took a few hours to make the trip to Turannia.

NSLICE-00P had contacted Uscfrea ahead of time, so he was prepared when the airship arrived above the former Legion keep in NSLICE-00P's lands. Still, Uscfrea found himself staring blankly at the ship floating in the air.

". . . Maybe I overestimated the Empire's decline. Or underestimated, if they had something like that and still couldn't respond to my attack . . ."

Behind him, Vopiscus shrugged.

"It's the latter. Utrad and Turannia have been requesting airship support for decades now, but after Magister Galenus's rebellion commandeered one, the Northern Court has refused to deploy its airships outside of the Imperial Heartland, save for short trips like this. Kind of defeats the purpose of having them if you ask me, but no one did."

Dux Augustalis gritted her teeth and clenched her fist. "It's decisions like that that drove us to desperation."

Uscfrea was about to make a smug comment when he remembered how the Dobhar's elders had refused his command to move the Home Fleet onto land. He slowly closed his mouth. He reminded himself that poor strategic decision-making was not limited to the Empire.

A smaller ship separated from the large one and landed in front of Uscfrea. The ramp extended, and then she walked out. NSLICE-00P had returned.

"All hail the queen of the Dobhar!"

Uscfrea struck the ground with his tail and bowed his head along with Wulver Chief Ceitidh Greumach and all other Dobhar and Wulver in the area. Dux Augustalis and Vopiscus hesitantly saluted in Imperial fashion, and their people followed suit.

Estrith, Ateia, Taog, and Princess Caecila's group also disembarked. Princess Caecila raised an eyebrow at the sight of the Imperial rebels in NSLICE-00P's territory but said nothing. Estrith walked up to Uscfrea with the pup strapped to her back and knelt.

"My king, I have returned."

Uscfrea nodded. "Welcome home, Warrior Estrith. You should probably call me steward or Uscfrea in public, you know."

Estrith frowned. "I could never!"

Uscfrea chuckled and shook his head. "Well, we'll talk about it later. Now, are you going to introduce the hunter on your back?"

Estrith lowered herself and gently took off the pack, then picked the pup up in her arms and rose to her feet. Uscfrea smiled at the sight.

"This is Eoforich, son of Elfswitha."

"Eoforich!"

The moment Estrith said the name, a Dobhar woman broke into a run. Eoforich's eyes widened, and he leapt from Estrith's arms as the woman approached.

"Mom!"

Elfswitha caught her pup and embraced him with all her might. Only after a long moment did she turn to Estrith and bow her head.

"I thought he was lost. I hoped, I prayed, but I never dared to imagine he might return to me. How can I ever repay you?"

Estrith frowned, then shook her head. "It . . . was not me, but the queen of the Dobhar who rescued your son."

Elfswitha's eyes widened, but she nodded and walked toward NSLICE-00P and began to thank her. Uscfrea nodded, turning to Estrith.

"How fares your trip, Estrith?"

Estrith furrowed her brow. "It is . . . confusing, my king. The Empire is as mighty as you always said. Yet, they are strange; they waste tremendous time and effort on things I do not understand. I . . . do not know what to think, if I am honest."

Uscfrea patted her shoulder. Estrith looked up to him.

"That is good, Estrith Edilddaughter. Our people are warriors, straightforward and honest. The Imperials are significantly more complicated. It will take some time to get used to them, but that is the point. We will need more than spears if we are to rise among them; it is good that you see how much we have to learn."

Estrith's eyes widened, and she nodded her head. Uscfrea then glanced over.

"What do you think of our queen so far?"

Estrith frowned. "I have no liege but you, my king. But, she uses her power to take care of what is hers, and she is powerful indeed. It . . . is good that she is on the Dobhar's side. She . . . she *is* the queen of the Dobhar, for now."

Uscfrea smiled at that. "I believe so as well; we will need to work to keep it that way. Come, let me show you how our people have grown."

Estrith smiled and nodded. "Of course, my king. I would be honored."

# 38

# A Slew of Offers

*"Why fight when you can profit?"*

—High Queen Melriel of Mirima, upon concluding a permanent nonaggression and trade pact with the Elteni Empire.

Aedile Hortensus laughed at the senator's joke. Helleria sat next to him, covering her mouth as she gave a small chuckle. Eventually, the senator stumbled off to refill his cup, and Aedile Hortensus smirked.

"It is fortunate the senator has more funds than he has wit."

Helleria gave an actual smile at that. "Speaking of senators, what do you think of the situation with Balbus?"

Aedile Hortensus's smirk grew. "Well, I know you hate it when I say I told you so . . ."

Helleria raised an eyebrow. "Really? Seems to me like she just stumbled about while the Magister Exploratore took care of it?"

Aedile Hortensus shook his head, clicking his teeth.

Helleria puffed her cheeks. "Don't be patronizing. Balbus was an idiot; don't tell me you're impressed the queen of the Dobhar escaped that poor excuse of a scheme."

Aedile Hortensus smiled as he shrugged. "The senator always had greater ambitions than means, so he fell into things he never should have approached. He was doomed the moment he got involved in Enlightened trafficking. So, my question to you is . . . why has he survived this long at all?"

Helleria shrugged. "He was never important enough for anyone to deal with. It would have been more beneficial to blackmail him than apprehend him . . ." She trailed off as she finished the sentence.

Aedile Hortensus nodded.

"Exactly. Magister Exploratore per Corvanus Appius, the man who got appointed as the head of the Northern Court's intelligence as a Mélusine due to his competence and sheer will to hold the Empire together, hated that man's guts. You don't think he put together all that evidence he presented only after the queen of the Dobhar got involved, do you? And yet, up until now, he made no moves whatsoever against the senator. Even with their intense personal hatred of each other and Balbus making every possible move to provoke him, Magister Appius tolerated his existence. And that is simply because Balbus was a useful pawn. He could be blackmailed at any moment should the magister have required an extra vote in the senate, an inside man to Consul Noxisius's faction, or even a bit of leverage over the consul himself."

Helleria frowned again. "And the queen of the Dobhar missed all of that."

Aedile Hortensus shook his head. "I think, rather than her having missed it, she didn't think of it in the first place. And that is my point of concern. If it had been me Balbus had targeted, I would have marched straight to Consul Noxisius to gain whatever concessions I could. Miss NSLICE-00P didn't care to do that, and so the Magister Exploratore blew the senator up before she could in a much more literal fashion. Which is why she must be addressed with the utmost care and courtesy. Because she just doesn't see things the way the rest of us do and is entirely willing to set it all on fire."

Helleria slowly nodded while Aedile Hortensus smirked.

"And so, how about you invite her to a meeting?"

Helleria nearly fell out of her seat, her face contorting as Aedile Hortensus chuckled.

"Like I said, we're going to address her with care and courtesy, not ignore her entirely. We have learned *something* about her in all of this: she does seem to care about the Dobhar she conquered. That gives us an angle for mutually beneficial arrangements. I simply wished to emphasize that we will remain *polite* about it. We will even be . . ." Aedile Hortensus took a deep breath, his face twisting in disgust as he spat out the final word, ". . . *honest.*"

Helleria gasped and laid her hand on Aedile Hortensus's forehead. He simply took a deep drink of his wine as she checked his temperature.

Magister Verrucosis rubbed his chin and grunted. The situation was . . . complicated. On the one hand, they had failed to integrate this NSLICE-00P into the Legion due to the complete lack of ambition and loyalty from Legate Lucceius. And now, NSLICE-00P had been revealed to have a powerful friend in Magister Exploratore Appius. Magister Verrucosis hated how the Exploratores thought themselves independent of the Legion from which they had been born, but he could admit the magister did good work. Any direct or uninspired moves against the foreign upstart could backfire with severe consequences, as Senator Balbus and his patron Consul Noxisius had recently learned.

On the other hand, Magister Ausonius had managed to spin the reports and downplay NSLICE-00P's accomplishments. The record now stated that it had been the Legion who had conquered the corrupted dungeon near Corvanus, with only a footnote mentioning any external assistance. That man had a good head on his shoulders.

Magister Verrucosis's eyes widened, and then he grinned.

"I've got it."

Magister Ausonius was smarter than he realized, for he had revealed the strategy his better could use. One that Magister Verrucosis had used himself on more than one occasion. He knew, best of all, the difference the wording of a report could make. The same report stating the same facts could be twisted to call the same battle as either a stunning victory or a humiliating defeat. Emphasizing certain aspects and downplaying others could completely change how an audience would receive the same fundamental facts.

Verrucosis knew the need to maintain morale by ensuring the public had an accurate view of his own achievements, as well as the need to restrict the impact of . . . less competent commanders by ensuring their own deeds were seen in the proper context. And he had no doubt the same had occurred regarding this . . . NSLICE-00P. After all, the only reports they had were scattered interrogations by frightened traitors. The facts were extremely sparse, which gave great leeway for interpretation. And how would the people involved in these reports have interpreted them?

A cowardly traitor who first betrayed their oaths and then fled after encountering the first resistance would of course want to play up the one who "defeated" them. Such would both justify their own cowardice while also diverting the Empire's attention to the new and powerful threat. Likewise, Emperor Lucius had an obvious interest in playing up this NSLICE-00P, given she represented his entire plan for gaining any real power of his own. A desperate play for control by a weak and powerless man.

So, Verrucosis had no doubt that NSLICE-00P's achievements had been exaggerated. Likewise, conquering a small corrupted dungeon with an entire Legion and the North's foremost battlemage present to handle the majority of the work was not a particularly impressive feat. All he had to do was find conclusive proof of the exaggeration. Not only could he cut the delusion that this random wanderer was somehow more impressive than the Legion that had forged the Empire, but he could reveal Emperor Lucius's duplicity. He could prove once and for all the need for a strong, well-funded, and independent Legion.

And he thought he had a good idea on how to do just that . . .

* * *

Since she was here, Uscfrea gave NSLICE-00P a rundown of her territory. She could observe the situation in the Otter Burrow at any time, but the dungeon only covered a small fraction of the territory, so the tour was still informative. In fact, Uscfrea quietly avoided any of the dungeon-related matters due to Princess Caecila joining the group.

The princess was still very impressed.

With the support of the people of Utrad, the Dobhar civilization was advancing at lightning speed. The beach was full of Dobhar training under the command of veteran centurions. Limitanei and architecti cooperated with Dobhar shamans to reshape the sandy beach into a stone port. At the top of the cliff, a small city now extended from the old Legion keep as the Imperials set up shelter while Wulver and former Exploratores scouted the surrounding area.

And while it was not part of the tour, NSLICE-00P could also see how Uscfrea was leveraging the Otter Burrow. The Otter Burrow's territory continued to expand over the Dobhar settlement and was now moving up toward the Legion keep at the top of the cliff. Uscfrea had added several dungeon rooms here and there, mainly to produce resources. There was a boneyard where the Dobhar could scavenge to make their harpoons, a cove leading to an underwater area with constantly respawning sea life to fish, and a kelp forest where the Dobhar harvested various sea plants. Uscfrea had also set up a more traditional dungeon slightly away from the Dobhar settlement, where young Dobhar were training in real combat.

And, in a secret room near the dungeon core itself, a trusted group of now Contracted Dobhar practiced firing with flintlock pistols. It appeared that even though the cyborg-related items were too technologically outdated for NSLICE-00P, Uscfrea was greatly curious about the new weapons. Well, at the moment, they were only experimenting with the most basic items and hadn't seen fit to bring them out into the open; it remained to be seen if the Cyborg affinity would unlock more advanced options.

Over the course of the tour, NSLICE-00P noticed a flash of light.

"MY QUEEN!"

A young Dobhar rushed through the halls of the Dobhar settlement and jumped toward NSLICE-00P. Or rather, a young Sacred Otterkin, given the streaks of golden and silver fur on her body and the glowing gem in her forehead. The young Aldreda tried to jump up NSLICE-00P's leg, but couldn't get a grip on her armor. NSLICE-00P responded by catching her, and the young Sacred Otterkin embraced the cyborg's arm, nuzzling her head against it.

Her mother, Aethelu, came running down the hall before she stopped with a smile and bowed.

"My queen, welcome home. We are most pleased to see you."

It turned out the young Aldreda was growing up well. The Dobhar had been worried when she had continued to absorb mana, much as a monster, and they'd had to give her some levels far earlier than a normal pup. But fortunately, beyond her quick growth and mana absorption, Aldreda acted like any other Dobhar pup.

Well, save for one very apparent characteristic.

Princess Caecila and her entourage had frozen solid.

"Um, Petronia, Typheras, is that . . . a Dobhar pup with Holy mana?"

Petronia rubbed her chin. "Um, it appears like that, Your Highness. I . . . am not sure. I have never heard of a Dobhar hero before, much less one that is practically an infant."

"Right. So . . . um . . ."

Typheras shrugged. "Maybe we're mistaken? She just has fancy fur, and she's hugging NSLICE-00P, right? Maybe we're getting the mana mixed up."

"My queen, my queen! Look at what I can do!"

"Observation: Unit Aldreda's magical capabilities beyond expected parameters. Updating potential combat effectiveness calculation."

Princess Caecila grew even more still.

"Oh. She just cast a Holy spell. Of course."

Petronia nodded.

"Your Highness, I believe it wise to maintain strong relations with Her Majesty NSLICE-00P."

Once they had toured the area, NSLICE-00P and friends bid farewell to Turannia once again. Estrith bowed before Uscfrea, and then they climbed aboard the airship to return to Corvanus . . .

NSLICE-00P spent the trip to and from Turannia analyzing the materials Sidonia had given her access to. As the Magus Major specialized in Elemental Magic with combat applications, she had access to most of the Academy Arcanum's military-grade spell circles. It wasn't the Spatial Magic NSLICE-00P had hoped for, but it was still a great boon for her general magical knowledge and her combat capabilities.

In particular, the classified military spells focused heavily on Strategic Magic performed via joint ritual casting. This was a method by which different mages could join together to cast larger spells than any of them was individually capable of. It was also the Empire's main tool for magical warfare, given its mages' individual inferiority to their primary opponent, the Empire of the Sun.

As such, NSLICE-00P was able to record several new Strategic Magic circles. Most notably, in her opinion, was the massive barrier spell Caelinus's rebels had used against her. A strategic-sized barrier spell would vastly improve her defense capabilities. In addition, there were several new offensive spells as well: a thunderstorm one like the one used against her, Water and Frost variants of her Rain of Fire spell, and an Earth-based spell that originated from the ground instead of the air.

The other piece of knowledge she had gained regarding ritual casting was perhaps even more important. It would, admittedly, not affect her own capabilities that much; her mana reserves and Mana Control were sufficient to solo-cast strategic spells without issue, after all. But, if ritual casting could be introduced and mastered by her growing NSLICE network, it would massively improve their capabilities. If her subordinates could cast Strategic Magic without her, they would gain powerful offensive—and defensive, if the strategic Barrier spell circle was viable—tools. That, in turn, would increase their operational freedom, since they could handle a much wider variety of threats without needing her to intervene.

NSLICE-00P had, unfortunately, not had the opportunity to test any of this knowledge. Strategic spells required a large, clear, secure location that had been confirmed free of all third parties. The risks of collateral damage or of explosive misfires were particularly high for spells meant to combat armies, after all. And while NSLICE-00P was fully confident in her ability to construct any magic circle with perfect precision, there was no guarantee that the spell circles recorded in the library were actually viable. She was confident she could identify and stop a misfire before it occurred, but there was still a small risk.

All of this meant she needed more space than normal before conducting live-fire tests, as she could not rely on a spell circle that had not been confirmed as working beforehand. She would need to arrange such a testing environment so she could employ the new circles in combat as needed.

And as for ritual casting? That was even less practical at present. Not only did it require the same conditions as testing Strategic Magic did, it also meant deploying all of her subordinates, including some who had not been registered with the Empire. The existence of those subordinates was currently classified even to her friendlies Ateia and Taog, much less Imperials she had no contracts with.

She could, of course, leave her friendlies behind and find an isolated location to conduct all this testing, but increases in combat capabilities in and of themselves were not a major priority at the moment. They did not outweigh the major directive or additional scans of academy materials for data relevant to the primary directive.

That was, until she arrived back in Corvanus, and several messengers arrived. NSLICE-00P was currently in a lounging room with Agedia, Ateia, Taog, and Estrith, debriefing with Agedia on anything that had occurred while they had been in Turannia, when the mansion's attendants delivered two scrolls to her. All conversation ceased and all eyes turned to her as she opened and read the scrolls. Ateia asked the question.

"What is it, Seero?"

"Answer: This unit has been invited to meet with Aedile Lar Paesentius Hortensus to discuss trade agreements between his business interests and this unit's subordinates in Turannia. This unit has also been requested to participate in Legion exercises by Magister Peditum Decius Considius Ausonius. Legion assistance with this unit's primary directive has been offered in return."

Agedia hummed and crossed her arms.

"What are you thinking, shiny girl?"

"Answer: This unit calculates both offers to be an efficient use of time. Exchange of goods and services between this unit's subordinates and Imperial business interests could improve economic and military capabilities of this unit's subordinates, and will provide opportunities for information gathering related to this unit's primary directive."

NSLICE units like NSLICE-00P had assisted in security and transportation for trade deals between her original organization and third parties, so NSLICE-00P knew that trade alone did not violate nonintervention protocols, depending on the terms of the agreements. But her protocols were not the only ones at play this time.

At this point, Estrith stepped forward with a frown on her face.

"My queen, you are talking about the Dobhar, are you not? I would not have us bound to any Imperial."

"Response: This unit is referring to all subordinates currently residing in the Dobhar secure home base, including but not limited to Dobhar units. This unit will not directly affiliate subordinate units to third parties; however, exchanges of goods and services are not classified as an affiliation with military obligations."

Estrith kept frowning. Agedia shrugged.

"Well, barbotter, I'd also feel uncomfortable interacting with Aedile Hortensus, as anyone who likes keeping their money should. But if I were you, I wouldn't reject it out of hand. The Empire *does* sell some of its weapons, you know?"

Estrith glared at her but fell silent. If the Dobhar could acquire some of the weapons she had seen . . .

". . . Fine. Do as you wish, my queen. I do request to be present for any conversations involving the Dobhar, however."

"Acknowledged. Query: Have any other units identified any vulnerabilities or issues with meeting with Aedile Lar Paesentius Hortensus?"

Agedia rubbed her chin.

"He specifically stated the meeting is for the trade talks?"

"Affirmative."

Agedia frowned.

"That's . . . really weird, to be honest. From what I understand, Aedile Hortensus *never* specifically states his intentions with anything he does."

"Query: Does the anomalous statement of intent indicate potential hostility?"

Agedia hummed for a while before slowly shaking her head.

"To be honest, I have no idea why he would do this. But . . . he might be a glorified con artist, but he is also insanely cautious, and he *does* fulfill his contracts, just not always in the way he leads you to understand. I can't see him trying anything particularly aggressive after what happened to Balbus. I think it's worth a try. Just . . . remember that he's always working an angle and searching for an advantage. Don't sign anything just because it seems good on the surface."

"Acknowledged."

Agedia slowly nodded.

"And then, what do you think of the other offer?"

"Response: Assistance with this unit's primary directive is appreciated. However, this unit requires additional details on the exact exercises and this unit's role within them, as well as the exact assistance being offered before calculating a response. Query: Have any other units identified any vulnerabilities or issues with meeting with Magister Peditum Decius Considius Ausonius?"

Taog frowned.

"I'm not sure. How common is it for the Legion to conduct exercises with non-Imperials?"

Agedia shrugged. "Depends on which non-Imperials. For close allies like the Dwarves or the kingdom of Mirima, there are ongoing annual drills. For a distant neutral party like, say, the Thunder Harpies of the Wild Lands? Unheard of. Shiny girl here is a bit of a mixed case in my opinion. Normally, someone as new as her wouldn't be invited to anything more practical than a parade, but she *is* technically an Amicitia Populi Elteni. And then there's the question of what Magister Verrucosis is thinking with all this. I can't imagine he simply wants friendly cooperation with shiny girl. Maybe he's hoping to try and one-up her in some way during the exercise."

Ateia tilted her head. "But, like, is that even possible?"

Agedia narrowed her eyes.

"Don't get complacent. Just because shiny girl has overwhelming power *doesn't* mean they have to acknowledge it, especially in an exercise where they aren't fighting to the death or anything. Plenty of ways to make her look bad."

"Requesting Clarification: The most likely threat is to this unit's reputation?"

Agedia slowly nodded.

"Requesting Additional Clarification: Could this unit's relationship with the Empire and current agreements regarding the primary directive be at risk as a result?"

Agedia frowned.

"Hm . . . indirectly, sort of? If people don't like you, they won't be enthusiastic about helping you. But with the Amicitia Populi Elteni title and with the other two as inquisitors, given Emperor Lucius's current position . . ."

Agedia took a deep breath and then sighed.

"I would say it's not a direct threat as long as you don't kill a bunch of people or something during the exercise. I don't see a way they could threaten your current titles with just an exercise, but they could make further negotiations more complicated for you, especially with the senate."

NSLICE-00P's robotic eye flickered for a bit.

"Analysis: This unit calculates that potential benefits outweigh expected risks and will agree to both meetings."

Agedia nodded.

"All right. Just be careful, okay?"

"Affirmative."

# 39

# Deal or No Deal?

*"Please comply immediately, or this unit will reengage termination protocols."*

—An NSLICE unit during surrender negotiations with a Resistance band.

The next day, NSLICE-00P found herself walking through a warehouse for construction materials. She noted more golem carriages moving stacks of brick, stone, and lumber about, supervised by organic workers as they worked tirelessly. There were also giant golem hands extending from the roof of the warehouse that could pick up and move large payloads anywhere within the facility.

It was an acceptably efficient arrangement by NSLICE-00P's analysis, though the lack of conveyer belts kept it a step below full automation. The golems also seemed to need regular verbal commands, so the organic workers were more heavily involved in the process.

The worker ahead led her to a side hallway, and eventually, to a small office. There was very little adornment, just a desk and a couple chairs with a mana-powered lamp and a couple of potted plants. Behind the desk sat a handsome man in a simple but high-quality toga, with a similarly dressed woman behind him. He gave a smile and rose to his feet.

"Ah, you must be Her Majesty, the queen of the Dobhar. I am Aedile Hortensus, pleased to meet you."

"Greeting: This unit is designated NSLICE-00P. It is nice to meet you."

Aedile Hortensus smiled and motioned to his seat.

"Please forgive me for my lack of hospitality, but shall we launch right into it? My impression is that you keep a busy schedule."

"Acknowledgement: This unit prefers efficient negotiations."

Aedile Hortensus nodded as the woman stepped forward, handing him a scroll.

"Wonderful."

Opening up the scroll across the desk, he spun it around and motioned to NSLICE-00P.

"I'll cut right to the chase, then. I am greatly interested in opening trade with your people, the Dobhar."

He gave a nod to Estrith, who simply growled at him. He put his hands up and turned back to NSLICE-00P.

"They have far greater access to the North Sea than any other race, and so I imagine they have all sorts of novel goods. Likewise, I imagine there are plenty of goods they might appreciate from various places in the Empire. I would like to send regular convoys to exchange whatever goods the Dobhar and my merchants see fit to trade."

Estrith frowned but fell silent. She knew her discomfort was simply from having to interact with Imperials in the first place, and the snake's warnings that this one was particularly untrustworthy. But despite that, she could not find wrong with his words at first glance. While organized trade between larger entities was unfamiliar to her, barter existed amongst all Enlightened societies, so she could understand the fundamental idea. And, ultimately, she knew that such an exchange fit within Uscfrea's goals for the Dobhar. Acquiring what the Empire had for themselves was her ultimate task, so she squashed whatever feelings she had and turned to NSLICE-00P, waiting for the queen of the Dobhar's response.

As for NSLICE-00P, her robotic eye flickered a bit.

"Affirmative Response: This unit calculates trade between her subordinates and subordinates of Aedile Hortensus to be potentially beneficial."

Aedile Hortensus's smile grew.

"Excellent. Then, for my proposal. Am I right to assume your territory does not currently possess significant port facilities?"

"Affirmative."

Aedile Hortensus nodded.

"Then, I would also like to offer my assistance in constructing a suitable location for trade. This here is a basic contract and preliminary proposal, though the exact details and numbers are subject to change based on the actual conditions of the site. You may pay in Idrint or in kind, although I am also willing to discount the price if you wish to offer favorable trade conditions to my subsequent convoys. I would also like to lease one of the warehouses and docks we will build if that is agreeable to you, and again, we can discount the upfront cost of construction if you will grant us favorable conditions on that."

NSLICE-00P quickly scanned the contract and proposal, then ran numbers. Her analysis quickly concluded that the agreement was favorable. The upfront cost was irrelevant to her due to her ability to generate Idrint on demand, so having a port constructed on her behalf was purely beneficial. While Aedile Hortensus had alluded to longer-term aspects of the contract, these were not mandatory if she was willing to pay the full amount upfront, so she did not need to consider such things. There were some provisions for providing reasonable housing and supplies to the construction workers, but that was par for course. All in all, the contract was simple, straightforward, and calculated as beneficial both to the Dobhar and to her primary directive.

However, she had specifically granted authority over the Dobhar's internal affairs and the administration of her territory to Uscfrea, so she contacted him now.

*"My queen? Do you have need of me?"*

*"Uploading potential contract with Imperial authority Aedile Hortensus. Please analyze and indicate whether the terms are acceptable."*

*"Hm?"*

NSLICE-00P waited as Uscfrea looked things over.

*"My queen . . . you are offering to pay for this?"*

*"Affirmative."*

*". . . Why, may I ask?"*

*"Explanation: Idrint is calculated as the most abundant and readily available of the proposed methods of payment. This unit calculated that the proposal itself is beneficial to Dobhar subordinates and provides opportunities for information gathering regarding her primary directive."*

*". . . I see. In that case, we would be grateful to accept, my queen."*

*"Acknowledged."*

Aedile Hortensus watched in silence, even when the woman behind him started glancing at him. He bided his time, though, even as NSLICE-00P just sat there silently for several minutes. He managed not to react, either, when NSLICE-00P began speaking without warning.

"Affirmative Response: This unit and subordinate units have calculated the proposal as acceptable."

Aedile Hortensus broke out into a wide grin and clapped his hands.

"Marvelous. I will arrange for an architecti to visit and survey locations at once, then."

"Acknowledged."

There was some further discussion of logistical details before the preliminary contract was signed. Aedile Hortensus was a bit surprised when NSLICE-00P offered to pay the full upfront amount in Idrint, but he accepted it without a fuss.

He waved goodbye as the group left the room. Only after the door shut did his eye start to twitch . . . and then a moment later, he collapsed on the table and heaved a massive sigh. The woman behind him, his aide Helleria, rubbed his back.

"Are you alright?"

He heaved another sigh.

"That was . . . *far* more difficult than I expected. That girl is *entirely* too honest and straightforward! Do you know how many times I had to hold myself back? How many holes I saw we could exploit that I'll have to just . . . let go?! I think this . . . *honesty* business is bad for my health."

Helleria nodded as she continued rubbing his back.

"There, there, just think of your ogre story."

Aedile Hortensus heaved another sigh.

And so, the first official economic contact between the Empire and the Dobhar was agreed upon.

# 40

# A Military Exchange

*"I, for one, welcome our new killer robot overlords."*

—A former US admiral, after NSLICE units intervened in a mutant assault for the first time.

Later that same day, NSLICE-00P made her way over toward the Imperial palace. Making her way to a side building, one housing Legion administrative personnel, she was quickly guided to a large office. She entered the room to find a fit, middle-aged man in Legion uniform. He also rose to his feet and saluted.

"I, Magister Peditum Decius Considius Ausonius, greet Her Majesty NSLICE-00P, Amicitia Populi Elteni and the queen of the Dobhar."

"Greeting: This unit is designated NSLICE-00P. It is nice to meet you."

Magister Ausonius nodded to her as he shook her hand.

"Likewise. Thank you for meeting with me today."

"Acknowledged. Request: Please provide additional details regarding proposed joint exercise and compensation."

Magister Ausonius nodded.

"Right away, Your Majesty. We were planning to run the Corvanus legions through an anti-Archon drill. Normally, we use Strategic Magic to mimic the power of an Archon, but that solution isn't perfect. It was reported to Magister Verrucosis, however, that you confronted an anti-Archon formation when you faced Caelinus's rebel legions. We were wondering if you would be willing to participate as the Archon."

"Requesting Elaboration: Please state all mission parameters."

Magister Ausonius stepped over to his desk and pointed to a map with a few carved figures on it.

"We would meet at the field of Sol Ruinam here. We would want to run through a couple of scenarios. First, we would set up the formation ahead of time and have you attempt to break it. Then, we would run some more constrained attempts, such as you ambushing our forces or vice versa, to see how the legions hold up under time pressure. Ah, please note that we expect there to be no casualties in these sorts of exercise if at all possible, so please make every attempt to avoid harming our troops. We would prefer you to hold back if you wouldn't be able to break the formation without doing so."

"Acknowledged. Statement: This unit will attempt to achieve simulated combat objectives with a zero-casualty parameter. Warning: This unit will utilize all acceptable means at her disposal but will withhold any classified capabilities. Exact replication of combat feats cannot be guaranteed during simulated combat as a result."

Magister Ausonius nodded at that.

"That's fine, we don't expect you to show us everything you have. Also . . . how would you feel about us potentially firing back? We would like as realistic a simulation as possible, but we obviously will not put you at harm or do anything you are uncomfortable with."

NSLICE-00P's robotic eye flickered.

"Response: This unit will request live-fire testing of offensive means against this unit's potential barriers before determining if live-fire counterattacks are acceptable."

Magister Ausonius raised an eyebrow.

"Truly? That's . . . quite generous of you. All right, I'll make a note of that. And then, let's talk about the compensation. If you participate in these exercises, Magister Verrucosis will pass the information on your people to all the legions of the North, who will be instructed to keep an eye out. He will also reach out to his contacts in the eastern Legions and the Sky Legion of the South to see if they have any information. Would that suffice?"

"Affirmative Response: This unit finds the proposed conditions acceptable. Please state the location and time this unit should report to."

Magister Ausonius blinked. "Um, really? Just like that?"

"Affirmative."

Magister Ausonius blinked again, and then frowned. Grunting, he heaved a sigh.

"Are . . . you sure about this, Your Majesty? I, um, well, let's say the exercises go really well for the Legion. You know your own reputation might take a bit of a hit, right? People might question if you really did what they say you did in Utrad if you don't break our formations here. Would you be okay with that?"

"Affirmative. Explanation: Assistance with this unit's primary directive is calculated as higher priority than public acknowledgement of this unit's capabilities.

Preventing wide-spread familiarity with this unit's capabilities is also calculated as beneficial for the sake of terminating and avoiding termination by potential hostiles."

Magister Ausonius stared for a moment.

"You . . . would *want* for people to think you're weaker than you actually are?"

"Affirmative."

After that, Magister Ausonius hammered out the rest of the details with NSLICE-00P. Once she had left, he stood up and walked over to his window. Letting out a deep breath, he held his head and chuckled.

"Prefers everyone to think she's weaker because it will make easier for her to kill and survive? Who would've thought she and Magister Verrucosis would be on the same page? She's definitely frontline military . . . and definitely not politically minded, that's for sure."

He heaved another sigh and shook his head.

"Well, hopefully, they'll both be satisfied by the results of all this . . . assuming the anti-Archon formation holds . . ."

The next day, Magister Verrucosis watched as his legions gathered and prepared at the designated location. The field of Sol Ruinam—the site of a decisive battle between a joint alliance of the city-state of Elteno, the kingdom of Mirima, and the Dwarven clans against the Empire of the Sun. The victory won there had ended the threat of the Empire of the Sun to the area and propelled Elteno into a major regional power. Where the first incarnations of the anti-Archon formation had made their debut and humiliated the Sun Elves' mightiest mages.

Magister Verrucosis hoped for a repeat of such events today.

He would not have to wait long. The Imperial family's plaustrum subterraneum soon rose from the ground, and off disembarked the woman herself, NSLICE-00P, along with her pet inquisitors and foreigner. Princess Caecila accompanied her.

Magister Verrucosis saluted to the princess.

"Welcome, Your Highness. Magister Utriusque Militia Septimus Vipstanus Verrucosis, at your service."

Princess Caecila nodded. "Thank you, Magister."

He dropped his salute. "Here to watch the exercises? It's rare for you to participate in Legion affairs while your husband is away, is it not?"

Princess Caecila raised an eyebrow. "Is that a problem?"

Magister Verrucosis grinned. "Not one bit. Come, Princess, and let me show you the might of our Legions!"

Unlike many, Magister Verrucosis had no issue with Princess Caecila. Sure, she was a naive and foolish girl way in over her head, but that suited the Magister

Utriusque Militia just fine. She knew better than to interfere with military affairs, which was more than he could say for a lot of *other* people he knew. Plus, her husband was a trained knight and popular amongst the Legion, so the magister looked forward to his eventual reign.

His only issue with the princess was her present company, for he knew she had been sent to keep an eye out for the upstart. But, he figured that would change today. If the princess saw with her own two eyes the duplicity of NSLICE-00P's reputation and the real and proven strength of the Legion, the Imperial family would then understand who it should place its hopes upon. And if Emperor Lucius insisted on his foolish plans, the princess at least could inform her husband of current events.

He turned to the woman in question.

"Greetings, Your Majesty NSLICE-00P, queen of the Dobhar and Amicitia Populi Elteni. I am Magister Utriusque Militia Septimus Vipstanus Verrucosis."

"Greeting: This unit is designated NSLICE-00P. It is nice to meet you."

Magister Verrucosis nodded and put a smile on his face.

"Thank you for joining us today. I hope it will be . . . *informative* for all parties involved."

"Acknowledgement: Improvements to participant efficiency is a major objective of the incoming exercises, which this unit will make all reasonable efforts to achieve."

Magister Verrucosis nodded.

"Good. In that case, I'd like to begin immediately."

"Affirmative."

Magister Verrucosis nodded to Magister Ausonius standing quietly behind him, and his subordinate stepped forward to instruct NSLICE-00P on where she should head for the first exercise. Magister Verrucosis couldn't help but crack a smirk.

His victory soon approached . . .

NSLICE-00P moved to a part of the field where the Legion was setting up. There were several mages gathered, as well as a handful of siege engines and their crews. Magister Ausonius turned to face her.

"Here we are, Your Majesty. We can test our offensive measures against your defenses here so you can decide whether or not you want to allow counterattacks and how many. Just to confirm, can you form barriers around targets other than yourself?"

"Affirmative."

Magister Ausonius nodded. "Good, then we shouldn't have any issue. Would you like to proceed with the testing?"

"Affirmative."

NSLICE-00P created a mana barrier over a target out in the field. The mages went first so they would have time to recover their mana for the actual exercises, casting a variety of small individual spells before finishing off with a ritual cast. A small, dark cloud formed overhead, and a large bolt of lightning struck her barrier, but it managed to hold strong.

Magister Ausonius watched with a serious expression before giving orders to the siege crews. A ballista fired an enchanted projectile that struck with greater speed and force than should have been possible, all focused into a single point. NSLICE-00P did not have enough time to reinforce the barrier, so she quickly formed another Supercharged one underneath, which managed to prevent the projectile from piercing the target.

Her robotic eye began to flicker, causing several of the Legion soldiers to back up and mutter among themselves. Magister Ausonius had seen it before, though, so he kept a professional expression.

"What do you think, Your Majesty?"

"Analysis: This unit's defenses should be capable of preventing harm against demonstrated measures for the proposed duration of the exercises. However, this unit calculates the risk of miscalculation as concerning. This unit will therefore provide a Clone protocol as an alternate target for tests of Legion offensive countermeasures."

Magister Ausonius nodded.

"A Clone spell? I agree; that would be for the best. Was there anything else you wanted to test before we begin?"

"Affirmative. Query: Can Magister Peditum Decius Considius Ausonius confirm the target field is clear of all affiliated life-forms and property? This unit would like to test new wide-area termination capabilities."

Magister Ausonius nodded.

"We cleared the area for the testing and the later exercises."

"Acknowledged."

With that, NSLICE-00P turned toward the empty field and began to form a new magic circle, one of the strategic spells from the classified materials Sidonia had shown her. She kept her sensors focused on the magic circle in case of leaks, entanglements, or potentially explosive buildups, but the circle completed without issue. It seemed the classified materials had been recorded with greater accuracy than the materials available to the general public.

A moment later, the ground began to rumble. A spike made of stone burst up from the ground with a crack. Then another. And another. Soon, spikes covered the entire field. The Legion soldiers stared with wide eyes and dropped jaws. Even Magister Ausonius's eyes opened a bit more than usual.

"It's one thing to hear about it, and another to see it in action . . ."

*You have learned the strategic spell Garden of Spikes!*
*Modular spellcasting detected . . . strategic spell Garden of Spikes upgraded into Prismatic Floor!*

She repeated another spell and soon, huge blobs of water were striking the ground. They were of such size and force that they left craters on impact.

*You have learned the strategic spell Crushing Rainstorm!*
*Modular spellcasting detected . . . strategic spells Rain of Fire and Crushing Rainstorm upgraded into Prismatic Rain!*
*The strategic spell Prismatic Rain is now Level 4!*

With the upgrade of the rain spells to a modular prismatic form, there was no need to cast the Frost variant. She considered testing the defensive spell, but she wanted to keep that capability classified for now. She also determined that she could observe the Legion's version to compare and determine if the circle she had recorded was viable.

Meanwhile, the Legion soldiers trembled, and even Magister Ausonius had begun to sweat.

"Um, Your Majesty, are your mana reserves okay? Wouldn't solo-casting two strategic spells in a row tire you out for the upcoming exercises?"

"Negative."

"I . . . see . . ."

Magister Ausonius's misgivings on this affair only grew . . .

# 41

# Exercise Able Terminator

*"There is what the reports say, and there's what actually happened. The reports are the opinions of the officers on the field. Officers with personal agendas, I might add. NSLICE units provide nothing but the data, the raw facts. I personally prefer fact to opinion."*

—Dr. Ottosen, on reports of NSLICE units causing excessive collateral damage.

Soon, the first exercise was ready to begin. The Legio Ianus III and Legio Arcanum I had assembled and prepared their formation. Magister Verrucosis, Princess Caecila, and NSLICE-00P's friendlies had boarded a Legion airship overlooking the battlefield, while NSLICE-00P herself flew in the sky nearby.

Magister Verrucosis's voice rang throughout the battlefield.

"Prepare formation!"

The legions below arranged themselves and began to cast their spells. The mages of the Legio Arcanum I formed a circle and began a ritual cast, sharing and harmonizing their mana, though they did not form any spell circles just yet. The soldiers of the Legio Ianus III began to form individual magic circles before a mage in their midst thrust a staff into the ground. A massive spell circle linked all the individual ones, and a barrier formed over both legions.

It was exactly the same process that Caelinus's legions had used against her previously. But this time, NSLICE-00P was not under attack or any threat of termination and could watch the process in its entirety. She recorded the circles with interest. The larger circle was identical to the one from the classified scrolls, so NSLICE-00P now predicted with ninety-three percent certainty that the spell she had on record would work.

"Begin exercise!"

And that was NSLICE-00P's cue. She cast a Prismatic Bombardment spell filled with Light Beams as per its original Aurora Barrage version, and then began a general assault upon the barrier. She had discussed with Magister Ausonius ahead of time and had a specific program of different attacks to cycle through to test the Legion's barrier. To begin with, she would conduct a sustained, unfocused barrage for a full twenty minutes.

Onboard the airship, Princess Caecila and her retinue gaped at the site before her. Beam spells fell from the sky like a deluge of rain, lightning up the field below.

"This . . . is one woman's work?"

Ateia and Taog glanced at each other, smiled, and shrugged. Estrith scowled and started to turn her gaze, for she did not have good memories of this particular sight. But she kept her eyes facing forward, for she wished to see how the Imperials would deal with the attack that had broken her people's assault.

Meanwhile, Magister Verrucosis smirked.

"It is impressive at first glance, but look. For all that might, the Legion holds."

Princess Caecila could only nod silently, while Estrith's scowl grew. The magister was correct. The barrier remained intact . . .

The full twenty minutes passed, and NSLICE-00P dropped her assault. She watched as the Legion cycled some of its soldiers in and out of the formation, refreshing the mana flowing through the barrier. Soon, Magister Ausonius waved a rod, and a light began flashing green: the signal for her to begin the next test.

This time, NSLICE-00P went all out to break the barrier in a single blow. She Supercharged the Prismatic Bombardment spell before firing all its beams at once. They struck one another and fused together, forming a huge ball of light that exploded into one truly massive fused beam so bright it dimmed the world around it. It struck into the barrier and created a blinding flash of light, as well as the sound of a roaring explosion.

And as the light faded and everyone's vision returned, the audience's eyes widened. Magister Verrucosis broke out into a massive smile.

The barrier had held.

As NSLICE-00P had predicted and assured Magister Ausonius of. This particular attack had failed to penetrate a similar barrier in real combat, after all, but it was still an impressive display of resilience by the anti-Archon formation.

From then on, NSLICE-00P cycled through several more attempts. She attempted a Prismatic Rain with both Fire and Water, neither of which performed any better than the Prismatic Bombardment. She then attempted a Prismatic Floor, which had been requested by Magister Ausonius. She noted that the mana from the barrier extended into the ground below, interrupting the spell as they both fought for control over the same area. The ground rumbled, but no spikes emerged from below the Legion.

In the end, none of NSLICE-00P's attacks broke the barriers. If she wanted to break a joint barrier, she would need to take advantage of her mana regeneration to wear it down over a longer period of time than was planned for this exercise, or else resort to the Equalizer and the Anti-Mana bombs. But the Equalizer was her trump card and the most classified weapon in her arsenal, and so she did not plan to reveal it in exercises with a third party such as this. The Legion would not learn how exactly she had broken their defenses today.

Then came the Legion's turn. NSLICE-00P formed a Clone with a defensive barrier and had it conduct evasive maneuvers. The Legio Arcanum began to cast various spells of their own, notably the thunderstorm Caelinus's Legion had used against her. NSLICE-00P recorded the circle with interest. The legions also attacked with their siege weapons, and their highest-leveled sharpshooters took some shots as well. NSLICE-00P noted with interest that the three groups were not firing at random but began to coordinate, utilizing the siege engines for area denial to control her clone's movement while the sharpshooters distracted and put pressure on her barrier, all so the mages could strike true with a strategic spell. NSLICE-00P was forced to layer several more barriers to prevent damage to the clone, which could no longer evade all the attacks coming its way.

Well, if this were a real engagement, she would also be engaging in counterfire to disrupt the attempt, but it was enlightening to see what the Legion had intended for her. She may eventually have suffered damage had she not quickly broken the stalemate with Caelinus.

Soon, the first exercise came to a close, and after a brief period of rest, the second began. The next was a bit less structured. It was intended to model a Legion ambush on an Archon. NSLICE-00P formed a clone and had it slowly march across the field. The two legions would then need to coordinate and act quickly, forming the barrier at the same time as ritual casting a spell in order to get the first hit without leaving themselves vulnerable.

NSLICE-00P had been instructed to begin disruptive counterattacks the moment the strategic spell activated. The exercise would be considered a success for the Legion if they managed to get their barrier up before her counterattack could arrive. Since she was using a clone as well, she would also not put her barrier up until after the ritual cast began, to see if they could get their spell off before her defenses.

They, again, went with the lightning. NSLICE-00P was able to form her barrier nearly immediately, so the spell failed to damage her clone. It was a subsequent close call, but the Legion managed to get their barrier spell up in time.

That was informative for NSLICE-00P. The knowledge that she could not count on counterattacking to an ambush before an Imperial joint barrier completed meant that she should make all attempts to be the initiator in potential conflicts with the Legion.

Well, that was when approaching the situation without the Equalizer, which would not be withheld in any real conflict, but it was still worth considering what she might do without it.

And then it was time for the final exercise. In this case, NSLICE-00P would ambush the Legion, and they would have to scramble to respond. The legions would be assembled into march columns and could only begin to set up their formations after NSLICE-00P began her attack. In this case, they did not need to work together; the exercise would be considered a success if either the Legio Arcanum retaliated with an accurately aimed strategic spell or if the Legio Ianus successfully formed their barrier.

NSLICE-00P, of course, was not permitted to cause actual casualties, nor to destroy the equipment used in the ritual formations. But she was permitted to do anything else she could think of to disrupt their efforts, and was also permitted to strike legion troops with low-level spells, in which case they would be counted as "dead."

NSLICE-00P formed her clone some distance away from the legions and, as soon as she received the signal, began her attack. She formed a Prismatic Bombardment overhead, and the Legion immediately scrambled into action. And then she struck . . . from the sides.

The Prismatic Bombardment had been a distraction. She had also Farcasted multiple Beam spells, which opened fire from ground level, striking the Legio Arcanum mages assembling into a circle and the Legio Ianus mage carrying the ritual staff. Another set of mages tried to take up the circle and the staff, but she struck those two. The legions then adapted to the attacks and began forming individual barriers around the two key targets . . . and that's when NSLICE-00P opened fire with the Prismatic Bombardment overhead.

Precisely aimed and fused Beam spells broke the smaller barriers and caused explosions near the gathered troops, knocking them to the ground as the smaller beams continued to pick off key targets. She switched some of them to the Fire element and swung these across the ground, creating waves of fire between parts of the Legion formation. She also cast some Fireball spells as well to create more noise and blasts, intending to disorient the troops.

It was not as effective as she'd predicted, as the disciplined Legion troops followed their training, and their officers kept them moving. So, she began to pick off the officers as well. She also began to add in some Earth Magic, raising walls and digging ditches that disrupted movement. Soon, the chaos started to affect the troops, and discipline began breaking down.

Eventually, Magister Ausonius signaled for her to cease fire. NSLICE-00P scanned the field and each of the Legion troops. The formations were shattered, and the troops were huddled in small groups, trying to duck and hide from the attacks all over. But she ignored morale effects and analyzed the soldiers' physical state.

*Imperials Terminated: 0.0*

Having confirmed compliance with the nontermination parameter and that no Legion targets were in need of medical attention, NSLICE-00P let her spells and mana fade.

Magister Verrucosis grinned and rubbed his hands together. This had been a *perfect* result. NSLICE-00P had sure made a mess of things when she had caught the Legion off guard, a bit of an embarrassing result that he would definitely be following up on, but that was it. When the Legion's formation was set up as planned, she couldn't break it.

Not only could Magister Verrucosis now report that the Legion had defeated NSLICE-00P in a direct confrontation, but he had also unlocked the secret of Caelinus's defeat. It was clear that either Caelinus had not set up the formation correctly, or more likely, that NSLICE-00P had ambushed him before he had a chance. Magister Verrucosis could now explain the factors that had allowed NSLICE-00P to personally overcome a Legion and why that success didn't matter in the slightest.

And yes, her mystical might was impressive on an individual level, but she was no worse than an Archon. She could clearly be handled with appropriate preparations. The Legion had no reason to fear her, and the Empire had no reason to bow to her. All was as it should be.

But as Princess Caecila, Magister Ausonius, and the troops on the ground looked across the cratered and burning field, they all came to a very different conclusion . . .

# 42

# The Gates of Obliteration

*"The end of the world? Killer robots and vicious mutants trying to kill us all? Here, we call that Tuesday."*

—Former US admiral while coordinating Resistance efforts.

Magister Peditum Ausonius finished reading the report. He held back a sigh as his audience, the Imperial senate, immediately began to whisper among themselves.

"So, the queen of the Dobhar . . . was stopped by the Legion?"

"In an exercise where no one was serious, you mean."

"But still, I heard she could break an anti-Archon formation without a sweat. Now you're telling me the Legion held? If that's true, then what of her deeds in Utrad? Something is not adding up here."

"Hmm . . . we all knew they were exaggerated, but to this degree . . ."

The senators glanced at the Emperor on his throne.

"It is somewhat suspicious, isn't it?"

Emperor Lucius held back his own sigh.

At least, until he was back in his private room, where he began to sigh all he wanted. He turned to the other person in the room, his daughter-in-law, Princess Caecila.

"Those idiots! A *friendly* exercise designed by Magister Verrucosis is obviously not a conclusive example of the queen of the Dobhar's abilities! Even if it were, someone who is *just* on par with an *Archon* is not someone you can disregard!"

Princess Caecila frowned. "Magister Verrucosis must have doctored the report. From what I saw that day . . . I feel we should be more wary of Her Majesty, not less."

Emperor Lucius sighed once more.

"And what does Her Majesty think of all this? We may need to smooth things over lest she take matters into her own hands . . ."

Princess Caecila shook her head.

"That's the thing; I am not sure if she is aware of what is being said about her, but if she knew, she would approve."

Emperor Lucius raised an eyebrow.

"She *approves*? She's *happy* about the senate now questioning her achievements?"

Princess Caecila slowly nodded.

"The Legion is assisting with her search in exchange, so she has already been compensated for the exercises. And when I asked about the effects on her reputation, she simply stated that inaccurate assessments of her capabilities would make it easier for her to slay her enemies."

Emperor Lucius held his face in his hands.

"That is not a reassuring statement. I suppose it beats her being angry, but not by much. No one is calling for an investigation of her status just yet, but this is going to severely restrict our own options if we can't counter the rumors—"

Fortunately, or unfortunately, it turned out Emperor Lucius would not have to deal with this tricky situation after all. At that moment, there was a loud knock on the door.

"Your Majesty! Urgent message from Velus's Pass!"

Emperor Lucius sighed. "It's just one thing after another." He straightened his back and adopted an imperious expression. "Enter."

The door opened, and a Legion soldier entered and saluted. Emperor Lucius nodded at him.

"Report."

But even as the soldier opened his mouth, another one rushed into the doorway.

"Your Majesty, urgent report from Viridi Pabulum!"

And before Emperor Lucius could even respond to that, a third one nearly crashed into the second.

"Your Majesty, urgent report from Elteno!"

At this point, Emperor Lucius lost his expression, and his eyes started to grow wide.

"What is going on?"

A group of soldiers was patrolling through the halls of the fortress guarding Velus's Pass, mostly checking the basement for monster rats. The wards could detect a monster that slipped into the fortress, but they couldn't catch a normal rat already inside that absorbed enough mana to become a monster, and normal rats always seemed to find a way inside.

But as they were walking, they heard hissing and crackling noises. Glancing at one another, they ran toward the noise. It was coming from a small room off to the side of the basement. They felt a wave of mana pass over them as they approached.

Throwing open the door, they gaped.

Right there, in the middle of the fortress guarding the way into the Imperial Heartland, was a dungeon entrance. And judging by the crackling lightning and waves of mana it was throwing off, not a stable one.

This scene repeated itself in the Silver Gorge and the Gap of Vindex. It happened again in the Dwarven hold of Dhor Thoram. It happened again in the cities of Viridi Pabulum, Mestaynga, and Durocobrivis. All across cities, Legion fortresses, and allied settlements in the Imperial Heartland.

One even appeared under Elteno, the former capital and birthplace of the Empire itself.

And of course, where there were dungeons, there were monsters . . .

Emperor Lucius convened his council in Corvanus. They gathered in the Legion keep, standing around a large table in a war room. The council included the leaders of the three major factions of the senate, Consul Noxisius, Magister Utriusque Militia Verrucosis, and Aedile Hortensus, along with Magister Exploratore Appius, Magister Arcanum Cnaeus, and Magister Peditum Ausonius. There was also the grandmaster of the Imperial knights and numerous Legion personnel.

The Emperor grimaced.

"How did this happen?"

Magister Exploratore Appius shrugged.

"Cult."

Magister Utriusque Militia Verrucosis raised an eyebrow.

"Really, Appius? Your answer to this situation is to spout conspiracy theories?"

Magister Exploratore Appius shrugged again. "I don't see any other viable explanation for a wave of corrupted dungeons spontaneously appearing under every major settlement and fortification in the province at the exact same time. It's either a one in a million cosmic fluke, a test sent to us by the Aesdes themselves, or it's an intentional attack. Take your pick which you believe."

Consul Noxisius crossed his arms. "And if it was the doing of a cult, was it not your job to warn us of such things?"

Magister Exploratore Appius stared at him with narrowed eyes. "Oh, I'm sorry. I was just a little busy with the rebellion stripping away all my eyes and ears north of Velus's Pass. Maybe if the Exploratores budget had been updated at any point in the last few *centuries*, I might have had a bit more leeway to investigate 'conspiracy theories', as Magister Verrucosis put it."

Emperor Lucius held back a sigh. "Magister Peditum, what is the situation so far?"

Magister Peditum Ausonius stepped forward.

"The only good news is that these corrupted dungeons seem fairly small, since they popped out of nowhere. The Legion keeps are all holding; Velus's Pass is already conducting a counter assault. But until the keeps clear their dungeons, the legions are tied up."

Consul Noxisius frowned.

"So we're just going to let corrupted dungeons run rampant in the cities? Do you understand what the consequences of that would be?"

Aedile Hortensus nodded. "Not to mention all of our allies requesting support. I'd imagine it would be costly if we snubbed the Dwarves, for example."

Magister Utriusque Militia Verrucosis scoffed. "My troops can handle this. A few small dungeons are nothing."

Aedile Hortensus nodded. "But of course. I do wonder how many people will die while they do, however."

Magister Utriusque Militia Verrucosis scowled.

"You dare question the might of the Legion? I'd like to see *you* handle this! Why don't you try and bribe the dungeon, huh?"

Aedile Hortensus smiled and held up his hands. "Of course, I would not presume to interfere with military matters, good Magister. I simply believe we should consider the costs imposed should our response be . . . delayed."

Emperor Lucius turned to the grandmaster.

"Grandmaster, what of the knights?"

The grandmaster frowned and crossed his arms.

"We've dispatched everyone in the province, and I've reached out to all the private orders. We can handle Viridi Pabulum and Mestaynga, but Elteno will have to wait."

Consul Noxisius shook his head. "That's not good enough. Elteno may lack in strategic value, but if we let the birthplace of the Empire burn to the ground, we will lose all our support among both the people and the other courts."

Aedile Hortensus rubbed his chin.

"We can't call back the legions from Utrad?"

Magister Peditum Ausonius shook his head. "We could, but these are corrupted dungeons we're talking about. They would grow *much* stronger in the time it takes those forces to return, and the damage dealt in the meantime could be catastrophic."

Consul Noxisius turned to Magister Arcanum Cnaeus.

"What of the Imperial academy? The support of the mages would enable the Legion to take on the threat, wouldn't it?"

Magister Arcanum Cnaeus shook his head. "There's one under the Imperial academy too, and *my* request for reinforcements has already been denied. I don't believe I need to inform you what occurs if a dungeon gains access to the resources of the academy. Until our dungeon is dealt with, the faculty of the academy are needed at home."

Emperor Lucius rubbed his chin.

"Then what about . . . the queen of the Dobhar?"

Everyone fell silent for a moment. Magister Utriusque Militia Verrucosis scoffed and shook his head. "I refuse. My Legions can handle this. We don't need her."

Magister Peditum Ausonius cleared his throat.

"Sir, I must point out she *has* cooperated with the Legion. I feel bringing her in would be a boon for the troops' morale."

Consul Noxisius rubbed his chin.

"Putting aside our current dilemma, she has already resolved several major situations for us and received a great deal of our resources in exchange. If we continue to rely on her any further, we will start to appear quite weak to the other courts . . . and everyone else, too. It would not be wise to have her solve all of our problems."

Aedile Hortensus shrugged. "I'm not sure I agree . . . but I do think we need to consider what we would need to pay her. You aren't going to give her everything in the treasury, are you, Your Majesty?"

Emperor Lucius heaved a sigh, his shoulders slumping.

"Then . . . we have no choice but to deploy the Imperial guard, and the legions of Corvanus."

Magister Utriusque Militia Verrucosis grinned.

"I will lead them personally and see to it that this crisis is put to an end."

Aedile Hortensus frowned. "Is that wise? That would leave us entirely exposed, wouldn't it? How do we know another dungeon won't appear in Corvanus?"

Emperor Lucius shook his head.

"If this council is not willing to request the queen of the Dobhar's aid, then I do not see any other choice."

Consul Noxisius nodded. "I concur. And in the worst case, we could hire her to protect the capital. If we truly cannot handle this ourselves, then so be it. But let us first make every effort to solve Imperial problems with Imperial means."

Magister Utriusque Militia Verrucosis smirked.

"Besides, is that not what the Magister Exploratore is for?"

Magister Exploratore Appius threw up his hands.

"Of course. Sure. Blame it on me when something happens because you were scared of the queen of the Dobhar showing you up, why don't you? Well, for the record, I think we should request her help immediately, so don't come crying to me if we can't handle it without her."

Emperor Lucius sighed, then nodded his head.

"Nothing for it. Let's deploy the guard, then, and pray to the Aesdes that we truly don't need the queen of the Dobhar's help."

And so, the Legions of the Northern Court, the Exploratores, and every knight order that would heed their call set out to strike down the great evil that assaulted the Empire.

Well, none of that mattered to NSLICE-00P, who had not yet been informed of the crisis. Besides, she would have agreed with Consul Noxisius's assertion that Imperial problems should be dealt with by Imperial means, although a wave of corrupted dungeons would have offered notable upgrade opportunities.

But she was not aware, so she simply considered her next move at her residence. And as she did, one of the attendants approached her.

"Excuse me, Your Majesty, we have received a delivery for you."

"Acknowledged."

The attendant handed her a letter and a scroll. Ateia glanced over her shoulder.

"What is it, Seero?"

NSLICE-00P opened the letter and read over it.

"Answer: Consul Noxisius has requested a meeting with this unit in order to offer a formal apology for the actions of his subordinate unit."

Ateia tilted her head. "Um, that's good, I guess?"

Another voice entered the conversation. "That stuck-up jerk apologizing to a foreigner? It's a miracle from the Aesdes."

The group turned around to see Agedia approaching.

Ateia nodded. "So you think Seero should go?"

Agedia took a deep breath.

". . . Yes, if I'm honest. This is a serious olive branch by the leader of a major faction. If you reject it . . . that's practically a declaration of hostility. So, if you want either to engage with Noxisius or to stay as uninvolved as possible, then you should accept this gesture. But if you *do* want to start a fight with the traditionalist faction, then do what you want."

NSLICE-00P's robotic eye flickered, but she came to a decision fairly quickly. She took Agedia's recommendation into account, as avoiding unintentional hostility was desirable. But ultimately, all of that ended up irrelevant compared to a second detail . . .

"Analysis: Benefits to primary directive identified. Additional contact determined as desirable."

Because alongside his letter, Consul Noxisius had sent NSLICE-00P a scroll on Spatial Magic.

# 43

# Deceived

*"And as concerning as the loss of irreplaceable technology is the fact that NSLICE-00P was presumably annihilated instantaneously, such that it could not even report an engagement to us? That indicates we are dealing with a more serious threat than we've ever encountered in this half of the world."*

—One of Dr. Ottosen's sponsors, on the sudden loss of NSLICE-00P.

On the evening of the next day, as the sun was setting, NSLICE-00P, Ateia, Taog, and Estrith moved out to meet with Consul Noxisius. Princess Caecila had apparently been called back to the palace for an emergency, and had not been included in the invitation in any case. Agedia followed at a distance with a drone to keep her abreast of the situation, since she was uncomfortable meeting with the consul herself.

The meeting was to take place at the villa of an unaligned senator, a neutral meeting ground that could still provide appropriate hospitality. Agedia took up position in the street nearby while NSLICE-00P and the rest made their way inside.

The senator in question led NSLICE-00P into an open courtyard with a fountain in the center, lit by the moonlight and a handful of torches. A woman with black hair sat at a small table, flanked by two guards. NSLICE-00P noticed a strange anomaly; there was a gap in her perception underneath the courtyard. All of her sensors—mundane and otherwise, and even her dungeon field—couldn't pierce through that specific area. NSLICE-00P assumed it was a dungeon.

The presence of a dungeon within Corvanus, especially underneath the villa of a senator, was unexpected. The history of the Empire she had recorded from the library had led NSLICE-00P to believe the Empire was generally hostile to dungeons and did not permit them to exist within major population centers, much less the capital city. But she was here for a diplomatic meeting, not a dungeon termination or a subordinate upgrade routine, so NSLICE-00P simply devoted some processing power to keeping an eye on things and moved on.

The black-haired woman rose to her feet and saluted.

"Hello. You must be NSLICE-00P. I am Vipstana Apelles, Consul Noxisius's assistant. I greet you and thank you for coming."

"Greetings: This unit is designated NSLICE-00P. It is nice to meet you."

Vipstana nodded her head. "Nice to meet you."

But Taog frowned and crossed his arms.

"Excuse me, Miss Apelles, but where is the consul? We were under the impression he would be here to apologize to the queen of the Dobhar in person."

Vipstana nodded her head.

"That is fair. Consul Noxisius deeply regrets that he could not be here; he has been called into an emergency meeting with the Emperor. He did not wish to cancel on Her Majesty NSLICE-00P, however, so has tasked me with entertaining her until he arrives. He will make his way here as soon as the Emperor releases him. In the meantime, I will take care of Her Majesty today and demonstrate our intentions in full. Do I have your permission to proceed, Your Majesty?"

Taog frowned, but NSLICE-00P's robotic eye flickered. From Taog's discomfort, NSLICE-00P predicted that diplomatic etiquette had been broken. But at the end of the day, the apology was secondary to NSLICE-00P. Her primary goal in this meeting was to determine what resources the consul possessed regarding Spatial Magic and to secure access.

"Affirmative."

And the moment NSLICE-00P responded positively, the anomaly sprung into motion.

It turned out what she had detected was not a dungeon, after all. The gap in her perception surged up out of the ground and wrapped around her, some sort of black amorphous substance. NSLICE-00P found her sensors cut off from the rest of the world. She was about to respond with the Equalizer . . .

"Hostile intent detected. Engaging termination—"

. . . but before NSLICE-00P, Ateia, Estrith, or Taog could react, the substance vanished.

And took NSLICE-00P along with it.

Ateia's eyes widened. "Seero! You! What did you do with Seero?!"

Estrith moved faster. The Dobhar scowled and immediately threw her harpoon at the woman, but the black substance wrapped around Vipstana, and she vanished just before the harpoon struck. She stepped out of the shadows in another part of the courtyard.

"With her permission, I have reverse summoned her to the Realms of Mana; the Realm of Eternal Night, to be specific. There, she will be cut off from the Aesdes and the power of the world. She will lose access to all of her skills and her Holy mana. There is no escape, even for a hero. She is gone. And now, the Heralds of the New Dawn will accomplish our mission."

Just then, water rose out of the fountain behind the group, and a figure jumped forward. Ateia shrieked as it grabbed her and pulled her back into the water. Taog turned, his eyes widening.

"ATEIA!"

He ran forward as fast as he could, but the two fell into the fountain with a splash. He peered over the edge as soon as he arrived.

Both Ateia and her attacker were gone without a trace.

"WHERE IS SHE?!" Taog spun around and snarled at Vipstana.

Vipstana motioned to the guards. "That does not concern you any longer. We have no use for you, and so you are about to die."

The woman's guards drew their blades and began fighting with Estrith, who was warding them off with her harpoon, but these were the elite guards of a consul. She blocked one strike and tried a counter stab, but the other guard stepped in and swung at her from the side. She snarled and leapt back, barely avoiding the blow, when the first soldier stepped in again and swung his sword up, knocking Estrith's harpoon out of her hands while his comrade stepped in for the kill.

Taog threw the Dark Blade at them, and the attacking soldier blocked on reflex. That gave Estrith time to pull her harpoon back with a mana-chain and jump back. She gripped her spear and gritted her teeth.

Just the first exchange, and she had nearly died. Taog had helped, but he was too low level to take on either of these guards alone . . . and he had already lost his best weapon. The situation was not in their favor.

The guards slowly approached. Estrith had failed to guard the queen of the Dobhar; she had failed her debt to Ateia . . . and now, it looked like she and the other Imperial were going to die themselves. She cursed.

"My king . . . I am sorry. This warrior was not worthy of you in the end. But I will not let these Imperial dogs hunt me like helpless prey. They will bleed before I die!"

"About that . . ."

A shadow passed over the moon and everyone looked up. The two guards stepped back as something crashed into the courtyard, tossing up a cloud of dust. A shining lance pierced out of the dust cloud and stabbed straight through one of the guards.

Agedia leapt out of the cloud and wrapped her snake half around the other one. One quick squeeze of her tail, and she snapped his neck. She narrowed her eyes.

"I didn't think you demon lovers would move on the shiny girl like this. I guess the joke's on me, huh?"

Vipstana tilted her head, placing a finger on her chin. "Oh. You're the failed Imperial knight, aren't you?"

Agedia glared at the woman, lifting her lance. "In the flesh. And you and I have a score to settle."

Vipstana stepped back into the shadows, appearing to melt into the darkness. "Several scores. You already failed to protect the mother. Now, you have failed to protect the daughter, even though heroes accompanied both. Evidence suggests your resistance was and still is completely irrelevant."

Agedia suddenly leapt back and swung her lance over Taog's head as Vipstana leapt out of a nearby shadow, swinging a knife toward Taog. Agedia's lance barely deflected the attack.

"Barbotter, take the kid and go! I can't protect you both!"

Estrith scowled but nodded and grabbed Taog, running for the entrance. Additional guards stepped out to block them, but Agedia tossed her lance across the courtyard. It pierced through several of the guards and pinned them to the nearby wall, opening enough of a gap in their formation for Estrith and Taog to jump through and escape.

Vipstana reappeared in front of Agedia. "Disarming yourself. Foolish."

And then, Agedia's tail wrapped around and slapped the woman on the side of the head, knocking her to the ground. Agedia scoffed, curling up her tail like a spring and launching into the air. She landed by her lance and pulled it out of the wall, taking down the remaining guards with a single swing.

"A Mélusine is never unarmed."

And so, Agedia faced off with one of the Heralds of the New Dawn . . .

Estrith and Taog ran through the hallway of the villa. Several of the guards had broken off and were chasing after them.

"Come, Imperial! The hunter who falls behind is left behind!"

Taog gritted his teeth and ran. Just then, a pair of guards stepped out in front of them. Estrith growled and leapt at them. Fortunately, these were the guards of the lower-ranked senator, so Estrith was not outclassed this time, stabbing into one before they could act. She growled as the other grazed her shoulder, but her tough fur prevented any serious damage. She spun around and bit the man's hand, retrieving her harpoon as he stumbled back and then stabbing him as well.

A third stepped out from the side of the hall and swung his blade toward her back. Taog let out a shout, stuffing as much mana into a Dark Slash as he could and swinging his remaining sword. The man grunted; Taog hadn't done much damage, but a skill slash to the back of the neck still hurt. As a result, Estrith had a chance to roll forward out of the way of the guard's attack and swept his feet with her tail. The man fell to the floor as Estrith scrambled to her feet and stabbed the guard before he could do the same.

She looked at Taog and nodded, and the two continued on. But then, Estrith cursed.

A full contingent of guards now barred the path before them. She and Taog turned around to double back . . . but the pursuing guards had caught up and now blocked the rear.

They were trapped.

# 44

# Heralding a New Dawn

*"Watch now. Your salvation approaches!"*

—The leader of the Atomic Cult.

Ateia flew out of a tub of water in the grip of her captor, coughing and sputtering. When she had gathered herself, she turned around and glared.

"Let me go!"

Her captor giggled. "Now then, Miss Ateia, don't be like that. Please behave yourself; I would hate it if I had to get . . . rough."

Ateia's eyes widened. The person was wearing a mask, but Ateia recognized her voice.

"Magus Major Sidonia?"

Sidonia smirked at her. "Why, hello there, Miss Ateia. Do be aware that I am known by another name here."

Ateia glared at her. "Why are you doing this?! Let me go; I have to go back and help Seero!"

Sidonia shook her head. "Oh, poor Ateia, you haven't realized it, have you? I'm afraid Her Majesty NSLICE-00P is gone for good."

Ateia gritted her teeth. "That's impossible! Seero . . . Seero will find a way! She always does!"

Sidonia smirked at her again. "Your faith is commendable but mistaken. No one can survive in the Realms of Mana for long; not even those blessed by them. And without access to the Aesdes, Miss NSLICE-00P wouldn't be able to escape even if she had the skills. But enough of that. I'm afraid you do not have time to worry about her. You have problems of your own, my dear."

Ateia tensed in preparation to act, but a tendril of water curled from the fountain and wrapped around Ateia's hands. Sidonia smirked as she pushed her forward. Ateia glanced around and found herself in a large basement, filled with hooded and masked figures. There was a large magic circle carved into the floor, surrounded by torches. One of the masked figures raised their hands as the others chanted and channeled their mana into the circle.

"Most excellent work, Herald of Rain. I assume our plan was successful?"

Sidonia, or rather, the Herald of Rain, smiled. "Like a charm, Herald of Twilight. Miss NSLICE-00P will not interfere any longer."

The Herald of Twilight chuckled. "Excellent, all is as the Herald of Dawn predicted, then. But where are my manners? We have a guest!" He spread his hands wide. "Welcome, Ateia Niraemia, Imperial inquisitor! It is my honor to welcome you to my home."

Ateia just glared at him. "Why are you doing this? What do you want with me?"

The Herald of Twilight chuckled again. "The Heralds of the New Dawn have but one purpose: To break free of the tyranny of the Aesdes and save the world. And you, Ateia Niraemia, will be the key!"

Ateia narrowed her eyes. "So, you're a crazy cult?"

The Herald of Twilight shook his head. "We are Enlightened; the only truly Enlightened. You see, the Aesdes are similar to the Domides in almost every way, save one: they enjoy the suffering of their charges. Every Domides shares their power freely with the denizens of their Realm, and their subjects are empowered by it. As a result, no living thing from a Realm of Mana ever truly dies, from the greatest of kings to the lowest of creatures. Even if their corporeal form is destroyed, they will simply return to their Realm until they have bathed in the power of their Domides and can take shape once again.

"But the Aesdes? The Aesdes hoard their power. Barely one in a million may even use the power of the Aesdes, the power of this world, the power of this Realm, I would say. And not even a hero can escape the cold clutches of death, much less the rest of us. Ours is the only Realm in all reality to suffer death, and it is the Aesdes who strive to keep it that way. Which is why we will tear down the wall the Aesdes have built and let the power of the Source flow freely into this world! And then, we shall become gods and taste the bitter poison of death no longer!"

Ateia stared at him. "Yeah, you're definitely insane. The Realms of Mana are filled with demons and evil! You're going to destroy the world! And I won't help you do it, no matter what you say!"

The Herald of Twilight stepped forward, grabbing her chin. "No, you won't. Rather, it is your blood that is the key, Ateia Niraemia. Or shall I say . . . Ateia Dilectia."

Ateia froze. "What?"

The Herald of Twilight chuckled. "Oh my. They never told you who your parents were, did they? Well, rejoice then, for I will tell you the truth."

The Herald of Twilight stepped back and straightened his spine.

"You, Ateia Dilectia, are the daughter of Aedinia Dilectia! Who herself was the secret daughter of Emperor Herius! And that makes you the purest descendant of Velus in the entire Northern Empire!"

Ateia's mouth dropped. "What? I'm . . . related to the Emperor? You're crazy. That's . . . impossible."

The Herald of Twilight chuckled. "Oh, but it is very possible. Your father was wise to hide you from us, but now, his failure is complete. And now, we have our key. You see, the masses of this day and age have forgotten the history of the Empire. They dismiss the stories of Velus as fanciful tales, myths to tell children before bed. But we know the truth. And the truth is more fanciful than any fiction. Velus's wife was not a saintess or a hero. She was one of the very Aesdes themselves! And so, the blood of the Aesdes runs through the children of Velus, even to this very day!"

He sneered under his mask. "And *that* makes them the ideal conduit for our ritual. Your innate connection to the Holy mana, the power of this world, means we can use you to connect to the boundaries of the Material Plane, and then to tear them apart! And while normally the Imperial family is too heavily guarded to approach, a secret, illegitimate daughter is another matter entirely!"

He sighed and shook his head. "But your fool of a mother killed herself to spite us. And so, we gave up on the Imperial family. Emperor Lucius's blood is too weak for our purposes, and the rest of the Imperial family is protected in the Eastern Court. Until one day, we found you."

He grinned again. "And you, dear Ateia, are the greatest prize of all! Not only are you a direct descendent of Velus and the Aesdes, your father was the Hero of Elteno himself! A mother with the blood of the Aesdes, and a father who was blessed by them! You have the strongest connection to the power of the world of any human in the past millennia! And so, with you as our conduit, our ritual's power will grow a thousandfold! The walls trapping us in this cold and horrid place will be torn asunder, and we will ascend to godhood!

"Prepare the ritual!"

Just then, the other figures finished channeling their mana, and the magic circle on the floor began to hum and glow. The Herald of Rain pushed Ateia forward, and the hooded figures bound her to the floor. The Herald of Twilight stood over her, pulling out a dagger covered in glowing patterns.

Ateia struggled, but she could not free herself from her bonds. She called upon her mana, she activated her skills, but she had none that would work in this situation. In desperation, she tried to activate the Radiant Shot skill, but channeled the mana through her body instead. The Holy mana reacted to the Herald of Rain's water bindings and broke them, and Ateia tried to leap away, but the hooded figures tackled her. She was once again bound to the floor, this time with mundane chains.

The Herald of Twilight grinned. "Let our chains be broken!"

He plunged the dagger into Ateia's torso.

Ateia started to scream. Her body started to glow, her mana pouring out of the wound as a golden-and-silver light that streamed into the air—and the ground. There, flowing rivers of golden-and-silver light began to appear. Ateia's mana connected to these streams, and they began to flow back into her. Ateia's screams grew as her body was obscured by light.

And then, the magic circle underneath her activated. A red-and-black light shot through her and into the golden and silver rivers, staining them red. The rivers began to twist and scatter, forming into a circle. Cracks of red light began to form in the air inside the circle.

And then . . .

The air itself shattered. The ritual had begun.

A Rift formed in the center of the room and continued to grow.

The Herald of Twilight began to cackle. The Herald of Rain smiled. The others in the room began to celebrate. And within the center of the storm, tears streamed down Ateia's face as the mana surged through her body. She tried everything she could think of. She tried to stop the mana flowing through her. She tried to direct it elsewhere. She tried to activate her skills. She tried to pull up the records of the Aesdes.

But nothing worked. There was too much mana flowing through her to stop; she couldn't even grab hold of it. Her whole body burned, she could barely even think, and she couldn't even see the records from the Aesdes anymore.

She couldn't do anything. She tried to cry out, tried to plead, but her voice wasn't working anymore. All she could do was plead in her heart.

*"Taog . . . Seero . . . Agedia . . . Father . . . anyone! Help me, please!"*

# 45

# Lost Once More

*"It appears the efficiency of the Geo-Oscillator has dropped notably in our satellites and would cease to function entirely once out of Earth's orbit. That's a bit of an obvious oversight. Fortunately, it will not impact current NSLICE operations, but we will need to address the issue should NSLICE units need to act in extraterrestrial environments."*

—Dr. Ottosen, reviewing a new satellite launch.

Once again, NSLICE-00P found herself in a pitch-black world. She couldn't feel anything. She was picking up soft whispers and the occasional growl, but her other sensors couldn't identify the source of the noises. Even her dungeon field couldn't pierce through the darkness around her.

And worse . . . her Geo-Oscillator Engine had once again lost contact with the planetary core.

Well, in many ways, the situation was better than the first time, the most important of which was that her systems could currently run on mana, and she had numerous Mana Capacitors that gave her significantly greater power storage than she had originally been designed for. That mana started flowing back from the capacitors into the Geo-Oscillator Engine, keeping it active for now.

But in other ways, the situation was worse.

Because previously, she'd found herself in an empty void with nothing in it. But now? She couldn't detect anything around her . . . but this void was not empty. The darkness itself appeared to have substance—and will. It was creeping into her armor plating and her systems. And everywhere it touched, she stopped being able to perceive.

Her robotic eye turned red.

"Hostility detected. Activating termination protocols."

And how exactly would NSLICE-00P terminate an amorphous substance she couldn't identify? One that seemed more like a dangerous energy than a living thing?

"Equalizer engaged."

NSLICE-00P opened fire with the Equalizer . . . and then, everything became clear. The Equalizer did, in fact, react with the hostile substance in its current configuration, confirming it was a type of mana. While NSLICE-00P still couldn't sense or record the hostile mana around her, she could record the reaction with the Equalizer. And because of that, she was able to make a reasonable approximation as to the attribute of the mana around her.

It appeared to be a type of Dark mana, only significantly more dense and powerful. And . . . there was another revelation.

As the Equalizer destroyed the Dark mana, it created a small, minuscule area where no Dark mana existed. Yet, the area was not empty. NSLICE-00P detected unattributed mana flowing into the gap before it contacted the Dark mana and joined with it, converting into more of the hostile energy.

NSLICE-00P's robotic eye flickered as she analyzed the situation. First of all, she appeared to be in a location filled to the brim with mana that was cut off from the planetary core she had calibrated her Geo-Oscillator Engine to. Secondly, this mana was a type of Dark mana, and was innately hostile to her, as well as jamming most of her senses. Thirdly, this mana could still be interacted with as normal mana, and when destroyed was replaced by attributeless mana that immediately took on the Dark attribute on contact.

And so, she determined the course of action with the highest probability to avoid eventual termination by either hostile mana or by running out of power.

She took out a metal sphere from her inventory, one of the anti-mana storage devices she had experimented with. She fired up the Equalizer and channeled it into the device.

When experimenting with anti-mana magic circles, she had run into certain limitations. She could guide the anti-mana down appropriately formed energy channels . . . but she herself had no contact with or control over the energy. This was an issue when attempting to replicate magic circles, as mana-based spellcasting appeared to have a mental element. Mana could be manipulated by the mind unassisted, and mana-based magic circles assumed this to be the case. Even something as simple as the Bolt spell had variables such as velocity that turned out to be determined, at least in part, by the caster rather than the circle. But since she couldn't interact directly with anti-mana, she could not impart those variables into the anti-spell.

But she did have one success.

The Barrier spell, at least in its simplest Arcane-attribute form, was a relatively static construct. It simply formed mana into a spherical shape and that was it, with very few adjustable components requiring mental input. So once she had determined the correct anti-mana circle to match the effect, she had found she could channel anti-mana into a barrier. She couldn't control the size, shape, or density of this barrier, and since the Equalizer power output didn't scale with her Mana Density, it was noticeably weaker than her Barrier spells, but she could surround herself with a sphere of anti-mana if she wished.

She fired up the Equalizer and channeled it into the anti-mana barrier projector she had made, forming this barrier now. This would create a small region around her where the Dark mana would be erased, and unattributed mana would flow in.

Of course, if she only erased the Dark mana, the unattributed mana would convert to Dark and replace it. So, she moved on to the second step.

If the attributeless mana took on an attribute on contact with the Dark mana, then she predicted she could simply cast a spell of a different attribute and so give the mana something else to convert to.

And which attribute did she pick?

The attribute which had proven itself against Dark mana in the past, as well as being generally effective against most attributes she had encountered.

The Holy attribute.

Interestingly, when NSLICE-00P attempted to cast the spell, the spell library from the foreign system didn't appear in her UI. NSLICE-00P double-checked the UI and found that the entire Personal Status section of the foreign system was missing.

But that didn't matter to NSLICE-00P. She had already recorded her spell library into the NSLICE network's joint protocol database, so she simply brought up the relevant spell file and let her cybernetic components guide the magic circle construction.

And so, NSLICE-00P created a Holy Barrier, just barely smaller than the anti-mana barrier.

As she predicted, the area within the barrier started to flood with golden-and-silver light as the attributeless mana contacted the Holy mana and took on that attribute. The Dark mana still within the barrier started to burn away, cut off as it was from the main source all around.

Of course, NSLICE-00P couldn't keep this up forever. Since her Geo-Oscillator Engine was running on her Mana Capacitors instead of supplying them, her mana wasn't regenerating. She would run out quickly at the rate she was spending it. Fortunately, she had calculated a reasonably likely phenomena that might resolve that issue. If the attributeless mana converted to a nonhostile attribute, she predicted she may be able to utilize it to power her core.

But it turned out she would not need to rely on the external mana, after all. Because as the Dark mana covering her body started to burn away, a message passed across her UI.

*Diagnostic Report: Attempting to recalibrate Geo-Oscillator Engine. Suitable planetary core located. Connection established.*

It turned out, she had not been moved out of range of the planetary core after all, but rather that the Dark mana had been jamming her connection to it. Once enough of the Dark mana was cleared, the Geo-Oscillator Engine was able to locate and reestablish a connection with that core, through the very source of unattributed mana that had been replacing the Dark mana.

And then mana started to flood NSLICE-00P's systems as the Geo-Oscillator Engine began producing power once again. In fact, her diagnostics reported the Geo-Oscillator Engine was now producing significantly more power than before. Her Dungeon Field Generator shone some light on the situation, revealing that her connection through the unattributed mana flow was apparently closer to the core than the surface of the planet, and that this connection was even stronger than the original one as a result.

And then . . . something happened that NSLICE-00P had not predicted. As the last of the Dark mana within her barrier burned away, there was a massive flash of light that blinded all of her senses. When the light faded and her senses began to respond, the Dark mana was gone. Instead, she found herself standing on a tiny rock floating in an empty void. Fortunately, her Geo-Oscillator Engine remained calibrated, and nothing in the area proved hostile toward her. It appeared she had avoided termination.

However . . . she had no data as to her current location, or how she might return.

She then, unexpectedly, heard a voice in this empty place.

*"Seero . . . help me, please!"*

She froze. That voice . . . was Ateia's. The dream she'd had after casting Divination played through her organic components once again. Something snapped into place, like a switch in a circuit had just been turned on, and bits of obscured information in the dream suddenly became clear.

She identified the voice calling for her help in that dream as Ateia's.

And the city burning around her was Corvanus.

NSLICE-00P's heart rate began to spike, and her body temperature increased. Her emotional control efficiency was rapidly deteriorating; somehow, her organic components were convinced that Ateia was currently at a high risk of termination. Her cybernetic components began to weave a Calm spell to reinforce her emotional controls, but her organic components grabbed hold of the mana and prevented the circle from completing. The cybernetic components began to calculate a response, when the organic components contacted them.

The organic components proposed an idea. And they reasoned that rather than spending resources and bandwidth trying to reestablish emotional controls, that she should dedicate all available resources to finding a way to move from this location. As long as she was trapped in this unknown place, she couldn't make progress on any of her directives, she couldn't prevent Ateia from being terminated, and she couldn't terminate the hostiles who had forcibly relocated her to a hostile environment.

Her robotic eye flickered . . . and her cybernetic components concluded that this proposal was reasonable. Reestablishing emotional controls was ultimately of lower priority than determining a return path from this location. If her organic components had a possible solution to the second issue, then the most efficient course of action would be to analyze and test it.

So that's what she did. She lay on the ground for safety, and then cast the Divination spell.

Her organic components had pointed out that the dream from the Divination spell had ended up matching her current scenario, and speculated that recasting the spell might provide relevant data. Her cybernetic components objected to the dangerous spell, but her organic components pointed to records from the library that indicated that historical figures of the Empire had cast the spell in the past without the side effects she'd experienced. They proposed the hypothesis that her earlier collapse had been due to her attempts to increase the data transfer from the spell, and that she may have bypassed built-in safeguards as a result. The cybernetic components concluded this hypothesis as reasonably likely, and so concluded it was worthwhile to attempt another casting with no modification to either the circle or the flow of mana.

The spell activated . . . and then, NSLICE-00P's organic eye blinked while her robotic eye flickered. The data transfer was many orders of magnitude smaller than before. And rather than any dreams or relevant data, it gave her a great deal of information about her surrounding space, including its current dimensions. Apparently, the size of the rock she was on indicated the entire dimensions of the current universe.

That . . . did not make any logical sense. But when she attempted to confirm via the Dungeon Field Generator and her sensors, all data recorded ended up supporting that conclusion.

*"Seero . . . anybody . . . help me, please!"*

But then she heard Ateia's voice again. And more than that, she *felt* Ateia's mana brushing up on the boundaries she had just identified. Her robotic eye began flickering rapidly.

Thanks to the data she had just received, she had recorded the existence of some sort of barrier around this tiny universe. And as Ateia's mana brushed up against it and tried to flow through their Contract bond, she recorded energy signatures from the reaction of the barrier to that mana.

And if NSLICE-00P could record an energy signature, then . . .

She lifted her hands and placed them together with her palms facing forward, connecting the energy channel outputs in either hand together. As she did, she heard Ateia's voice once more. Her heart pounded, and her body temperature increased as her metabolic rate began to rise.

The edge of her mouth curled down slightly as her organic eye narrowed.

"Equalizer engaged, full power."

# 46

# Counterattack

*"You're not the only one with assistance from greater beings!"*

—Hero Viridia Sollemnis,
while confronting a Cult of Mana.

Taog and the Dobhar stood back-to-back as the guards carefully closed in from either side. Taog heaved a sigh, then gritted his teeth.

It looked like he was going to die. And it was only right that he did. After all . . . he had failed to protect Ateia, the one thing in the world he couldn't afford to lose. He had let Seero die, without ever once repaying her for all she had done on his behalf. He had failed to protect everything he'd ever cared about. And now, he would fail to protect himself.

But then, he felt the Dobhar's tail slap the back of his ankles.

"Steel yourself, Imperial. If I am to die at your side, then you will die with honor. Do not give them your life; hold your head up high and make them take it from you. Even cornered prey does that much."

Taog took a deep breath and lifted his sword. He thought back on his life, on every moment he had been beaten and battered and just let it happen. A fire began to burn within his stomach. Lar's stupid face overlapped with the guards' ahead of him, and he began to growl subconsciously.

That's right. He had already failed. He was going to die. So . . . there were no more consequences to be feared. There was no reason for him to control himself any longer. If he was going to die anyway, then wouldn't it be nice to try fighting back for once?

The Dobhar nodded.

"Better. You are a Wulver's pup, the son of the hunters of the land. You should not whimper and cower like prey."

Taog smirked as he lifted his sword. "You know, I never got your name."

The Dobhar gripped her harpoon.

"Estrith Edilddaughter."

Taog smiled. "Heh, Taog Sutharlan. Nice to meet you, Estrith."

Estrith scoffed. "This is the first time you've acted like a warrior worth meeting. Now, die well, Taog Sutharlan!"

Taog responded with a shout. Estrith shouted as well, and the two began to charge.

Only for one of the walls to explode. Taog shielded his face as the stone flew past him.

Armored knights in full plate armor stepped through the hole, bowling over one set of the guards, who were quickly outmatched and fell back.

"There's the Dobhar and the inquisitor. Retrieve them!"

Two of the knights stepped past Taog and Estrith on the other side and held shields up in between them and the second group of guards. Two more grabbed Taog and Estrith by the shoulders and pulled them outside. Taog's eyes widened.

A full squad of armored knights stood around the hole in the villa, and with them stood Magister Exploratore Appius and a group of Exploratores. The magister's eyes narrowed.

"Where're the others?"

Taog ran over to him. "They took Ateia! I don't know where! Seero . . . they did something to her! They said they sent her to the Realms of Mana!"

Magister Appius scowled and turned to a group of Exploratores bringing up the rear. "Find the other inquisitor! Scour the entire city; tear it apart if you have to!"

The Exploratores saluted and immediately began scattering as the knights backed out of the villa. The guards didn't pursue.

Taog gasped again.

"Agedia! She's still fighting someone inside!"

Magister Appius nodded. "Got it."

And then he turned to leave. Taog blinked. "Where are you going? We have to help her!"

Magister Appius glanced back at him with a small smirk. "No, Dia's not the one who needs help."

Back in the courtyard, the black-haired woman melted back into the shadows. Agedia swung her lance down toward the ground, knocking the knife out of Vipstana's hand as the woman tried to ambush Agedia from her own shadow.

Agedia yawned. "Let me guess, Herald of Predictability?"

Vipstana reappeared on the other side of the courtyard and frowned. "No."

A pitch-black magic circle formed in front of her, and then, all the torches in the courtyard went dark. A black veil stretched over the open space above, blocking the light of the moon and the stars as well.

"I am the Herald of Night."

Agedia scoffed. "Ah, so you channel the Realm of Eternal Night, huh? Thanks for the tip."

Agedia grinned when the Herald of Night did not respond. "What, you thought I haven't spent every partially sober moment of the last decade researching your little club and dreaming of all the ways I would tear the flesh from your bones? Because I have. And when you have a Mélusine's innate poison resistance, it takes a *lot* to get drunk, you know?"

"Irrelevant. All that time, all that effort, and still, you failed yet again. Now you will fade into the night, never to be seen again. All your life is destined to fall into shadow. Nothing will remain of you but your failure."

Agedia's eyes narrowed. "Oh, really now?"

Two spots on Agedia's cheeks began to glow. Hoisting her lance, she curled her snake half down before she spun around and thrust with her lance.

There was a wet thud, and then the Herald of Night gasped. The veil overhead vanished, revealing the light of the moon once again. Agedia sneered as she pushed the lance deeper into the Herald's torso.

"I've seen this trick before, Herald of Predictability. From what I've read, Eternal Night represents the endless darkness of nighttime, blocking our perception and obscuring all the terrors we can't see until we fall into an eternal sleep. But did you know? Snakes are perfectly happy living in the night . . . and have plenty of ways to hunt in the dark. All I had to do was represent that with my mana, and suddenly, your Eternal Night's not so scary."

The Herald of Night did not respond as she slumped over and breathed her last. Agedia spat and then tossed her fallen opponent aside.

NSLICE-00P opened fire with the Equalizer. The rainbow beam shot through the air and struck empty space above the edge of the rock, and then slowly, ever so slowly, a circle of light began to grow around the point of impact. It began to expand.

But then, it stopped. NSLICE-00P detected massive amounts of mana flowing into the barrier, trying to repair the damage dealt by the Equalizer. And since the Equalizer was already running at full power, she would not be able to create more than a tiny hole in the barrier.

Her heart raced even faster. Her mouth curled down a bit more. Her organic eye narrowed a bit tighter.

Her organic components grabbed hold of her mana and attempted an idea. And since her emotional controls were deactivated, and her priority was making escape attempts, her cybernetic components did not resist despite the lack of analysis and reasoning regarding the idea's viability.

Her organic components grabbed her mana and thrust it into the hole in a manner vaguely reminiscent of the Transfer protocol. It was sloppy, haphazard, barely even close to what she had observed. There was no way it would even come close to the skill.

But at that moment, another wave of Ateia's mana flowed through the barrier . . . and linked to NSLICE-00P's.

Ateia was a person with Holy mana in her blood who was currently being used as a conduit to assault the barriers of the world directly, so at the moment, her mana was connected to the power of the Aesdes flowing through the world.

NSLICE-00P was a hero, a proven defender of the Material Plane, who had a contract connecting her and Ateia. And a dungeon, a construct intimately connected with the boundary between the world and the Realms of Mana.

So, in that moment, NSLICE-00P's mana connected to the mana of the wider world via Ateia. NSLICE-00P's organic components pulled on the mana as her cybernetic components tried to support and turn the haphazard motion into something vaguely legitimate.

The closest thing they could come up with was when the black-haired hostile had forcibly relocated her. And though she did not have enough data to replicate the process exactly, the Holy mana, the power of the world, responded when it found its defender cast adrift.

So now, a mass of Holy mana streamed in through the hole and wrapped around NSLICE-00P. It was then sucked back in through the hole . . .

. . . And once again, NSLICE-00P disappeared with it, leaving the tiny universe empty. With the Equalizer gone, the hole closed up completely.

Taog, Estrith, and Magister Appius suddenly heard shouting and crashing. Another part of the villa exploded, sending stone and one of the guards flying into the street, before Agedia slithered out of the hole with a scowl.

She nodded at Magister Appius. "Shiny girl's gone. Cult took Ateia. We need to find her, *now.*"

Magister Appius nodded back. "Exploratores are scouring the city as we speak."

Agedia frowned. "Have they checked Consul Noxisius's place? He's the one who called shiny girl here."

"A group is already on the—" Magister Appius fell silent. Everyone turned to look in the direction he was facing. Glowing lights were shining from the hole Agedia had made, one that led directly to the courtyard. The group rushed over and looked inside.

Rivers of golden-and-silver light appeared in the courtyard. They began to swirl around, and then condense and bulge out. A mass of light dripped out of the rivers, and then there was a bright flash.

And when the light died down and everyone's vision cleared, their eyes all widened. Taog's heart began to pound.

"Seero! You're alive!"

Estrith's eyes went wide. "Queen of the Dobhar . . ."

NSLICE-00P now stood in the courtyard with a full-on scowl on her face.

Her helmet then fully covered her head, and both of its eyes glowed bright red.

"Status Report: Successful return to area of operations confirmed. Critical priority termination protocols activated. This unit will now terminate all confirmed hostiles with extreme prejudice."

Her boosters fired, and she shot into the sky, rocketing across the city. Agedia glanced at the others and grinned.

"*Don't mess* with the shiny girl. LET'S GO, PEOPLE!"

The group took off running in the direction NSLICE-00P had flown.

# 47

# Terminate with Extreme Prejudice!

*"Furious Statement: Let's teach him a lesson."*

—NSLICE-00P's new commander, while initiating an ambush.

NSLICE-00P had identified Vipstana's corpse, and so confirmed that hostile had already been terminated, so she prioritized determining Ateia's status. She now soared through the air, tracking Ateia through their Contract. The link was barely needed, as NSLICE-00P was detecting massive mana signatures that were intertwined with Ateia's own.

As these foes had pulled off a potentially effective termination attempt on her, any considerations of respecting local regulations or obscuring classified capabilities were now significantly lower priority than terminating the threat. And that was before she even considered the risk of failing her major directive. So, NSLICE-00P rocketed through the sky at maximum speed with no compromises for concealment.

She approached a large villa where Ateia was being held, apparently in a basement or cavern below the surface. Her sensors detected a large mana barrier over the structure, so she took out one of her anti-mana storage containers and charged it up at full blast, reaching critical capacity just as she approached the barrier. She tossed and detonated it ahead of her, and a wave of sparkling rainbow light ripped a hole right in the barrier, which NSLICE-00P shot through.

She didn't know for sure if the residents of this place were affiliated with Vipstana, so her initial plan was to pass through unless hostility was confirmed. She intended to smash straight through the floor of the villa's courtyard into the basement below, but she detected a gap in her perception that was rapidly approaching her. She took evasive action as the undetectable projectile passed her by, only for a Fireball to soar through the air toward her.

NSLICE-00P formed a mana barrier, but the Fireball burned the spell structure. NSLICE-00P boosted away, landing on the ground, and turned toward a slightly pointed-eared man in a red robe. She opened fire with her machine guns, but a warrior in wooden armor stepped forward, lifting a shield of tangled branches and vines. The vines grew rapidly and blocked the bullets.

"We are the knights of the New Dawn, and now we can freely use the blessings of the Domides! You will fall here, barbarian!"

NSLICE-00P responded by forming a Prismatic Bombardment circle that covered the sky. Yellow, red, and blue beams rained down, all with golden-and-silver highlights.

"Status Report: Hostility confirmed. Terminating hostiles."

The warrior grinned and raised his shield as a red beam struck it, channeling Overgrowth mana to infinitely regrow his leafy shield . . .

His eyes widened. The shield burst into Holy flames, the vines shrieking as they burned away. He quickly dropped the shield, but he was too late. The flames had spread to his wooden armor . . . and all his abilities focused on Overgrowth's rapid regeneration. He could only scream as he burst into flames that nullified his corrupted growth.

*You have slain Human (Level 94)!*
*Gained 3 Personal XP!*

The mage launched mana-burning Inferno Fireballs toward the Prismatic Bombardment circle, but NSLICE-00P wiped them out with the Equalizer. The mage then quickly formed an Inferno Barrier to protect himself, but the flames of Inferno could not burn through Holy Water. A jet of water shimmering with a golden-and-silver glow pierced straight through the barrier and the mage.

*You have slain half-Elf (Level 89)!*
*Gained 3 Personal XP!*

Meanwhile, NSLICE-00P continued to dodge the hidden projectiles, forming Holy Barriers to protect herself as well. She couldn't detect the sharpshooter . . . but she could detect a gap in her dungeon field's perception that was extremely familiar to her.

And she already knew how to handle the mana of Eternal Night.

Bright beams of Holy and Light mana pierced through the gap in her perception from every direction, saturating the entire area. The veil of Eternal Night faded away, revealing a small woman with a crossbow . . . who was now riddled with holes.

*You have slain Dwarf (Level 92)!*
*Gained 3 Personal XP!*

Additional guards streamed into the courtyard, but these were even lower level and no threat to NSLICE-00P. Having confirmed that the entire villa was hostile, she bombarded the entire structure and set it aflame, then used Earth Magic to open a hole directly in the floor of the courtyard. She jumped down into the basement, the heart of the mana signatures she was reading.

All eyes turned to her as she floated down. A massive Rift was forming in the center while a bunch of masked and hooded figures stood around the room. They gaped at her, and the Herald of Rain went completely pale. The Herald of Twilight sputtered.

"But that's . . . impossible! No one can escape from the Realms of Mana, especially not the Realm of Eternal Night!"

Meanwhile, the Herald of Rain had already started running. Leaping into the tub of water in the room, she vanished from the area. Fortunately for her, NSLICE-00P wasn't paying attention to her at that particular moment. The cyborg's organic eye narrowed under her helmet, her organic components forcing all of her processors and sensors onto a single target.

In the center of the room lay Ateia, screaming as massive amounts of mana flowed through her and into the growing Rift. Burning flames shot from the hole in reality as the Realm of Inferno intruded upon the Material Plane.

NSLICE-00P immediately fired the Equalizer into the magic circle underneath Ateia. The red-and-black mana stopped flowing into the girl, and the Rift's growth slowed considerably.

NSLICE-00P also already knew how to deal with a Rift. In fact, she had just refined her Rift termination protocols with the data from the Realm of Eternal Night. So, she tossed an improvised anti-mana bomb directly into the Rift, then formed a massive Holy Barrier over it. She calculated if she replaced the Realm's power with a nonhostile attribute, it would be significantly easier to absorb the Rift's mana.

The Equalizer-powered bomb pushed back the mana from the Rift, and then the unattributed mana that replaced it converted to Holy instead. And in this case . . . the Holy mana connected to the rivers of golden-and-silver light flowing around Ateia. The mana poured from these rivers into the Rift, and the wound in the world healed within seconds. NSLICE-00P didn't even need to absorb excess mana to close the Rift this time.

The Herald of Twilight reached out for the Rift as it vanished. "NO!"

But before the Herald of Twilight could react, he was covered by a massive Holy Light Beam, along with every other figure in the room. No trace of them remained when the beams died down.

*You have slain 12 hostiles!*
*Gained 18 Personal XP!*

NSLICE-00P scanned the area, but found no further life signs, mana signatures, or gaps in her perception within the room.

"Hostiles terminated. Retrieving friendly."

NSLICE-00P walked over to Ateia, but she froze as she looked over the girl. Her heart began to pound as her robotic eye analyzed Ateia's status.

Ateia was dying. The massive amount of mana flowing through her was causing her body to collapse; she was already missing some parts, and others were flickering and fading. NSLICE-00P immediately cast Recovery Magic, but it failed.

A mana overload like this did not simply damage the body. It overwhelmed the matter making up the being and made it lose cohesion on a conceptual level. Ateia's body couldn't be healed because it couldn't *remember* the parts that had faded.

NSLICE-00P rushed over and focused on her dungeon field. She used the Equalizer to cut off the rivers of mana pouring into Ateia and tried to absorb as much of the mana afflicting the girl as possible. But while she succeeded, the damage was already done. Ateia's body had absorbed too much already and had lost its integrity, so she continued to fade away.

NSLICE-00P's organic eye went as wide as it could go and started to quiver. Her heart pounded in her chest; she felt as if she were about to be terminated. Moisture began to build in her eye.

Meanwhile, her robotic eye continued to flicker. A Calm spell began to form once again.

NSLICE-00P's organic components grabbed the mana and were about to rip apart the spell circle when her cybernetic components sent them a message. They had calculated a potential method by which to fulfill the major directive. They'd also calculated that the situation was extremely delicate and required maximum precision. All available bandwidth was necessary to achieve a significant probability of success, and the current emotional disruptions would reduce that probability.

Her organic eye narrowed. And then her organic components completed the Calm spell on their own.

In fact, not only that, but the emotional controls suddenly jumped in efficiency. The organic components voluntarily submitted themselves to the cybernetic, and all separate threads gathered into one.

NSLICE-00P immediately got to work. She had already dealt with a mana-overload scenario once, but Ateia's state was significantly worse than the Dobhar pup's had been. She calculated that the original method would not be sufficient here, and that she did not have time to iterate on it, especially given the delicate nature of the operation. Additional measures were required to stall Ateia's degradation.

So NSLICE-00P formed a Contract in the air. The default one provided by the skill; one with no additional provisions for the contractee. The one automatically applied when she accepted dungeon master surrenders.

"Request: This unit has a potentially viable treatment method but requires friendly Ateia's approval to proceed. Please respond."

At that moment, Ateia slowly turned her head. Her eyes widened, and she stretched out her hand. She practically mouthed the words, only the tiniest whisper escaping her lips.

"Seero . . . please . . . help . . ."

And that was enough.

**New Contract signed! Existing Contract updated!**
**Ateia Niraemia added as a full subordinate!**

And with that, the phenomena NSLICE-00P predicted came to pass. Mana from her core streamed into Ateia and automatically attempted to maintain her in optimal fighting condition as it did with her monster subordinates. All lingering excess mana within Ateia drained through the connection while the dungeon's mana stabilized her remaining body. Ateia ceased fading away.

But she was still missing large parts of her body. Since she wasn't a full contract prior to this, the dungeon couldn't restore her prior state. The mana was struggling to prevent her death even now. The Contract had only bought a short amount of time.

But NSLICE-00P wasn't finished yet. Because as it turned out . . . NSLICE-00P already knew a way an organic being could survive with missing body parts. In fact, a method that *intentionally* removed body parts to improve efficiency.

She could rebuild Ateia. And she already had the technology.

NSLICE-00P focused her dungeon field perception . . . on herself. Of course, a combat enforcer didn't walk around with her full blueprints in memory, so instead, she analyzed the structure of her own implants. She began recreating them as closely as she could with Metal Magic and the Item Foundry, forming them directly on Ateia's body. A robotic arm connected to Ateia's missing shoulder. A metal leg grew from her knee. A metal helmet covered half of her head.

And then . . . all the mana swirling within Ateia reacted. The cybernetic components had not fully linked to Ateia, as NSLICE-00P didn't have enough data on NSLICE processing to replicate the procedure in the field. But NSLICE-00P no longer lived in a world of science and technology, where magic was but a rare anomaly. She now lived in a world of magic and mana down to its very roots. And in such a world, stories had physical power.

The dungeon mana wanted to restore Ateia to optimal combat condition, but it could not, as it did not have an adequate record to rebuild. But now . . . a new and viable option had presented itself. One that perfectly synergized with the Primary affinity of NSLICE-00P's core and Ateia's own bloodline. It combined the records of NSLICE-00P's existence with Ateia's, including the potential that flowed in Ateia's veins. And with the excessive amount of mana poured into Ateia by the ritual, there was more than enough spare power for a transformation.

Ateia's body and the new cybernetic components began to glow until she could no longer be seen . . .

And then . . .

The light faded.

Ateia had now fully bonded to the cybernetic components. Most of her body was now covered in metal armor, much like NSLICE-00P's, but with golden and silver highlights all over. Two metal wings extended from her back with glowing tendrils of light instead of feathers. A bright golden-and-silver light shone in the center of her chest.

A light slowly grew in her robotic eye, and then her organic eye slowly opened. She turned her head, and her organic eye widened.

"Seero . . . ? Confused Query: What . . . happened?"

**Subordinate Ateia Niraemia has evolved into . . .**

**Wait . . .**
**What?**
**. . .**
**I need to report this.**

## EPILOGUE

# Mission Report: ???

There is a plane of existence separate from the Material Plane, yet intimately connected to it. Rivers of golden-and-silver light stream from the world below up into a field of clouds upon which rises an island the size of a continent. Upon this island, life and nature flourishes and grows, not merely as a reflection of the world below but as the paragon of what it can become.

Golden and silver trees the height of mountains rise into the sky. White horses seem to glide across vast fields. Golden dragons soar among flocks of songbirds, adding their mighty voices to the chorus. Schools of fish glimmer in pristine lakes, silver scales reflecting the sun like polished jewels. Buildings blend directly into the landscape as civilization and nature come together in perfect harmony, neither dominating the other but both working together to elevate each other to new heights.

This is no Realm of Mana, nor any corner of the mortal world. This is the Blessed Land, from which the Aesdes watch over the world.

And at the center of this place rises a mighty mountain, larger than any that exists in the land below. It rises high above a second layer of clouds such that its peak cannot be seen even from the Blessed Land, yet its summit glows with such light that all the residents of this place and even the world below know where it lies, a gentle star that warms the day and soothes the night. At the top of this peak lies a solemn temple, carved from the stone of the mountain.

This is the home of Anualë, Lord of Light and Sky, the protector of the world and everything in it, the First of the Aesdes, and appointed steward of the Blessed Land.

Anualë himself appeared as a kindly old man with a beard of light and white robes that fluttered as if in a breeze. He sat upon a large chair in his main hall, masterfully crafted yet flat on the floor, for the First of the Aesdes did not elevate himself above his kin, or any other. From here, he watched the world and the Blessed Land, and gave counsel to all who sought him out.

Said Anualë was currently staring with his eyes half open and his shoulders slumped. He heaved a sigh before rising to his full height.

As he did, his appearance shifted, for the Aesdes are not defined by their material flesh so much as by the weight of their existence, and so are able to appear as they desire, contingent on their stature. In this case, Anualë changed from a kindly old man to a stern warrior in his prime, clothed in golden armor with a glowing sword upon his back. Wind picked up around him as he rose into the sky, gazing down upon the two individuals who stood in his hall. Before him stood a beautiful human woman with golden hair and a crown of leaves, silver robes, a golden sword, and a bright aura of light around her, and a pitch-black cat wearing a tiara filled with countless gems of every color.

"Colleöne, Lady of Courage and Victory, She Who Guides the Champions of the World. Shialnor, Lady of Mana and the Boundary, She Who Cultivates the Gardens of Mana. Let us start from the beginning and confirm my understanding of the situation."

Colleöne and Shialnor both gulped as Anualë began his review.

"When we received word of the Walking Dungeon, we were deeply concerned. But as we turned our gaze to her, we discovered that she is a traveler from another reality entirely, and her situation was the result of her unique existence. For such a being to have arrived on our shores is something beyond even our ken. We decided it was the will of Elséró and that we should not interfere, but that we would celebrate an existence we had not conceived of before. In any case, the . . . *timing* of the discovery would have precluded any intervention."

Colleöne glared at Shialnor, but Shialnor looked away and started cleaning her paws.

"Then, she became a hero dungeon, the first of its kind ever to exist. Our hearts were troubled by this, but such doubts were easily whisked away. She performed a great service to us and to the world, at great risk to her own being. Your judgment was right, Colleöne, and though our hearts trembled at the possibilities, we were glad to see this traveler defend her new home, and concluded it was only right to reward her as her deeds deserved."

Colleöne nodded. Shialnor continued her cleaning. Anualë then frowned.

"And then . . . she forged a new race entirely, one that innately accesses the power of Elséró that flows through the world. We still cannot see what effect this will have on the future, and have not come to an agreement on how we should look after this new race. But the birth of new life is to be celebrated, so celebrate it we did."

Anualë now took a deep breath. "And that . . . brings us to today."

He held his head with his hand.

"Please, enlighten me if you will . . . *why* exactly is there a *second* Material Plane now? Not to mention . . . the *birth of a new Aesdes*? Please explain the events that led to this outcome in a manner that I can understand—and accept."

Colleöne and Shialnor glared at each other. Colleöne crossed her arms. "You explain it."

Shialnor tilted her head. "Ehhh, me? No thanks. You do it."

"You're the Lady of Mana and the Boundary! This is *clearly* your jurisdiction!"

"Eh, but like, it's all about Holy mana, right? Isn't that *your* job?"

"Enough." Anualë gave a stern look to both of them, then turned his gaze to Shialnor.

Shialnor gulped and nodded. "R-Right, so . . . the boundaries between Realms in the Source are more metaphysical than geographic, right?"

Anualë nodded. "So they are."

"And . . . the power of Elséró is currently expanding the Material Plane when it comes into contact with the Source at the edge of the world, right?"

Anualë nodded again. "As Elséró wills, so that all life new and old may find a home to call their own."

Shialnor slowly nodded. "Right. And . . . you know about that whole 'anti-mana' thing she does, right?"

Anualë nodded. "A sobering thought, but yes, a key part of her unique nature. The power of another reality, proof of her otherworldly origin."

Shialnor gulped. "Right, so . . . she, um, got sent to a Realm of Mana. The Realm of Eternal Night to be specific. If she . . . um . . . used the anti-mana thing, she might have cleared a small area of that Realm's attribute, returning it to base Source. If she then applied another attribute and completely filled a space around her with it . . . she could have sectioned off a new Realm. And if that attribute was Holy . . . well . . . then upon contact with the Source . . ."

Anualë sighed. "It would have extended the Material Plane, only in a separate place, and so formed a new one instead. But within that idea lies another question. If she was sent to the Realm of Eternal Night, even our power would have struggled to reach her, given that Realm is shrouding darkness made manifest. And I thought we designed the Holy Magic circles to be practically impossible for the mortals to cast unassisted? How was it she was able to cast Holy spells while cut off from our support?"

Shialnor frowned. "That has to do with the nature of her existence. From what I can tell, these 'cybernetic components', particularly the ones bonded to her mind, are designed to store and process information. They have been assisting her with casting magic circles from the very beginning and are largely responsible for her rapid growth in the mystic arts. So . . . if she had recorded a Holy Magic circle ahead of time, her own unique characteristics could have assisted her in forming the circle. Not to mention her Holy Dungeon Core affinity. She would have had the ability to generate Holy mana in her core, and so could still cast the spells even if she was cut off from the Material Plane."

Anualë sighed again. "Well, what's done is done, I suppose. The fact is there now exist two Material Planes, one of which appears to belong to NSLICE-00P. But . . . I suppose it's not *that* different from how the normal dungeons operate. Shialnor, you must integrate this new plane into NSLICE-00P's dungeon record. Now that it exists, it is our responsibility; I would not see it destroyed by collision with the first or by subsumption into a Realm of Mana."

Shialnor bowed her head, holding back a sigh. Anualë took a deep breath.

"Now, that brings us to our second issue."

Shialnor immediately turned to Colleöne. "Your turn."

"Me?"

Shialnor nodded. "It's your fault, after all."

Colleöne glared at her. "*My* fault? You're the one responsible for the whole Hero Dungeon situation!"

Shialnor nodded. "And you're the one who spread the blood of the Aesdes among the mortals because one was too handsome for you."

Colleöne's face fell, and she hung her head. Shialnor smirked, but Anualë cut her off.

"Enough. Colleöne, can you explain what happened here?"

Colleöne gulped. "Well, um, it seemed the human girl, Ateia, was disintegrating from mana overload. NSLICE-00P attempted to save her by Contracting her and then conducting a manual evolution to restore her missing body. It . . . appears to have succeeded."

Anualë raised an eyebrow. "That leaves out a great deal of detail, including the most concerning. How exactly did a dungeon evolution produce an *Aesdes*?"

Colleöne averted her gaze. "Well . . . um . . . if I understand it correctly, the dungeon monster evolution process reads all of the records regarding the individual to extrapolate how they can become a greater version of themselves. And, um, because of her . . . *lineage*, the human girl had the blood of the Aesdes within her. Not only that, but NSLICE-00P has a Holy affinity, and the ritual conducted on Ateia flooded her with Holy mana. And, um . . . since there aren't exactly normal evolution options for either humans or Holy-attributed beings, the, um . . . only example record of greater stature that resembled her state at the time was . . . well . . . her ancestor . . ."

Anualë took a deep, long breath. "And now, a human has been elevated to an Aesdes while still living in the Material Plane, and under the contract of a dungeon to boot . . ."

Colleöne gulped. "W-Well . . . Aesdes might be a bit of an exaggeration. She's, um, something similar in type, but she is obviously much lesser in stature. She is what a lizard is to a dragon when compared to even the lowest of the citizens of the Blessed Land."

Anualë narrowed his eyes on her. "It is the type that is important here. An individual's stature may grow or diminish over time. You should know this most of all, wife of Velus, the Ascended One."

Colleöne just hung her head. Anualë sighed deeply.

"We will need to discuss exactly what should be done. But what I can say now is that this Ateia and her savior are both on a path none of us have ever seen before and none of us can see the end of. It is clear that we must pay closer attention to them than we have. It would not do to let one of our own stumble her way through the world without counsel or aid. I believe this situation will call for a more direct hand."

And then, Anualë gave a small and mischievous smile. "Besides . . . she is your family, Colleöne. I suppose it would be boorish of us to withhold her from you."

Colleöne blushed and looked away. Anualë chuckled for a bit, but then his smile dropped.

"Well, let us join the others, then, and discuss the other problem in all of this. These 'Heralds of the New Dawn' are much greater in both power and lore than we thought possible for mortals of their age and stature; we must determine how exactly they have come so far so quickly."

The Herald of the New Dawn himself entered into the communication device once more, connecting through the Realms of Mana.

This time, only one other person joined him: the Herald of Rain, the only survivor among the Heralds present in Corvanus.

The Herald of the New Dawn frowned. "You are certain of this?"

The Herald of Rain nodded her head repeatedly. "Positive. I saw the Herald of Night banish NSLICE-00P to the Realm of Eternal Night with my own eyes! She was gone; I would not be here if I had made a move on the girl with her still around. I barely got out of there in time when she returned."

The Herald of the New Dawn took a deep breath and closed his eyes. Decades of planning after centuries of preparing the conditions, all to come apart in under a year. All due to this one girl who had come out of nowhere.

They thought they had accounted for her and all other factors. The hero was banished to the Realms of Mana, the Legion and the Imperial Guard were all drawn away from Corvanus, the Imperial mages were occupied, and they had the hidden princess in their grasp to make the ritual even stronger than they had planned for. They'd even triggered the ritual and opened the Rift, and he had even obscured and deflected the sight of the Aesdes so that they would not realize the danger until it was too late! It *should* have been impossible for anyone to stop them at the point they had reached.

And yet, for all that, this NSLICE-00P had still found a way to stop them. Somehow, she'd returned from the Realm of Eternal Night, entirely intact, then punched through their defenses in an instant and disrupted the ritual. And then, she'd somehow managed to personally close the Rift that had *already formed.*

At this point, the Herald of the New Dawn wouldn't be surprised if she'd saved the hidden princess too, even *after* the princess had been sacrificed as the ritual's conduit. "Impossible" seemed like barely an inconvenience for this girl.

The Herald of Rain clutched her head. "Just . . . who is she?! I thought it was impossible to escape from the Realm of Eternal Night!"

The Herald of the New Dawn rubbed his chin. "It should have been . . . for any human of this world, at least."

The Herald of Rain tilted her head. "What do you mean, 'from this world'? That's . . . where else would she have come from?"

"Where indeed."

The Herald of the New Dawn looked up and hummed for a minute.

"I believe I will need to look into this personally. Clearly, we have gravely underestimated this NSLICE-00P, and we have paid a heavy price for doing so. Go, head out east and take refuge with our brothers and sisters there. It is no longer safe for you to remain here."

The Herald of Rain frowned. "Sir . . . will you be alright?"

He smiled at her. "Of course. She's never met me, after all, and I do not plan to move against her again until we understand her completely. I will exercise extreme caution."

The Herald of Rain nodded. "Then I will head out immediately. Good luck, sir."

The Herald of the New Dawn exited the space, his consciousness returning to his body. He rubbed his chin.

"NSLICE-00P, huh? You had my curiosity before, but now, you have my attention. I suppose I only have myself to blame for moving forward without investigating you properly. But now it's time to find out who exactly this outsider is, and where exactly she came from."

He gave a small smirk. "After all, is it not the job of the Aesdes to protect the world from intruders?"

He stood up, then vanished in a flash of light.

# NSLICE-00P's Final Status

**NSLICE-00P's Dungeon Management**

| Overview | |
|---|---|
| Name | The Walking Dungeon |
| Level | 419 |
| XP | 52/100 |
| Available Perk Points | 313 |
| Mana | 261/261 (375/375) |
| Exterior | Human/Automata Hybrid (LOCKED) |

| Dungeon Affinities | |
|---|---|
| Type | Strength |
| Cyborg | Primary |
| Holy | Medium |
| Fire | Minor |
| Water | Minor |
| Beast | Minor |
| Metal | Minor |
| Nature | Minor |

| Rodent | Minimum |
|---|---|
| Earth | Minimum |
| Arachnid | Minimum |
| Slime | Minimum |
| Light | Minimum |
| Dark | Minimum |

| Implants | | |
|---|---|---|
| **Type** | **Mana Upkeep** | **Description** |
| Bionic Prosthetics +3 | 0 | Overwrites STR and SPD, Values: 130 STR, 65 SPD |
| Armor Plating +5 | 0 | Overwrites DEF and RES, Values: 150 DEF, 75 RES |
| Bonded AI | 0 | Enables direct contact with the System. Overwrites DEX, Value: 1000 DEX |
| Techno-Organic Interface | 0 | Enables conscious control over organic and emotional functions. Resists mind-influencing effects. |
| Advanced Sensors +2 | 0 | Vastly expands scope and effectiveness of senses. |
| Internal Weapon Bays | 0 | Enables use of dungeon traps as weapons. |
| Repulsors +1 | 0 | Enables flight and tactical boosts. |
| Energy Channels +2 | 0 | Enables user to channel internal energy into external attacks. |
| Dungeon Field Generator +2 | 10 | Surrounding area counts as dungeon territory. Enables mana absorption within area of effect. |
| Monster Hangar (Small) +1 | 2 | Provides 10 living spaces for small monsters. Unlocks subordinate summoning. |

| Item Foundry +1 | 3 | Unlocks Item Creation. |
|---|---|---|
| Mana Capacitor +2 (x7) | 0 | Boosts maximum mana by 30 each. |
| Drone Hangar (Small) | 1 | A Monster Hangar specialized for nonorganic monsters of limited sentience.<br>Trades amenities for boosted storage capacity.<br>Provides 5 storage spaces. |
| Monster Hangar (Medium) | 5 | Provides 5 living spaces for medium-sized monsters. Unlocks subordinate summoning if not available. |

| Inventory | |
|---|---|
| Name | Description |
| ??? dagger | A dagger, likely enchanted given the amount of mana held within. Further information could not be determined. |
| Ursanus pelt | The pelt of an ursanus alpha. Tough, well-insulated, and full of mana. |
| Ursanus bones | The bones of an ursanus alpha. Extremely durable, and full of mana. |
| Idrint | Quantity: 5,000.<br>Basic solidified mana, now a standard medium of exchange. |
| Mana Iron Sword | A sword made of mana iron. Sharper than normal, and well suited to further enchantment. |
| Rod of Command | A rod used to command golems. This one may control up to ten at once. May take control of unbound golems via physical contact. Also functions as a potent spell focus, particularly for Earth and Metal Magic. |

| | |
|---|---|
| Grimoire of Arofinas Leolar | The magical techniques and knowledge of Arofinas Leolar, High King of Mirima, as recorded and annotated by himself.<br>This is a copy transcribed by the Elteni Empire. |
| Anti-Mana Storage Device | Quantity: 5.<br>A metallic sphere with an inverse mana-storage enchantment circle, capable of storing anti-mana energy. May explode if overloaded or damaged while full.<br>Eh, close enough. You built it, so you don't need me to tell you, right? |

| Subordinates | | | | |
|---|---|---|---|---|
| Name | Species | Level | Mana Upkeep | |
| Rattingtale | Cyber-Rat | 16 | 1 | Check Status |
| Lilussees | Cyber-Spider | 17 | 1 | Check Status |
| Ateia Niraemia | ??? | ??? | ??? | ??? |
| (TEMPORARY) Taog Sutharlan | Human/ Wulver | 29 | -- | (Status locked) |
| 01R | Cyber-Rat | 17 | 1 | Check Status |
| 02R | Cyber-Rat | 14 | 1 | Check Status |
| 03R | Cyber-Rat | 15 | 1 | Check Status |
| 04R | Cyber-Rat | 15 | 1 | Check Status |
| 05R | Cyber-Rat | 14 | 1 | Check Status |
| 06R | Cyber-Rat | 11 | 1 | Check Status |
| 07R | Cyber-Rat | 10 | 1 | Check Status |
| 08R | Cyber-Rat | 12 | 1 | Check Status |
| 09R | Cyber-Rat | 9 | 1 | Check Status |

| | | | | |
|---|---|---|---|---|
| **10R** | **Cyber-Rat** | **8** | **1** | **Check Status** |
| **01S** | **Cyber-Spider** | **16** | **1** | **Check Status** |
| **02S** | **Cyber-Spider** | **15** | **1** | **Check Status** |
| **03S** | **Cyber-Spider** | **14** | **1** | **Check Status** |
| **04S** | **Cyber-Spider** | **9** | **1** | **Check Status** |
| **05S** | **Cyber-Spider** | **10** | **1** | **Check Status** |
| **06S** | **Cyber-Spider** | **8** | **1** | **Check Status** |
| **07S** | **Cyber-Spider** | **11** | **1** | **Check Status** |
| **08S** | **Cyber-Spider** | **9** | **1** | **Check Status** |
| **09S** | **Cyber-Spider** | **10** | **1** | **Check Status** |
| **10S** | **Cyber-Spider** | **11** | **1** | **Check Status** |
| **00B** | **Cyber-Bear Adolescent** | **20** | **15** | **Check Status** |
| **Uscfrea Ymmason** | **Dobhar** | **95** | **--** | **Check Status** |
| **Estrith Edilddaughter** | **Dobhar** | **62** | **--** | **Check Status** |
| **Aldreda Aetheludaughter** | **Sacred Otterkin** | **1** | **--** | **Check Status** |
| **00C** | **Cyber-Dog** | **16** | **3** | **Check Status** |
| **01C** | **Cyber-Dog Ignis** | **14** | **4** | **Check Status** |
| **02C** | **Cyber-Dog Aqua** | **15** | **4** | **Check Status** |

| | | | | |
|---|---|---|---|---|
| 00F | Cyber-Cat | 15 | 3 | Check Status |
| Melion | Metal Slime | 65 | 15 | Check Status |
| Ceitidh Greumach | Wulver | 32 | | Check Status |
| Snuan Covenwalker | Monster Rat | 8 | 1 | Check Status |

| Non-Sentient Units | | |
|---|---|---|
| Name | Quantity | Upkeep |
| Stealth Mini Drone Golem | 25 | 0.2 each (5 total) |

| Traps | | | |
|---|---|---|---|
| Name | Number Active / Deployed | Mana Upkeep | Description |
| Assault Rifle +3 | 2/2 | 2 | Rapid-fire projectile weapon with high penetration. |
| Autopistol | 2/2 | 2 | Rapid-fire projectile weapon with medium penetration. |
| Anti-Armor Missile Launcher +2 | 2/2 | 2 | Homing explosive designed to penetrate armor. Very high penetration. |
| Anti-Personnel Missile Launcher +2 | 6/6 | 6 | Homing explosive designed for area damage. Medium penetration. |
| Stun Ray | 1/1 | 1 | Nonlethal electric weapon. Can inflict stun and paralysis statuses. |
| Wrist Blade +2 | 2/2 | 0 | Wrist-mounted blades that can be deployed at high speed. |
| Flamethrower | 2/2 | 2 | Deals fire damage and applies burn status in a large cone. |

| | | | |
|---|---|---|---|
| The Equalizer +1 | 1/1 | 0 | Huh? What the heck is this? Some kind of weird metal that doesn't even exist here?<br><br>Um . . . well . . . best I can tell it's some sort of antimagic field generator? Eh . . . well, it's yours, not mine, so you don't need me to tell you, right? Like, you already upgraded this thing yourself, so you're good, right? |

| Dungeon Skills | | |
|---|---|---|
| Name | Level | Description |
| Analyze | N/A | Check the status of a target. More detail for targets within the dungeon. Details depend on level difference. |
| Contract | N/A | Bind a consenting target to the dungeon, per terms agreed upon by both parties. |
| Transfer | N/A | Move yourself, a subordinate, or a consenting target within your dungeon. |

| Dungeon Perks | |
|---|---|
| Name | Description |
| Human-Dungeon Hybrid | Enables Implants tab.<br>Enables unique Dungeon Combat skill.<br>Enables direct manipulation of dungeon mana.<br>+100 HP<br>Rooms tab locked.<br>Exterior locked. |
| Affinity Sharing | Can share Primary and Major affinities between subordinates' cores and master core. |

| Dungeon Feats | | |
|---|---|---|
| **Name** | **Description** | **Effect** |
| Dungeon Victor | To the victor go the spoils.<br>Unlocked by destroying or subordinating another dungeon. | +1 Perk Point<br>Unlocks Dungeon Warfare category perks. |
| Dungeon Overlord | A master of masters.<br>Unlocked by subordinating another dungeon master. | +2 Perk Points<br>Unlocks Subordinate Core category perks. |
| Raid Boss | Fine, I'll do it myself.<br>Unlocked by destroying or subordinating another dungeon with no assistance. | +2 Perk Points<br>+1 level in HP Regen skill<br>+1 level in MP Regen skill<br>+50 HP<br>Unlocks Raid Boss category perks. |
| System Upgrade | Unlocked by manually performing a system upgrade. Which is not supposed to be possible.<br>Ugh, this is going to get complicated, isn't it? | Um, I don't know. Just have +20 Dungeon Perk Points or something. Whatever. You're figuring this out yourself anyway, so close enough. |
| Purifier Dungeon | Dungeons are supposed to protect the world; you took that duty more literally.<br>Unlocked by destroying a corrupted dungeon core. | +20 Perk Points<br>Unlocks Purifier category perks. |

| | | |
|---|---|---|
| **Monster Creator** | **Granted to a dungeon master who has created a new, never-before-seen monster species.** | **+20 Perk Points Unlocks Monster Customization.** |
| **Matron of the Sacred Otterkin** | **Thanks to your efforts, a new intelligent species has been born.** | **+40 Perk Points Additional Perk Points may be granted based on the development and contributions of your client species.** |

**NSLICE-00P's Personal Status**

| Personal Status | | | |
|---|---|---|---|
| General Information | | Physical Attributes | |
| Name | NSLICE-00P | STR | 130* (Overwritten) |
| Species | Human/ Dungeon Core/ Automata Hybrid | DEX | 1000* (Overwritten) |
| Level | 151 | SPD | 65* (Overwritten) |
| XP | 80/100 | DEF | 150* (Overwritten) |
| Perk Points | 215 | RES | 75* (Overwritten) |
| HP | 235/235 | Magical Attributes | |
| MP | 274/274 | Mana Density | 102 |
| | | Mana Control | 185 |

| Active Skills | | |
|---|---|---|
| Name | Level | Description |
| Infused Mana Beam | 15 | Focus mana into a channeled energy attack.<br>Infused: May infuse Mana Beam with attributed mana. |
| Sneak | 1 | Move quietly to avoid notice. Makes it harder for others to notice the user. Effectiveness highly dependent on environment. |
| Multicasting | 13 | Can cast several spells at once. Number of simultaneous spells increases with level. |
| Anti-Mana Channeling | 4 | My best guess is that this projects a kind of inverse mana that reacts destructively with normal mana, including HP. While it can fully deplete HP, it does not harm matter itself.<br>Requires The Equalizer. |
| Power Strike | 1 | Infuse mana into a weapon for heavier damage. Power and range increase with level. |
| Farcasting | 10 | Allows the user to manipulate mana and create magic circles at far distances. |
| Strategic Magic | 5 | Governs the use of Strategic Magic spells. |
| Supercharge | 9 | Fill a spell with additional mana to boost its effects. May cause the spell to misfire. Effect boost depends on the amount and density of mana added. Misfire chance depends on Mana Control and amount of mana added. |
| Continuous Casting | 3 | May use additional mana to retain a spell form, allowing the spell to be instantly recast. |

| | | |
|---|---|---|
| Spell Fusion | 11 | Allows the user to combine compatible spells. |
| Intense Purifier Flame | 10 | Imbue a weapon or Flame-attribute attack with purifying Holy-attribute fire, dealing extra damage to corruption, monsters, dungeons, and beings from the Realms of Mana.<br>Intense: Boosts mana density of affected flames. |
| Heroic Power | 4 | To handle great responsibility, a hero needs great power.<br>Doubles Mana Density for a short time. May damage user if reused too quickly due to strain from excess mana. |
| Holy Strike | 1 | Infuse Holy mana into a weapon strike for heavier damage. Power and range increase with level. |
| Spell Shaping | 19 | Enables user to understand and modify the portion of spell circles related to shapes.<br>User may utilize known spell shapes with any available and compatible school of magic. |
| Spell Modification | 5 | Enables user to understand and modify the portion of spell circles related to spell modifiers.<br>User may utilize known spell modifiers with any available and compatible spell. |
| Blessed Growth | 1 | Imbue a weapon, Nature-attribute spell or skill, or compatible living thing with Holy-attribute life force. Vastly increases speed, scale, and health of plant growth.<br>May have other effects depending on target. |

| Passive Skills | | |
|---|---|---|
| General | | |
| Name | Level | Description |
| Dungeon Combat | -- | Dungeon traps and skills count as personal weapons and skills. |
| HP Regen | 7 | Automatically recover HP pool. Increased regeneration speed for damaged body parts. |
| MP Regen | 7 | Automatically recover MP pool. |
| Presence Detection | 4 | Detect living entities around the user. Range and scope of detection increases with level. |
| Trap Detection | 4 | Detect traps. Range and scope of detection increases with level. |
| Challenger | -- | Damage dealt x1.5 against targets of higher level. Damage received x0.75 against attacks from targets of higher level. |
| Hero Dungeon | -- | Unique Hero Skill for NSLICE-00P.<br>PLEASE don't do anything bad with this!<br>Removes dungeon vulnerability to Holy attribute.<br>Grants Dungeon Affinity: Holy (Minor). |
| Magic | | |
| Name | Level | Description |
| Spell Penetration | 8 | Enable spells to bypass a portion of RES. May spend more mana to boost the effect. |
| Geomancy | 7 | Elemental spells reduce the target's resistance to that particular element. May spend more mana to boost the effect. |
| Mana Shield | 1 | When active, may convert HP damage received into Mana damage. Mana Density will be used instead of DEF/RES in that case. HP damage will resume if Mana is fully drained. |

| Utility | | |
|---|---|---|
| Name | Level | Description |
| Enchanting | 14 | The art of infusing objects and beings with mana. |
| Mana Crafting | 3 | Crafting items through mana rather than physical processes. |
| Resistances | | |
| Name | Level | Description |
| Poison Resistance | 2 | Resist and recovery from poison status. Resist Poison-attributed damage. |
| Schools of Magic | | |
| Name | Level | Description |
| Arcane Magic | 11 | The school of magic governing the manipulation of unattributed mana. A solid foundation for students of the mystic arts, though somewhat less mana efficient than the more specialized schools. |
| Earth Magic | 9 | The school of magic governing the manipulation of Earth-attribute mana. One of the basic elemental magics, strong at defensive spells and spells that deal physical damage. |
| Fire Magic | 12 | The school of magic governing the manipulation of Fire-attribute mana. One of the basic elemental magics, strong at offensive spells and spells that inflict the burn status. |
| Water Magic | 9 | The school of magic governing the manipulation of Water-attribute mana. One of the basic elemental magics, fluid and flexible with many applications. |
| Air Magic | 3 | The school of magic governing the manipulation of Air-attribute mana. One of the basic elemental magics, fast and wide reaching. |

| | | |
|---|---|---|
| Light Magic | 13 | The school of magic governing the manipulation of Light-attribute mana. One of the basic elemental magics, quick and precise spells that are excellent against Dark-aligned foes. |
| Dark Magic | 2 | The school of magic governing the manipulation of Dark-attribute mana. One of the basic elemental magics, powerful and obscure, though dangerous if not treated with appropriate caution. |
| Nature Magic | 5 | The school of magic governing the manipulation of Nature-attribute mana. Focuses on growth and living things. |
| Poison Magic | 6 | The school of magic governing magical poisons. Excels at spreading poison status and dealing damage over time. |
| Metal Magic | 11 | The school of magic governing the manipulation of metal. Generally focuses on manipulating existing metal, though may create metal directly at great cost. |
| Lightning Magic | 3 | The school of magic governing the manipulation of lightning. Extremely fast and powerful, though somewhat expensive to cast. |
| Frost Magic | 3 | The school of magic governing cold and ice. Excellent at controlling and slowing. |
| Recovery Magic | 7 | The school of magic governing healing through magic. |
| Illusion Magic | 4 | The school of magic governing the manipulation of senses and emotions. |
| Holy Magic | 14 | The school of magic governing the manipulation of Holy-attribute mana, the attribute of the Aesdes that protects the world. |

| Hero | | |
|---|---|---|
| Name | Level | Description |
| Heroic Challenger | 3 | A hero never gives up, no matter the odds. Attacks ignore a small percent of target's DEF/RES/Immunities and always deal a minimum amount of damage. Gives a small chance to survive a fatal hit with 1 HP. |

| Spells | | |
|---|---|---|
| Spell Shapes | | |
| Name | Level | Description |
| Armor | 2 | Coat a target in mana, generally for defensive purposes. |
| Bomb | 5 | Pack mana into a dense package that explodes. |
| Barrier | 13 | Form mana in a defensive surface or wall. |
| Beam | 15 | Concentrate mana into a precise, fast-moving beam. |
| Blade | 6 | Form mana in a sharp sword that may be held. |
| Blast | 12 | Condense mana, then release it in an explosive blast. |
| Bolt | 18 | Form mana into a package that can be launched. |
| Chain | 8 | Form mana into a binding that wraps around a target. |
| Clone | 5 | Form mana into a shape similar to the user that will execute simple orders. Increased skill will increase the power and substance of the clones and the complexity of orders they may accept. |

| | | |
|---|---|---|
| Cloud | 3 | Condense mana into a gaseous form that lingers in an area. |
| Curse | 3 | Infuse a target with hostile mana. Exact effects depend on the attribute used. Use of alchemic ingredients or conduits related to the target may increase duration, effects, and potency. |
| Dash | 3 | Coats user in mana and propels them forward. Behavior may change based on attribute applied. For example, Earth attribute will cause the user to travel underground and then burst out at the target location. |
| Fist | 3 | Concentrates mana on the user's fist. Generally produces powerful, if short-ranged attacks. |
| Floor | 3 | Fills the ground with mana. Exact effects will depend on the attribute chosen. May be spread out in a wide area or concentrated on a single point. |
| Infusion | 13 | Fill a target with mana. |
| Prison | 3 | Entrap a target in mana that will attempt to prevent movement or action. May also interfere with outside attacks on the target depending on attribute used. |
| Rain | 3 | Create a mass of mana in the air that will bombard an area over time. |
| Siphon | 3 | Establish a connection between the user and target's mana. Generally used to forcibly transfer mana, but exact effect may vary with attribute. Can be resisted depending on target's Mana Control. |
| Spike | 7 | Shape mana into a thin point meant for piercing. |
| Sensing | 3 | Replicate or extend senses via mana. Exact sense and method depends on attribute used. |

| | | |
|---|---|---|
| Twister | 3 | Rapidly spin and cycle mana. |
| Spell Modifiers | | |
| Name | Level | Description |
| Dense | 18 | Condense mana even further, increasing the mana density and effect of the spell. |
| Fusion | 19 | Spell can combine with itself or other compatible spells. |
| Hardened | 1 | Improves spell defense against piercing/ disruption effects. |
| Lasting | 3 | Reduces speed at which mana disperses, increasing spell duration. |
| Piercing | 3 | Increases spell penetration against RES and magic barriers. |
| Wide | 3 | Increases spell's area of effect. |
| Channeled | 1 | Spell increases in intensity the longer it is cast. |
| Unique Holy Spells | | |
| Name | Level | Description |
| Holy Ward | 1 | Protect an area with Holy mana, warding off monsters and evil.<br>Also boosts HP and Mana recovery. Does not protect from attacks. |
| Banishment | 1 | Attempts to return a target creature to its origin realm.<br>No effect on inhabitants of the world. |
| Divination | 1 | Attempt to read the state of the world. May reveal things that were, things that are, or things that yet may be. What, exactly, none can predict, only that what is revealed should not be dismissed. |

| Illusion Aspects | | |
|---|---|---|
| Name | Level | Description |
| Calm | 5 | Dampen target's emotions, calming them down.<br>Higher levels may dampen specific emotions. |

| Strategic Spells | | | |
|---|---|---|---|
| School | Name | Level | Description |
| Modular | Prismatic Bombardment | 8 | Continuously rains Beam spells on the target area. Attributes may be chosen or swapped per circle at will.<br>If Fusion modifier is available, beams may be combined at will. |
| Modular | Prismatic Rain | 4 | Bombards a wide area with large compatible projectile-type spells; default is Bomb shape. |
| Modular | Prismatic Floor | 1 | Infuses a wide area to apply effects from below. Exact effects may vary with attributes used. |

| Personal Feats | | |
|---|---|---|
| Name | Description | Effect |
| Against the Odds | Do not ask how many there are, but where they are.<br>Unlocked by winning a fight when outnumbered by equal or higher-leveled opponents. | +1 Perk Point |
| Solo Conquest | I am the dungeon master now.<br>Unlocked by conquering a dungeon alone. | +1 level in HP Regen skill<br>+1 level in MP Regen skill<br>+1 level in Presence Detection skill<br>+1 level in Trap Detection skill |

| | | |
|---|---|---|
| Arcane Prodigy | The career of a supreme sorcerer does not start on the beaten path.<br>Unlocked by learning a high-tier magic skill under level twenty without spending Perk Points. | +3 Perk Points<br>Unlocks more advanced magic perks. |
| Enchanter | The first step on the path of the magic craftsman.<br>Unlocked by manually accomplishing a Mana Infusion. | +1 level in Enchanting skill |
| Skill Creator | You don't just master the path. You define it.<br>Unlocked by creating a brand-new skill. | To be honest, this normally happens when you're a MUCH higher level, so I'm a bit worried about passing you this much this early, but, um, okay.<br>+20 Perk Points |
| Healer | Anyone can deal in death. It takes an expert to deal in life.<br>Unlocked by using mana to heal a wound. | +1 level in Recovery Magic skill |
| Challenger | Levels and odds are just numbers.<br>Unlocked by defeating an who is the greater of level 10 twice your level while alone. | +3 Perk Points<br>+ Challenger skill |
| Strategic Mage | A strategic mage is king of the battlefield.<br>Unlocked by affecting a hundred or more equal-size opponents (or equivalent mass of other-size opponents) at the same time with magic. | +1 level in Strategic Magic skill<br>Unlocks Strategic Spells. |

| | | |
|---|---|---|
| World Defender | You have protected the world itself, at great risk to yourself. | +20 Perk Points<br>+1 level in Holy Magic skill |
| Hero | You faced terrible odds for the sake of the world and proved victorious. You are truly a champion of the world. Please, please, please keep it that way! | +20 Perk Points<br>Grants Unique Hero Skill: Hero Dungeon |
| Most Worthy | Whosoever wields this skill, who is clearly worthy, shall possess the power of their opponent's weapon.<br>Unlocked by taking control of an artifact bound to someone else. | +10 levels in Enchanting skill |
| Hero of the Sacred Otterkin | So . . . we normally give this when someone has done something that protected the existence of an entire species. And like, you just *created* a new species, so . . . I guess that means you are, in fact, responsible for their continued existence.<br>You know what?<br>Whatever. | +20 Perk Points<br>+1 level in Holy Water Ball spell<br>+1 level in Holy Strike skill |
| Spell Shaper | Mana may take many forms, but the true mage knows that the mana remains the same.<br>Unlocked by manually adjusting a magic circle into a new spell. | Grants Spell Shaping skill. |

| | | |
|---|---|---|
| Spell Adjuster | Magic is the art of changing reality. So why would a spell be static and immutable?<br>Unlocked by manually applying a spell modifier to a magic circle. | Grants Spell Modification skill. |
| Magic Crafter | Both crafters and mages reshape reality to fit their needs. One just does it faster.<br>Unlocked by crafting an item purely through mana (excepting default spell shapes such as Blade)! | +1 level in Mana Crafting skill |
| Dungeon Conqueror Feats | | |
| Name | Description | Effect |
| Dungeon Conqueror (Rat Cave) | Unlocked by conquering the Rat Cave Dungeon. | +1 Perk Point<br>+1 level in Sneak skill |
| Dungeon Conqueror (Earth Tunnels) | Unlocked by conquering the Earth Tunnels Dungeon. | +1 Perk Point<br>+1 level in Earth Magic skill |
| Dungeon Conqueror (Spider Tree) | Unlocked by conquering the Spider Tree Dungeon. | +1 Perk Point<br>+1 level in Poison Resistance skill |
| Dungeon Conqueror (Slimy Pit) | Unlocked by conquering the Slimy Pit Dungeon. | +1 Perk Point<br>+1 level in Poison Bolt spell |
| Dungeon Conqueror (Glimmering Grove) | Unlocked by conquering the Glimmering Grove Dungeon. | +1 Perk Point<br>+1 level in Light Magic skill |
| Dungeon Conqueror (Nature's Wrath) | Unlocked by conquering the Nature's Wrath Dungeon. | +1 Perk Point<br>+1 level in Nature Magic skill |

| | | |
|---|---|---|
| Dungeon Conqueror (Beast Lair) | Unlocked by conquering the Beast Lair Dungeon. | +1 Perk Point<br>+1 level in Power Strike skill |
| Dungeon Conqueror (Darkest Dungeon) | Unlocked by conquering the Darkest Dungeon Dungeon. | +1 Perk Point<br>+1 level in Dark Magic skill |
| Dungeon Conqueror (Metal Armory) | Unlocked by conquering the Metal Armory Dungeon. | +1 Perk Point<br>+1 level in Metal Magic skill |
| Dungeon Purifier Feats | | |
| Dungeon Purifier (Inferno) | A dungeon is dangerous to everyone in the world. A corrupted dungeon is dangerous to the world itself. And you conquered it all the same.<br>Unlocked by purifiying the Corrupted Dungeon (Inferno Realm). | +5 Perk Points<br>+1 level in Purifier Flame skill |
| Dungeon Purifier (Overgrowth) | A dungeon is dangerous to everyone in the world. A corrupted dungeon is dangerous to the world itself. And you conquered it all the same.<br>Unlocked by purifiying the Corrupted Dungeon (Overgrowth Realm). | +5 Perk Points<br>+1 level in Blessed Growth skill |

# About the Author

Icalos is a lifelong fan of sci-fi, fantasy, and video games, and the author of the Terminate the Other World! series, which was originally released on Royal Road. To learn more, visit his website at icalosbooks.com.